BRUTALITY

BRUTALITY

Ingrid Thoft

G. P. PUTNAM'S SONS | NEW YORK

G. P. PUTNAM'S SONS
Publishers Since 1838
An imprint of Penguin Random House LLC
375 Hudson Street
New York, New York 10014

Copyright © 2015 by Ingrid Thoft
Penguin supports copyright. Copyright fuels creativity, encourages diverse
voices, promotes free speech, and creates a vibrant culture. Thank you for
buying an authorized edition of this book and for complying with copyright
laws by not reproducing, scanning, or distributing any part of it in any
form without permission. You are supporting writers and allowing
Penguin to continue to publish books for every reader.

Library of Congress Cataloging-in-Publication Data

Thoft, Ingrid.
Brutality / Ingrid Thoft.
p.   cm. — (A Fina Ludlow novel ; 3)
ISBN 978-0-399-17118-5 (hardcover)
1. Women private investigators—Fiction.   2. Women—Crimes against—Fiction.
3. Criminal investigation—Fiction.   I. Title.
PS3620.H58B78   2015   2015002565
813'.6—dc23

Printed in the United States of America
1   2   3   4   5   6   7   8   9   10

BOOK DESIGN BY AMANDA DEWEY

For Doug Berrett and
Judith Stone Thoft
and in loving memory of
Richard A. Thoft, M.D.

BRUTALITY

PROLOGUE

Liz Barone had come to the conclusion that if her illness didn't kill her, the medical and legal bills just might. She tore open the latest invoice from her attorney and unfolded the piece of paper inside. Compared to the lawyers in downtown Boston, his fees were reasonable, but reasonable didn't mean cheap. She smoothed the latest onto a stack with the others and rested her head in her hands. Where was she going to find an extra thirty-seven hundred dollars? There was also the three-hundred-dollar bill for lab tests that the insurance company was refusing to pay. Add to that their usual expenses, and Liz felt they were rolling downhill without brakes, picking up speed with each passing moment.

The day had started badly: She'd woken with a dull, heavy ache in her head, and it had only intensified. It was too soon to take another pill, but if she didn't, there was no way she'd get through her to-do list: cook dinner, bathe children, pack lunches, review the reports from work, gather materials for the lawyer, choose a birthday gift for her mother. It was a list that any parent could relate to, but Liz had to do it all while contending with what felt like a vise on her skull.

Her options were either to cry or soldier on. She'd never been one to cry *and* soldier on, so she pushed her chair back from the table and went to the cabinet above the stove. She took down a bottle of Tylenol, fished out two pills, and filled a glass at the sink to wash them down.

The January sun had already set, and the backyard was cloaked in darkness, the window providing an unwelcome mirror.

How had she gotten here? Of all the futures Liz had imagined for herself, she'd never imagined this one. She sighed. That's how life works: You worried about a hundred different scenarios and outcomes, but it was the one you never imagined that was your downfall. Life didn't just exceed your wildest dreams; it also exceeded your wildest nightmares.

Liz detected movement on the other side of the window and took a step just as there was a knock on the back door. Jamie and the kids weren't due home for at least another hour, and she really wasn't in the mood for a visitor, but whoever it was had already seen her. Too late to pretend she wasn't home.

She unlocked and opened the door.

"This is a surprise," she said. Liz opened the door wider, letting in her visitor and a blast of frigid air.

She was puzzled, but once again, her imagination failed her.

She never could have predicted that ten minutes later she would be lying on her kitchen floor in a pool of blood.

1.

"I can't believe Haley is missing this," Fina Ludlow said, crumpled in a ball in a snowbank. "You all right, buddy?" she asked her youngest nephew, Chandler, as he burrowed out from underneath her.

"That was awesome! Let's go again!" He grabbed her hand as she struggled to her feet. A chunk of snow had wormed its way up her parka and into the small of her back. Fina looped the rope attached to the toboggan around her free wrist and struggled to fish the snow out. Some had already melted and was making a cold, wet trail down her butt. She was having fun, moving into the hot and cold sweaty phase that marked any good sledding excursion.

Back at the top of the hill, her brothers Scotty and Matthew were prepping for another run. Scotty had his middle son tucked between his legs. Matthew was lying chest-down on the sled, headfirst. Scotty's eldest son was lying on top of him in the same position.

"You're going to allow that?" Fina asked Scotty. "Patty would not approve." Scotty's wife had married into the Ludlow family, thereby rendering her the rare voice of reason. Patty had opted to stay home with their niece, Haley.

"She won't know," Scotty said.

"Not until you call her from the ER," Fina commented. "Did you guys bring any business cards? There must be a market for sledding-related lawsuits."

Her brothers grinned.

"Don't spoil our fun," Matthew said, pushing off, his nephew clinging to his back like a tortoise's shell.

It was a rare day that the Ludlows had a couple of free hours together, when the demands of the family firm, Ludlow and Associates, didn't take priority. Winter had been a bitch so far, dumping snow and caking ice on every surface, prompting the governor to close down government offices and delay court business for days. Fina's father, Carl, had grumbled about the loss of billable hours, but his children and grandchildren were happy to have a brief reprieve from the daily grind.

Fina sat down behind Chandler and shoved off the icy surface and over the crest of the hill. Their ride was fast and bumpy, the boy hollering all the way down. As they approached the bottom of the hill, Fina tipped to the side; rather than let the ride peter out, they rolled over and off the sled in a dramatic wipeout. Chandler was elated.

Fina was cleaning snow out of her boot laces when her phone rang from the inner pocket of her parka. If she were in a different line of work she might ignore the call, but as a private investigator, she never knew who might be on the other end of the line. Fina had to welcome every potential job and every potential lead, even if nine times out of ten it was a telemarketer trying to sell her aluminum siding.

"Fina Ludlow," she said, wiping at her runny nose. She listened to the caller and made a few comments before hanging up.

The reprieve was over.

Although most of Fina's cases came through Ludlow and Associates, she didn't have a dedicated space at the firm. She used conference rooms and empty offices on the premises as needed, but she preferred to meet clients—especially potential clients—on their own turf or at least a turf of their choosing. She learned a lot about people from their environments and how they interacted with them. That's why she was happy to meet her caller from the day before at Mass General Hospital, despite her general dislike of hospitals.

At the ICU reception desk, she encountered an administrator who could have blocked for the Patriots, so advanced were her skills.

"Who are you here to see?" She peered at Fina.

"Liz Barone." That wasn't strictly the truth, but oh, well.

"Are you family?"

"I'm her cousin." That definitely wasn't the truth.

The receptionist printed out an ID badge, which Fina affixed to her jacket. She gave Fina a stern lecture that cell phone use was not allowed and pointed her to a small waiting room.

The space overlooked an inner courtyard, and although the windows promised natural light, it was nearly impossible to see the sky given the size of the building. Across the courtyard, hallways and rooms were brightly illuminated, offering a montage of hospital life.

Fina took off her coat, stuffing her gloves and scarf into her pockets before taking a seat in a straight-backed chair. A woman of about forty was lying on a sofa wrapped in a thin blanket. She appeared to be sleeping, but every couple of minutes, she would toss and turn on the unforgiving couch. A Japanese family occupied the chairs opposite Fina. They were deep in conversation, their voices low but insistent.

Rather than contemplate the personal disasters that had brought her roommates to this place, Fina scanned the landscape across the way. In one room, a man sat up in bed, eating off a tray, his eyes trained on the TV mounted on the wall. A woman sat in a chair next to him, flipping through a magazine. Another room held half a dozen people, their smiling faces amongst a sea of flowers and balloons. Fina pondered the vista offered by the waiting room. It seemed cruel to force devastated family members to gaze upon others' more mundane or joyful recoveries.

Fifteen minutes later, Fina was thoroughly engrossed in a CNN story about National Tortilla Chip Day when a woman entered the room. She was dressed in street clothes rather than medical attire.

"Ms. Ludlow?"

Fina stood and offered her hand. "Yes. Are you Mrs. Barone?"

"Call me Bobbi." Her handshake was firm, and her skin felt dry. "There's a meeting room that we can use."

Fina followed her down the hallway, trying not to stare at the occupants of the glass-fronted rooms. In some cases, it was difficult to even see the patients amidst the medical equipment. Machines and endless tubes and cords snaked around the beds that seemed as large and as complicated as luxury sedans. Each room boasted a dedicated nursing station right outside its door. The level of care and attention was extraordinary. If you had to be in critical condition, this was the place to do it. In the hallway, a uniformed Boston Police officer sat on a chair, flipping through the *Herald*.

Bobbi led her to a small nondescript room with a round table and four chairs. There was a poster on the wall about patients' rights and another extolling the virtues of hand washing, but little attempt had been made to decorate or warm up the space. If you were sitting in this room meeting with doctors, the life of your loved one was in serious peril. No one was going to pretend otherwise.

"Do you want some coffee? Water?" Bobbi asked.

"No, thank you, but can I get you something?" Fina sat down across from her. "I should have offered to bring in some food. I know that hospital food can get old fast."

"I haven't felt like eating. This is the most successful diet I've ever been on." She gave a wan smile. Bobbi Barone looked to be in her sixties, with short, dark brown hair, and a complexion that was more olive than fair. She was very attractive, with smooth skin and lovely teeth. Her face was round, but not chubby, and her features were delicate. Fina guessed she was about five feet five inches and carried a bit of extra weight evenly throughout her body. A modest diamond ring and wedding band encircled her left ring finger.

"Is Liz's husband going to join us?" Fina asked.

"He's getting some air, but we can start without him." Bobbi squeezed her hands together as if trying to warm them. The ICU was chilly, which brought to Fina's mind a morgue.

"So what can I do for you?" Fina asked, pulling a notebook out of her bag. She had a tablet computer with her, but she still liked pen and paper when conducting interviews.

Bobbi took a deep breath. "I don't know if you've been reading the papers, but my daughter was attacked a couple of days ago."

"I did see that." Fina had only glanced at the item in Friday's paper, but had gone back and read all the coverage after Bobbi called her. Liz Barone, a thirty-eight-year-old married mother of two, was attacked in her home in Hyde Park. She'd suffered a major head injury, and her prognosis was uncertain. "How is she?"

"She's in bad shape. She suffered a subdural hematoma"—Bobbi gestured toward her head—"and there's a lot of bleeding in the brain."

"Is there anything they can do?"

"They're considering surgery to relieve the pressure, but we'll have to see."

"I'm so sorry," Fina said. "How can I help?"

"Well," Bobbi said, "I want to know who did it."

"Of course." Fina paused. "I assume the police are investigating?"
Bobbi nodded.

"Which division is handling the case?" Fina asked.

"Major Crimes."

Fina felt a mixture of relief and dread. Lieutenant Marcy Pitney was the head of Major Crimes and Fina's sometime nemesis. Detective Cristian Menendez was also a member of the unit. He was Fina's good friend and sometime date.

"Lieutenant Pitney?" Fina asked.

"Yes. Do you know her?" Bobbi looked searchingly at Fina. The woman was desperate for a shred of hope.

"I do, and she's an excellent detective, as are her colleagues, particularly Detective Menendez. I'm not sure what I can do for you that they can't."

"I don't mean to question their skills, but there are only so many hours in the day, and they have so many cases. I want someone who's focused only on Liz."

Fina had heard this before. Clients generally trusted the police, but they couldn't accept their limited resources in terms of manpower. Like most things, if you were willing to throw money at a problem, you got more—though not necessarily better—results.

"Okay. Well, tell me about your daughter."

"She's married with two kids and works in a lab at New England University."

"Has anything unusual happened in her life recently? Has anyone threatened her or has she been engaged in any conflict you can think of?"

Bobbi shook her head. "The only thing that's different is the lawsuit, but I can't imagine that has anything to do with it."

"What lawsuit?" Fina asked just as the door swung open. A man in faded jeans and a black pullover sweater walked in and dropped down into a chair. He rubbed his eyes with the heels of his hands.

"This is Liz's husband," Bobbi said. "Jamie Gottlieb."

Fina extended her hand. "Sorry to meet under such difficult circumstances."

"I was just telling Fina about the lawsuit," Bobbi explained.

Jamie made a gesture indicating she should continue. Fina listened and studied him at the same time.

She'd done some preliminary research on Jamie in preparation for the meeting. He was a project manager at a local interactive firm, but most of the information Fina found online was related to his band. Jamie was the guitarist for the group, which had enjoyed modest success in the nineties, but seemed largely inactive these days. They were called Wells Missionary, a name that made no sense to Fina, but was probably an ironic reference to art and the capitalist machinery. Jamie was trim with longish brown hair that dipped down toward his eyes. He wasn't traditionally handsome, but with his square jaw and hazel eyes, he looked slightly tortured, which for some reason was often a draw to the opposite sex. Sitting across from him, Fina could imagine he attracted the ladies when armed with a guitar.

"Liz was working with an attorney," Bobbi continued. "She was going to sue New England University."

"Why?" Fina asked.

Jamie studied his fingernails.

"She played soccer there when she was a student, and she's developed health problems. She thinks they're related to her time on the team."

"What kind of problems?" Fina thought she knew what was coming next, but she wanted to hear it from Bobbi.

"Cognitive health issues. MCI, to be exact."

MCI was mild cognitive impairment, the diagnosis most often given to athletes who suffered sports-related concussions. It was the affliction that so many NFL players were contending with, and although *mild* was part of the name, the impairment could be devastating.

"I'm familiar with MCI. What sort of symptoms was she experiencing?"

"I don't see how this is relevant," Jamie interjected. He bared his teeth in a look between a smile and a grimace. "This has nothing to do with her current situation."

"We don't know that, Jamie," his mother-in-law insisted.

"This is a waste of time, Bobbi. No offense," he said to Fina.

"None taken. What do you think happened?"

"I have no idea, but the world is full of crazy people. Liz didn't have any enemies. This had to have been random. She probably opened the door to the wrong person."

"That doesn't make any sense, Jamie," Bobbi said.

"I know you want to do whatever you can, but I don't see how hiring her"—he gestured at Fina—"is going to help."

"I don't expect you to pay for it," Bobbi said, a touch of irritation creeping into her voice.

"That's not what I meant," Jamie said.

Fina knew that some people didn't like the idea of an investigator snooping into their lives. Some people were more private than others, and then there was the group that actually had something to hide. Fina wondered which category Jamie occupied.

"I want to get back to Liz." He rose from his seat. "Do what you think is best," he said to his mother-in-law before leaving the room.

The two women sat in silence for a moment.

"I'm sorry," Bobbi said. "We're under a lot of stress, and clearly, he doesn't want to hire you."

"Why is that, do you think?" Fina asked.

Bobbi tipped her head back and studied the ceiling. "Jamie tends to take the path of least resistance in life. Right now he doesn't have the energy or the emotional resources to do more than sit by Liz's bedside."

"But you do? You still want me to investigate?"

She met Fina's gaze. "Absolutely. She's my child. I'd do anything for her."

"What about Liz's father? Is he in the picture?"

"My husband died five years ago. Thank God for small favors; this would have killed him."

Fina stashed her notebook in her bag and pulled out her business card. "Do you have an e-mail address?" Bobbi nodded. "I'll send you my rate information, and I'll get started as soon as you say the word," Fina said.

Bobbi folded her hand around the card as if it were a talisman.

"I'll want to speak with you again—and Jamie. I'll try not to irritate him too much."

"Good luck with that," Bobbi murmured.

"I'll also need the contact info for the attorney Liz was working with. He'll be a good place to start."

"He's in Natick. Thatcher Kinney." She laced her hands together. "You don't think I'm wrong about the lawsuit being an issue?"

Fina stood. "I don't know, but it represents a change in your daughter's routine and contacts. It would be foolish to dismiss it without taking a closer look."

"Thank you." Bobbi stood and gave Fina a hug. It wasn't the usual way her meetings ended, but this was an unusual circumstance. Bobbi Barone needed a hug, and Fina was happy to oblige.

"Hang in there," Fina said after pulling away.

"I am. By a thread."

In the hallway, Fina headed for the exit, and Bobbi went in the opposite direction, presumably toward her daughter's room. Fina hit the button that unsealed the hermetically sealed unit and took a deep breath once the doors closed behind her. That medical purgatory gave her the creeps.

While most of Fina's caseload came directly from Ludlow and Associates, occasionally she tried to throw in a job independent of the firm. There were a few reasons she might seek out other work: a case was interesting on its own merits; a case offered a potential payoff for Ludlow and Associates down the road; Fina felt like pissing off her father and asserting her independence. Liz Barone's case hit all three of these marks, though Fina would emphasize the potential payoff when selling it to her father.

Ludlow and Associates was located on the forty-eighth floor of the Prudential Tower. Carl had started the firm not long out of law school and built it into not only a family business, but one of the most successful personal injury firms in the country. All four of the Ludlow children had followed Carl's footsteps to law school, with varying degrees of success. Rand, the eldest, was a successful lawyer whose recent bad behavior had landed him in a family-enforced exile in Miami. Her other brothers, Scotty and Matthew, were partners in the family firm, but Fina hadn't made it past the first semester of law school. Instead, she found her niche as the firm's investigator. It was a competitive, lucrative, and sometimes distasteful line of work, but it was theirs, and they were good at it.

Fina breezed past the security guard at the front desk and wound through the hallways to her father's office. Since it was Saturday, his assistant wasn't in, and Fina strode directly into his office. It wasn't as much fun when she didn't have to evade his gatekeeper.

Her father was seated behind his desk, his brows knit together as he studied his computer screen.

"Look at these," he commanded his daughter.

"You know, Dad, other people say 'hello' and 'please.'"

"You're lecturing me on manners?"

Fina walked behind her father. She leaned over his shoulder and looked at the screen. It was odd being in such close physical proximity to him. Her parents weren't huggers. In fact, Fina couldn't remember the last time she and her father had embraced.

"What am I looking at?"

"Your mother's birthday gift."

"Don't you think you should ask Patty?" she said, referring to Scotty's wife. "She has a better eye for these sorts of things."

"I don't have time for that."

Fina scanned the bracelets on the Tiffany website. Her relationship with her mother was difficult, at best. In Fina's estimation, coal was always the perfect gift for Elaine.

"She likes blue," Fina noted, pointing at a delicate bracelet of diamonds and sapphires.

Carl grunted. "It's a little understated for your mother."

Fina reached for the mouse and scrolled down the page. She inhaled her father's cologne, crisp and faintly woodsy. Carl was a handsome man who put a lot of effort into his appearance. He was trim, with a muscular upper body and thick dark gray hair that was developing some flecks of white. Carl was also charismatic. He had a "take no prisoners" attitude people found immensely appealing. Most people wanted to believe that someone, somewhere, was in charge.

Fina bypassed all the tasteful, elegant options and clicked on a chunky diamond bracelet interspersed with gold Xs. "That looks like something she'd wear." She stood back and took in the astronomical price. "But doesn't she have a diamond bracelet already, Dad?"

Carl clicked on the purchase button and directed her back around the desk. "She has a few, but she can never have too many. So what's going on?"

Fina sat down in the chair across from him. "I've got a potential case that I thought might be of interest to you."

He frowned. "Not one of our clients?"

"No, but there may be something in it for us."

"Go on."

"Have you heard about the woman who was attacked in her Hyde Park home this past Thursday?"

"It's vaguely familiar."

"Well, her name is Liz Barone, and I just met with her mom and husband at MGH. Liz is in the ICU."

"That sounds like a criminal matter," he said. "Nothing to do with us."

"Just wait," Fina said, rising and walking over to the small but well-stocked bar on the other side of the room. She pulled a diet soda from the fridge and returned to her seat. "She was working with an attorney before she was attacked. She was planning to sue New England University."

"For what?" Carl's eyes flicked from his phone to her, his curiosity piqued.

"She played on their soccer team twenty years ago and has since been diagnosed with MCI."

"Concussions?"

"Bingo."

Carl tapped his fingers on his leather blotter. "Who's representing her now?"

"A guy named Thatcher Kinney in Natick, but I gather that her mom isn't happy with the job he's done."

"Never heard of him," her father said, indicating that Thatcher Kinney couldn't possibly be important if he wasn't on his radar screen. "Does the mom think the attack is linked to the lawsuit?"

"She doesn't know, but she wants someone to investigate, independent of the cops."

"She doesn't trust the cops?"

Fina shrugged. "She does, but she's doing anything she can to help her daughter. I think she wants to feel useful."

"Why'd they contact you?"

"Because I'm the best." Fina pulled out her elastic and gathered her hair into a tidier ponytail.

Carl gave her a withering look.

"And because of all the press from the Reardon case," she admitted. Fina's most recent case had involved the murder of a prominent Boston businessman. The case generated a lot of press, and Fina and the firm got their share of ink.

"And why would I want you to spend time on this?" her father asked. Carl liked to do this. He liked to make you state your case and win the argument, even if the argument was obvious and he'd already been convinced.

"Because if I figure out who attacked Liz Barone, her family will be eternally grateful, thereby wanting us to represent them in the case against NEU. A case that has potential to be huge, given all the athletes who are reporting cognitive issues due to sports injuries."

"What about the husband? You haven't said much about him."

"He seems reluctant to have me involved, which is peachy as far as I'm concerned. Maybe he did it, and I can wrap this thing up pronto."

Carl considered her for a moment. "Fine. Take the case, but I still may need you for something else."

Fina rose from her chair. "Of course, Father."

"Smart-ass," Carl murmured as she turned to leave.

She smiled. That was practically a term of endearment in the Ludlow family.

2.

Fina was feeling weary and sore, which could be partially attributed to the previous day's sledding excursion, but which she also chalked up to a general winter malaise. Everything was harder in winter, especially a snowy winter. You couldn't just walk down the sidewalk or pop out to the store for something. Every movement required more energy and attention, and it added up at the end of the day. Fina understood the wisdom of hibernation given the current conditions. Home was where she wanted to be.

For almost a year, Fina had been living in her late grandmother's condo overlooking Boston Harbor. Carl had originally purchased the condo to keep his mother and wife out of each other's hair, and Nanny had loved the prime location her perch provided for plane-spotting at Logan Airport. Before Carl could contemplate selling it after Nanny's death, Fina had moved in. She and Nanny had always been thick as thieves, and she knew her grandmother wouldn't mind. It had been suggested to Fina that she might want to update the décor, which smacked of old lady, but she couldn't be bothered. As long as she had a comfortable couch and a sizable TV, she was good. And the décor wasn't the first thing that visitors noticed, anyway; it was the view. And then the clothes, files, books, and magazines that Fina left strewn about the space.

She took a hot bath and pulled on sweats before checking her e-mail. Bobbi Barone had already responded to the e-mail Fina had sent from

Ludlow and Associates detailing her rates. Bobbi wanted to proceed, so Fina named a new folder on her desktop and opened a Word document. She contemplated the blank page for a moment, then wandered into the kitchen. A leftover container of pad thai appealed, as did a pint of Ben & Jerry's Karamel Sutra. Decisions, decisions. Fina grabbed the pad thai and a pair of chopsticks, feeling virtuous.

In the living room, she plopped down onto Nanny's overstuffed blue velvet couch and scooped up a mouthful of peanutty noodles. She chewed, then reached for her phone.

"Menendez," Cristian answered after the first ring.

"Hey. What are you up to?" Fina asked before taking another bite.

"I'm interviewing a man who believes that he can talk to God through his espresso machine."

"Huh. That's too bad."

"It is."

"I can barely get my coffeemaker to make a cup of coffee, let alone deliver a message from our Lord."

"If our Lord ever starts communicating through appliances," Cristian said, "I assure you, he won't start with yours."

"So cynical."

Fina could hear phones ringing in the background, and the rise and fall of conversations. She didn't know how Cristian ever got anything done in the squad room, which seemed more like a three-ring circus than a place of work.

"So I wanted to give you a heads-up." She plucked a shrimp from the container and dropped it into her mouth.

"I don't like the sound of that," Cristian said.

"I can't win with you."

"What are you up to?"

"Well, I don't think you're going to like it."

"Uh-huh."

"Bobbi Barone has hired me to investigate her daughter's attack."

There was a pause on the other end of the line. "Why?"

"Not because she thinks you're incompetent," Fina rushed to explain, "but because she's worried that you guys can't devote the necessary time to the case. Why are you on the case, anyway? You usually do more high-profile stuff."

"This is high profile. The mayor recently launched his Home Safe Initiative, and less than thirty days in, a woman gets clobbered in her kitchen—her kitchen in her family-friendly neighborhood."

"Got it. I think Bobbi just wants to feel like she's doing something, and hiring me fits the bill."

"You should just join the BPD," Cristian suggested. "Then you and I and Pitney could work together officially. Oh, wait. That's right. They'd never let you in."

Fina laughed. "That's me, harboring a fantasy to work for the man."

"So what do you want from me?" he asked.

"This really was a courtesy call, but now that you mention it, if you have anything to give me, I would be most appreciative."

"I don't."

"I'm sure I could give you something in return," Fina said.

They were quiet as they mulled over the options. Sexual favors were out given Cristian's current interest in a speech pathologist named Cindy. Fina had recently suggested that Cristian find a hobby other than obsessing about his ex-wife's love life. Bolstering his own love life, however, was not what she'd had in mind.

"How about Bruins tickets for you and Matteo?" she asked. The Ludlows had boxes at Fenway, Gillette Stadium, and the Boston Garden—she didn't care what anyone said, it would always be the Boston Garden to her even if some new corporate sponsor bought it tomorrow—and distributed tickets as thank-you gifts and bribes.

"He's three and a half. I don't want to take him to a hockey game." Cristian murmured thanks to someone.

"Well, how about *Disney on Ice*? That show is like a bad penny; it keeps turning up," she said.

"Admit it. You loved it when we took him last summer."

Fina had scored tickets months earlier and accompanied them to a show that was heavy on *Beauty and the Beast*. She spent most of the performance worrying about the physics related to the Beast's enormous head and those skinny blades.

"That show was beyond ridiculous, but I did like watching Teo have a good time," Fina said.

"Well, get on the horn to Goofy," he said, "and I'll let you know if anything comes up."

"And you'll soften the blow with Pitney?"

Cristian scoffed. "I'll do my best."

"That's all I can ask," Fina replied.

Fina sent an e-mail to Scotty's secretary—for some reason Carl's assistant wasn't very helpful, perhaps because Fina paid no attention to her—inquiring about Disney dates at the Garden.

She dropped the empty takeout container in the kitchen trash and grabbed a spoon and the Karamel Sutra. Back on the couch, she typed "Liz Barone" into a search engine. There was nothing revelatory in the results. The most recent links were related to the attack, and the handful of others referenced her work at an NEU lab or her involvement in soccer. Fina narrowed her focus; there was a lot you could find out online if you knew where to look. After an hour, Fina had determined that Liz had never been arrested nor had she ever been involved in a civil suit. Her driving record was clean, and she and her husband had purchased their Hyde Park house seven years earlier.

Fina had to wonder: If Liz Barone was such an upstanding citizen and a contributing member of society, why would someone shove her head into a kitchen counter?

Fina wanted to speak with Jamie and Bobbi again before diving into the case, but they were both unavailable on Sunday. Liz was undergoing a battery of tests, and her mother and husband wanted to stay close throughout the day. Bobbi promised to call Fina on Monday when they had a free moment, and in the meantime gave her the contact information for Thatcher Kinney. Given that he was a small-town lawyer, Thatcher Kinney wasn't even answering his phone on Sunday, let alone scheduling meetings.

It was hard to get work done on a Sunday, and Fina supposed if the Lord was allowed to rest, then so was she. Perhaps she took it a little far by not showering, dressing, or leaving the condo, but by Monday morning, she was ready to jump into the case.

Savvy and powerful people often went out of their way to avoid speaking with a private investigator, which was why Fina was a fan of dropping by unannounced and planting herself in their waiting rooms. But if an interviewee didn't fall into the savvy and powerful category, it was often better to schedule an appointment. The effort of calling ahead would be misconstrued as respect, and the subject wouldn't know better than to agree to the meeting. It was a win-win as far as Fina was concerned, so she called Thatcher Kinney first thing on Monday and was told by his sunny secretary that he could see her at eleven A.M.

The appointment time left her with a couple of hours to burn, so she threw on some workout clothes and headed down to the building's fourth-floor gym. Fina didn't enjoy working out, and her fast metabolism deemed it unnecessary in order to maintain her weight, despite her unorthodox diet. However, with each passing year and physical skirmish, she was increasingly aware that being fit wouldn't always be a given, so she was trying to exercise more often. Her on-the-job pursuits weren't consistent enough to qualify as cardio training.

Fina logged a few miles on the treadmill, lifted some weights, and was back upstairs with enough time for a shower, breakfast, and a quick review of Thatcher Kinney's bio. He didn't have an online presence with the exception of a mention in the Roger Williams University School of Law alumni bulletin. Assuming he attended law school not long after graduating from college, he was probably in his midfifties. Thatcher Kinney didn't seem to generate many headlines, which was great when discretion was required, but it rarely was in personal injury lawsuits.

There was a backup on the Mass Pike, proving Fina's theory that rush hour no longer existed; traffic was a reality of urban living that followed no tidy schedule or predictable pattern. She spent forty-five minutes cursing her fellow drivers and scanning the dial for anything that approximated music. The Top 40 station was repetitive, and the hip-hop option featured lots of moaning and "slap it here, girl," "work that booty, baby." Who said romance was dead?

Natick Center, where Thatcher's office was located, was a hybrid of the past and the present. The main street featured mom-and-pop businesses fighting the good fight against bank branches and chain coffee shops, but the newest additions to the area were large municipal buildings constructed to look old. The railroad tracks bisected the area, a testimony to the town's role as a bedroom community for Boston's professional workforce.

Fina found a parking space next to the town common and fought to open her car door against a snowbank. She squeezed out of the car, only to have to climb the hillock of dirty snow that was blocking her path. With no time to spare, she dashed across the street to a Victorian-style house that was the home of Thatcher Kinney, Attorney at Law, as well as a dental practice and an independent insurance agency.

Inside the front door was a small separate foyer with a row of mailboxes built into the right-hand wall. Fina stamped the slush off her boots and turned the doorknob leading into the hallway. A steep flight of stairs carpeted in industrial-looking gray rose directly in front of her. The door to her left was ajar, with a discreet black-lettered sign identifying it as Thatcher Kinney's digs.

Fina knocked and pushed the door open to find a small waiting room dominated by a metal desk and a seating area with two chairs. A coffeemaker stood on a trestle table with a mini fridge next to it. There was a fireplace, but rather than crackling flames, a potted plant stood in its hearth. Some people found wood fires messy and too much work, but Fina loved them. There was something sad and bereft about an empty fireplace in the dead of winter.

An open door gave a view into another office where a man sat behind a large wooden desk. Fina tapped on that door before crossing the threshold.

"I'm sorry to interrupt, but your secretary seems to be MIA."

The man looked up at her, small glasses slipping down the bridge of his nose. "Shirley's at the bank. Is there something I can help you with?"

"You can if you're Thatcher Kinney."

"I am."

"I'm your eleven o'clock appointment. Fina Ludlow."

She crossed the worn Oriental carpet and extended her hand. Thatcher rose partway out of his chair to shake and then gestured for her to sit in one of the wooden chairs in front of his desk. The Roger Williams seal was emblazoned on the back of both. Fina appreciated the school spirit, but doubted there were less comfortable chairs in the world.

"Nice to meet you."

Fina glanced around the room. The décor was typical single proprietor fare: framed diplomas, nicely matted prints of ducks and outdoor scenes, venetian blinds made homier with curtains. Thatcher's desk was tidy, with just a couple of piles of folders at the corners. He had a desktop computer that looked like it dated from the late nineties. It spoke volumes about his technical prowess, but maybe some clients found it reassuring; Thatcher Kinney was old-school and wouldn't be distracted by any newfangled technology.

"Can I offer you some coffee?" he asked, rising from his chair.

"Sure. Cream and sugar, please."

Thatcher went to the waiting room and returned a minute later with two mugs, one of which he handed to Fina.

"Thanks."

He took his seat and smoothed down his blue-striped tie before resting his ankle atop the opposite knee. He was wearing khaki pants, a white shirt, and a blue blazer. He looked like he should be attending his private school graduation, not practicing law.

"How can I help you, Ms. Ludlow?"

"Call me Fina, first of all." She smiled at him. "I'm a private investigator, and Bobbi Barone has hired me to investigate the attack on her daughter Liz. I was hoping you could provide some information."

"What kind of information?" Thatcher asked. "You must know I'm bound by attorney-client privilege."

"Of course. I'm not asking you to violate privilege, but if there is anything you can tell me about your work with Liz that might help my investigation, I would appreciate it."

He sipped his coffee and seemed to contemplate her request. Fina's calculations had been accurate: Thatcher was probably in his midfifties. He had strawberry blond hair that was cut short, with a hint of wave to it. His skin was freckled, and wrinkles were starting to assert themselves on his forehead and around his eyes.

"Why don't you tell me what you know," Thatcher said, "and I'll fill in the broad strokes where I can."

"Sure. Liz has been suffering from MCI, possibly a result of her soccer-playing days at NEU, and she wanted to sue the university. Bobbi wonders if the attack is related to the lawsuit."

Thatcher took off his glasses and massaged the bridge of his nose. "I wish I had more to add to that, but I don't."

"Because of privilege?"

"Because there isn't much to tell."

"Well, have you filed a suit yet?" Fina knew the answer to the question already, but she was always interested in hearing things from the horse's mouth.

"Not yet. I'd reached out to some people at NEU, put out some feelers, but that's as far as we've gotten."

"How long have you been working the case?"

"A month or so." Thatcher put his glasses back on.

Fina couldn't tell if he was dumb or just ignorant, but Bobbi Barone had been right to worry; this guy was completely out of his league.

She sipped her coffee. "If I may ask, what is your practice area?"

"A little of this, a little of that. I've had the practice—been in the same office—for twenty-seven years."

"Imagine that. So does 'a little of this' include personal injury cases? Med mal?" Fina asked.

"I've had one or two." Thatcher straightened up in his chair, perhaps deciding that offense should be taken. "My knowledge base is broad. I do some estate planning, real estate transactions, small claims. That sort of thing."

"Any class action?"

Thatcher studied the space over Fina's head. "Nope," he said, shaking his head.

Fina shifted her weight in her seat. "I'm surprised you wanted to represent Liz. Her case seems like a departure from your usual work."

He adjusted in his chair. "I've known Liz's family for many years, and we have friends in common. They hired me because I'm not a faceless lawyer in some downtown high-rise who'll bankrupt them. They trust me."

Not anymore, Fina thought.

There was a noise out in the waiting room, and a voice carried into the office.

"You would not believe the line at the bank, Thatcher, and then when I finally got to the counter, Rusty Atkins talked my ear off!" A woman stepped into the room. A surprised look crossed her face. "I'm so sorry. I didn't know you were in a meeting."

"Not a problem, Shirley. Do you mind pulling the door closed behind you?"

"Of course." She smiled before stepping out.

"Where were we?" Thatcher asked. He took a long draw of his coffee.

"Is there anyone you can think of who wanted to harm Liz? Either related to the lawsuit or otherwise?"

"Not to my knowledge. It must have been random," he said. "No one I know would do such a thing."

Why did people always think that murderers, liars, and thieves were loners with no human contacts? We all knew terrible people; we just didn't necessarily *know* that they were terrible. This insistence that nobody in one's universe would do anything wrong belied a real lack of imagination, as well as woeful ignorance. Where did everyone think the bad people were? Marooned on some island in the middle of the ocean, occasionally furloughed to commit bad acts back on the mainland?

"So no one?" Fina asked. "There was no one with whom she had any conflicts?"

Thatcher leaned forward and folded his hands on the desktop. "I don't know what to tell you, Ms. Ludlow. Do you want me to make something up?" He smiled, but the expression fell short of his eyes.

"Of course not."

Nobody had *no* conflicts. If they did, they weren't breathing, which would make any lawsuit moot. A good lawyer ferreted out the conflicts early on, even if they seemed minor. Fina knew that her father and brothers could be ruthless, but when they represented a client, they did due diligence and then some. They didn't judge or particularly care about their clients' transgressions, but they understood the best way to represent someone was to make sure there were no secrets or surprises. Being an attorney with high-stakes cases meant you had to ask tough questions; if you didn't, you could be sure opposing counsel would in open court.

Fina put her coffee cup on the desk and grabbed her bag from the floor. She handed a business card to Thatcher Kinney, who gave her one in return.

"If you think of anything useful, let me know," she told him.

Thatcher rose and came around his desk. "Come to think of it, Liz did give me some materials that I'm happy to pass along. They're not of a sensitive nature."

"Terrific." Fina wasn't hopeful. There was nothing promising about Thatcher Kinney.

He opened a file cabinet next to his desk and thumbed through the folders. "Here it is," he said, pulling out a file folder about an inch thick.

"Do you want to make copies for me?" Fina asked, taking the folder from him.

"Nah. Why don't you make them when you have a chance and send the originals back to me?"

"Great. Thanks." A folder of original materials would never make it out of Ludlow and Associates without a comprehensive record of where it was going and with whom. Thatcher wasn't just practicing law in another town, he was practicing in another decade.

In the waiting room she waved at Shirley, who was on the phone. Shirley smiled and waved back.

Gosh, they were nice.

Everybody knew how far nice got you in the world of personal injury lawsuits.

Fina pulled into a Dunkin' Donuts drive-thru on Route 9 and ordered a hot chocolate and a glazed donut. She was tempted to pull back onto the road and make some calls on her speakerphone, but the prospect of spilling a hot liquid on her lady parts was enough of a deterrent. Instead, she pulled over into a space in the lot and took a sip. Placing the cup in the cup holder, Fina reached into the paper bag and broke off part of the donut. She chewed it slowly, allowing the glazed sugar coating to linger on her tongue for a moment. Man, she loved sugar and fat.

She washed the rest of the donut down with more hot chocolate, then replaced the cup and wiped her hands on a napkin. She made follow-up calls to Bobbi and Jamie, but neither answered, which Fina chalked up to the "no cell phone" rules in the ICU. When leaving messages for them, she tried not to sound too impatient, but she was anxious to conduct more in-depth interviews. Family members were always prime suspects and had the most information about a victim's other relationships. Many times it was what family members failed to discuss that was most critical; unanswered questions or tactful evasions often pointed Fina in the right direction.

Rather than twiddle her thumbs, she reached into her bag and pulled out the folder that Thatcher Kinney had given her. The top document was a basic intake sheet that he probably gave to all of his clients, requesting personal data like the client's name, address, spouse, children, place of employment, and any other relevant contact information. Fina glanced over it and shuffled it to the back of the pile. Next was a stack of faded NEU student newspapers. They were all dated from 1994 to 1998. Fina did a cursory examination of each issue, but the only common thread was lengthy articles about the NEU women's soccer team and accompanying photos. Liz Barone was captioned in a few of the pictures and appeared in some of the group shots.

Beneath the newspapers, there was a sheaf of documents on NEU letterhead. They seemed to be fund-raising appeals, all of them signed by a development officer named Pamela Fordyce. The letters themselves were form letters, standard higher-ed missives begging for money, although a few of them mentioned the women's athletic program in particular. On the most recent one, someone had scribbled a large question mark and an exclamation point with a black Sharpie.

A question mark alone could be translated as "Huh?" and an exclamation point might be interpreted as "OMG!"

But both?

To Fina, it screamed, "What the hell?"

3.

Bobbi Barone asked to meet her in the hospital cafeteria, which Fina preferred to the ICU. She found Bobbi sitting near a window overlooking Storrow Drive and the river beyond it. The tray in front of her held a turkey sandwich, a dill pickle, an unopened bag of chips, and a can of soda. Contrary to conventional wisdom about institutional cafeterias, the sandwich looked like something you might find in an upscale deli. It was plump with turkey on a brioche-type roll, a leaf of green lettuce peeking out. The tomato slice was the color of salmon, but this was January in New England. One couldn't expect miracles.

Bobbi's complexion looked sallow, and her hair was flat.

"I'm sure everyone's telling you to eat," Fina said, sitting down across from her with a diet soda, "but it really is important."

"And I really am trying, but everything tastes like cardboard to me."

"That's not surprising. How's Liz?" Fina popped open the can and took a long drag of soda.

Tears welled in Bobbi's eyes and rolled down her cheeks. "She's not good."

"Bobbi, I'm so sorry." Fina reached out and squeezed her hand.

"They aren't going to operate. The doctors think the hematoma is too big and surgery won't help."

Fina was silent. It sounded pretty hopeless.

"You know what they told me?" Bobbi asked. "That if Liz had been found sooner, she might have had a better chance at survival. They figure she was on the kitchen floor for an hour or so before Jamie came home, maybe in and out of consciousness."

"That's awful."

"If you get to the ER right away, they can drill a hole or take off part of your skull and relieve the pressure." She shook her head. "I can't stand to think about it."

"There's nothing I can say that won't sound trite, but I am truly sorry you and your family are suffering."

"Well, thank you." Bobbi took the top off her sandwich and used a fork to pick off some turkey. She put it in her mouth and chewed slowly, then washed it down with some soda. "I realize you only started Saturday, but do you have any news?"

Fina smiled. "Are you kidding? Some of my clients expect the case to be solved in twenty-four hours. A request for an update is perfectly reasonable. I've spoken with Detective Menendez and let him know I'm on the case. Obviously, we'll share information whenever possible."

Bobbi nodded.

"And I met with Thatcher Kinney this morning," Fina said.

"Did he have any ideas about who might have done this?"

"No, not really." He didn't really have any ideas at all, but Fina didn't want Bobbi to ruminate about Liz's choice of attorney. "He gave me some background materials, but it didn't sound to me like the lawsuit—potential lawsuit—had gotten very far."

"So how can I help?" Bobbi asked.

"I need some background about your family and any information you can give me about Liz's friends, contacts, that sort of thing." Fina pulled her notebook out of her bag. "I don't want you to feel you're being cross-examined, but sometimes, when you're tired, it's easier to answer questions than provide general information."

"Ask me whatever you'd like," Bobbi said, pulling off another scrap of turkey.

"Does Liz have any siblings?"

"Yes. My other daughters are Nicole and Dawn."

"Do they live in the area?" Fina asked.

"Nicole's in Hartford, and Dawn is in western Massachusetts."

"Is Liz close to her sisters?"

"More Nicole than Dawn. Liz and Dawn have always been extremely competitive."

Fina sipped her drink. "Did Dawn play soccer as well?"

"Yes, for UMass."

Bobbi had bigger problems right now, but Fina imagined she must have contemplated the possibility of MCI devastating her other daughter's health. Whoever said the good Lord didn't give you more than you could handle was full of beans.

"Who knew about the potential lawsuit?" Fina asked.

"Our family and at least one friend that I know of, Tasha Beemis-Jones."

The name was familiar, but Fina couldn't place it. Her attempt to thumb through her mental Rolodex must have been evident, because Bobbi filled in the blank.

"She's an attorney, and her husband is a surgeon. Their picture is on the society page of the paper sometimes."

Fina's brain clicked in recognition. "Oh, right. I think she works for Sims and Lancaster?"

"I guess. Is that a big firm downtown?"

Fina nodded. Tasha Beemis-Jones and Dwayne "D" Jones were one of the city's African-American power couples. They were exceedingly attractive, smart, and well connected.

"Are Liz and Tasha especially close? Is that why Liz confided in her?"

"That, and they were soccer teammates at NEU." Bobbi picked up the pickle and contemplated it for a moment before placing it back down on her plate.

"Does Tasha have any cognitive health issues?"

"Not that I know of." Bobbi seemed like a decent person, but she must have wondered why her kid was suffering from MCI and someone else's wasn't. It was human nature to wonder why you drew the short straw.

"I should definitely talk to Tasha," Fina said. "Do you know the best way to reach her?"

"I might be able to dig up her cell number, but her office is your best bet. I think I have it."

"Don't worry about it. I can find it."

"You should try Kelly, also."

"Kelly?"

"Kelly Wegner."

"Was she a teammate, too?"

"Yes. They live a couple of streets from each other now, and their kids are close in age. Liz and Kelly see each other frequently—you know, carpools, birthday parties. They help each other out a lot."

It had started to snow. Large flakes floated by the windows, making Fina feel she was trapped in a large, dirty snow globe.

"Any other friends come to mind?"

Bobbi thought for a moment. "No. Most of Liz's time was spent at work or with her family."

"Were any of Liz's teammates going to join the suit?"

"She hadn't gotten that far, but she hoped they would."

"What about their neighbors?" Fina asked. "Is Liz friendly with any of them?"

"She and Jamie get along with everyone. People are friendly, but at this time of year, there isn't much social interaction. Sometimes Liz helped out the elderly woman across the street, Mrs. Barbatto."

"And Jamie?" Fina asked. "How are things with the two of them?"

"Fine, I suppose. As stable as any couple with young children and demanding jobs," Bobbi said, sipping her soda. "Those are stressful years."

"You probably don't want to contemplate your son-in-law harming your daughter," Fina ventured, "but the statistics are clear: Most violent crime victims know their attackers."

Bobbi looked her in the eye. "Make no mistake where my loyalty lies, Fina. If I find out that he or anyone else I know hurt her, I'll want Massachusetts to bring back the death penalty." She pushed her plate away. "But I don't actually think Jamie would hurt her. He's not a violent man."

"Okay. Did they fight much, or was either of them seeing other people?"

"Like an affair? I don't know when they'd find the time," Bobbi said. "Liz works and is with the kids, and when Jamie isn't working, he's playing music."

"Right. I read about his band." Fina tipped back the soda can to get the last drops. "Speaking of Liz's work, can you tell me what she does exactly?"

"You'll have to speak with her boss to get the specifics, but she's an administrator at a lab at NEU."

"Was she a science major?" Fina asked.

Bobbi nodded. "She considered going into medicine, but decided that the time commitment and the expense were too great. I think it worked out, though. The job at the lab has reasonable hours, and administration suits her; she's very organized."

"Does she like her job?" Fina asked.

"She does, but it's stressful. Their funding is always being cut, and the scientists, most of them are type A's and can be difficult."

"Isn't it awkward? Her suing her employer?"

"I raised that with her, but Liz thought there was enough distance between the lab and the athletics department that she could compartmentalize her job from the case. She also didn't feel she had a choice. She was growing desperate."

Fina jotted down some notes, and Bobbi glanced at her watch. "Is that enough for now?" she asked. "I really want to get back downstairs."

"Just one more question. Thatcher gave me some materials that Liz had given him, including some solicitations from the NEU development office. Did Liz mention them to you?"

"Yes," Bobbi said. "She was extremely upset that they were begging her for money."

"Do you know if she contacted them?"

"I don't know." Bobbi's head was tilted to the side, as if she was having difficulty staying upright. The poor woman was exhausted.

"Thanks for taking the time." Fina stowed her notebook. "I really want to speak with Jamie, but I understand that circumstances make that difficult."

"I've asked him to be in touch, but I don't want to nag him."

"It's okay," Fina said. "You've given me other avenues to explore."

Bobbi deposited her tray onto a conveyor belt and they walked down the hallway to the elevator bank, which afforded a wide view of the Charles. All sorts of people in all sorts of medical uniforms were going about their business: janitors, orderlies, doctors, and nurses. Fina was glad that there were other people willing to perform all those jobs. She didn't have the stomach or the courage to do what they did.

The elevator doors opened, revealing a gurney and a handful of people. Fina held the door open with her hand and gestured for Bobbi to get on. "I'll take the next one."

"Thank you, Fina," Bobbi said, hugging her tightly before stepping into the car. The doors closed silently behind her.

Good Lord. This was more maternal affection than Fina had experienced in the entire previous decade.

Fina wandered over to the windows and pulled her phone out of her bag, searching for Sims and Lancaster. The operator connected her to Tasha Beemis-Jones's office, and the assistant told her that Ms. Beemis-Jones was in conference and would be for the remainder of the day. Fina made her pitch as an emissary of Bobbi's and hoped that she wouldn't have to make the plea too many times before she finally connected with Tasha.

Her phone rang before she'd slipped it back into her bag.

"I'm very stressed," the voice on the other end of the line confessed.

"What's going on, Risa?" Fina asked.

"I'm waiting to have some tests done, and I'm having second thoughts."

Fina wasn't someone who surrounded herself with girlfriends, but Risa Paquette was a recent welcome addition to her inner circle. Although they'd grown up together, their friendship had really taken hold when both women stepped into the breach left by the death of Fina's sister-in-law Melanie. Fina and Risa were committed to getting Fina's niece, Haley, on the path to a less dysfunctional life. Most recently, they'd been grappling with Risa's dysfunctional life, featuring a long-lost aunt who needed a kidney—Risa's kidney. Fina had investigated her aunt and discovered that Fina's impulse to protect her family extended to her friend.

"You're having the preliminary tests, right?" Fina asked. "That doesn't commit you to donating your kidney to Greta."

"I know, but I feel like every step I take down this road is going to make it harder to say no to her."

Fina pressed her hand against the window. It was ice-cold. "I understand, but you have to keep reminding yourself that you are not obligated to do this. You may not even be a match."

"I'm kind of hoping I'm not," Risa confessed. "Does that make me a terrible person?"

"Hardly. It makes you a human person. What are you having done today?"

"Just blood work. Then I have to come back for an EKG, a chest X-ray, and some other stuff, depending upon the results."

"Risa, if you don't want to do this, don't."

There was a pause at the other end. "I do want to. I'm just having a moment of weakness."

"It's not weakness. It's indecision, and there's nothing wrong with that." Fina glanced at her watch. "Where are you?"

"MGH."

"Hey, so am I! I'll meet you. What time is your appointment?"

"It's in half an hour, but you have better things to do than hold my hand."

"Not really."

Risa hesitated. "You're sure?"

"Yes. Let me distract you."

"That would be great. I'm in the transplant center on the eighth floor."

"I'll be right there."

Fina took the stairs up two flights and navigated her way past the nephrology and rheumatology departments. The transplant center was a study in contrasts: sickly, sallow patients amidst blush-colored walls and prints of flower arrangements by Monet and Matisse. Risa was the picture of health, seated by herself in a small grouping of chairs. She kissed Fina on the cheek and patted the chair next to her.

"Now that you're here," Risa said, "this seems so silly."

"Maybe it seems silly *because* I'm here," Fina suggested, picking up a copy of *AARP* magazine.

"You're probably right." Risa leaned back in her chair and inspected her nails. They were short and polished in a nude shade. Risa was a superlative cook, and her hands were busy every day. It wasn't digging ditches, but she definitely raised a finger.

"My hair's a little darker," she said, twisting to give Fina a 360-degree view. "Do you like it?"

Fina shrugged slightly. "Sorry I didn't notice. You look great. You always look great." In her midforties, Risa was very pretty, with short ashy brown hair and hazel eyes. She never looked overdone, but Fina supposed that required a lot of work.

"Here," Fina said, handing her a copy of *Ranger Rick* magazine. "Tell me something I don't know about white terns."

"What *do* you know about white terns?"

"Nothing. It'll be easy."

Risa rolled her eyes and pulled out her phone instead.

Fina turned to an article on knee replacement, and Risa scrolled through her e-mail. She was typing when her name was called.

"Do you want me to go back with you?" Fina asked.

"No, I'm okay."

"I'll be here."

Fina tossed aside the magazine and pulled her tablet from her bag. She ran a search on Liz's sisters, Nicole and Dawn. There was one mention of Dawn in a newspaper article about an adult soccer league in Amherst. Nicole came up in links related to her employer, a Hartford-based advertising agency. Fina didn't learn anything new from the search and soon found herself distracted by a news story about a woman who had been discovered dead in her home—eight years after she died. And people thought Fina was a loner.

Risa reappeared ten minutes later. "I'm all done." She stopped in front of Fina's chair and pulled on her coat.

"How was it?"

"Easier than childbirth."

"Isn't everything easier than childbirth?" Fina asked.

"Yes, but it's a good yardstick."

"I'll take your word for it." Fina slipped her tablet back into her bag and followed Risa to the elevator.

"Now, how about you let me buy you a drink at the Liberty?" Risa asked. The Liberty Hotel was next door to the hospital, partly consisting of the former Charles Street Jail. Fina remembered when it was a jail and Buzzy's Roast Beef was the only fine dining in the neighborhood.

"I would love to, but I've got work to do," Fina said. "A client of mine is a patient here."

"A rain check?" Risa asked.

"Definitely."

The elevator doors opened, revealing two men, one of whom was glued to his phone.

At the ICU floor, Fina gave Risa a hug before stepping off and holding the door open with her hand. "You're going to be okay?"

"Yes. Thank you. I really appreciate it."

"No problem. Just remember: You're not committed to anything."

The man without the phone shifted impatiently, which gave Fina the urge to perform a monologue from *Hamlet*.

"Talk to you soon," Risa said as Fina released the door.

"Bye."

Fina walked to the ICU reception area hoping that Jamie was available. She was leaning against the desk pleading her case when he came down the hall, his posture slumped, his eyes trained on the floor. He looked startled when she called his name.

"I don't suppose you have ten minutes," she asked.

"No, not really."

"I don't know if you've been getting home at all, but I could always stop by your house."

"I guess you could come by later, assuming nothing changes here."

"Why don't I text you, and you can let me know what might work. I don't want to disrupt your time with your kids." *But I do really want to talk to you,* Fina thought.

"Sure." He rattled off his number.

"Were you on your way out?" Fina asked, gesturing toward the automatic double doors.

"In a minute," he said. "Don't wait for me."

Fina nodded. "I'll try you later."

"Yeah." Jamie stood at the desk and watched Fina leave.

The more he put off their conversation, the more intrigued she became. Fina wasn't sure why Jamie didn't want to talk, but she'd get to the bottom of it. Avoiding her indefinitely wasn't an option.

K evin Lafferty wanted to patronize Hamlin's shoe store, but their hours weren't convenient for anyone who held down a job. He and Sheila had purchased the kids' first baby shoes at the local store, and he knew the place was barely holding on, but who had time to shop for shoes in the middle of a weekday?

So instead, he found himself in the aisle of a big-box sporting goods store on a Monday night, trying to make sense of rows upon rows of sneakers.

"Robby! Casey! Stay with me, guys," he called out to his young sons.

Two smaller versions of Kevin came careening around the corner, nearly knocking over an end display of men's basketball shoes.

"Easy, guys. Don't tear up the place." He mussed the light brown hair on their heads and shooed them over to a bench in the middle of the aisle. "What size are you?"

"How are we supposed to know?" five-year-old Casey inquired.

"Well, pull off your sneakers and tell me what size those are. We know those are too small, so we'll move up from there."

The boys each pulled off a shoe and examined the tongue.

"I'm a one, Dad," Robby, the eight-year-old, offered.

"I don't know what I am," Casey moaned.

"Robby, help your brother while I look for you." He searched the stacks of boxes looking for size two.

A woman came into the aisle trailed by a young boy. "Excuse me," she said, squeezing past Kevin in the tight space.

He returned her smile and watched her walk away. *Not too shabby. Not too shabby at all,* he thought, admiring her slim body. Kevin hadn't noticed if she was wearing a ring, but he knew that he only need follow her and strike up a conversation to get the ball rolling. Not that Kevin was looking, but he was well aware of the effect he had on women. He had light brown hair and bright blue eyes. His smile was easy and his teeth straight. Women responded to Kevin like a fighter to smelling salts.

"Dad. Dad!" Robby interrupted his reverie. "Casey's size eleven."

"Thanks, kiddo." He reached up to grab a box off the top shelf. "Here's your size, and these"—he dropped down to a squat and plucked another box—"these should work for Case."

Of course the shoes weren't laced, so Kevin sat down and made quick work of them. At least that meant the boys would have practice tying them. There was a whole generation of kids being raised who had no idea how to tie a shoelace. It was ridiculous. Pretty soon they wouldn't be able to read analog clocks anymore.

Robby worked his feet into the shoes, but Casey needed Kevin's help to pull his on.

"What do you think?" Kevin asked as Robby ran up and down the aisle. Casey followed suit, never wanting to be left behind by his big brother.

"I like them," Robby said.

"Come over and let me check your toes," Kevin said. He reached down and depressed the end of the sneaker, checking that Robby's toes weren't too squished or swimming in the shoe. "I think that's good. What about you, buddy?" he asked Casey.

"They make me run superfast, Dad," his youngest said, tearing by him.

"The shoes don't make you faster, dummy," Robby remarked.

"Hey, watch it. Don't call your brother names. Say you're sorry."

Robby looked down at his highly engineered sneakers. "Sorry," he grumbled.

"Let me take a look, Casey." Kevin performed the same toe test on the boy and declared them a perfect fit. "Do you want to wear them out?"

"Yes!" they exclaimed in unison.

"All right. Let's go pay." Kevin boxed up their old shoes and tucked the boxes under his arm. He thought they should just be pitched in the trash, but he did that last time and Sheila was not happy. She wanted to keep the shoes for when it was wet or muddy, which seemed unnecessarily frugal to him. They did okay; why did they need to recycle smelly sneakers?

Back at the car, he helped the boys get buckled in. He was in charge of dinner since Sheila was on a late shift at the hospital, but he didn't feel like cooking.

"Who wants McDonald's?" he asked.

There were cheers of assent from the backseat. They got bags of burgers and greasy fries at the drive-thru and drove home, where they sat and ate in front of the TV. After a couple of episodes of *SpongeBob SquarePants*, Kevin put them both in a warm shower and then tucked them in with a chapter of Harry Potter.

What was Sheila always grousing about? The boys didn't seem like such hard work to him.

4.

It was six thirty P.M., and Fina needed food. She was dreaming of sausage and mushroom pizza when her phone dinged with a text. Jamie Gottlieb was ready to talk. He was on his way home to Hyde Park and wondered if Fina could swing by in an hour. She put her pizza dreams on hold and pointed her car toward the Barone/Gottlieb household.

Technically still within the city of Boston, Hyde Park looked more suburban than urban, with small single-family homes and tree-lined streets. Liz and Jamie's house was a modest colonial with a white picket fence and an oak tree in the front yard. A swing hanging from a large bough gently rocked in the wind, and the remnants of a snowman teetered on the lawn. Their last snowfall had been a few days ago, and they'd entered the yucky phase of a winter wonderland: brown snow, slushy salt that stained your boots, and crusty snowbanks that made walking nearly impossible.

There was an old Passat and a minivan in the driveway. The light by the front door burned brightly. Fina checked her watch and, since she was early, decided to check in with the neighbors. Canvassing door-to-door was tedious work that rarely garnered useful information. People like to believe their memories are like steel traps, but actually, they're more like sieves and highly unreliable. Fina knocked on eight doors, five of which were opened. Two of the neighbors hadn't been home at the approximate time of Liz's attack, two were eating dinner or helping with homework, and Mrs. Barbatto, the elderly neighbor, was watching the news. They all had nice things to say about Liz and Jamie, but Fina gained nothing from the outing other than frozen feet.

She rang the bell at Liz's and did a little dance to keep the blood flowing to her extremities. She was greeted a minute later by a gray-haired woman in black pants and a thick pullover sweater.

"Hi, I'm here to see Jamie."

"Is he expecting you?" she asked.

"Yes. I'm Fina Ludlow."

The woman studied her, then stepped back and invited her into the house. The door opened directly into the living room, which was comfortably furnished, but cluttered. There were toys and children's books on the floor, and messy stacks of newspaper had overtaken the coffee table. An overflowing laundry basket stood by the TV, and a Tupperware container with art supplies balanced precariously on the arm of a chair.

"Could you wait here for a moment?" the woman asked. Her face was lined with fatigue.

"Of course."

Fina pulled off her boots and jacket once her hostess had retreated; if Jamie had had a change of heart, it would be harder to ask her to leave if she had already shed her layers.

The woman returned to the front hall. "He's in the kitchen. Come on back."

Fina followed her through a dining room that doubled as a home office and into the kitchen, which overlooked the backyard. Jamie was sitting at the kitchen table.

"I'm going to check on the kids," the woman said before making herself scarce.

Fina watched her leave and let her eyes wander around the room. There were no signs of the violence that had occurred there only days before. Someone had done a good job cleaning up.

"That's Mrs. Sandraham," Jamie explained. "She babysits. She wanted to be sure I was up for a visitor."

Fina took a seat across from him. "How are the kids doing?"

"They miss their mom. Luckily, Mrs. Sandraham and Liz's friends have been helping out."

"It takes a village, even under the best of circumstances," Fina murmured.

Jamie got up and pulled a bottle of beer from the fridge. He waggled it in Fina's direction, and she nodded. Clients and interviewees always felt more comfortable if you followed their lead, so mimicking their drink order was an occupational hazard. If Fina had a dime for every beverage she didn't actually want, she'd be a rich woman and have to pee much less often.

"How are you holding up?" Fina asked.

"I'm okay. Just waiting." Jamie popped the tops off the two bottles and handed one to Fina before slumping back into his seat.

Fina knew that you didn't watch and wait indefinitely. At some point, the doctors would determine if Liz had any brain function. If she did, the family had a long road ahead of them. If she didn't, they had an agonizing decision to make. Both options were odious.

"I appreciate your taking the time to speak with me. I know you're exhausted and want to spend time with your kids."

Jamie took a long swallow rather than respond.

"When we spoke on Saturday," Fina continued, "you seemed convinced that the attack was random."

He nodded.

"So you can't think of anyone with whom Liz had a conflict or some kind of grudge?"

"No."

"What is her relationship like with her family?"

"It's good," Jamie said. "She gets along well with her mom and sisters."

"Is she closer to one sister than the other?"

"Nicole, but she gets along fine with Dawn. They're so damn competitive." He shook his head. "It's ridiculous."

"How so?"

"They compare road race times and do impromptu push-up contests."

That sounded like the kind of thing Fina and her brothers would do. She had no doubt that if she proposed a push-up contest, Matthew and Scotty would drop to the floor like lead balloons. Carl might even join in—anything to allow him to prove his prowess.

"What about friends and coworkers?"

"She's got some friends in the neighborhood. I can give you some names, and she's still tight with Tasha Beemis-Jones."

"I left a message for Tasha this afternoon. How about at work?"

Jamie picked at the label on his beer bottle. "She likes her colleagues. Her boss is a jerk, but I think that's just work stuff."

"What kind of work stuff?" Fina asked.

"I don't know the specifics, just that Vikram rides her ass."

Fina drank some beer. "I'm kind of surprised you don't know the specifics," she ventured.

"Why? Liz doesn't know all the details of my job and my office politics. We don't get a lot of time to talk, and when we do, we don't talk about work."

"Do you enjoy your work?" Fina asked.

Jamie looked at her quizzically. "I don't get why that's important."

"I'm just getting the lay of the land."

He shrugged. "I like it."

"But not as much as playing music."

"No, not as much as playing music, but I couldn't make a living doing that, and the benefits package is nonexistent." He grimaced.

Fina took a swig of beer before reaching into her bag. She pulled out one of the old NEU newspapers. "Can you take a look at this picture and tell me if you recognize anyone?" The paper was folded to highlight a large photo taken on the sidelines of a soccer game. It featured players and others in street clothes.

Jamie pulled the paper toward him. "That's Liz, obviously." He pointed at a younger, healthier version of his wife. "Tasha, Coach Adams, and that's Kelly." He indicated each of them.

"Kelly Wegner?"

"Yeah. How'd you know?"

"Bobbi mentioned her."

He nodded. "She and her husband live a few streets away. The kids are playmates."

"That's nice," Fina said. "I love living close to my college best friend." Speaking of which, she owed Milloy Danielson, her BFF, a phone call. He was usually up for sausage and mushroom pizza. "I met with Thatcher Kinney this morning."

"Oh yeah?"

"Yeah. Have you met him?"

"I went to Liz's first meeting with him," Jamie said. "I'd met him before at a Christmas party or something like that."

"And what did you think?"

Jamie tore off another strip of the bottle label. "He seemed like a nice guy."

Fina squinted at him. "Did you think he was doing a good job? Was he a good advocate for Liz?"

"I'm not really involved in the lawsuit, but he seemed fine to me."

She nodded. Jamie's lack of interest in—or at least awareness of—Liz's activities struck her as strange. She didn't think spouses should know every shred of information about each other, but this seemed especially hands-off.

"What about her interactions with the development office at NEU? I got hold of some correspondence that suggests they were prodding Liz for a donation."

"Alma maters are always asking for money."

"Sure, but it seems pretty insensitive to ask her to support a program that she held responsible for her condition."

"Liz is mad at everyone at NEU," he said. "I wouldn't narrow it down to one department."

Fina tapped her nail against her beer bottle. "I'm sorry to ask this because I know it's nosy and indelicate, but how were you and Liz doing?"

Jamie paused, his nearly empty bottle halfway to his mouth. "Are you asking me if I clobbered my wife?"

"No, but I assume your answer would be no if I were asking."

"Yeah, that's exactly what my answer would be. Liz and I are good. Everything's fine on that front."

"Glad to hear it." Fina swallowed the rest of her beer and carried the empty over to the sink. "Could you give me Kelly's contact info? I need to ask her a few questions."

Jamie grabbed his phone and read off Kelly's number.

"What about Coach Adams?" Fina asked.

"A dead end, literally. He died about seven years ago."

"Okeydoke. I'll be in touch when I have news."

"Great," Jamie said unenthusiastically, trailing her to the front door, where she struggled into her outerwear.

"Did the cops take Liz's computer?" she asked, her hand on the doorknob.

"Yes."

"I'd love to take a peek when you get it back."

Jamie shrugged. "Sure."

Sitting in her car with the vent blasting hot air, Fina thought about the conversation. Bobbi was the one actually paying her bill, but it struck her as odd that Jamie hadn't asked Fina for a progress report. Didn't he care who attacked his wife? Did he already know who did? Was he the one who attacked her, which would explain his disinterest?

But shock and trauma were such curious things; sometimes it was hard to determine if weird behavior was the result, or just plain weird.

Fina went home and called Milloy, her best friend, massage therapist, and overall Renaissance man. They'd met in college and discovered during orientation week that they were kindred spirits. They were both loyal and dependable, and neither enjoyed analyzing their feelings. Sometimes their relationship was romantic, and sometimes it wasn't. It depended on the day.

She invited him over for pizza and a massage—provided by him, not her—but he took a rain check.

"Maybe you should plan ahead a little," he suggested. "Not assume that I'm available at the last minute."

"I didn't assume that. I hoped. You know, 'hope springs eternal in the human breast.'"

"Leave your breasts out of this."

"Are you available on Thursday evening, good sir?" she asked.

"I'm waiting to hear back from a client, but I think so."

"Good. I look forward to it."

Picking up the phone and ordering pizza seemed like too much work, and cooking would have been a Herculean effort, so she grabbed a handful of Ritz crackers and smeared them with peanut butter.

Fina finished eating and snuggled under Nanny's afghan on the living room couch. She pulled her computer onto her lap, marveling at the heat provided by the machine. What did the pioneers do without electronics to warm their nether regions?

HGTV was airing a showcase of unusual homes that provided nice background noise as she researched Kelly Wegner, whom she hoped to interview the next day. Cyberspace offered little of interest: Her husband, Josh, worked for an insurance company, they were active in the Methodist church, and Kelly participated in a number of charity road races.

Fina picked up her phone and dialed Emma Kirwan, her guru for all things computer-related.

"Yes?" Emma answered.

"Not even hello?"

"Did you really call me for conversation, Fina?"

Emma was extremely conservative and rigid, except for the myriad illegal activities she performed on her computer. Fina had yet to give her a computer quandary she couldn't crack, and she'd proved invaluable in past cases. Despite that, Fina always stumbled over her cashmere twin sets and sensible shoes. Emma looked like she should be leading a book group discussion about Glenn Beck's newest tome, not hacking into secure networks.

"I need you to look into someone for me," Fina said. "Her name is Liz Barone. She was attacked in her home a few days ago, and the cops have her computer."

"Well, that limits me."

"I know, but can't you float up into the cloud or whatever it is and find me some dirt?"

"Yeah, that's exactly what I'll do," Emma said dryly.

"I can hear your eyes rolling, Emma. Just do what you can," Fina said. "She also works for NEU in a lab."

"What kind of lab?"

"I don't know, but I don't think she was developing deadly viruses or anything like that."

"I'll see what I can do, but labs are usually well protected, and it's too risky."

"Like I said, just do what you can. I'm particularly interested in anything related to the NEU development office and a woman named Pamela Fordyce."

"I'll let you know when I find something," Emma said, ending the call.

Fina put down her phone and grabbed the folder that Thatcher Kinney had given her. She pulled out the school newspapers and studied the photos more carefully, identifying Kelly and Tasha in a number of them. Other players wearing the NEU uniform were pictured, as was the man Fina assumed to be Coach Adams, wearing an NEU jacket and those ill-fitting slacks—yes, slacks—that seemed to be the favored attire of coaches.

As she studied the photos, two other people caught her eye. They were both white men, one who looked to be in his midtwenties, the other about a decade older. The younger one was handsome, and in a couple of the pictures, he had his arms slung around the players in a pose of easy familiarity. The older man stood off to the side a bit, but was also smiling. His posture was more upright, and he wore a suit jacket and a tie. Other than the players and the coach, these two were the only consistent faces on the NEU sideline.

Just who were these super-fans?

Fina called Kelly Wegner shortly after eight the next morning. Interviewees who were parents were always up early and had generally crossed more off their to-do lists by nine A.M. than some people did all day. This was precisely why Fina admired them and had no interest in joining their ranks.

Kelly had just dropped her kids at school and was at the grocery store. She had to swing by the dry cleaner and the post office, but would be happy to meet Fina at Liz and Jamie's house in two hours.

Fina dragged herself down to the gym and logged a few miles on the treadmill. Back upstairs, she showered off the sweat and pulled on a pair of jeans, a sweater, and thick wool socks, her go-to outfit these days.

When she pulled up to Liz and Jamie's house, the exterior light was burning brightly just as it had been the night before. There really was no point in turning it off for the mere eight hours of milky daylight with which they were graced this time of year. A gray minivan was parked in the driveway next to the minivan from last night. There were a couple of kid-related decals on the rear window, but a quick glimpse of the interior didn't reveal any empty juice boxes or smooshed-up Goldfish crackers. Fina walked to the front door and rang the bell. A minute later, she was greeted by a compact woman with a blond bob.

"Kelly? I'm Fina Ludlow."

"Nice to meet you," Kelly said. She wasn't much over five feet three inches, but she looked solid, with short, stocky legs. Her jeans were tight, and her sweater showcased broad shoulders. Stepping back from the door, she ushered Fina into the house.

"You can leave your boots and stuff here," she offered. "I feel like this winter is never going to end."

"Technically, I think it just started," Fina commented.

"I know, but it feels worse this year, don't you think?"

"It definitely feels colder." Fina placed her boots on the plastic boot tray and pulled off her coat.

"It makes running a real pain," Kelly said, smoothing her hand over the back of an upholstered chair.

"You're a runner?" Fina asked innocently. Some people were flattered to know that you'd done some research on them, but others found it creepy. It was too soon to tell which camp Kelly lived in.

"Yup, but it's tough when the streets are such a mess and the sidewalks aren't shoveled."

"And it's icy," Fina said. "Sounds dangerous."

"That's why I've been spending a lot of time on the treadmill these days."

The cluttered living room from the night before had been transformed into a room that could be featured in a home-decorating magazine. The only newspaper in evidence was the day's *Globe*, and the container of art supplies had been stowed on a bookcase. There was no sign of laundry, the pillows looked fluffed, and a throw had been neatly folded and laid over the back of the sofa. A mild cooking scent perfumed the air.

Fina followed Kelly to the kitchen.

"Is there any news from the hospital?" Fina asked.

Kelly shook her head. "Just watch and wait. Do you want some coffee?"

"Please." Fina took a seat at the table.

"So I have to admit," Kelly said, her back to Fina, "I don't quite understand why Jamie hired you."

"Well, technically, Bobbi Barone hired me, but they both want to know who hurt Liz."

Kelly brought a steaming mug of coffee over to the table and pushed milk and sugar in Fina's direction. "Isn't that what the police are for?"

"Yes, but I'm an extra set of eyes and ears. And I have some contacts they don't."

"Don't get me wrong," Kelly said, "I'm glad they hired you. I just wasn't sure how it worked."

Fina wrapped her hands around the hot mug. "How did you find out that Liz was hurt?"

"Jamie called me. I live a few streets away. Liz and I went to NEU together, and our kids are friends." Kelly bustled back over to the sink and ran the tap. She picked up a clump of steel wool and began scouring a cookie sheet.

"Do you have any idea who might want to hurt Liz?" Fina poured milk into her mug and dropped in a generous spoonful of sugar. "Any enemies that you're aware of?"

"She's a soccer mom," Kelly said over her shoulder. "What kind of enemies would she have?"

"Lots of people have enemies. Sometimes the people you least expect have the most complicated relationships."

"Not Liz. The most complicated thing in her life was that lawsuit, and I'm not convinced anything was going to come of it."

"What makes you say that?" Fina asked.

"It just seems like David and Goliath."

"How long have you known about it?"

"She's been talking to the attorney for a month or so, but she'd been after NEU for about six months." Kelly shook the cookie sheet over the sink and slotted it into a drying rack. "She told me about it when she started having issues."

"Cognitive issues?"

"Yup." Kelly wrung out the sponge and began wiping down the counters. She hadn't made much progress when a timer beeped. After donning two pot holders, Kelly reached into the oven and pulled out what looked like a lasagna. The white cheese on the top was lightly browned and bubbling. Kelly seemed more familiar with Liz's kitchen than Fina was with her own, but perhaps that wasn't saying much.

"It's nice of you to come over here and help out," Fina commented.

Kelly gave a pained smile. "Do you think it's too much? I don't want to overstep, but I thought I should make myself useful until it's time to pick up the kids."

"I'm sure Liz and Jamie appreciate it."

"Liz and I try to help each other when we can. When I had foot surgery last year, she was a lifesaver."

"Sounds like you're good friends to each other."

"This"—Kelly made a sweeping motion—"is also kind of selfish. Cooking and cleaning keep me calm. I know it sounds crazy."

"That does sound crazy," Fina said, "but thank goodness there are people like you in the world."

Fina sipped her coffee, which was still too bitter despite her ministrations. She preferred her hot beverages to be sweet, ideally with a thick coating of whipped cream. "Anyone else you think I should talk to?"

Kelly returned the pot holders to a drawer and leaned her hip against the counter. "Like who?"

"Friends, colleagues. I'm just trying to get a better sense of Liz outside the context of the lawsuit."

"You should call Tasha. She's one of Liz's closest friends from college."

"Tasha Beemis-Jones?" Fina asked. Kelly nodded. "Jamie and Bobbi mentioned her. She played soccer with you guys, right?"

"Yup. She's an attorney now, downtown." Kelly left the room and returned a moment later with an overflowing laundry basket.

Fina was getting worn out from the dervish dance of homemaking activities. "Anyone else?"

"I'd have to think about it," Kelly said, taking a seat at the end of the table. She grabbed a soccer shirt from the basket and shook it out before neatly folding it and placing it on an empty chair.

Fina reached into her bag and pulled out a couple of the school newspapers. "Do you recognize these two men?" She pointed at the mystery fans she'd identified the night before.

Kelly craned her neck to get a better look. "That's Kevin Lafferty." She pointed at the younger of the two.

"Who's he?"

"He worked for NEU for a year or two, and now he's president of the booster club."

"What's that?" Fina asked.

"It's a group of alums who support the athletic programs. They're all sports nuts and have lots of school pride. They attend the games and do fund-raisers, and as president, Kevin interacts a lot with the coaches and the student athletes."

"Sounds like a full-time job."

"It's a volunteer position, but he devotes a lot of time to it."

Fina looked skeptical. "Huh."

"It's a social thing," Kelly explained, "and people get to pretend they never left college. There's also a certain status attached to it on campus. The top boosters are treated like VIPs."

"Got it. So what's he do the rest of the time?" Fina asked.

Kelly scrunched up her face in thought. "I think he works in the pharmaceutical industry."

"Do you know how to reach him?"

"No, I can't remember the name of the company, but Tasha might."

"And him?" Fina pointed at the older man.

"That's our team doctor, Gus Sibley." Kelly smoothed down the stack of clothes that she'd already folded.

"Is he still alive? Jamie mentioned that Coach Adams died."

"I think Dr. Sibley's alive, but I don't know for sure."

"Last you heard was he still at NEU?"

"I think so. He was still there when we graduated."

"So these two were at every game?" Fina pointed at the men in the photo.

"Well, Dr. Sibley had to be, and I think Kevin attended most of them. To be honest, I was focused on what was happening on the field. I didn't pay much attention to the sidelines."

"Of course. That makes sense." Fina sipped her coffee. "What about Liz's job? Did she enjoy it?"

"I think so. I mean, she felt the guilt that all working mothers do, but she seemed to like it. I know that sometimes the politics could get heated, but Liz was no shrinking violet."

"Any coworkers in particular you think I should speak with?"

Kelly folded a tiny pair of briefs. "She's mentioned a woman named Dana before. She also talked about her boss; they don't get along."

"Vikram?" Fina asked.

"Yeah."

Fina stood and took her coffee cup over to the sink. She poured the contents down the drain, washed it, and left it upended on the drying rack. "Did Liz act any differently the past few weeks? Was she upset or distracted?"

Kelly shook her head. "Not that I noticed. The lawsuit was definitely weighing on her, but that was nothing new. Obviously, she was worried about her health. It's a mother's worst nightmare, thinking she might not be around for her kids."

The comment gave Fina pause. Although her mother, Elaine, seemed largely inconvenienced by her kids, Fina wondered if that had always been the case. Fina's older sister, Josie, had died before Fina was born, when she was two and a half. Had the death of her eldest child permanently changed the kind of mother Elaine was, or was this version of Elaine the version that Fina would have gotten regardless of Josie's death? She would never know.

Fina returned to the front door, and Kelly waited as she put her boots and jacket back on.

"Let me give you my card," Fina said, reaching into her bag. "If you think of anything that might be relevant, don't hesitate to be in touch."

"Of course."

"Do you know if Jamie is going to be at the hospital all day?"

"I imagine." She winced. "Please take it easy on him. He's having a terrible time."

Fina paused. "I'm not sure what he told you, but I promise, I'm not being hard on him. Unfortunately, asking tough questions is part of an investigation. It can't be helped."

Kelly nodded. "Right, right. I just don't want him to suffer any more than he has to."

"Nor do I."

Fina climbed into her car and made a U-turn in the street, waving to Kelly as she took off. She turned the heater to high and felt the dry, hot air blast out of the vents.

If Liz didn't regain consciousness soon, her house would be unrecognizable.

5.

Pamela Fordyce studied the items on a shelf in her display cabinet. She supposed she could make room between the millefiori glass duck from her trip to Italy and the ceramic dragon she'd purchased in Shanghai. She spent a few moments shifting around her treasures, then placed the framed photograph in the newly vacant space. A couple of steps back and a tilt of her head told her all she needed to know. It wasn't quite right.

Returning the items to their original spots, Pamela took the photo back to her desk and lowered herself into the deep leather chair. It was a nice photo, she thought, running her fingertip around the frame. She looked thinner than usual, and Deb looked pretty, but she just wasn't ready to put it on display. Not yet.

She stowed the gift in her right-hand top drawer and pushed it closed. She'd have to remember to put it out if Deb stopped by the office. Deb had purposefully given her two pictures—one for Pamela's home and the other for the office—and Pamela knew Deb would be angry if she didn't put the office version on display. But Deb really didn't have a right to be so impatient with her. She wasn't a teenager in love, and she wasn't interested in committing to a serious relationship—not now, and maybe not ever—with Deb.

Pamela searched the top of her desk for her reading glasses, which seemed to always be either on her nose or lost. A string around her neck was the obvious solution, but that would make her really feel old. She was only fifty-four, and the fewer reminders of that, the better. That's what no one ever told you about working at a university: You spent your days surrounded by energetic young people who required little sleep. At least when she'd worked in development in the hospital she'd felt like the picture of health compared to the population she was serving. Here, she was given daily reminders of her advancing age. It's not that Pamela didn't like being around the kids; she enjoyed the company of the work-study students who provided support in the development office. But sometimes their youth was so . . . What was the right word? Abundant, obvious. There was no moderation or temperance, like a radio that had only one volume setting—extremely loud.

Glancing at her schedule, Pamela saw that she had five minutes before her next meeting. She wandered over to the kitchenette a few doors down from her office and poured herself a cup of black coffee. There was a box of Munchkins open on the countertop, and she studied the contents. The glazed and chocolate were always the first to go, but even plain cake Munchkins were better than no Munchkins. She placed three on a napkin and brought them back to her desk, where she sipped her coffee and popped them into her mouth in quick succession.

The first committee member strolled in a minute later, and Pamela took her time tidying her desk and consulting her computer. In her experience, it was better to wait until everyone had arrived before she left her desk and took her place at the head of the conference table. If she were already sitting there, it would suggest to them that she had nothing better to do than wait around for them, which couldn't be further from the truth. Some of the attendees might outrank her in the university hierarchy, but the dean had appointed her the head of this particular committee, and Pamela was savvy enough to know that every move was an opportunity to garner new authority.

She waited until five minutes after the appointed meeting time and then called things to order. Stragglers would just have to catch up.

"Welcome, everyone," she said, and made eye contact with her colleagues. "We have a lot to discuss in limited time. Let's begin."

F ina was tooling up Hyde Park Avenue when her phone rang with a
summons. If she wanted to speak with Tasha Beemis-Jones, she
should present herself at the Elite Sports Club in the Financial District
in forty-five minutes. Tasha's assistant informed her this was the only
window in Tasha's schedule, emphasizing that it was a one-time offer.
Fina gladly accepted.

The club had valet parking, which Fina generally disliked. Private
investigators' cars were their mobile offices, and giving someone unob-
served access was akin to unlocking your office door for a stranger and
then heading out to lunch. Unfortunately, her options were few and exorbitant at midday in downtown Boston.

A doorman held the door for her—that was five calories she wouldn't
be burning—and directed her to a sleek counter. The lobby was small,
but its ceiling rose up the equivalent of two stories. There was little
décor except for two leather chairs in an intimate sitting area, but the
focal point of the space was what appeared to be a wall of plants climbing nearly to the ceiling. The variety of texture and hue was stunning,
and Fina imagined there was an intricate irrigation system behind the
plants making them appear as if they were sprouting spontaneously
from the wall.

"May I help you?" a young man behind the counter asked. He was
wearing slim black pants and a T-shirt so tight, Fina thought she could
see blood pumping through his heart.

"I'm meeting Tasha Beemis-Jones," Fina replied.

"Your name, please, and a picture ID."

Fina handed over her driver's license—no need to alert him to her PI
status—and he tapped at his keyboard for what seemed like an inordi-
nate amount of time. It was how Fina always felt at the airline counter:
What were they doing? Writing *Moby Dick*?

The receptionist was probably in his twenties and was handsome in
a *GQ* kind of way, with a strong chin, sharp cheekbones, and full lips.

Fina wondered what he'd looked like as a baby. Obviously, his features would have been proportional, but what made him striking as an adult could not have made him snuggly as an infant. He was probably making up for it now.

"What size are you, ma'am?" He smiled at her, revealing perfect white teeth.

"Huh?"

"Your size? For your gear?"

Fina looked at him askance, recalling the three miles she'd run only hours before. "I'm not here to work out. I'm meeting someone."

"I understand, but street clothes aren't allowed in the club."

"I have to change right here?" Fina asked, pointing at the large windows fronting the busy street.

He chuckled. "Of course not. You can change in the women's locker room, but you will have to change."

Fina sighed. She should charge Bobbi time and a half for this. "Size eight clothes and shoes."

The young man reached into a wardrobe hidden in the wall behind him and pulled out some items.

"Once you get upstairs, if something doesn't fit, just ask the attendant to swap it for you."

He slipped the goods into a large tote emblazoned with the club logo and ushered Fina over to the elevator. "The women's locker room will be on your right when you exit the elevator." He handed her a key attached to what looked like a thin, short bungee cord. "This is for your locker. You can change, and Ms. Beemis-Jones will meet you on the fitness floor."

"Wonderful," Fina said.

Upstairs, she proceeded to the locker room and unlocked her assigned locker. "Locker" was a misnomer; it was actually a small walk-in closet outfitted with a floor-to-ceiling mirror and an upholstered chair. The room itself was made of highly polished black wood and brought to mind a humidor rather than a gym.

Fina pulled on a sports bra, designer leggings, a T-shirt, and socks, and what looked like a brand-new pair of sneakers. Good thing, because she didn't share shoes with people unless she was related, and even then some people didn't make the cut. She locked her belongings away in the changing room and headed to the fitness floor.

A group of glowing, sculpted women came through a door looking as if they'd just finished filming an exercise DVD. They were a tribe: the same perfect bodies, highlighted blond hair, sleek workout clothes. Fina ducked past them and surveyed the room before her. It wasn't a huge space, but it was filled with every type of equipment you might need: treadmills, stair-climbers, and ellipticals, as well as free weights and weight machines. Most of the walls were mirrored, creating fit doppel-gängers everywhere Fina looked.

Fina scanned the room and recognized Tasha from the photos on-line. She hopped onto the treadmill next to her. There was an unopened bottle of water sitting in the cup holder and a fresh towel hanging over the handrail.

Tasha was close to six feet tall, her black hair pulled back in a pony-tail. Her ebony skin was slick with sweat, but the makeup outlining her brown eyes was impeccable. If there was an ounce of fat on her, Fina couldn't imagine where it might be.

"Ms. Beemis-Jones? I'm Fina Ludlow."

Tasha was running at a clip, but offered her hand across her body to shake.

"You can call me Tasha." She glanced at Fina. "Fire up your tread-mill. We can do two things at once."

Goddamnit. One of the few days Fina decides to work out, and her witness insists on a treadmill-based interview. Fina punched the keys, and the belt rolled to life. "Thanks for agreeing to meet with me."

"Sorry we have to do it here. My schedule is a nightmare, but obvi-ously I want to help Liz any way I can," Tasha said.

"Have you spoken to Bobbi or Jamie recently?" Fina upped her speed. She might not be a star athlete, but she had her pride.

"I called Bobbi this morning, but there's no change."

"That's what Kelly Wegner said. I met with her this morning."

"How's she doing?"

"Hanging in there," Fina said. "Cleaning a lot."

Tasha made a noise that was somewhere between a chuckle and a snort. "She's always been that way. You should have seen her dorm room in college. Her CDs were alphabetized, and her underwear drawer looked like a display at Victoria's Secret."

"Hmm. I'm definitely missing that gene," Fina admitted.

"Well, Kelly's got it in spades."

Fina waited a minute before launching into her line of questioning. "Do you have any idea who might have hurt Liz?"

"I've been racking my brain, but I'm coming up empty," Tasha said. "Liz didn't really have enemies."

"Were there people she didn't get along with?"

"Enough to kill her? I would say no, but obviously I'd be wrong."

Fina was starting to feel warm, moisture rising from her pores. "What's her relationship with Jamie like?"

Tasha shrugged. "It's fine."

"That's pretty lukewarm."

"Well, they've never struck me as the most passionate couple, and they both work long hours."

"So even in the beginning they didn't seem head over heels?"

"I'm not saying they don't love each other, just that neither is especially demonstrative, and the music stuff always created tension." Tasha increased the incline of her treadmill. Show-off.

"Oh right, he was in a band."

"Technically, he still is, but it got to the point that he had to choose. He realized he wasn't going to be a rock star, and you can't raise a family on an amateur musician's salary, not to mention the lack of health insurance and paid vacation time."

"Was that a bitter pill to swallow?" Fina was feeling the strain of running and talking at the same time. Tasha moved effortlessly next to her.

"Definitely. I'm not sure it's been completely digested yet."

"Does he blame Liz?" Fina asked.

Tasha eyed her. "Well, she's the messenger, right? It's easy to blame her for his dashed dreams, but I'm not suggesting he would hurt her. Jamie is a fairly passive guy. I've rarely seen him get worked up about stuff."

"What did you think about her potential lawsuit against NEU?" Fina asked.

Tasha smirked. "I thought she needed to get herself a real lawyer."

"Like you?" Fina smiled.

"I'm a commercial litigator. I don't do personal injury," Tasha said.

"You don't think Thatcher Kinney is up for the big leagues?"

"Have you met him?"

"Yes. Why did Liz hire him in the first place?" Fina asked.

"He knew her mom, and they had friends in common. I think she was worried about hurting his feelings or causing some brouhaha in town."

"You can't worry about hurt feelings when it comes to legal representation."

"You should know, Fina Ludlow," Tasha said, emphasizing *Ludlow*.

Fina ignored her. "What did you think about the lawsuit itself?"

"Liz is not litigious by nature, but she was sick of getting the runaround from NEU. She felt like they weren't leaving her any choice."

"Does the case have legal merit, in your opinion?"

"Unfortunately, there wasn't any concussion protocol when we were playing. People didn't know better, and I don't think you can hold someone responsible for not knowing they should know something."

Fina grabbed the water bottle from the holder and took a swig. She needed the hydration, but it also bought her a moment to catch her breath. "Had you noticed a difference in Liz, cognitively?" she asked Tasha.

"Some small things, but we don't see each other as often as we'd like. Mostly, she recounted things to me," Tasha said, staring at her reflection in the mirror. "You just never think that something like this is going to happen."

Fina wasn't sure if she was referring to the MCI or the attack. "I know. It's awful." They were silent for a minute. "What about at work?" Fina asked. "Any problems there?"

"I think there was some issue with her boss recently, but I don't know the specifics. It wasn't a personal issue, though, not a reason for someone to attack her."

Sadly, physical attacks sometimes were related to workplace issues, but those generally occurred at work. It would have taken effort to track Liz down at her home.

"What's her boss's name?"

"Vikram . . . I can't remember his last name." Tasha adjusted the incline of her treadmill again.

Fina's legs were aching, and she could feel a blister developing on her right heel. "I showed Kelly some old NEU newspapers this morning, and she pointed out two men that showed up in a lot of pictures: Kevin Lafferty and Gus Sibley."

Tasha maintained her stride, but Fina saw her fingertips briefly touch the railing of the treadmill. She didn't say anything.

"They were at most of the games?" Fina prompted.

"Dr. Sibley was since he was our team doctor, and Kevin was always hanging around."

"Hanging around sounds kind of bad."

"I don't mean it to," Tasha said. "He was just there a lot."

"Have you had any contact with either of them since your playing days?" Fina asked.

"Intermittently. We bump into each other at NEU fund-raisers, that sort of thing."

"Do you know how I could reach them?"

"I'm not sure what the point would be. Do you really think Liz's attack has something to do with NEU?"

"I don't know. That's what I'm trying to figure out," Fina said. "Speaking with them is due diligence; I'm sure you can appreciate that."

Tasha nodded. "Gus is still affiliated with NEU, and he has a private practice in Chestnut Hill, and Kevin's the president of the booster club."

"Do you know where he works?" Fina asked.

"Barnes Kaufcan, the pharmaceutical company."

"Did you ever get the sense that Dr. Sibley had any misgivings about concussions when you and Liz were playing soccer? Was he pressured to play injured players?" Fina blotted her face with the towel. A dull pain radiated up her shins. She hoped to God this wasn't a distance training day for Tasha.

"Not to my knowledge."

"What was your experience with injuries?" Fina asked.

Tasha grabbed her water and chugged it. She dropped the bottle back into the cup holder before answering. "We got hurt. We were competing at a high level. What the staff said or didn't say didn't matter. I was competitive, and I made the choice to play hard," Tasha said, staring straight ahead.

Before Fina could respond, an older black man wandered over and planted himself in front of Tasha's treadmill. "We need to reschedule the exploratory meeting," he said to her without any preamble.

Tasha glared at him. "Reed, this is Fina Ludlow. She's a private investigator."

The man looked spooked for an instant, then recovered and exchanged hellos with Fina.

"Call my office to reschedule, won't you?" Tasha said tersely.

"Of course. I'll be in touch." He beat a hasty retreat.

Fina didn't say anything for a moment, nor did Tasha.

"Mayor or city council?" Fina asked.

"I'm sorry?" Tasha peered at her.

"People convene exploratory committees when they're thinking of running for office. So which office do you have in mind?"

Tasha decreased her speed and slowed to a walk. She grabbed the towel from the handrail and mopped her sweaty brow. Her makeup still looked untouched.

"No comment."

"You'd make an excellent candidate," Fina said. She hopped onto the sides of the moving belt before pressing the stop button.

"Uh-huh."

"You can tell me. I'll be discreet."

Tasha rolled her eyes and pulled one foot toward her butt to stretch her quadriceps muscle. "Discretion is not the first thing that comes to mind when I hear the name *Ludlow*." She stretched the other leg before stepping off the treadmill.

Fina followed her to the water cooler. "Is there anyone else you think I should talk to about Liz?" she asked.

"No, but I'll let you know if I think of anyone." Tasha took a long gulp from her refilled water bottle. "I've got to go, but you're welcome to stay and work out some more."

Fina pretended to seriously consider the suggestion. "I think I'm good."

Tasha smiled. "Well, in that case, they have amazing products in the locker room, plus a Jacuzzi and a sauna. Take your time in there."

"That sounds infinitely more appealing. Thanks."

"If you hear anything about Liz, give me a call," Tasha said before disappearing into the locker room.

"Of course."

Fina refilled her bottle before wandering into the locker room, where she stayed in the Jacuzzi until her fingers got pruney.

She wasn't quite sure what she'd gleaned from the conversation other than an elevated heart rate and sore hamstrings.

6.

Fina retreated home—given the arctic temperatures and her muscle fatigue, a nap seemed like the right course of action, but she staved off the urge. She called Scotty's assistant, Michelle, to get an update on the Disney ticket situation. Fina joked about trading favors, but she was a big believer in quid pro quo. Sometimes people were altruistic and selfless, but more often they were looking to further their own interests or the interests of the people they cared about. Even so, most people clung tightly to the idea that relationships were equal and neither party should have the upper hand. No one wanted to feel like they were getting the short end of the stick. That was what drove lawsuits, after all: making someone "whole" after they'd been wronged. Cristian was her friend, and she liked making him and Matteo happy, but she also knew it was good for business.

Fina grabbed a diet soda and plopped down on the couch before dialing Cristian.

"Menendez."

"Hey. How's it going?"

"Fine. How are you?" It was quiet in the background, which suggested he wasn't at the station.

"I'm good." She sipped her drink.

There was a pregnant pause.

"Good news: There's a *Disney on Ice* show coming up," Fina said. "It's called 'Let's Celebrate!' It's—and I quote—a 'magical medley of holidays, celebrations, and festivities from around the globe,' including a luau, Mardi Gras, and Valentine's Day. It sounds absolutely horrific."

"Which means Teo will love it. Let me check the custody schedule and I'll give you some possible dates."

"Is there any way we could meet up today?"

"What do you want?" he asked suspiciously.

"I want to share my progress on the Liz Barone case with you."

Cristian laughed. "Of course you do. I'm pretty busy working on that case myself, so why don't you just tell me over the phone?"

"It's so much more fun to give you updates in person," Fina said. It was true: Flirting with Cristian face-to-face was way more satisfying than on the phone.

"I'll be at the Jim Roche ice rink in West Roxbury at five P.M. I'll have ten minutes or so."

"Why are you going to an ice rink when it's ten degrees outside?"

"Why do you think, Sherlock?"

Cristian hung up, and Fina cursed her miscalculation.

Even Cristian wasn't worth freezing her ass off.

It was about twenty-five degrees in the rink, and loud. The place was crawling with kids, most of them lumbering under the weight of hockey pads and helmets. Fina arrived just as the Zamboni emerged to smooth the shaved and pitted surface into a glassy, wet layer.

A couple of the benches in the locker room area were occupied by men and women wearing pads and police department hockey shirts. Fina spotted Cristian and caught his eye. People on the force knew they were friends, but she didn't want to put him on the spot in front of his colleagues. Some cops had nothing but disdain for PIs, and it was a relationship best kept on the down low.

Cristian threaded his way over to her, and they found a spot on a bench. He dropped his bag onto the rubber floor and pulled off his boots.

"Forget the cold, why are you playing hockey when you're on a case?" Fina asked.

"It's part of the community outreach thing. It's only an hour, and Pitney catches hell if we don't put in the time. It's also a good way to blow off steam."

Fina eyed the competition. "You're blowing off steam playing against a ragtag group of neighborhood kids?"

"I meant the other cops." Cristian forced his foot into a skate and tugged on the laces. "The teams are mixed."

"Well, you're a good man and a role model. I still don't understand the appeal of a sport where you freeze your ass off."

"Never mind that. I only have until the ice is clean."

"All righty. Were there any signs of forced entry at Liz Barone's house?"

Cristian paused his lacing efforts. "Hold on. I thought you were going to update me."

"I am," Fina said, "but I thought you could start."

He shook his head, winding the laces around the small hooks at his ankle. "No, there were no signs of forced entry."

"So either the door was unlocked, the perpetrator had a key, or Liz let the person in."

"Jamie says that they always lock the door."

"That rules out one option then. Did Jamie find her?"

"Yes. Luckily, the kids were at a neighbor's house so they were spared."

"Who has a copy of their house key?" Fina asked.

"When's the part where you give me information?" Cristian asked, moving on to the other skate.

"So impatient. If you insist, I've spoken with Bobbi Barone, Jamie, Kelly Wegner, Tasha Beemis-Jones, and the attorney, Thatcher Kinney."

"And?"

"And the attorney is clearly not the man for the job, but it's not clear yet if the lawsuit had anything to do with the attack," Fina said.

"That's great, but you're not telling me anything I don't already know."

"But I will, eventually. Maybe not today, but someday." The Zamboni was turning the corner, making its final pass. "You got any alibis?" Fina asked.

"Nothing airtight. We need a few more suspects in the meantime." Cristian tucked his shoes under the bench and zipped up his bag. He stood and bounced lightly on the skates. "What's next on your agenda?"

"Gus Sibley and Kevin Lafferty."

Cristian blinked at Kevin's name.

"Oh, so maybe you don't know everything," Fina said.

"Enlighten me."

"He's a booster for NEU athletics, and he spent a lot of time hanging around the women's soccer team back in the day."

"Does he have a current relationship with Liz?"

"That's not clear. Speaking of relationships, how's Cindy?"

"She's good."

"Just good?"

"Just good." He pulled on his oversized gloves.

"Well, I'm glad we're going to the Disney thing. I feel like I haven't seen you much recently, not since your dating life took off."

Cristian frowned at her. "I don't have that much time to begin with, you know that. It's work and Matteo, mostly."

"I understand," Fina assured him. "I'm not complaining. I just miss hanging out."

"Me too."

Silence hung in the air between them.

"At least we're working together again," Fina offered, grinning.

"We do have that," Cristian said.

"You act like you don't approve of my methods, but secretly you think I'm a stellar investigator."

"Whatever you need to tell yourself," he said. "See ya."

He waddled over to the edge of the rink and stepped onto the ice. Fina hightailed it to her car and sat for a moment letting the hot air blow over her, reassessing her earlier conclusion: Even a little bit of Cristian was worth freezing her ass off.

Fina decided to make a stop before heading home and pointed her car toward Newton. The MetroWest suburb was one of the wealthiest in the region, but it also had its share of ranch houses and Cape Cods. Fifty-six Wellspring Street was one of those ranch houses, with a tidy yard and a flagpole by the door that always held a season-appropriate flag. Fina pulled over in front of the house and swore at the sight that greeted her.

Once she was out of her car, she hollered at the man in the driveway. "What are you doing?"

"What does it look like I'm doing?" Frank Gillis responded.

"It looks like you're trying to have a heart attack!" Fina went over and took the shovel out of his hand. "First of all, you're not supposed to be shoveling. Second of all, I don't even understand *what* you're shoveling. This is all going to melt in a day or two."

"There was a little patch of ice, and I didn't want the mail carrier to slip."

"Stop worrying about everyone else." Fina gently nudged him toward the front door, where she leaned the shovel against the house. "If Peg sees you doing this, she'll kill you."

Frank Gillis was the former Ludlow and Associates investigator who'd taught Fina everything she knew—except for the illegal stuff, which she'd learned on her own. Frank was her professional mentor, and he and his wife, Peg, were her second family. They filled the hole in her life created by Carl and Elaine's lack of parenting skills.

Fina followed him into the house, where they deposited their outer layers before heading into the kitchen.

"Do you want some coffee?" Frank asked, pulling the pot from the coffeemaker and pouring himself a cup.

"No, thanks." She reached into the fridge and grabbed a diet soda instead.

They walked into the family room, where Frank lowered himself into a recliner. Fina took a seat on the couch next to his chair.

"Seriously, didn't the doctor tell you not to do any demanding manual labor?" she asked.

"Sweetie, it really was just a patch of ice."

"So what? Do you think your heart can differentiate between a big patch and a little patch?"

Frank sighed. "You're overreacting."

"I really don't want to visit you in the hospital if you have a heart attack or a stroke. I'm not great with illness; you know that."

He reached out and patted her hand. "I know. It's all about you."

Fina glared at him. "So you don't mind if I tell Peg what you were doing?"

Frank held up a finger. "What did I teach you about discretion? Let's talk about something more pleasant: What are you working on these days?"

"You know that woman, Liz Barone, who was attacked in her house in Hyde Park?"

He nodded. "I saw it on the news."

"Her mother has hired me to investigate."

"Through the firm?"

"No, she came to me independently."

"Carl doesn't mind?"

"Only because there may be something in it for him. The victim was in the early stages of filing a lawsuit against NEU. Carl wants a piece of that action."

"What kind of suit?"

"Liz was suffering from cognitive issues, allegedly from concussions she got while playing soccer at NEU."

Frank squinted in question. "When was this?"

"About twenty years ago, but I'm not worried about the lawsuit. I'm just trying to figure out whodunit."

"Are you having any luck?"

"It's early days, but I can always use a hand if you're looking for something to keep you busy," Fina said hopefully.

Occasionally, Frank took on a job for Fina, but mostly his detecting days were over, which suited him just fine. He always said that investigating was a young person's game, but Fina hoped that wasn't true; she wasn't getting any younger.

"I'd love to see Peg," she said, glancing at her watch, "but I have things to do."

Frank raised an eyebrow. "Do you have a date? Nothing would make Peg happier."

"No," Fina said, rising from the couch and stretching her arms overhead. "I do not have a date."

"I'll tell her you stopped by," Frank said, walking her to the door.

Fina pulled on her jacket, reached over, and kissed him on the cheek. "You never know when I might drive by, so you better not try any more snow removal."

"You're very bossy. Maybe that's the reason you don't have a date. You might want to give that some thought." He tapped the side of his head.

"Yeah," said Fina. "I'm sure that's the only thing standing between me and wedded bliss."

Fina sat in the car until he closed the front door, and she saw him reclaim his spot in his recliner. It wasn't that Frank was in poor health, but he'd had a small scare with his heart last winter, and he wasn't supposed to take any chances.

And Frank and Peg were not allowed to die. It was out of the question.

Fina decided to head home via Scotty's house in Newton.

She knocked on the front door and then used her key to unlock it.

"Patty? Haley? Anyone home?" She closed it firmly behind her and once again started stripping off layers. It was exhausting, the endless dressing and undressing required by a New England winter.

"Hey," her fifteen-year-old niece said from the top of the grand staircase.

"Hey. What's shakin', bacon?" Fina asked.

Haley gave her a pitying look. "Nothing. Aunt Patty is in the kitchen." She skipped down the stairs, her ponytail bobbing behind her. Looking at her, you'd never guess that her mom had been murdered last summer and that she'd been taken in by her aunt and uncle.

Fina pulled her niece into a hug. "How's school?" Fina followed Haley through the large first floor to the combined kitchen/great room at the back of the house.

"Aunt Fina's here," she announced before flopping onto a couch next to Chandler.

Fina greeted her nephews and sister-in-law, who had the accoutrements of dinner prep laid out before her. Patty stuck to a strict dinner and evening routine; she was a firm believer that limits and consistency made for happy children.

Fina climbed onto a stool at the kitchen island and rotated to face her niece. "You didn't answer my question, Hale. How's school?"

"I cannot wait for spring break," Haley said dramatically.

Fina spun back and looked at Patty, who rolled her eyes.

"What's going on with you?" Patty asked. There was a loud thump as Fina's older nephews, Ryan and Teddy, spilled over the back of the couch and landed in a heap on the rug, wrestling enthusiastically.

"I'm not taking anyone to the emergency room tonight," Patty announced.

"You're so mean," Fina commented as the boys separated and

squeezed past Haley to dig out two Xbox controllers from the bottom shelf of the coffee table.

"I'm just making my expectations clear," Patty said. "It's called good parenting."

"I was in the neighborhood. Thought I'd stop by," Fina said. "Did the boys tell you about our awesome sledding?"

"They did," Patty said, giving Fina the hairy eyeball. "It sounded like terrific fun and needlessly dangerous."

"That's how we Ludlows roll," Fina said. She hopped off the stool and went around to the refrigerator to gaze at the contents.

Patty looked over her shoulder into the oversized stainless steel appliance. "Anything?"

Fina closed the door and screwed up her face in concentration. "I'm not sure what I'm in the mood for."

"How old *are* you?" Patty asked.

"Ha!" Haley exclaimed from the couch, her fingers flying across her phone keyboard.

"Never ask a lady her age," Fina cautioned.

"Says the woman who gets in more fights than a professional boxer," her sister-in-law offered.

Fina opened a pantry door and grabbed a bag of tortilla chips before reclaiming her spot at the island. Thirty seconds after she had the bag open, the children flocked to her side, digging their hands into it.

"You're a terrible influence on my children," Patty said, slicing through a green pepper with a knife.

"I like to think of myself as more of a cautionary tale. I'm not offended if you use me as an example of what not to do."

Patty took the bag and shook some chips into a bowl, then sealed the top of the bag with a large clip. "Enough snacking. You need to save room for dinner." The kids each grabbed another handful and dispersed. "Are you staying?" Patty asked.

"I'd like to, but I have work to do." Fina gave her sister-in-law a hug. "Sorry for corrupting the children."

"I'd be worried if you didn't."

"Good-bye, children," Fina called, and made the rounds giving kisses. "Haley, let's do something soon."

"Okay." She didn't look up from her phone.

"I'll call you. You better answer."

"I said okay," the girl whined.

Was there anything more delightful than the teenage years?

7.

Getting in to see Kevin Lafferty the next morning wasn't nearly as difficult as Fina thought it might be. She called his office at Barnes Kaufcan, the pharmaceutical company where he worked, and when the receptionist heard Fina was connected to NEU, a window in his schedule magically opened. Fina didn't say how she was connected, and the assistant didn't ask.

Before setting off, she called Emma Kirwan, who hadn't been in touch since their conversation on Monday night.

"I was just about to send you an e-mail," Emma said.

"Did you find something?"

"I'm not done, but I found a couple of e-mail exchanges between Liz Barone and Pamela Fordyce."

"What did they say?"

"You can read them yourself. They should arrive in a second. Let's just say there wasn't a lot of love lost between them," Emma said.

"Excellent. Keep looking and keep in touch."

Fina clicked open the e-mail from Emma and scanned its contents. Liz had written an e-mail to Pamela requesting that her name be removed from all fund-raising appeals. Liz had received a form e-mail in return promising to do just that. Apparently it hadn't happened, because Liz sent a second request that she be removed from the list. The same form e-mail was sent in return. Fina was growing irritated just reading the exchange; she could only imagine how Liz felt.

Enraged was how Liz felt, according to her next communication. She'd sent Pamela a vitriolic missive berating her for her insensitivity, greed, and inability to perform a simple administrative task. Liz claimed that she had hired an attorney and he would be in touch regarding what Liz felt was a campaign of harassment. Fina didn't think it was a campaign, but clearly Liz was feeling desperate, and who could blame her? As far as she was concerned, NEU owed her, big-time.

The Barnes Kaufcan manufacturing space was located in an office park on Route 128 in Waltham, but the administrative offices were located downtown, close to the Federal Reserve and South Station. Fina decided to drive there for the sake of convenience, despite its being within walking distance of Nanny's condo. She was also feeling sore and tired from the miles she'd logged on the treadmill the day before, and wasn't recovery one of the most important components of exercise?

Fina signed the visitors' log at the security desk in the lobby and got directions to the Barnes Kaufcan office. She took the elevator to the seventeenth floor and was greeted by an illuminated sign featuring the company logo and glossy pictures of "people from other places." This was a category of PR that Fina found prevalent with companies that were involved in global business. The photos—whether on office walls, company websites, or the annual report—showcased lots of nonwhite people, usually in brightly colored native outfits, beaming as if they'd swallowed a month's worth of antidepressants. Fina didn't doubt that these people existed; she just marveled at their ubiquitous presence in the marketing strategies of high-earning international corporations.

She gave her name to the receptionist, who must have been twenty-one if she was a day, and accepted a glass of water before taking a seat in the waiting area. The reading material on offer was mostly health-related magazines, the *Wall Street Journal*, and the *Globe*. Fina opted for a brochure about Barnes Kaufcan's efforts to bring their products to developing nations, which seemed a tad suspect since the company was known for their arthritis drugs. She tried to imagine how infants suffering from chronic diarrhea might benefit from less creaky joints.

"Mr. Lafferty will see you now," said a young man who appeared in front of Fina. He, too, looked to be in his early twenties. He was fit and neatly dressed in pants and a button-down shirt and tie underneath a sweater.

"I'm Colin, Mr. Lafferty's assistant." He directed her down the hallway.

"Nice to meet you, Colin. I'm Fina Ludlow." She made some chitchat about the weather and learned that Colin was originally from Alabama.

"I just can't get used to the cold, even after five years," he explained.

"Did you come up here for college?" Fina asked.

"Yes. I graduated from NEU last year."

"Right. I know that Kevin is very involved in all things NEU."

"I lucked out. I love working for him. So many of my friends work for assholes." A blush rose on his cheeks. "Sorry."

"No worries, Colin. I've heard it before," Fina assured him. "And you're right to feel lucky. Having a boss you like can make all the difference in the world." Fina knew it was tough having a boss who ate his young, especially if you *were* his young.

"Kevin, I have Ms. Ludlow for you." Colin left her at the threshold of his boss's office, and Kevin Lafferty came around the desk to greet her.

"Ms. Ludlow, I'm so glad to meet you." He gave her a firm handshake and directed her to a chair across from his desk. The office didn't boast a view of the Fort Point Channel or anything else particularly memorable, but it did show a glimpse of sky, which wasn't easy to come by in the thick of the city. The space was furnished in sleek, contemporary furniture, but its most prominent feature was the collection of sports memorabilia that festooned the walls. There were framed newspaper articles and features from *Sports Illustrated*. Team pennants took pride of place next to photographs featuring a smiling Kevin amongst various NEU athletes. There was one photo of Kevin standing next to the Patriots owner, Bob Kraft, but everything else was NEU-related, including the signed collection of balls in a display case against the wall.

Fina took a detour to the case and examined the souvenirs more closely. "Wow. I heard you're the NEU sports guy, but I had no idea."

"I'm also the Barnes Kaufcan guy," he said, gesturing to a different shelf featuring professional accolades and recognition of Barnes Kaufcan's charity work.

"Of course."

Fina settled into her chair and studied Kevin as he sat down across from her. He was handsome in an easy, familiar way, like your brother's best friend growing up, the one you secretly hoped would be staying for dinner if only so you could stare at him across the table and name your future babies in your head. Kevin's sandy-blond hair and blue eyes radiated good health, as did his wide smile. He was trim, but not skinny, and although Fina knew he was close to fifty, he could easily pass for a decade younger.

"So what can I do for you, Ms. Ludlow? You're here on NEU business?" He folded his hands together and gazed at her.

"Well, first, you can call me Fina."

"Fina, then, and I'm Kevin."

"I don't know if you're aware of recent events involving Liz Barone, who was attacked in her kitchen. She was a soccer player at NEU, and I think you were involved with her team."

Kevin frowned. "I heard about Liz; it's all over the papers. I'm not sure what it has to do with me, or NEU for that matter."

"I'm a private investigator, and I've been hired by Liz's family to look into the situation. I'm trying to get a clearer picture of Liz."

Kevin leaned back and ran his hands through his hair. "Sure, but I still don't know how I can be helpful."

"Just by answering some questions. It won't take long."

He nodded his assent.

"When was the last time you spoke with Liz?" Fina asked. "My understanding is that you were a regular presence at her NEU soccer games."

"Sure, but that was twenty years ago. I'm still a presence at the games, but Liz isn't."

"So you haven't had contact with her recently?"

Kevin shook his head slowly. "Not for at least a year or so."

"And where was that?" Fina asked.

"I think it was at an NEU fund-raiser. Aren't the police looking into the attack?"

"They are, but sometimes people feel better knowing there are extra boots on the ground, as it were. Bobbi Barone wants to do something for her daughter, and her options are limited right now."

"Liz's condition hasn't improved?" Kevin asked. "I never know if I should believe what I read in the papers."

Fina smiled. "You shouldn't believe what you read in the papers, but no, she hasn't improved."

"It's a hell of a thing." He gazed out the window. "It just doesn't make any sense."

"So you haven't seen Liz for about a year?"

"That's right."

"Would you consider her a friend?"

"Not really. An acquaintance, at best."

"What was she like in college?"

"She was great." Kevin picked up a globe-shaped crystal paperweight and rotated it between his hands. "She was an amazing soccer player and a good student."

"Were you aware that she wanted to sue NEU?"

He glanced out the window again before returning his gaze to her. "I'd heard rumors about it."

"From whom?"

Kevin shrugged. "From the rumor mill. I don't remember who told me, but those sorts of things tend to get around."

Fina wasn't getting any traction, so she changed directions. "So I heard you're the president of the booster club. What does that involve?" she asked.

He smiled. "Anything that supports the athletic department and the student athletes."

"Like what? I've never talked with a booster before."

"I get the word out about games, help with fund-raising, and attend events to show team spirit. I sit on some committees. That sort of thing. Boosters supplement the support provided by the university."

"So being the president is kind of a big deal."

"I love NEU, and I love sports."

Fina grinned slyly. "Do you think you'll ever have a building named after you? The Lafferty Field House or something like that?"

"I don't have thirty million dollars lying around, but you never know. Money is only one part of being a booster. I wouldn't do it if I didn't love the sports."

"You have quite a collection," Fina said, nodding toward the memorabilia.

Kevin grinned. "There's nothing better than a good game. Do you like sports?"

"I do. I'm not a fanatic, but I follow our teams and go to a few games each season. Do you have a favorite sport at NEU?"

"That's like picking a favorite child." He smiled. "But I do love basketball. Anything that's on the national stage is especially exciting," Kevin said, "but I try to give where I'm needed. The least publicized teams are often the ones that benefit most from our attention."

"That makes sense," Fina said, "but you're limited by NCAA rules, right?"

"Absolutely. The club can't approach athletes for recruitment purposes or give them or their families gifts. The rules are there to keep the playing field level, so to speak, and I would never break those rules or jeopardize the programs." He delivered the sound bite with a smile.

"So no gifts or loans or anything like that?"

"Nope." There was a hint of testiness in his reply.

"Do you attend practices or just games?" she asked.

"Both. Depends on the sport and the season and the coach."

"How involved are you with the women's soccer team these days?" Fina asked.

"I really don't understand how that's relevant to Liz's current situation," Kevin said. He gave her a smile most women would have found appealing. "I have to admit, Fina, I feel like you're on a fishing expedition."

"I want to know who hurt Liz Barone." She smiled. "In fact, I think I opened with that. I'm sorry if my questions seem irrelevant or impertinent, but that's how I get answers, by asking questions."

"If you say so." Kevin pushed his chair back and planted his hands on the desk. "Sorry I couldn't be more helpful."

"You've been very helpful," Fina said, rising to her feet. She pulled a card from her bag and placed it on the blotter in front of him. "I appreciate your taking the time to talk to me. Please be in touch if you think of anything that might be useful."

"Of course." He picked up the card and flicked it against the palm of his other hand. "Colin will show you out."

Ten minutes later Fina tucked the parking receipt into her expenses folder and pulled out of the garage.

Kevin Lafferty seemed like a nice guy with a nice life. Nice guys didn't always finish last, but in her experience, they rarely finished first. Unless, of course, they weren't really that nice.

Fina was summoned to Ludlow and Associates by Carl, who insisted she come in immediately to provide information on a different case. He was in the midst of an intense phone conversation when she arrived, so she grabbed a diet soda from the fridge and plopped down onto his couch.

"Dad, technically, I'm not on your clock," she said once he hung up.

Carl peered at her. "I said you could take this case, but I didn't say you could shirk your regular duties."

"But why am I here? It's not a deposition, so it could have waited."

"Not as far as I'm concerned. The associate on the Haynesworth case needs to interview you."

Fina knew this was his way of testing her and reminding her who was boss. She found it both annoying and unprofessional, not to mention typical.

"Fine," she replied, "but every minute I spend here, I'm not making progress on the Liz Barone case. The one that may give us a huge payday."

"Then you'd better get going." Carl gestured toward the door. "Shari will tell you where to go."

"Always a pleasure, Father," Fina said, leaving his office.

She got her marching orders from his assistant only to find herself in a deserted conference room. Being kept waiting was particularly irksome.

She put in a call to Pamela Fordyce's office and was told that her assistant was away from her desk, did she want to leave a message? Fina left word that she had an important development-related matter to discuss and would like to meet with Ms. Fordyce as soon as possible. She was checking e-mail on her tablet when her brother Matthew walked past the glass-enclosed space. He reversed his direction ten seconds later and entered the room.

"How's it going, Sis?" Matthew, the youngest Ludlow brother, was two years older than Fina. He had that Ludlow sparkle—the just-right wavy hair, the dimple, the impish grin. Much to their mother's chagrin, he was single, and Fina didn't expect him to settle down anytime soon. Matthew had his pick of women and didn't have to balance work and family. A steady stable of dates and friends with benefits kept him quite satisfied.

"I'm good," Fina said. "You?"

"Can't complain. Working like a dog, but nothing new about that. You waiting for Dad?"

"No. I'm waiting for some associate who needs info on the Haynes-worth case."

Matthew's brow scrunched up. "Remind me which case that is?"

"The asbestos in the nursing home."

"Right." He adjusted the Omega watch on his wrist. "What are you getting Mom for her birthday?"

Fina sat back in her chair. "I thought I could go in on something with you guys."

He folded his arms across his chest. "You always do that. Piggyback on our gift at the last minute."

"I always pay you," she said. "It's not like I'm a freeloader."

"You're an idea freeloader," Matthew insisted. "You never think of anything, and then you jump on our idea bandwagon."

"Your idea bandwagon? You sound like a ten-year-old pioneer. So what are you getting Mom?"

Matthew looked at his shoes before making eye contact. "Haven't decided yet."

"Haven't decided or don't know because Patty is the one choosing the gift?" Fina asked.

He grinned. "I take the fifth."

"Where do you think I learned how to jump on the idea bandwagon anyway? My big brothers taught me everything I know."

A young woman tapped on the glass wall of the conference room and motioned for Matthew to join her.

"Catch you later." Matthew gave her a quick kiss on the cheek and squeezed by the associate who was there to pick Fina's brain.

After several hours spent discussing all things asbestos, Fina grabbed a burger and fries in the Prudential Center food court. Back in her car, she called Gus Sibley's private practice, but was told that he was at his NEU office for the remainder of the day. She made her way there, only to find that she'd just missed him. Undeterred, Fina hopped online and found his home address in Brookline.

She decided to make the most of the Wi-Fi connection she'd found in the NEU parking lot and did a quick search on the good doctor. The Internet confirmed that Gus was a well-respected orthopedist who had a private practice and also worked for NEU as a team doctor. There were pictures of him with the women's soccer team and at various charity events with his wife, Margie. Fina pulled up the Massachusetts medical board website and searched his record. There were no pending claims against him, nor had he made any malpractice payouts in the last ten years. Next, Fina logged on to the Ludlow and Associates database. There was one mention of him as a potential expert witness on a case, but there was no indication that he'd ever testified.

A ten-minute drive brought her to the Sibley house, a brick center-entrance colonial located a few streets off Route 9 in Brookline. It was close enough to the thoroughfare to make it convenient to the hospitals and NEU, but far enough away that you didn't hear cars speeding by. The neighborhood consisted of medium-sized colonials with fenced-in backyards. Ten miles west and the houses probably went for five hundred thousand dollars, but Fina imagined the Sibley abode—and its neighbors—would fetch over a million.

Fina picked her way up the concrete path to the front door, encouraged by the smoke curling out of the chimney. She rang the doorbell and knocked her feet against the front stoop to dislodge any sandy slush from her boots.

A moment later, the door was opened by a man in a blue suit, a folded-up tie peeking out from the pocket. His white shirt was unbuttoned at the neck, and a pair of black wingtips dangled from two fingers of his left hand.

"Yes?" he inquired.

"My name is Fina Ludlow. I'm a private investigator. I'm looking for Dr. Gus Sibley."

"I'm Dr. Sibley." He leaned against the door.

"I wonder if I could ask you a few questions." Fina rubbed her hands together, hoping to send a subliminal message about the likelihood of hypothermia if she were to remain on the front step.

"Questions regarding what?"

"It's about Liz Barone."

A pained expression washed over his face. He glanced over his shoulder toward the interior of the house. "What exactly about Liz?"

"As you may know, she was critically injured during an attack in her home. I've been hired by her mother and husband to investigate the attack. I know you're her friend and hoped you would be willing to answer a few questions."

Gus considered her for a moment and then stepped back into the foyer. "Of course. Why don't you come in?"

"Thanks. It's freezing out."

"Do you have some ID?"

"Sure." Fina pulled her PI license from her bag and held it up for his inspection.

He studied it and nodded. "If you don't mind taking off your shoes. We're trying to win the war against sand and salt." He held out his hand and took Fina's coat, which he hung over the doorknob of the front hall closet. Fina reached out and steadied herself on the chair rail as she struggled out of her boots.

"I'm with my grandson," Gus said. "Are your questions child-friendly?"

"I'll make sure they are," Fina said, following him into a room to the right of the staircase. The temperature was noticeably warmer, largely due to the fire that was crackling in the fireplace. A large TV was mounted on the wall, and a sizable coffee table sat between two couches. The surface of the table was strewn with LEGO pieces, and a young boy kneeled in front of it, studying the cover of a cardboard box.

"Grampy, I can't find this one." The child pointed to a picture of a tiny gray piece.

"It'll turn up," Fina said. "Someone will step on it by the end of the night, experiencing more pain than any piece of plastic should ever inflict."

Gus smiled. "You build a lot of LEGOs?"

"I have a niece and three young nephews. Is that the airport fire truck?" Fina tilted her head to get a better look at the box. Whose bright idea was that? Here, kids, let's build the truck that will save you when your plane crashes!

"I can't find this part for the jet engine," the boy said, thrusting the box toward Fina with one hand and wiping his nose with the other.

"Ah yes, the jet engine that has detached from the fuselage," Fina said, exchanging a look with Gus. "Let's see what you have." She kneeled down in front of the table. "I'm Fina. I'm just here to ask your grandfather a few questions."

"This is Archer," Gus said. He sat down next to Fina on the carpet, his legs tucked awkwardly to the side. Everything about Gus was slightly oversized—his head, his thatch of grayish-white hair, his torso. He wasn't overweight nor was he particularly tall, but there was a thickness, a solidity to him that couldn't be ignored.

"Do you have a cookie sheet?" Fina asked. "That's how we usually sort the pieces. They're easier to see that way." Fina wasn't good at most child care–related tasks, but give her a LEGO kit and she'd give you a city or a high-speed police chase or the space shuttle lickety-split.

"Go ask Nana for a couple of cookie sheets, Archer," Gus instructed the child, who popped up from his knees as if he were spring-loaded. "It's just horrible what happened to Liz," Gus said when Archer had left.

"It is," Fina said, scouring the tabletop for the fake flames.

"How can I help?"

"I'm gathering background information, and I'm interested in Liz's playing days at NEU."

"How would that relate to her injuries?" Gus asked.

"Well, Liz was going to sue NEU because of cognitive deficiencies she was experiencing, allegedly from the concussions she sustained playing soccer. Were you aware of the lawsuit?"

"She had mentioned it to me," Gus said.

"When was this?"

"We last spoke a few weeks ago."

"So you've kept in touch all these years?" Fina asked.

"I consider it one of the perks of my job," he said. "The friendships I make with players and their families."

"What did you think about the lawsuit?"

Gus prodded a piece with his fingertip. "I hadn't given it much thought, really," Gus said.

"Really? You were—are—the team doctor. You must have some opinion."

Archer came running back into the room with two cookie sheets banging together. The threesome gathered up the pieces and spread them out on the metal sheets.

"I follow all the protocols provided by the CDC," Gus said after a moment. "I always have."

Fina looked at him. He was wearing glasses, and the reflection of the fire in his lenses made it hard to make eye contact. She decided not to press the point, and they worked in silence for the next couple of minutes.

"I still don't understand what the lawsuit has to do with Liz's injury," Gus said, breaking the silence.

"A lawsuit like that is high stakes," Fina said. "The university—and the people associated with it—would have a lot to lose." Her eye was drawn to the NEU pin glinting on Gus's lapel.

Gus scoffed. "You think someone did *it*"—he eyed Archer—"because of that? I'm sorry, but that strikes me as absurd."

"Okay. Why do you think someone did *it*?"

"I haven't a clue. Liz is a wonderful person." Gus popped two LEGOs together that looked like the cab of the fire engine. "I can't imagine a scenario that would lead to that particular outcome."

"And yet we have reached that particular outcome," Fina noted. Gus was silent. "So there's nothing you can tell me? No one who had a beef with her? No conflicts that you're aware of?"

Gus turned a piece over in his hand. "None, I'm afraid."

"Do you know her husband, Jamie?"

"I've met him, but I can't say I know him."

"Any sense what their relationship is like?" Fina asked.

"Again, no."

"Was there anyone else from the team or NEU who Liz kept up with? Another teammate? A coach?"

"The head coach passed away more than five years ago, so that won't help." Gus set aside a couple of stickers meant to decorate the sides of the fire engine. Archer continued sorting through the multicolor pieces.

"An assistant coach?" Fina popped a fire helmet onto one of the tiny LEGO men.

Gus shook his head. "I think these are part of the hose apparatus, Archer." He handed a few black LEGOs to his grandson. "Can you snap those together?"

"Do you have an airplane to go with this?" Fina asked the boy.

"Uh-huh. I have two planes, and Santa just brought me the cargo terminal for my airport."

"That comes with the conveyor belt, right?" she asked.

"Yup." He swiped at his nose again. "And you could build that with us, too."

Gus glanced at Archer.

"I don't think you two need much help," Fina said. "Dr. Sibley, you must know Kevin Lafferty."

Gus frowned. "Everyone knows Kevin, or rather, Kevin knows everyone."

"I spoke with him this morning. He's quite the NEU supporter."

"He does a great deal for the NEU teams." Gus peered at her. "Are you related to Carl Ludlow?"

Fina smiled. "I am, but don't hold it against me."

Gus sighed. He leaned on the table and pushed himself to standing. "We appreciate your LEGO expertise, Ms. Ludlow, but I think you should probably be going."

"I understand." Nothing like the mention of Carl's name to kill the moment. Fina clicked a wheel well into place before rising. She shook her leg, which was thrumming with pins and needles. "Archer, keep up the good work, buddy."

"Uh-huh," he murmured, his head bent over the task at hand.

Fina followed Gus to the front hall and tried to avoid the small puddles her boots had deposited during their conversation. Sweaty boots were bad enough, but they were particularly unpleasant when paired with wet socks. Gus handed over her coat, which she pulled on, fishing her scarf and gloves out of the pockets.

"If you think of anything that might be helpful, please be in touch." Fina gave him her card.

Cold air greeted Fina on the front step, and her back muscles tightened in response. She'd never given much credence to the concept of mild weather being good for your health, but as she got older, it was beginning to make sense. Who wouldn't prefer sunshine and frozen drinks to darkness and frozen toes?

8.

The ringing phone was a rude awakening at 7:23 the next morning. The screen indicated the call was from NEU, so Fina struggled to a sitting position to answer. Why do we assume that we think better sitting up?

"Hello."

"I'm trying to reach Fina Ludlow. This is Jill from Pamela Fordyce's office at New England University."

"This is Fina."

"A slot has opened up in Ms. Fordyce's schedule. She can see you at ten thirty this morning."

"That's terrific."

They dispensed with the details regarding directions and parking, and Fina hung up the phone. She reset her alarm, giving herself another hour of sleep.

After showering and throwing on some sweats, Fina grabbed a strawberry frosted Pop-Tart and munched on it while reviewing Pamela Fordyce's bio.

A graduate of NEU and Stanford, Pamela was a senior member of the development team and traveled extensively representing the university. She was involved with some charities and had been married once, many years ago, according to the public records that Fina tapped into. She had no arrests, and according to property records, she owned a small condo in Charlestown. Everything about Pamela Fordyce indicated a straightforward interview.

Standing in front of her open closet, Fina contemplated her clothing options. Her years as an investigator had taught her that first impressions could be the difference between gaining access and being excluded. She was all for individuality and personal expression, but people who thought that their appearance didn't have any bearing on the opportunities afforded by life were kidding themselves. You needed to get a place at the table, and then you could change the menu.

In light of this, she chose a conservative black pantsuit that she'd picked up at Ann Taylor and a cranberry silk blouse. The outfit felt like a straitjacket; maybe subconsciously she'd flunked out of law school to avoid the accompanying wardrobe. Fina pulled her hair back in a low bun and applied more makeup than usual, albeit tastefully. Her black leather tote bag had been an attempted bribe by Elaine years before. If Fina wasn't going to stay home barefoot and pregnant, could she at least have a respectable job? No, apparently not.

In the NEU parking lot, she swapped her boots for low heels. As she struggled out of her boots, something caught Fina's eye. A large dark sedan was idling at the end of the row. Fina looked around, but didn't see any soon-to-be-free parking spots, which might explain the driver's behavior. The tinted windows prevented her from seeing the driver, but perhaps he was on the phone or searching for something in his bag. There was something about the car that felt threatening, and Fina thought it warranted further investigation. Cristian had taught her that contrary to popular belief, when you were walking on the street late at night and felt insecure, you should make eye contact with the people you passed. *Let them know you see them* is what he said. If they thought you were unaware of their presence, they were more apt to take advantage. Unless, of course, they were nuts and were going to kill you either way.

Betting that wasn't the case, Fina climbed out of her car and approached the sedan. She was about five feet from the driver's-side door, staring at the outline of the driver's silhouette, when the engine roared and the car sped away. It was possible the driver was just shy or late for an appointment, but Fina doubted it. Unfortunately, she hadn't gotten the license plate number, and paranoia was an occupational hazard. She'd just have to stay on her toes.

NEU's development office was housed in a traditional brownstone on a side street close to Huntington Avenue. Offices occupied all four floors and were accessed by an elderly elevator or a narrow, curved staircase. Once Fina was upstairs, Pamela Fordyce's assistant directed her to a small waiting area and provided a glass of water to quench her thirst. The walls were decorated with large photographs, all NEU-related: the student center designed by a celebrity architect, action shots of the football team, a gaggle of students representing every color in the racial rainbow. It looked like a happy, engaging place to spend your time—kind of like the land of Barnes Kaufcan. Fina picked up a copy of the alumni magazine from the coffee table and flipped through its glossy pages. She was scanning the profile of an alum who made it big in the semiconductor business when she was retrieved by the assistant and ushered into Pamela's office.

"Ms. Ludlow?" A woman rose from behind a large walnut desk and came around to shake Fina's hand.

"Yes, and you must be Ms. Fordyce."

"Pamela. Please, have a seat." She waited as Fina took a seat on an upholstered sofa. Pamela sat in a Louis XVI–style chair facing her and placed a delicate teacup and saucer on the table next to her.

Pamela's office suite—one half of the fourth floor—topped the building. Broad windows afforded views of Back Bay and the South End, depending upon which direction you looked, and a large fireplace served as a focal point. A fire burned in the grate, making the space feel more like a home than a place of business. The fireplace was flanked by display shelves, which held photos and tchotchkes.

"Would you like some coffee or some more water?" Pamela asked, tugging her suit jacket together over her middle.

"No, I'm fine. Thank you."

Pamela launched into small talk, which was probably development office protocol. After a few minutes of chitchat, she got down to business.

"I apologize; Jill wasn't clear about the reason for your visit," Pamela said. "What is it that I can do for you?"

Fina had been purposefully vague when requesting the appointment. There was no point in getting Pamela's hackles up before she even walked in the door.

"I imagine that you are aware of the situation with Liz Barone?" Fina asked.

A vein in Pamela's neck began to pulse. "Of course. We take an interest in all our alumni."

"Of course." Fina sipped her water, drawing out the moment. "Liz's mother and husband have hired me to investigate the attack on her." She reached into her bag and pulled out her PI license.

Before Pamela could examine it, her office phone rang.

"Excuse me." She answered it at her desk and engaged in a brief conversation. Fina took advantage of the moment to take stock of the woman. She guessed Pamela was an inch or so shorter than she was and in her midfifties. Her pantsuit was slightly ill-fitting, and her dark brown hair was cut into a graduated bob, a style that never made any sense to Fina. Why would you want the back of your head to look like a wedge of cheese? The front of her hair came to her chin, a length that few women could pull off without looking like a LEGO lady. Her makeup was understated, and with her clear skin and white teeth, Pamela was reasonably attractive.

She hung up the phone and returned to her straight-backed chair. She looked at Fina quizzically. "And this situation with Liz concerns the university how?"

"Actually, it concerns you." Fina returned her license to her bag. "Liz had retained an attorney and was taking steps to sue NEU. Among the materials the attorney provided to me were a number of fund-raising letters with your signature."

Pamela sighed, a smile turning up the corners of her mouth. "Fina, I send out thousands of those appeals every year. They're generated by a database."

"Right, but Liz also e-mailed you directly a number of times." She pulled out copies of the e-mails that Emma had found. Pamela took them from her and scanned them. She handed them back to Fina, then picked up the teacup and sipped from it. Fina had to give her credit; she was as cool as a cucumber.

"So what is your question exactly?" Pamela asked.

"I'm wondering what contact you've had recently with Liz, and if the subject of her pending lawsuit was ever discussed."

"Those e-mails are the last contact we had."

"You never spoke in person?"

"Why would we?" Pamela asked.

"I don't know. Liz was very angry, and you didn't seem to be getting the message. Maybe she decided to deliver it in person."

"Liz was misguided regarding the lawsuit. The athletic department was not responsible for her situation," Pamela said. "There's no evidence linking her difficulties to her athletic career at NEU. In terms of the fund-raising requests, she wanted to be off the list, and an administrative error kept her on the list. It was a minor misunderstanding."

"If I were suffering from a debilitating disease and someone repeatedly asked me to fund the very thing that I believed caused the disease, I'd be bullshit," Fina said.

"The NEU athletics program is one of the best in the country." Pamela perked up, launching into an overview of the various teams and their winning ways. Her description was so positive, it was hard to imagine that anyone got hurt or lost a game when sporting the NEU colors. She made it sound like rainbows arced over every playing field and unicorns frolicked at halftime.

"Our goal," Pamela concluded, "is to have a positive relationship with all of our alumni."

"I don't doubt it, but the threat of a lawsuit and bad publicity must have concerned you," Fina said.

"NEU is a large institution with an extremely diverse population. It's not always smooth sailing, but that's just part of the territory for a school of our caliber."

"So you weren't worried?"

"Not especially." Pamela smiled, but there was no warmth in her expression.

"So just to clarify, you never spoke with Liz in person or on the phone?"

Pamela didn't speak for a moment. "She called me a couple of weeks ago."

"What did you talk about?" Fina asked.

Pamela put up her hands in frustration. "She reiterated the request that her name be removed from the fund-raising database. I took care of it myself as soon as I hung up the phone."

"And that was it?"

"That was it. Sorry to disappoint you."

"Had you ever had contact with Liz before this issue arose?" Fina asked.

"We'd met at a couple of fund-raising events, but we certainly didn't know each other."

Fina nodded. "Is there anyone at NEU who might have some useful information?"

"About Liz? I have no idea. As I said, our contact was limited."

"But she worked here."

"So do eighteen thousand other people," Pamela said. "I don't know them all."

"What about Kevin Lafferty?"

Pamela looked at her wristwatch. If she thought a social cue like that would get rid of Fina, she had another thing coming. "He's a booster in the athletic program."

"How well do you know him?" Fina asked.

"I've known Kevin for a number of years."

"And he knew Liz?"

"You should ask him."

"I have. I wanted to get your opinion."

"I wish I could be more helpful, but I really have nothing to add."

She didn't envy Pamela her position. Since everyone was a potential donor, you couldn't offend anyone. Fina wouldn't last five minutes in that job.

Fina stood and gathered her belongings. "I don't want to take up any more of your time." She stepped over to the display cabinet to take a closer look. "This is quite a collection."

Pamela looked uneasy with the change in conversational direction, but she was either too polite or too savvy to halt it. "Yes. They're from my travels. I've had the privilege of visiting some wonderful places. Do you travel?"

"No. The idea appeals, but work and family always seem to require my attention."

"You have to make time for it. There will always be something keeping you from doing what you really want." Pamela's gaze trained itself on the door.

"I suppose that's true," Fina said.

Pamela followed Fina to the reception area, where Fina handed over her card. "If you think of something that is relevant, please be in touch."

"I can't imagine I will." Pamela folded her fingers around the card and retreated into her office.

Fina returned to her car, where she kicked off her shoes and stuck her feet next to the air vent. The conversation hadn't been a rousing success, but at least she hadn't been removed by security.

All in all, not a bad result.

You need to come by the station," Cristian told Fina when she answered her phone on the way home.

"Why?"

"Why do you think? Because the brass want to give you an outstanding citizen award."

"Finally! Someone's noticed. I'm on my way."

Fina headed toward police headquarters, not relishing the thought of what was to come. Historically, when she was summoned to the police department it meant she was in trouble. Not legal trouble—like most people who were summoned there—but professional trouble. Cristian's boss, Lieutenant Marcy Pitney, and Fina had overlapped on a number of cases, and their relationship could best be described as contentious. Pitney rarely approved of Fina's methods, and Fina thought Pitney didn't give her due credit for her investigative chops. They were both smart and stubborn, and in an alternate universe might have been friends.

At headquarters, a uniformed cop escorted her upstairs to the Major Crimes division and left her in an interview room to stew. The metal table and chairs were bolted to the floor, and a camera winked in one of the corners of the ceiling. Fina wasn't a germophobe, but these rooms always made her feel particularly unclean. Interview rooms and ERs were the giant petri dishes of modern society. She was trying not to focus on a dark stain on the floor and to distract herself with a game of solitaire when Pitney came in ten minutes later.

"Hello, Lieutenant. How are you?" Fina asked, stowing her phone.

"I'm fine. Where's Menendez?"

"Contrary to what you may believe, we aren't actually joined at the hip."

Pitney gave her a withering look and popped her head out of the room. "Will someone find Menendez and tell him to come to interview three?"

Pitney closed the door and took the seat across from Fina. "Do you think it's possible," she asked, "for you to do your job without being a pain in my ass?"

Fina considered the question. "Possible, but not probable."

"That wasn't the answer I was looking for."

"What?" Fina asked. "You want me to lie?"

"No," Pitney said slowly, as if to a small child, "I want you to stay out of my way."

The lieutenant crossed her arms over her ample chest. Today she wore a magenta sweater and forest green pants. Pitney made no attempt to blend in and bore no resemblance to the female cops on prime-time television. She was barely five feet two inches with a mop of curly hair that looked orangish or purplish depending on the lighting. She wore pants and tops that were garishly colored, and her nails were always painted in an equally bold hue. Fina wouldn't be caught dead in her outfits, but she had to hand it to her—Pitney was a sartorial risk-taker.

"Perhaps you could be more specific in detailing my transgression," Fina said.

The door opened and Cristian came in cradling two coffees and a diet soda between his hands. He put the coffees down on Pitney's side of the table and slid the soda over to Fina.

"This doesn't help, your providing room service," Pitney said, eyeing him.

"Believe me, hydrating her will only make her more agreeable," Cristian said, taking the seat next to Pitney.

"How'd the hockey game go?" Fina asked, popping the top on the soda and reveling in the faint hiss indicating maximum carbonation.

"It was good. Everyone had fun, no major injuries."

"That sounds like the antithesis of Ludlow sporting events."

"All right, enough chitchat," Pitney cut in. "I was just telling Fina that she needs to stop getting in the way."

"You were about to tell me what I'd done wrong *this* time," Fina reminded her.

"I got a call from Gus Sibley this morning." Pitney blew on the surface of her coffee before taking a tentative sip.

"Uh-huh."

"He wanted to know why you were running a parallel investigation to ours and bothering him."

"Did you explain that's what private investigators do?" Fina asked.

"Oh, I explained that you bother people."

"Lieutenant, our meeting was completely cordial. I asked him some questions and helped him and his grandson build a LEGO set. Did he mention that part?"

Cristian grinned behind his coffee cup.

"He left that part out," Pitney said.

"I'm confused," Fina said. "Some guy—who welcomed me into his home of his own free will—decides that wasn't such a good idea after the fact, so he calls the cops on me? And you do his bidding for him?"

Cristian raised an eyebrow, knowing Pitney wouldn't like the characterization of doing anyone's bidding.

"Fina, if you annoy witnesses, it makes our job more difficult," Pitney said.

"I understand that, but when I left, he wasn't annoyed. And why would some innocuous questions from me make him so jumpy?"

"What did he tell you?" Pitney asked.

"Very little. He said he followed the player safety protocol when Liz Barone played at NEU. He last spoke with her a few weeks ago, and he knew she was filing a lawsuit. That's it."

Pitney tapped a coral-colored nail on the tabletop. "So you think he's involved?" she asked.

"Is that really why I'm here?" Fina asked, her gaze moving between Pitney and Cristian. "So you can pick my brain?"

"You're here," Pitney said, "because I want you to lay off Gus Sibley and report any information you have. You always seem fuzzy on the concept of obstruction of justice."

"I am crystal clear on that concept." Fina sipped her drink. "May I go now?"

"Is there anything else you want to tell us before you leave?"

Fina studied the ceiling for a moment. "I think the Pats have a good chance in the playoffs."

"Go," Pitney said, rotating out of her seat. "Before I have you arrested for criminal obnoxiousness." She strode out of the room.

Fina took a long drink and swallowed. "There's something weird about Gus Sibley calling you guys. Our conversation really was benign."

"Apparently not to him."

"What a baby."

"Not everyone is as tough as you," Cristian said.

"Ain't that the truth." Fina rose from her chair, and Cristian followed her into the hallway. "Keep in touch."

"I know you will if I don't," he said, giving her a gentle nudge in the direction of the exit.

Bobbi Barone had left a tearful message on Fina's voice mail. Fina was used to bearing witness to people's misery, but generally it was after the fact, when she had the benefit of a little distance from whatever terrible event she was investigating. This time was different, and Fina tensed up when she listened to the message. She was witnessing the unfolding of Liz's fate, and it was miserable to see, even though she didn't know the woman. When she was hired to find a missing person or investigate a botched surgery or even look into a murder case, the worst had already transpired. Fina wasn't convinced that the worst was over in this case, and the waiting and wondering added a whole new level of stress. She couldn't imagine how Bobbi and Jamie were holding it together.

Fina returned the call, and Bobbi suggested they meet at a pizza place a couple of blocks from the hospital. Fina was relieved to avoid the bright hallways and antiseptic smell of MGH, but felt guilty for even thinking such a thing. Bobbi had no choice but to return to that building.

Bobbi was sitting at a round table in the back, nursing a coffee, when Fina arrived. Three other tables were occupied, one by a group of orderlies and the other by men and women in white coats. It was a casual place where you ordered at the counter and your name was called when your food was ready. A beefy young man behind the counter in a too-tight white T-shirt got her a diet soda. His hair was slicked back in a modified pompadour. It was an interesting choice for the early twenty-first century.

"Do you want anything else, Bobbi?" Fina asked before he rang her up.

"No, thank you."

The young man and Fina exchanged a look. Their proximity to the hospital suggested he was used to the medical population, both the staff and those related to patients. Bobbi's hunched posture and sad face suggested her membership in the latter group. Fina gave him a tight smile and accepted her change.

She brought her drink over to the table and set it down across from Bobbi's mug of coffee.

"Sorry I didn't answer when you called," Fina said. "I was talking to the police."

Bobbi's head lifted slightly. "Any news?"

"Nothing concrete, but I'm starting to annoy people. In my experience that means I'm making progress." She sipped her drink. The nearby table of orderlies erupted in laughter. "How is Liz?"

Bobbi opened her mouth to speak, but the only thing that came out was a small, strangled sound. It wasn't even a cry, just the mangled suggestion of it. Tears streamed down her cheeks. Fina pulled some napkins out of the metal dispenser and handed them to her. She reached across the table and grasped Bobbi's hand.

"I am so, so sorry, Bobbi, and I know that is a woefully inadequate thing to say."

Bobbi just nodded and cried. Nobody in the place seemed to take notice, perhaps because they were used to displays of emotion.

Bobbi cried silently for another minute, Fina clasping her hand. She didn't say any of the platitudes she found to be obnoxious or insensitive that people often trot out on such occasions. Nobody wanted their loved one to be in "a better place." They wanted their loved one sitting next to them, happy and healthy.

Finally, Bobbi blew her nose and took a deep breath. "She's still alive, but not really," she said, gesturing toward the hospital. "She's brain-dead."

Fina felt an ache in the pit of her stomach. "How is Jamie handling all this?"

"He's shell-shocked. He's completely overwhelmed."

Fina nodded, but remained silent. She had lots of questions, but she knew that if Bobbi wanted to say more she would.

"We have to make a decision," Bobbi said after taking a deep breath.

Fina looked at her. "That's a horrible thing to have to do," she said.

"It is."

"Are you and Jamie on the same page?"

"I think so, but it's difficult having these conversations with him. I realize it would be difficult for anyone, but Jamie doesn't generally take the bull by the horns."

"I'm sorry to interrupt, ladies." The young man from the counter had appeared at their table. "But we have an extra order of our famous garlic bread, and I'd hate for it to go to waste." He placed it on the table in front of them. A strong garlic aroma tickled Fina's nose. "And I brought you a fresh coffee and some water," he said to Bobbi.

"Oh, that's so nice, thank you," Bobbi said, patting her moist cheeks with a napkin.

Fina looked at the guy, who was probably in his midtwenties, and felt a powerful urge to marry him or adopt him on the spot. She wasn't sure which one, but she knew he was a keeper. "That's very sweet. Thank you very much," she said, giving him an appreciative smile.

"My pleasure," he said, returning to his post behind the counter.

"It does smell good," Fina said, pushing the plate in Bobbi's direction.

Bobbi picked up a piece and took a bite. She chewed it thoughtfully before taking another.

Fina took a piece for herself and marveled at the restorative powers of butter, cheese, and garlic. She and Bobbi sat eating quietly for a few minutes.

"Do you want specifics about what I'm working on?" Fina finally asked. "Or do you prefer I wait until I have something significant?"

"I don't need specifics right now. Jamie and I need to figure this out, but maybe after . . ." Bobbi trailed off.

"That's fine. Just let me know."

There was a gust of cold wind as the door opened, and Jamie walked into the pizza shop.

"Bobbi," he called over to her. "The kids are here with Mrs. Sandraham."

Bobbi looked up. "I've got to go, Fina. We're doing a handoff. We don't want the kids to spend too much time without either one of us."

"Of course."

Bobbi rose and gathered her belongings before coming around the table to give Fina a hug. Fina gave her an extra-tight squeeze to make up for her loss of words.

Jamie and Bobbi exchanged a few words before Jamie came over to the table. Fina really didn't know what to say to him; end-of-life decisions were intensely private, and she didn't presume that he wanted to discuss it with her.

"I'm heading over to the hospital," he said.

"Right. I was just touching base with Bobbi." Fina sat back down, but Jamie remained standing. "She told me about Liz's condition. I'm sorry."

He nodded. Really, what was there to say?

"Have you found something out?" he asked.

"There haven't been any major developments," Fina said, "if that's what you mean. I've been talking to a lot of people, which may not seem like much, but it's important."

"Who have you been talking to?"

"Kelly Wegner, Kevin Lafferty, Tasha, Gus Sibley. The development officer at NEU, Pamela Fordyce."

Jamie pursed his lips at one of the names on the list, but Fina couldn't be sure who had elicited the reaction.

"What was that?" she asked.

"What?"

"You just reacted to one of those names."

"No, I didn't," he said.

"Jamie." Fina pulled off part of the garlic bread. "Don't try to bullshit a bullshitter. Sit down for a minute and tell me what's going on." She popped the morsel of bread into her mouth.

He hesitated.

"Talking to me is a concrete way to improve this horrible situation," Fina said.

Jamie considered this before dropping into the chair that Bobbi had vacated.

"So who on that list bugs you?" Fina asked.

He massaged the back of his neck with his hand before answering. "Kevin Lafferty."

"I didn't realize you knew Kevin Lafferty."

"Not well, but I don't like him."

"Why not?"

"I think he's slimy."

"He's definitely a smooth operator, but what makes you so sure he's a bad guy?"

Jamie shook his head. "I don't know, I just don't like him. I think the whole booster thing is weird."

Fina shrugged. "I agree, but people have all kinds of hobbies. It's not that different than people who are passionate fans of a pro sports team."

"Yeah, well, I don't understand that, either."

"Some people might not understand your love of music and the sacrifices you were willing to make to play."

Jamie was silent.

Fina took a deep breath. This was like pulling teeth. "That can't be the only reason he rubs you the wrong way."

He lightly kicked at the empty chair next to him with the thick toe of his boot. "He had a thing for Liz," he said a moment later.

"What makes you say that?" Fina chewed another bite of garlic bread and washed it down with a pull of diet soda.

"Any time they saw each other, he flirted with her. He called her a couple of times, but she acted like it was no big deal."

"This was recently? He called her recently?" Fina asked.

"A month or so ago."

"Did she say what the calls were about?"

"Something about the NEU soccer program," Jamie said, "but she never said more than that."

"So, what? You think they were having an affair?"

"I don't know," he snapped. "What would you think in my position?"

"Fair enough," Fina said.

"I need to go."

"Wait, one more thing. Why didn't you identify Kevin when I showed you the old NEU newspapers?"

Jamie picked at the skin around his thumb before answering. "I didn't recognize him," he said. He stood, and she watched as he swayed ever so slightly, reaching for the back of the chair to steady himself.

"Are you okay?" Fina asked. "Maybe you should sit down again."

"I'm exhausted. That's all."

He left Fina at the table to contemplate his claim that he hadn't recognized Kevin. She found it hard to believe, but maybe he genuinely was too distracted at that moment, or maybe he was too embarrassed at the prospect of his wife and Kevin being involved.

Fina pitched her can in the recycling bin and placed the empty plate and mug on the counter. She reached into her wallet and pulled out twenty bucks, which she slid toward the young man.

"Thank you," she said. "That was very kind."

He slid the bill back in her direction. "On the house."

"If you insist," Fina said, depositing the money in the tip jar.

Outside, she jogged to the parking lot as the frigid wind sought out every available inch of exposed skin. She was dismayed to think that Jamie wasn't being up front with her, but she could cut him some slack, given that his life was falling apart.

But Kevin Lafferty?

There was no excuse for the lies he'd told her.

9.

Fina searched the NEU website and found the address for Liz's workplace, the Schaefer Lab of Environmental and Chemical Engineering. She also learned that the director of the lab—presumably Liz's boss—was Dr. Vikram Mehra. She located the lab on the map and navigated her way to the nearest parking garage.

Fina never felt bad about racking up expenses when she was on a case for Carl, but this case was different. She cringed every time she paid for parking or contemplated Emma's exorbitant fee. Bobbi Barone didn't strike Fina as living high off the hog, and these expenses added up. Perhaps Carl would have to subsidize the case—unbeknownst to him, of course.

Fina pulled into the garage and locked her gun in the trunk. She had a permit to carry a concealed weapon, but she knew it would cause a brouhaha if she had to go through a metal detector. Her gun was probably the least dangerous thing in the lab.

"I'm here to see Dr. Mehra," she told the security guard behind the desk in the lobby.

"Who are you?" He was a black man with heavy-lidded eyes. He did a visual inventory of her, a slow and exhaustive process.

"I'm a private investigator." She held up her license for his inspection. "I've been hired by Liz Barone's family."

The man made a phone call, which Fina couldn't overhear despite her best efforts.

"Dr. Mehra is unavailable. You're welcome to try back in an hour."

Fina looked around the lobby. "Is there any place I can sit and wait?"

He stared at her. "No."

"No?"

"There is a coffee shop around the corner. I imagine you would be welcome there."

"All righty then. I'll be back."

Fina understood that they might not want people hanging around in a lab building for security reasons, but he could have been a little more chipper.

She found the aforementioned coffee shop and bought a hot chocolate, which she nursed while she caught up on e-mails. An hour and fifteen minutes later, she walked back to the lab, hoping her luck had changed.

"I'm back," she said, handing him her license.

"Hmm. Well, aren't we the lucky ones," he said.

"Well, I think so, but I'm biased," Fina responded.

He picked up the phone and had another hushed conversation. He replaced the receiver and keyed her information into the computer.

Fina glanced at the name tag on his navy blue blazer. "Louis, can I ask you a question?"

"Do I have a choice?"

"You don't have to answer, I suppose."

He kept typing, but didn't respond.

"As I mentioned an hour and fifteen minutes ago, I'm investigating the attack on Liz Barone. Did you know her?"

"I know everyone who works here," he said.

"So you'd know if someone wanted to hurt her."

He raised his lids and studied her. "I don't know their personal business."

Fina leaned her elbows on the counter separating them. "Oh, come on. You see everyone who goes in and out of this place. You know who's sneaking out early, and I bet you know who's fraternizing when they shouldn't be."

Louis shook his head. "I know nothing."

"What's Dr. Mehra like?" Fina asked.

"You are quite the chatterbox," he said, placing a visitor's ID badge in front of her.

"Liz is in critical condition. If you know anything that could shed some light on the situation, I know her family would appreciate it."

"Through the metal detector, take the elevator to the eighth floor." He gestured toward the elevator bank.

"Let's stay in touch," Fina said, slipping her card toward him.

Louis picked it up and deposited it in the trash can by his feet.

"Oh come on, Louis. Humor me!" She grinned and walked through the metal detector.

Fina's boots squeaked on the shiny linoleum of the eighth floor. She followed a sign to the Schaefer Lab and found a small grouping of desks in an open area halfway down the hallway. Three were unoccupied, but a young woman in a lab coat was seated at the fourth.

"I'm looking for Dr. Mehra's office," Fina said.

"Last door on the right," she answered.

"Thanks." Fina continued down the hallway and stopped at the last door, which was ajar. A man was seated with his back to the door, studying something on his computer at a workstation. Fina knocked and poked her head in.

"Dr. Mehra?"

"Yes, come in." He rotated his chair around so he was facing his desk and the doorway.

"I'm Fina Ludlow. I'm a private investigator." She walked to his desk and extended her hand. He looked at her blankly, then shook it. His skin was cool and dry.

"May I sit down?" Fina asked when an invitation was not forth-coming.

Vikram gestured at one of the chairs in front of his desk.

The office was tidy, but lacked any warmth or personality. Most of the surfaces were bare, and the floor was clear of boxes and piles. Magazine files, each neatly labeled, filled the open shelving units. There was a cof-fee mug on the desk and one framed photo showing Vikram, a woman, and two teenage children; no one was smiling. The window overlooked roofs of smaller buildings, and the sill held two potted succulents.

"I was wondering if you could provide some information," Fina asked.

Vikram tilted his head and opened his mouth in an expression that brought to mind the wolf in *Little Red Riding Hood*. His white teeth glimmered against his skin. "First, I'd like to hear exactly who you are and why you're here," he said.

"Of course." It was a simple and legitimate request, and Fina was al-ways surprised by how infrequently it was made of her. She wouldn't always be transparent, but there was a greater chance she would be if only people asked.

"As I said, my name is Fina Ludlow. I'm a private investigator, and Liz Barone's family has hired me to investigate the attack she sustained."

"Are you working with the police?" Vikram asked. He was wearing a white lab coat over a pair of khakis and a plaid button-down shirt.

"Of course. Lieutenant Pitney and I have spoken about the situation, and I'm in frequent contact with Detective Menendez. I assume they've spoken with you."

"Yes, and I didn't have anything of value to share," Vikram said.

Fina smiled. "Well, I'm sure they told you that it's hard to know what's of value until a lot of information has been gathered."

"That's exactly what they said."

"Can you spare a few minutes?" Fina asked.

Vikram sighed and looked at his watch. "I suppose."

"Could you tell me what Liz's job entailed?" Fina asked.

"Liz is the administrative manager of the lab."

"What does that mean specifically?"

"She orders equipment, manages the budget, that sort of thing," Vikram said.

"And what's your position?"

"I'm the scientific director. I oversee all aspects of the lab, including the actual research projects."

"What do you study here?" Fina asked.

Vikram launched into a spiel on pesticides, and Fina filed it under *information she really didn't want to know*. That was one of the benefits of a largely processed diet; she rarely worried about the chemicals on her fruits and vegetables.

"Did Liz have conflicts with any of her colleagues?"

Vikram shrugged. "When you're in charge of managing the budget and other resources, it's not unusual for someone to be unhappy with you."

"But there was no one in particular?"

"Not to my knowledge."

"And your relationship with Liz?" she asked.

"It was professional," he replied, stony-faced.

"I assumed as much." It would be hard to have an intimate relationship with an ice cube, after all. "My understanding is that you had a conflict with Liz."

He peered at her. "Where are you getting your information from, Ms. Ludlow?"

Fina smiled at him. "From a variety of sources. Is it true?"

"You've been misled, I'm afraid," Vikram said. "You'll need to leave now. I'm very busy." He picked up a pen and uncapped it in anticipation of her departure.

"Thanks very much for your time."

Fina started down the hall, knowing that that wasn't the last she would see of Vikram Mehra. She was passing the grouping of desks when a loud voice echoed after her.

"Dana, I need to see the latest readings!" Vikram hollered to the young woman who'd directed Fina to his office.

Dana pushed back her chair and rolled her eyes. Fina smiled in solidarity and made her way to the elevator.

Downstairs, Fina pulled off her visitor's badge and swung by the front desk.

"Louis, you should have warned me that Vikram Mehra has a bug up his ass."

For an instant, the hint of a smile crossed the security guard's face.

"Gotcha!" she said, and left the building.

Fina had had her fill of difficult personalities, but the day was not quite done. Tonight was Elaine's birthday dinner.

Fina picked up Milloy from an appointment in Back Bay and stopped at a florist on Route 9 to get a large bouquet for her mother—not that she expected her to appreciate it. Elaine went through life keeping score of the things that didn't measure up. She was perpetually disappointed, and Fina had concluded that this approach gave her some twisted satisfaction. Sometimes, Fina wondered if her mother had been like this as a child. Was Elaine the little girl who never wanted what was for dinner? Whose shoes always pinched? Who always wanted to play with the classmate who didn't want to be her friend? Or had she been an agreeable child whose personality was ruined by the death of her toddler daughter? Some families might talk about such things, but the Ludlows were not one of those families.

"Thanks for this," Fina said to Milloy. "I know it wasn't what you had in mind when we made dinner plans."

"Your mother doesn't bug me the way she bugs you," he said.

"That's because she likes you."

Milloy didn't argue with the implied suggestion that Elaine didn't particularly like her own daughter. Fina appreciated that he didn't sugarcoat things, but that didn't mean it felt good.

"I promise, when your parents are in town," she said, "I'll return the favor."

Milloy's Chinese mother was anxious for her son to settle down and give her grandchildren. During his parents' biannual visits, Fina made herself available to play the role of his date. They never expressly said they were dating, but neither did they disabuse Milloy's mother of the notion that they were a couple. The ruse would only hold up for so long, but in the meantime, it eased the pressure on Milloy.

Carl and Elaine lived in an enormous house in Chestnut Hill. The stone and shingled manse provided way too much space for two people, but perhaps that was the point. It enabled her parents to be together, separately, which might be why they were still married after all these years. Both had difficult personalities, although Elaine was more trying as far as Fina was concerned. Carl was demanding and controlling, but you knew where you stood with him. Elaine was a master of passive-aggressiveness.

"Looks like the gang's all here," Milloy said as they pulled into the driveway that led to a four-car garage. The area was littered with luxury automobiles. The house was newly built, and the architect must have needed corrective lenses; the windows were too big, especially a circular outcropping of glass that looked like a growth on the front of the house.

They got out of the car, and Milloy stood for a moment, evaluating the structure.

"Huh."

"Were you hoping it had grown more attractive since your last visit?" she asked.

Fina steered them to a side door with the hope of sneaking in through the kitchen, perhaps fortifying herself with an adult beverage before facing the birthday girl.

A maid, decked out in full regalia, shooed them from the kitchen. Fina didn't recognize her, but that wasn't surprising; Elaine went through hired help like newborns went through diapers.

Chatter and laughter floated down the hallway and beckoned them to the media room, a sunken space that overlooked the backyard. The youngest family members were sprawled on one part of the enormous sectional watching the Bruins on the flat-screen TV. There were built-in bookcases and shelves on one wall and a small bar where Matthew and Scotty were deep in conversation. Elaine had some kind of catalog open on the dark wood coffee table and was showing something to Patty.

"Happy birthday, Mom," Fina said, stepping down into the room. She reached over the back of the couch and handed the flowers to her mother.

"Those are gorgeous, Fina," Patty remarked.

Elaine buried her nose in them and sniffed. "Not much of a scent, though."

Fina walked over to her brothers and picked up a corkscrew. She turned her back on the others and mimed thrusting it into her heart. They snorted with laughter.

"Milloy!" Elaine stood up and came around the couch to give him a hug. "What a treat!"

"Happy birthday, Elaine. You don't look a day over fifty."

"You spoil me, Milloy, but I love it." She smiled shyly. Fina looked on with distaste.

Milloy and Elaine returned to the couch, and Chandler, Scotty and Patty's youngest, quickly climbed onto Milloy's lap. Milloy was fit and muscular and thought nothing of picking up Fina's nephews and rough-housing with them. Scotty wasn't really into that kind of thing, and they relished the opportunity to play on a human jungle gym.

"How's Liz Barone?" Scotty asked, handing Fina a glass of wine.

"She's brain-dead. There's nothing they can do for her." The siblings didn't speak as they let the information sink in.

"Where's Dad?" Fina asked after a moment.

Matthew gestured with his head. "In his office."

"I'll be right back," Fina said, downing half of her wine in one gulp.

"Easy, killer," Matthew said.

"I have a designated driver. I can drink as much as I want, which, believe me, is going to be a lot."

Fina walked to Carl's lair at the other end of the house. His office had a high coffered ceiling and a wall of windows that looked out on a pond and the woods beyond it. Carl was sitting behind a large glass desk that faced the door, a huge painting mounted behind him. Like his interest in wine, Carl had adopted the art-collecting hobby because it was the thing to do. As far as Fina knew, her father couldn't tell the difference between a Kandinsky and a Dr. Seuss.

She rapped on the open door and took a seat on one of the leather couches that sat perpendicular to Carl's desk. He held her gaze for a long moment before speaking.

"How's it feel to return to the scene of the crime?" he asked.

"Huh?" Fina asked.

Carl gestured to a painting on the wall. Fina looked at him.

"My safe," he said. "Where you got the dirt on Rand."

Fina snorted. "Which dirt are you referring to? His professional malfeasance or the fact that he molested his daughter?"

Carl's face flooded with color. "We're not discussing that."

"Of course not. That would be the healthy thing to do, but we're not big on that."

"I took care of it."

"Temporarily," Fina said. "You took care of it temporarily."

Carl had exiled Rand to Miami, under the guise of opening a satellite office of Ludlow and Associates. Rand had threatened to return to the family fold a few months ago, a possibility Fina found intolerable. Haley was living with Scotty and Patty, putting her life back together, and her father had no place in it. No one else in the family was going to keep him away—at least that's what Fina was led to believe—so she dug around until she found incriminating information to hold over him. Information she found in Carl's safe.

Fina studied her father. "You wanted me to find that dirt."

Her father snorted. "Be serious."

"Rand's exile has been extended, and it's all because of me. You didn't have to be the heavy. I'd be annoyed, except that I fulfilled my objective at the same time."

"You make life much more complicated than it is, Fina, what with your conspiracy theories."

"Why didn't you cast him out yourself?" she asked. "Why'd you involve me?"

"*I* didn't involve you," Carl said.

"Of course you did. You knew I wouldn't let him be around Haley. Why am I the only one in this family with balls?"

He pointed a finger at her. "Watch it."

She said nothing, but maintained eye contact.

"Did you have something to report?" he asked.

"I'm making progress on the Liz Barone case."

"Glad to hear. The faster you're done, the faster you can get back to real work."

Fina shook her head. "This is real work, Dad."

"Firm work," he said.

"Well, if everything goes well, you should have a big fat lawsuit against NEU when I'm done."

"I'm looking forward to it. In the meantime, I have files for you to review. I'll have them messengered over in the morning."

Fina felt her neck muscles tighten. "Dad, I need to focus on this case."

"Just get your work done, Fina. It's not that complicated."

"Fina! Carl!" Elaine's voice cut into the conversation. "Dinner is ready! Now!"

Fina rose from the couch. "How can you stand her summoning you like that?"

"Hmm?" Carl had turned his attention to his computer.

Ah. That's how.

10.

The NEU student union was the bounty reaped from a $20 million alumni bequest. Pamela had been instrumental in securing the donation from an alum who'd made his fortune manufacturing and selling household cleaning products. She always felt a flush of pride when she entered the building: The NEU community enjoyed a state-of-the-art facility, and the alum would forever be associated with something other than toilet bowl cleaner.

Occasionally, Pamela had meetings in the food court portion of the building, although "food court" was a poor description of the space. Dozens of eateries were spread over two floors, interspersed with pool tables, comfortable seating areas, and study nooks. The center was always buzzing with activity, no matter the time of day.

Pamela had purposefully scheduled this early morning meeting outside of the office. She was a few minutes early, so she ordered a caramel flan latte and found a chair in a sunny corner. She peeled the lid off her drink and blew lightly across the steaming top.

Two Asian students a couple of chairs away giggled and conversed in a language that sounded jarring and stilted. Some lanky young men were tossing a Nerf football between couches. A large television that anchored the seating area was tuned to the local cable news station. Pamela pulled a file out of her briefcase and flipped through it. She was meeting with the finance committee later, and the gathering had the potential to be contentious. She wanted to be as prepared as possible.

"Pamela, can I get you something—oh, I see you've already got a drink." Kevin Lafferty placed his briefcase on an empty chair and unwound his scarf from around his neck.

"I do, but thank you for the offer."

"I'm going to grab some coffee. Be right back."

Pamela watched him walk to the café counter and chat up the pretty barista. To her knowledge, he'd never met a woman with whom he didn't flirt. Men also seemed to fall under his spell. Not in a sexual way, but in the way charismatic people have in charming whomever they deem worthy of their attention.

Kevin returned to the table with a cup of coffee and took a seat across from her. "What can I do for you?" he asked, taking a sip.

"Has that private investigator been to see you?" Pamela asked.

"The Ludlow gal?"

"She's not a gal, Kevin. Fina Ludlow is a grown woman who probably carries a gun."

Kevin rolled his eyes. "She stopped by the office. What about it?"

"She came to see me, too. I don't like her digging around."

"Why'd she go to see you?"

"Liz Barone sent me some angry e-mails, and Fina got her hands on them. They don't paint me in a very flattering light."

"What were you two e-mailing about?" Kevin asked.

"Liz kept getting annual fund solicitations and was incensed. We meant to take her off the list, but there was an administrative error, and it didn't happen as quickly as she would have liked."

"So, you explain that she was angry," he said, "but you handled it."

"Yes, thank you for that advice. That's exactly what I told Fina, but the lawsuit is a different story," Pamela said, spooning up some caramel from the bottom of the cup.

He shook his head. "We have nothing to do with the lawsuit."

"Except that it could have a negative impact on both of our lives."

"You're getting way ahead of yourself," Kevin said.

"Really? You haven't thought about what might happen if that suit goes forward?"

"It's not going to go forward. There's no proof," Kevin said. "There's nothing to worry about."

"I'm sorry, but I don't share your optimism."

"This is all going to die down, and we'll just get back to doing what we do."

"What did Fina want to talk to you about?" Pamela asked.

"She wanted to know about my contact with Liz and my role as a booster." His gaze wandered off as a trio of attractive undergrads walked by. He wasn't leering, but Pamela still wished she had a cattle prod with which to get his attention.

"And what did you tell her?"

"That there was nothing to tell." He looked at her. "Pamela, you've got to get a grip. NEU is going to be fine. We're all going to be fine." Kevin pushed back his cuff and looked at his watch. "I've got to run. See you at the silent auction."

He got up and draped his scarf around his neck. He walked away, depositing his cup in a recycling bin on the way out.

Maybe she did worry too much, but clearly, some people didn't worry enough.

Fina kicked off her workday with a call to Hal Boyd, her money guru. She used a CPA to file her taxes and oversee her business finances, but when it came to investigations, Fina needed someone who had a more flexible interpretation of the law. Hal was that someone.

He showed up at Nanny's an hour later, his puffy parka making him look even more rotund than usual.

"Do you want something to drink?" Fina asked. "Water? Tea? I might have some instant coffee."

"Water, please," Hal said, lowering himself into the easy chair next to the couch. Fina got him a glass of water and grabbed a diet soda for herself.

"Wow, you start drinking that stuff early," he commented when Fina sat down on the couch and popped the top.

"It's one of my few vices. Everything else, I do by the book," she said, taking a long slug.

Hal looked askance at her.

"I'm kidding, Hal! I don't do anything by the book."

He grinned. "What do you need?"

"I need some information about the Schaefer Lab at NEU."

Hal pulled out a notebook from his briefcase and jotted something down. "Anything in particular you're interested in?"

"How it's financed, any red flags related to money. That sort of thing."

"Sure." Hal picked up his water and took a sip. In addition to his ample girth, Hal was also short and balding. He had a nice face and a warm smile to go with his kind heart. Hal proved the tenet that a good personality really could make someone seem more attractive.

"For instance," Fina said, "if the university were to be sued, could that have an impact on the longevity of the lab?"

"Are we talking about a lawsuit directly involving the lab?" Hal asked.

"No, not necessarily. And what about grants and government funding?"

"Okay. Sounds good."

Fina tugged on the end of her ponytail as she ran through her mental to-do list. "The other thing I need is info on some personal finances."

"Ah. I was wondering why you needed me to do the NEU stuff; most of that is on public record."

"Sure, but I want you to find anything that isn't," Fina said, "and I need you to do some other digging that isn't completely aboveboard."

"Name it."

"I have a client named Liz Barone. I want you to take a look at her and her husband, Jamie Gottlieb."

"You think she's keeping something from you?" Hal asked.

"She's brain-dead, so she's keeping everything from me," Fina said, arching her brow.

"Oh God, Fina. That's horrible, even for you."

"Don't go soft on me, Hal," she said with a smile. "I think her husband might be keeping something from me, but he may just be grief-stricken or garden-variety difficult. It's hard to tell."

"So what do you want? The usual stuff?"

"Yeah. Debts, assets, general money habits."

"Done."

Fina loved working with Hal. He was terrific at his job, and he never gave her sass like Emma did.

"And I need the info as soon as possible, please."

"You usually do," he said.

"And you always deliver, Hal. You're one of the few reliable things in my life."

Hal struggled out of the chair and tugged on the bottom of the thick-stitched navy blue sweater that was already stretched tightly over his barrel-shaped torso. "You know I'm always happy to help you, Fina," he said, shrugging on his coat.

After he left, Fina brought his glass and her can into the kitchen and left them in the sink. She tended to wash dishes on an as-needed basis: When she needed one, she plucked a dirty one from the sink and cleaned it. The idea of using dishes, washing them, and putting them away only to use them again made no sense to Fina. It seemed wildly inefficient.

She was sitting down in front of her computer when Risa called, asking to meet. Fina was facing down the stacks of files Carl had sent over and figured she'd need a reward by midafternoon. She'd be hungry when she was done, and when she was hungry, there was no better place to be than Risa's.

ina's back was aching and her stomach was growling when she arrived at Risa's home for a late lunch. The family's Victorian gingerbread-style house was at the other end of the luxury spectrum from Frank and Peg's modest ranch. It boasted three stories and an addition out back that blended seamlessly with the original design. The shingles were painted in an intricate design of mossy green, white, and wine.

The front walkway and porch were mostly cleared of snow, with the occasional icy patch. The house was in its full glory in summer, when the large wraparound porch was festooned with hanging baskets dripping with fuchsias, lobelia, and petunias.

Fina rang the bell, and a moment later spotted Marty, Risa's husband, through the pane of glass on the door.

"Hi, Marty." Fina leaned in for a kiss on the cheek after he invited her in. "I didn't expect to see you home at this hour."

"I'm off to New York. Just stopped at home for my bag and a good-bye kiss." Marty worked in finance and traveled to Manhattan regularly.

He made small talk as they walked toward the back of the house. Risa's husband was a sweetie, but in Fina's estimation, one of the most boring men she'd ever met. She was aware, however, that what was boring to some was stable to others.

"Fina's here," Marty announced as they entered the kitchen.

The addition to the house had been designed to give Risa a kitchen worthy of her talents. The updated space was a combination kitchen, eating area, and family room, and the family spent most of their time there. The six-burner stove and granite island were where Risa worked her magic, while the kids watched TV and did their homework on the other side of the breakfast bar. It was very similar to Patty's setup, and it made Fina wonder when parents decided they needed to see their kids at all times. When Fina was young, her parents were quite happy to have them in a separate room with no sight lines or opportunities for interaction. Maybe they would poke their heads in if there were screams or the sounds of glass shattering. Maybe.

"Hey." Risa turned from the sink, her hands dripping with suds.

"I'm going. I'll call you when I get to the hotel," Marty said, giving Risa a kiss on the cheek.

"Have a good flight," Risa said.

"Nice to see you, Marty," Fina added.

He went into the attached garage, and they listened as the door rumbled to life.

"When's he coming back?" Fina asked. She pulled off her outerwear and laid it over the back of the couch.

"Day after tomorrow."

"It's nice he isn't gone for long stretches."

"It is. It's short enough that the boys barely notice."

Fina took a seat on one of the bar stools at the counter.

"I tried a new recipe," Risa said.

"You know I would have come over even if you didn't offer to feed me." Fina grinned.

"You say that, but I'm not sure I believe you. I'm on a Vietnamese kick; I made caramelized ginger chicken with sticky rice."

"Sounds delicious."

Risa reached into one of the white cabinets and pulled out two plates. "I have seltzer, iced tea, milk. Sorry, no diet soda."

"Seltzer sounds good."

The walls of the kitchen were painted a mossy green, which contrasted nicely with the earth-toned floor and backsplash. The space reminded Fina of Tuscany without the cheap Olive Garden vibe.

"How's the family?" Risa asked, busying herself around the stove.

"We had Elaine's birthday party last night."

"And? How was it?"

"There were tears, a broken picture frame, and diamonds—a typical Ludlow celebration."

"Who was crying? Elaine?"

"God no. Chandler, when Ryan broke the frame and blamed it on him."

"I'm sure your mom was happy to have you guys there to celebrate," Risa said.

"You're projecting the love for your own children onto my mother."

"Fina," Risa said, slipping a plate of food in front of her. "Of course she loves you. She's your mother."

"That's what functional mothers always say."

The chicken leg was a deep brown color and sticky with sauce. The rice grains clung to one another, their white interrupted by the occasional scallion. Fina inhaled the aroma.

"This smells amazing."

Risa put down two glasses of seltzer and a second plate of food before climbing onto the stool next to Fina.

"So, what's going on with you?" Fina asked, cutting off a bite of chicken and placing it in her mouth. There was some zing from the ginger, which interplayed nicely with the sweetness of the sauce.

Risa rotated her glass and straightened out her silverware. "Well, I got some news from the doctor's office."

"Okay."

"My test results have come back positive, meaning I can proceed with the transplant testing."

Fina swallowed a bite of chicken. "But you don't know if you're a match yet, right?"

"Correct."

"So what are you thinking?"

Risa sighed. "Well, that's my problem. I can't think straight."

Fina smiled. "Okay, why don't we break it down into manageable chunks?"

"Please do."

"Well, don't worry about the transplant for now. Before Greta got in touch with you, had you ever considered tracking down your birth family?"

"Not seriously. It's one of those things that you think, 'maybe, some-day,' but I never felt the need that some adopted people feel." Risa dipped her head. "Also, I didn't want to hurt my mom and dad."

"That's understandable. So you're minding your own business, and your biological aunt finds you." Fina assembled a perfect forkful of chicken, rice, and scallion and put it in her mouth.

"Exactly, and I'm having to think about something that I never really wanted to."

"Have you had any contact with Greta?" Fina asked.

"We've exchanged a few letters."

"Does she have any other family around?"

"No. She never married. Elizabeth did, and she had a son, but he died when he was nineteen in a boating accident."

Fina looked at her. "So you've also learned that you had a half sibling."

Risa nodded.

"That's a lot to process, even if you don't throw an organ transplant into the mix. Speaking of which"—Fina gestured to Risa's plate—"you need to eat something unless your plan is to take yourself out of the running with a hunger strike."

Risa took a bite. "That brings us to the kidney situation. I feel like Greta's feelings shouldn't figure in to the equation, but I'm getting hung up on them."

"What do you mean?"

"I mean, did she ever think about me all this time? Did *she* want to find me, but my birth mother wouldn't let her? If she didn't need a kidney, would she have contacted me, or is that the only reason she tracked me down?"

Fina put down her fork. "Risa, how could those questions *not* figure into this? You have every right to wonder about those things and take them into account when making your decision. It would be naïve not to."

"Really?"

"Of course. Look, if I were in your shoes and I thought that my aunt had no interest in me except as an organ donor, I would have serious reservations about handing over my kidney," Fina said. "It's great that people choose to make donations, but that's very different from being manipulated into doing so."

"I just feel guilty thinking that way," Risa said.

"Don't."

"Maybe her illness is a chance to have a relationship we might not have otherwise."

"Her illness," Fina clarified, "or your donation?"

"Both." Risa avoided Fina's gaze.

They were silent for a moment. "What if you had more information about Greta's motives?" Fina asked. "Would that make you feel better?"

"Maybe."

"What does the next round of tests entail?"

"A general physical, an EKG, a psych evaluation, a kidney function test. There's more, but that's just off the top of my head."

"So it gets more involved and more invasive."

"Yes. This is good, don't you think?" Risa asked, eating another bite.

"It's fantastic." Fina sipped her drink. "I think you need to figure out where your kids fit into this, weigh the likelihood of them ever needing your kidney. I assume you'd want them to have first dibs, but the chances of either of them needing it are probably incredibly small."

"I've been discussing that with the transplant coordinator," Risa said, chasing some errant grains of rice around her plate.

"Good," Fina said. "Remember, Risa, just because someone asks for something, it doesn't mean you're required to give it to them."

"I know, but it's hard to break out of that mind-set."

"That's why I'm here: to call into question your unwavering generosity."

"Is that why? I thought it was to appreciate my cooking." Risa slipped off her stool and brought their empty dishes over to the sink. She rinsed them before stacking them in the dishwasher.

"What if we did a little digging around to find out more about your birth family and Greta's story?"

"You could do that?"

"Well, *I* can't, I'm on another case, but I know someone who can."

"But I don't want anyone to know about this."

"I'm thinking of Frank Gillis," Fina said. "He'd be perfect. He's discreet, and he's a great investigator. People love telling him things. He wouldn't need two hours in Greta's local diner before he got the scoop."

"I don't know." Risa looked doubtful.

"Listen, if he doesn't find anything out, you're just a few bucks poorer, but maybe he'll learn something that has a bearing on your decision."

Risa grabbed a bottle of blue liquid and sprayed the countertop. She tore off a couple of paper towels and wiped the surface clean.

"Okay. Talk to Frank."

"Good." Fina slid off the stool and grabbed her things. "Remember, it's just more information, and information is power."

"I thought money was power," Risa said, trailing her to the front door.

"That, too, but you've got that covered."

They hugged, and Fina picked her way down the steps and returned to her car. Fingers crossed, Frank was interested in doing some sleuthing.

Fina arrived at Frank and Peg's house and was relieved to find that Frank wasn't shoveling snow, cleaning the gutters, or painting the exterior. She wasn't sure what her next move would be if he didn't heed her pleas to moderate his physical activity. You couldn't make someone do something they didn't want to, but it would be so much easier if you could.

She knocked on the door and poked her head into the small entryway off the den.

"Frank? Peg?"

What if they didn't answer? What if they were involved in a private moment? The idea gave her the heebie-jeebies, but maybe that was reason enough to stop letting herself in uninvited.

"We're in the kitchen," Peg called out.

Frank was sitting at the kitchen table, a cup of coffee in front of him. Peg was at the counter, cutting up an apple. Peg was a school nurse and was still wearing her uniform of dark blue scrubs and a patterned scrubs jacket.

"Snazzy scrubs you've got there," Fina said, slipping into a chair next to Frank.

"Believe me, you have people vomit on you on a regular basis, you're not going to wear your Sunday best."

"They look good and very comfortable. What are these?" Fina asked, looking at some glossy travel brochures on the table.

"We're going to visit Billy in Alaska," Frank said. Frank and Peg had two sons, one of whom lived in New York City, the other in Alaska. He'd gone out to the Last Frontier for college, had been enchanted by the natural beauty, and had never left.

"Not in the winter, I hope," Fina said.

Peg came over to the table with a plate of apple slices and took a seat. "We're thinking July," she said.

"That makes sense." Fina took a wedge of apple and bit off the end.

"So were you just in the neighborhood?" Frank asked.

"I was in the neighborhood, but I also have a question for you."

"Shoot," Frank said.

"I could use some help with a case, and I thought you'd be the man for the job."

Peg raised an eyebrow.

"It's not dangerous," Fina assured her, "and it's not a big time commitment."

"What is it?" Frank asked, picking up an apple slice. "Any sugar to go with this?" he asked his wife. Fina had also grown up dipping her apple slices in sugar, in the dark ages before everything was bad for you.

"No, Frank." Peg batted his hand playfully. "There is no sugar for dipping."

"Sorry," Frank said to Fina. "Go ahead."

"Obviously, this is confidential."

Frank nodded.

"I did some work for Risa Paquette in the fall." Frank and Peg knew Risa from various Ludlow family gatherings. "She was adopted as a baby, and she was recently approached by a woman claiming to be her biological aunt."

"Uh-huh." Frank bit down on an apple slice.

"I did some digging, and it turns out the woman *is* Risa's aunt, and . . . she needs a kidney."

Peg winced. "Which she'd like Risa to supply?"

"Exactly," Fina said. "Risa's not sure what to do, but she's started the testing process to determine if she's a match."

"There's no one else in the family who could donate?" Peg asked.

"Nope. The only other person from Risa's generation was her half brother, but he died a long time ago in a boating accident."

"So where do I fit in?" Frank asked.

"Risa would like to know more about her aunt and get some sense of her motives. Is she truly only interested in Risa's kidney? That sort of thing."

"And you think that kind of information is available?"

"Risa's maternal birth family is from a small town in Maine, just over the border. I've been there, and my sense is that everybody knows everybody else's business. I was thinking you could take a day trip—take your lovely wife, if you like." Fina gestured at Peg. "Do a little nosing around."

Frank drank some coffee.

"There's a town center with maybe one restaurant," Fina added, "and I bet if you chatted up a few locals, you could find something out."

"Sometimes small-town people circle the wagons," Frank said.

"But there's usually at least one Chatty Cathy, and if there isn't, no big deal." Fina grinned. "I'll pay you either way."

"You bet you will, sweetie." Frank looked at Peg. "What do you think? Are you up for a little day trip?"

"I suppose it can't be postponed until leaf peeping starts?" Peg asked hopefully.

"We've got a ticking clock, Nurse Gillis," Fina said.

Peg grinned. "Why not? Sounds like fun."

"You could stay overnight, my treat," Fina suggested. "Make a romantic weekend of it."

Frank's eyes lit up. "Sold!"

Fina was distracted when she got in her car and didn't notice the piece of paper on the passenger seat until she was a few streets away from the Gillis house. She kept her car relatively tidy and didn't remember leaving anything there. At a stoplight she scanned it; a lump caught in her throat. The annoyed driver behind her sat on his horn until she pulled over to examine it more closely.

It was a piece of plain white paper, and scrawled in a childish hand was:

FUCK YOU MIND YOURE OWN BUSSINESS BITCH

The poor grammar, spelling, and lack of punctuation were upsetting enough, but knowing that someone had been in her car was even more alarming. She knew that the note hadn't been there when she'd arrived at Frank and Peg's. Reaching over, Fina confirmed that the doors were locked. She looked around, but there were no cars idling nearby. It was an awful feeling, realizing that someone had been in your personal space, but it was even worse to think they'd been near the people you love.

"You miss me already, hon?" Frank asked when he answered the phone.

"Always, but I'm calling to give you a heads-up."

"What's happened in the four minutes since you left here?"

"I think someone's keeping an eye on me, so you should be extra careful."

There was a long pause at his end of the line.

"What happened?" Frank asked.

"I'm fine, really, but I would be remiss if I didn't suggest you and Peg keep an eye out."

"I need some specifics."

"I don't have any," Fina insisted. "Can you just be careful? I considered not saying anything at all, but that didn't seem like the right thing to do."

"This makes me very uneasy, Fina."

"Yeah, you and me both."

"You worry so much about my heart," Frank said. "But this sort of conversation is much more detrimental than a little snow shoveling."

"Frank, c'mon." She knew he was right, but it was the life she had chosen.

"Fine, but promise you'll keep me in the loop."

"I will."

"And text me to let me know you got home safely."

"Promise."

Back home, Fina wrapped her hand around her gun for the elevator ride upstairs. She made sure the condo was clear, then texted Frank and got ready for bed, her gun never out of reach. She laid it on her bedside table, but sleep didn't come easily.

Was the note connected to the sedan with tinted windows? Was it unrelated? Did she have two threats to worry about? Who had she pissed off this time?

11.

Fina wasn't prepared for the text message she got the next morning. In between spam for a sweepstakes and a plea from Haley to take her shopping was a brief entry from Bobbi Barone: They were going to take Liz off life support sometime that day.

Fina sat down at the dining room table, her phone gripped in her hand. She gazed out the large windows overlooking the harbor and Logan. Planes glinted in the cold January sunlight as they inched along the tarmac before barreling down the runway. People died every day, but it was rare that you woke up knowing that on this particular day, this particular person was going to die. Death sucked, whether or not you had advance notice.

Fina wanted to drop some kind of offering by the Barone-Gottlieb household. She knew that everyone brought food on these occasions; they would be drowning in a sea of lasagna, sweet rolls, and deli platters. She ruminated about the right gift while she showered and ate and decided finally to stop by a bookstore on the way to Hyde Park. Liz's kids probably needed distraction more than calories right about now.

There were no bogeymen in her car or lurking near the bookstore, so Fina tried to put last night's warning out of her head. She'd be more vigilant, but she couldn't let it distract her from the case, despite the note writer's best effort.

When Fina pulled up to Liz's house two hours later, Kelly Wegner was climbing out of her minivan in the driveway. She was laden with foil-covered casserole dishes confirming that Fina's choice of books and stuffed animals had been a good one.

"Kelly, let me help," Fina said, jogging over and taking the dishes from her as Kelly rummaged in her purse.

"Thanks," Kelly said. She fished out a set of keys and opened the front door. Fina put the dishes down on the floor and returned to her car for the kids' gift baskets. Back inside, Kelly had already shed her boots and coat and was banging around in the kitchen.

"Kelly? I don't want to track slush in the house," Fina called out.

Kelly emerged from the kitchen with a dish towel in hand. Her approach gave Fina the opportunity to take stock of her appearance, which, quite frankly, was awful.

"You look exhausted," Fina said. "I hate it when people tell me that, but are you getting any sleep? You can't help Jamie and the kids if you wear yourself out."

"I know. I'm trying, but I'm just not sleeping well." Her blond bob looked flat and unwashed, and dark circles under her eyes underscored her fatigue.

"That's understandable," Fina said. "I don't want to intrude, but I wanted to drop these off for the kids." She gestured toward the baskets, which she'd placed on the floor.

"Oh, that's so nice. They'll love them."

"Well, who knows, but maybe it will distract them a little."

Kelly stared at the baskets.

"Kelly?"

She didn't respond. She seemed to be in a fog.

"Kelly?" Fina repeated. Kelly looked at her. "Is there anything I can do for you?"

She shook her head as if clearing out the cobwebs. "No, thank you. It's just . . ." She trailed off.

"What?"

"I just can't even think about it."

Fina assumed that Kelly had been updated on Liz's status, but she wasn't sure, and it didn't seem like her news to share if she hadn't.

"Well, if you need something or think of something useful to the case, you know where to reach me." Fina put her hand on the doorknob.

"What?" Kelly looked confused.

"The case. I'm still trying to find the person who did this to Liz."

"Of course. I'm sorry. I can't think straight."

Fina reached out and squeezed her arm. "Take care of yourself."

"I will." Kelly smiled faintly. "Thanks, Fina. It was really sweet of you to get the kids something."

"It's the least I can do," she said, pulling the door closed behind her.

Had this been a TV show, Fina would have promised Kelly that she would bring Liz's killer to justice, but she'd learned early on in her career to avoid such promises. She would always do her best to solve a case, but there were too many variables beyond her control to promise a particular outcome. And nobody wanted to hear that she would try really hard. This wasn't kindergarten; you didn't get a prize for trying.

W hy are we meeting here?" the young woman asked Kevin later that afternoon.

"What's wrong with it?" he asked, grinning.

She wrinkled her nose and slid into the booth next to him. "It's kind of seedy."

"It's not that bad," he said, planting a kiss on her lips. She grabbed hold of his lapels and extended the kiss. When she pulled away from him, she had a big smile on her face.

Kevin blotted his mouth with a napkin and looked around the restaurant. It was a Chinese place he used to frequent when he was younger, a windowless space in a strip mall in Watertown. The establishment split once you were through the front door: a dining room with tables on one side and a bar with TVs and a cloudy fish tank on the other. The food was the typical greasy American interpretation of Chinese food, but nobody came here for the food. They came for the anonymity and the stiff drinks.

"Are you hungry?" Kevin asked.

She picked up the menu and flipped through the plastic-coated pages. "I really shouldn't eat this stuff."

"I'm sure they could steam some vegetables for you."

"Are you eating?"

"Let's get a pu pu platter," Kevin said, and gestured to the bored-looking young man standing by the front desk. "Can we get a pu pu platter and two head hunters, please?"

The waiter made a note on his small pad and disappeared through a swinging door into the kitchen.

"So, how are you?" Kevin asked the young woman, stretching his arm behind her on the booth.

"I'm good." She shrugged. "The same as usual."

Kevin didn't have the longest attention span in the world, but he still hadn't tired of looking at her. She was pretty, in a wholesome, all-American way. She had long brown hair and hazel eyes, and her teeth were white and straight. Her left eyebrow was interrupted by a small scar, but that only added to her appeal. She was unique-looking, but didn't deviate too far from the standard of beauty. It went without saying that her body was amazing; he wouldn't be doing this with someone who didn't knock his socks off.

"How are *you* doing?" she asked seductively, leaning in to nibble on his bottom lip.

The waiter put down two drinks in faux coconuts, each with an umbrella and a striped straw.

Kevin took a long sip before speaking. "I'm good, but something's come up that we need to talk about."

She sipped her drink and looked at him.

"There's some stuff going on, and in the interest of being cautious, we need to take a step back."

She blinked slowly and put down her drink. "What's going on?"

"There are some things happening in the media and the administration, and the athletic program may get some extra attention."

"But what does that have to do with us? We always try to keep a low profile."

"I know. We need to be extra careful right now."

"Why?" she asked. "We're not doing anything illegal, and if some people don't approve, who cares?"

Kevin took her hand in his. "We both should care. We need to do what's right for our relationship in the long term, not just what feels good today."

She sat back against the booth, a pout emerging on her face. This was one of the downsides to youth—an inability to compromise or delay gratification.

Kevin took a long drink of his head hunter and dropped his hand down to her knee. He rubbed it for a moment. The waiter returned to their table bearing a faux wooden dish with various small compartments surrounding a blue flame.

"Pu pu platter," he announced, and left.

Kevin spun the dish around to examine the offerings before grabbing a fried wonton and dipping it into a dish of duck sauce. "Umm. That's good. Here, try one," he said, placing one on her plate.

"So what does that mean exactly, 'take a step back'?" she asked, crunching on the fried tidbit.

"Just that we should see a little less of each other and meet in places where we're less apt to run into anyone I know."

"Places like this?" She gestured toward the mural on the wall that depicted some version of Shangri-la.

"It's just temporary." Kevin gnawed on a sparerib, licking the sweet sticky sauce off his fingers.

"Are you going to make it up to me?" the young woman asked.

Kevin smiled his winning smile and kissed her deeply, the grease and sauce lubricating their lips. "I promise."

"You better," she said, gnawing on a chicken wing like a vulture.

C ristian didn't answer his phone, so Fina left a message and checked her voice mail. She returned a call from Hal and offered to stop by his place to get an update. Fina had never been to Hal's home and was impressed when she pulled up to a well-maintained Victorian a few blocks from Porter Square in Cambridge. There were two front doors on the porch. Fina knocked on the left-hand door and waited a moment before there was a shadow behind the curtain-covered window.

"Hi, Fina," Hal said. He stepped back into a small hallway that opened into the living room, which boasted three large bay windows. The shiny wood floor was partially covered by an Oriental rug and a couch in a neutral microfiber. That room flowed into what was supposed to be the dining room. Hal had repurposed the space for his office; there was a desk pushed against one wall, its surface dominated by two large computer monitors. Beyond this was an open-plan kitchen that was tidy and bright. A hallway off the kitchen probably led to the bathroom and bedrooms.

"Let me take your coat," Hal offered.

Fina took off her outerwear and handed it to Hal. He hung it on a coatrack near the front door.

"Have a seat," he said, directing her to the couch.

"I like your place, Hal. It's very bright and cheery."

"Thanks." He beamed. "Can I get you something to drink?"

"No, I'm good, thanks."

Hal grabbed a laptop from his desk and joined her on the sofa. On the side table, there was a scattering of photos featuring Hal and a young girl. She looked to be about five years old.

"Is this your daughter?" Fina asked, picking up the photo.

"Yup. That's Sarah."

"How did I not know you have a daughter?" Fina wondered.

"I don't usually talk about her with clients. Some of the people I do business with, I'd rather they not know about her."

Fina nodded. Haley had been targeted by a creep during her last investigation, and she understood the inclination to protect one's family. It was hard enough protecting Haley from her own father; Fina tried to avoid external threats whenever possible.

"Does she live with you?" she asked.

"Every other weekend and Wednesday nights," Hal said. He looked at the photos and smiled.

"She's really cute," Fina said. "You know, I can get tickets to most everything that comes to the Garden. I'm getting *Disney on Ice* tickets for Cristian and his son. If you ever want to take Sarah to something, let me know."

Hal thought about it for a moment. "You know what she'd love? That Irish clog-dancing group. If they come to town again, I'll take you up on that."

"You are a good dad," Fina said. "That show seems like a guaranteed migraine."

Hal shrugged. "She loves all kinds of dance."

"I will keep my eyes open and let you know." Fina sat back against the couch cushions. "What do you have for me?"

"I'm still working on the finances of that couple," he said, "but I did poke around the NEU lab."

"Okay."

Hal clicked a few keys on his laptop. "NEU is a private school, so they don't get any tax money for support."

Fina nodded.

"They depend on the annual fund and other donations for most of their operating budget, but the labs get government and private support in the form of grants and other charitable programs."

"Did you get a sense of the financial health of the Schaefer Lab?"

"Their budget seems pretty tight, but that's not unusual for a research facility."

"Was there anything that jumped out at you?" Fina asked.

He scooched forward on the couch. "I did come across one thing that was interesting."

Hal loved reporting his findings, and time willing, Fina tried not to rush him. It seemed to be one of the highlights of his job.

"So there's a big grant given out by a consortium of pharmaceutical companies every five years to support long-term studies," he explained. "The Schaefer Lab was on the short list of finalists this year, but didn't get the grant."

"How long was the short list?" she asked. "Presumably there were other labs that also lost out."

"There were five other labs that didn't get funding, but what was interesting was the chatter, for lack of a better word, that I found on some scientific forums."

"What kind of chatter?" Fina asked.

"Rumor has it that there was some internal conflict at the Schaefer Lab that had an impact on their application. A couple of people were suggesting it's the reason the lab wasn't awarded funding. It sounded like it was theirs to lose, and they did."

"So it wasn't just a matter of it being a tough break, but they did everything they could. Better luck next time. That sort of thing?"

"That's not what it sounded like, but you never know. They may just be sore losers," Hal said.

"Did any names come up?" Fina asked. "Was there anyone in particular being blamed?"

"No, but that didn't surprise me. These boards usually have a lot of innuendo and few facts."

"Doesn't mean they're inaccurate," Fina noted.

"No, but they should be taken with a grain of salt. Does this make any sense in the context of your case?" He looked hopeful.

"I think so. It's definitely a good lead." Fina gazed at the plants crowding the sills of the bay windows. They looked healthy, their leaves deep green and shiny. Fina had never had much luck with houseplants. Even the ones that were supposed to be impervious to a brown thumb had succumbed under her care, or lack thereof. "Which pharmaceutical companies are part of the consortium that gives out the grant?" She decided not to name Barnes Kaufcan specifically; sometimes it was good to see what Hal found on his own, without any prompting.

"I don't have that info," Hal said, tapping away. "I can find out, though."

"That would be good. And by the way, the couple you're looking into, the woman is going to die within the next twenty-four hours."

Hal looked stricken. "How do you know that? That's so creepy."

"Because she's been removed from life support," Fina said. "The police are going to get more involved once that happens because it will be a murder case, not just assault. I just wanted to give you a heads-up so you know what you're stepping into."

"Thanks. I appreciate the warning."

Hal helped her into her coat and opened the front door.

"Thanks, Hal," she said. "Great work, as always."

He blushed and studied his stocking-clad feet. "Thanks, Fina. I'll let you know as soon as I have more info."

"Looking forward to it," Fina called over her shoulder. "And I'll keep you and Sarah in mind for show tickets!"

Hal waved at her from his spot at the front door.

Hal was such a sweet man. Fina really hoped he never ended up in jail. He wouldn't last a day.

Oh my God. That feels amazing. Don't stop."

It was early evening, and Fina was lying on Milloy's portable massage table under a sheet. He was working on her back.

"Everybody is tight in this weather," Milloy commented, his large hands kneading her flesh.

"I think we need to put a regular appointment on the books. No more of this 'as needed' business," she said.

"I'm happy to. Your schedule is the one that's so unpredictable."

"You work with athletes, right?" Fina asked a minute later, her voice muffled by the face cradle.

"Yes."

"Professional athletes?"

"A few, and also people who take their fitness routines seriously— triathletes, skiers, rowers. Why?"

"This case has got me thinking," Fina said. "I spoke with a woman the other day who played college soccer, and she basically said that she would have played even with a head injury. I can't imagine being that consumed by a sport or exercise."

Milloy held the sheet away from her as she flipped over onto her back. "I think that's because you're lazy," he said, starting down one leg.

"But don't you think some of those people are obsessed? Isn't their training excessive?"

"Sure, but if you're a pro that's how you pay the bills, and the ama-teurs think it's worth the trade-offs." Milloy adjusted the sheet, tucking it under one leg.

He worked silently, and Fina allowed her mind to wander. It cycled through its usual topics: work, family, and food. Milloy had tried to get her into meditation, which was just one facet of his strategy for healthy living. He'd given up after Fina kept popping up to add items to her to-do list. She could never just let her thoughts float by and observe them without judgment. If they were taking up space in her brain, the solution was getting them out of there, not giving them the run of the place. They agreed to disagree about the purpose of the practice.

"All set," Milloy said five minutes later, giving her scalp a quick massage.

"That was heavenly." Fina rolled over on her side and sat up, pulling the sheet around her.

Milloy wandered into the kitchen. He returned a minute later, drying his hands on a dish towel.

"What do you want to eat?" he asked.

"You choose." Fina slid off the table and padded into her bedroom, where she put on old sweats and thick socks before coming back to the living room.

Milloy ended a call on his cell. "Sushi in twenty minutes." He folded up his table and rested it against the wall near the front door.

Fina gathered soy sauce, chopsticks, and beers from the kitchen and placed them on the coffee table.

"Haley seemed pretty good the other night," Milloy said.

Fina sat down next to him on the couch. "She seems okay."

"That's good, right?"

"It makes me nervous," Fina said.

"Why?"

"I'm waiting for the other shoe to drop."

"Fina, a lot of shoes have dropped already. Melanie's murder, Rand's stuff, Haley's troubles. There may not be any more shoes to drop," he said.

"There are always more shoes."

"Stop being so pessimistic. Whatever happens is out of your control."

"So you say." Fina reached for the TV remote and clicked it on. There were no enticing sporting events, so she let Milloy channel surf. He settled on a baking competition in which sugar artists had to sculpt a Wonder of the World out of sugar. They paused it for a moment when their food arrived, but started back up again once they were situated with their dinner.

"I don't think you can compare the Taj Mahal and the Christ the Redeemer statue," Fina commented after chewing on a slice of raw tuna. The sugar artist on the screen was wrestling with a cupola.

"Why not?" Milloy asked. "Which one do you think is more difficult?"

"The Taj Mahal. If you screw up Christ, you put another fold in his robe or claim that he's just as God made him."

Fina's phone rang, and she glanced at the screen.

"I need to take this," she told Milloy. "It's work." She pressed the answer key. "Hey. What's up?" she asked Cristian, wiping wasabi off her finger.

"I've got some bad news."

Fina got up off the couch and walked over to the window. "Go ahead."

"Liz Barone died about half an hour ago."

Fina swallowed.

"You there?" Cristian asked.

"I'm here. I'm just trying to wrap my head around it."

"I know. She's not much older than we are," he said.

"Oh God," Fina said. "I hadn't even gone there. Who gave you the news?"

"The hospital. She was a crime victim, and now she's a murder victim."

"You haven't spoken with Bobbi or Jamie?"

"Not yet. We're trying to leave them in peace for a little while."

"That sounds like a good idea." Fina looked out and spotted what she thought of as a ghost ship. The large tanker was only illuminated at its stern and bow, leaving most of the ship blanketed in darkness. It looked clandestine, but was really anything but.

"I just wanted to let you know," he said.

"Thanks, Cristian. I appreciate it." She should tell him about the note, she knew, but Fina hesitated. She didn't have the strength for a lecture from Cristian or Milloy.

"What's going on?" Milloy asked when she rejoined him on the couch.

"The woman who was attacked? She was taken off life support this morning, and she just died."

"Sorry," Milloy said, reaching over to rub her leg.

They kept watching the competition as one creation fell to the floor and shattered into a million pieces.

"Life is very sucky sometimes, Milloy."

"I know, Fina. I know."

12.

"Fina, you should come out here," Milloy called from the living room.

She rolled over in bed and felt around on the floor for some clothes. They'd somehow reached the same conclusion the night before—without any discussion—that Milloy should spend the night. Their relationship was very complicated or very simple, depending upon your point of view. Sometimes they supported each other in a more intimate way, and other times, they didn't.

"What is it?" she asked, pulling on some sweats. She padded out into the living room, where Milloy was showered and dressed, sitting at the dining room table. He was eating toast and an omelet.

"I have eggs?" she asked, gazing at his plate.

"Do you want me to make you some?"

"No, thanks. What's so important that you had to interrupt my beauty sleep?" She sat next to him and grabbed a piece of toast from his plate. Milloy pointed the remote at the TV and pressed play.

"The woman who was attacked in her Hyde Park home more than a week ago died from her injuries last night at Mass General," a perky reporter said, trying hard to mask her enthusiasm with a note of gravitas. "This morning, Liz Barone's mother, Bobbi Barone, announced that Liz had left her brain to the Brain Bank affiliated with Boston University, where it will be studied for signs of degenerative neurological disease. At the time of her death, Liz Barone was pursuing a lawsuit against

New England University related to brain damage she allegedly suffered as a student athlete at NEU."

"Did you know about this?" Milloy asked. He muted the broadcast, which had moved on to a story about a new diet guaranteed to rev up your sex drive.

"It's the first I've heard." Fina chewed a bite of toast. "A heads-up would have been nice, but there you have it."

"Is this good or bad news?"

She considered the development for a moment. "I think it's good. It's good for science, obviously, but it's good for the case, too."

"How so?" Milloy asked.

"If BU looks at her brain and finds evidence of damage, that will have huge ramifications in terms of the lawsuit, the prospect of which has to make a lot of people nervous. When people are nervous, they get sloppy. Sloppy works in my favor."

"Sloppy is also more dangerous," Milloy noted.

"Murder cases are dangerous," Fina said. "It's the nature of the beast, and I'm always careful."

"And yet, you still get jumped."

"I said I was careful, not omniscient," Fina said. "I promise to stay on my toes."

"I wish that were more reassuring than it is."

Fina squeezed his biceps, which was smooth and sculpted. "I'd go with it, if I were you." She rose and went into the kitchen.

"Sure I can't make you some eggs?" Milloy asked from the other room.

"And waste perfectly good Nutter Butters?"

The first time Fina walked into Barnes Kaufcan, she hadn't any preconceived notions, but things had changed. Liz's death had soured her mood, and Kevin Lafferty had lied to her and wasted her time. Both were transgressions she didn't easily forgive.

On Monday morning there were two security guards at the lobby desk, one of whom looked fresh out of high school, the other approaching retirement. The older guard was standing, pulling on his coat, so Fina fiddled with her phone. She couldn't be sure that the older guard was the more conscientious of the two, but sometimes you had to gamble, and her instincts told her that the younger one would be more likely to succumb to her charms. Fina watched him for a few moments after the older guard had left. The manner in which he eyed the young female visitors, and his lack of a wedding ring, gave her confidence in her assessment.

She walked over to the desk and leaned toward the young man.

"I was wondering if you could help me," Fina said, signing in to the electronic visitors' log, smiling. She looked around surreptitiously and pulled out her PI license. "I'm doing some work for a client"—she let him have a quick glance at her ID before putting it away—"and I'm wondering if you could check something on your visitors' log."

"You're a PI?" he asked.

"I am."

"That's cool."

"I like it. So, the visitors' log?" Fina asked.

"I'm only supposed to give access to the log when there's a written request."

"I don't actually need access. I just need to check for a name. It's electronic, right?"

"Yeah, yeah. It's all here." He gestured toward the computer in front of him, and his sleeve rode up his arm. Fina could see a tattoo peeking out.

"Another good thing about being a PI? You don't need to cover your ink," she said conspiratorially.

"That would be awesome," he said. He considered her for another moment before relenting. "What were you looking for?"

"I just want to confirm that a woman named Liz Barone visited in the past two months." Fina leaned even closer. "My client, he's a young guy and thinks his fiancée has been cheating on him. The wedding's in March."

"Seriously?"

"Yeah, I'm hoping to save him a lot of grief and money." Fina grinned and brushed some hair back from her face. "If I can give him the proof he needs, he can call the whole thing off."

"How do you spell the last name?" he asked.

Fina spelled it out and waited. She hoped the older guard had gone for a long lunch break, not just a quick cup of coffee.

"Here it is," he said. "She was here twice. Do you want me to write down the dates for you?"

"That would be great. Let me guess: She was visiting Kevin Lafferty at Barnes Kaufcan."

The guard smirked. "You got it. Bummer for your client."

"Yup." Fina smiled and took the Post-it from him. "You should think about being a PI. I bet you'd be good at it."

"You think?" He beamed and sat up straighter in his chair.

"Definitely. I can tell you've got good instincts." Fina winked at him and went to the elevator.

Louis, at the Schaefer Lab, would have a stroke if he witnessed such a dereliction of duty.

I have an appointment with Kevin Lafferty," Fina told the receptionist. "My name is Fina Ludlow."

Fina stood at the desk while the young woman picked up the phone and engaged in a brief conversation.

"Ms. Ludlow?" She hung up the phone. "Mr. Lafferty's assistant doesn't have you on the schedule."

"Did you speak with Colin?" Fina asked.

"Yes, but he wonders if you got the wrong day."

"I'll just go back and clear things up," Fina said, leaving the reception area.

"You're not supposed to—"

"I don't mind!" Fina called out cheerily over her shoulder. She arrived at Colin's desk to find him hanging up the phone, a queasy look on his face.

"Ms. Ludlow, I'm so sorry, but there's been some mistake. Mr. Lafferty doesn't have an appointment with you today."

"Trust me, Colin. He's expecting me."

Colin glanced down at his computer screen. "I'm happy to find another time for you."

"No need. Now is good."

He glanced between her and his boss's closed door.

"You can call security and have me thrown out," Fina said, "but I think a better course of action would be to let Kevin know I'm here."

The young man came around the desk and tapped lightly on Kevin's door, then stuck his head inside the office. He gave Fina a glance before stepping into the room and closing the door behind him. Fina took the opportunity to examine what he'd left up on his screen. It was Kevin's schedule, and lo and behold, she wasn't on it.

A moment later, the door opened and Colin reemerged. "He's ready to see you, Ms. Ludlow. Can I get you something to drink?"

"No, Colin, but thank you for asking." Fina crossed the threshold and closed Kevin's door. He was sitting behind his desk, the crystal paperweight in one hand.

"Your manners are lacking, Ms. Ludlow."

"That's what my parents always say, but wasn't that kind of *their* job?" Fina took a seat across from him.

"You could have called and made an appointment," he said. "I would have been happy to make time."

"I know, but that's what I didn't want you to have—time. I didn't want to give you a chance to get your ducks in a row."

Kevin smiled. "What are you talking about?"

Fina smiled back and leaned toward him. "You lied to me. I hate it when people lie to me. Firstly, because it wastes my time, and secondly, because then I can't trust anything they tell me."

"Maybe people lie to you because it's none of your business." He rotated the paperweight in his hand.

"Well, sure. In your opinion it's none of my business, but that is just a matter of opinion." Fina pulled the Post-it the guard had given her out of her bag. "Were you and Liz Barone having an affair?"

"I'm sorry?" He raised an eyebrow.

"You know, making the beast with two backs?"

Kevin glowered. "No, we were not having an affair, and that really is none of your business."

"You told me you hadn't been in contact with Liz in over a year."

"I haven't," he said, looking her squarely in the eye. Either Kevin Lafferty was a good liar or he'd convinced himself he wasn't lying.

"I've heard otherwise," Fina said.

"Oh yeah? Who told you otherwise?"

"Her husband, Jamie Gottlieb."

Kevin replaced the paperweight on his desk and got up from his chair. He wandered over to the display cabinet of NEU memorabilia. "Jamie Gottlieb is mistaken."

"Really?" Fina asked.

"Really."

Kevin plucked a signed baseball from one of the shelves and brought it over to Fina. "This was from the fourth game of the Founders series. Damon Lackey threw a no-hitter."

"Fascinating." Fina took the proffered ball and looked at the signatures scrawled around the dirty leather. It looked like it had been signed by a bunch of preschoolers. "Why are you so sure that Jamie is mistaken?"

"Because I was not having an affair with his wife." Kevin took the ball back and replaced it on the shelf.

"And you haven't seen her for over a year?"

"That's correct." He sat back down behind his desk.

"Can I have one of those?" Fina asked, pointing at a row of bottled waters on a credenza.

"Be my guest."

Fina got up and grabbed one of the bottles. "Do you want one?" she asked Kevin, who shook his head. She sat back down, twisted off the top, and took a long gulp. She could tell that Kevin was losing patience, just as she'd hoped.

"So how do you explain the fact that Liz Barone came to see you in this very office twice in the last six weeks?" Fina drank some more.

Kevin's smile faded, and he rubbed his temple with his hand.

Fina tipped her head. "Comments? Questions?"

"What does that have to do with Liz's situation?"

Fina screwed the top back on her water. "Her death, you mean. I assume you heard that she died."

Kevin sneered. "You have no tact, you know that?"

"I can be extremely tactful, Kevin, but frankly, you haven't earned it. This is about to become a murder case, and I suggest you tell me what you and Liz were discussing during your visits."

He sighed and looked bored. "We weren't having an affair. We were discussing the lawsuit."

"What about it?"

"I didn't think it was a good idea."

"Well, obviously it's not a good idea from your perspective or NEU's, but why wouldn't it be a good idea for Liz?"

"Because there would be a lot of publicity, and she wouldn't want to expose her family to that."

"So you were trying to protect her from the harsh glare of the media? Why? Why did you care what happened to her?"

"We were old friends. I didn't want to see her put through the wringer."

"So your attempts to dissuade her had nothing to do with the potential fallout for the athletic program if the suit went forward?" Fina asked.

"Of course I wasn't thrilled at the idea of a messy lawsuit," he said, "but I was concerned for Liz."

"You were right to be concerned for her."

"What's that supposed to mean?"

"Well, you were worried about her well-being, and she ended up in a coma."

"I didn't have anything to do with what happened to her."

"That's not what I said," Fina clarified.

"It's what you implied."

Fina had some more water. She considered asking Kevin point-blank if he was the mysterious note writer, but there was nothing to be gained from that line of questioning. He wouldn't tell her if he was, and she didn't want to clue him in if he wasn't. "Anything else you want to tell me?"

"I have nothing to tell you, and I have a meeting." Kevin stood and walked over to the door where his suit coat was on a hanger. "I really wish I could help, but I can't."

"All righty then. Give me a call if anything else comes to mind." Fina got up and slipped the water bottle into her bag. "Just to satisfy my curiosity, where were you on the night that Liz was attacked?"

Kevin smirked. "I was at the annual Medical Society benefit dinner at the Westin. You can check with one of the hundreds of other people who were there."

Kevin pulled on his coat and waited for Fina to exit the office before him.

"Colin," Kevin said, closing his office door. "Would you please see Ms. Ludlow out? To the lobby downstairs?"

"I can find my own way," Fina assured them, smiling. "I'm good at finding things." She walked back to the elevators.

She hadn't learned much, but she was definitely going to keep an eye on him.

———

Fina parked her car in the garage close to the Schaefer Lab and locked her gun away in the trunk. She entered the lobby, pleased to see Louis at his usual post.

"Good morning," Fina said. The security guard looked up at her, expressionless. "Louis," she said, holding up her hand as if to quell his excitement. "Stop being so emotional. I know you've missed me."

"What do you want today?" he asked.

"I need to see Dr. Mehra again." She propped her elbows on the desk. "I know you'll find this hard to believe, but I think the good doctor has been lying to me."

"Is that so?"

"I need to speak with Dana, also. Maybe you could see if she's available first?" Fina did need to speak with Dana, but she also knew Dana provided access to Vikram, which would come in handy if he'd already tired of their relationship.

"When did I become your social secretary?" Louis mumbled under his breath, picking up the phone.

Fina pulled off her gloves and scarf and tucked them into her bag while he had a brief conversation.

"Dana says wait at her desk. She's finishing something up in the lab. ID, please."

Fina handed over her credentials. He typed something into the computer, and then a visitor's pass was spit out by a printer underneath the desk.

"You know where you're going?" he asked.

"Indeed. I will see you soon." Fina affixed the pass to her jacket and headed toward the metal detector.

She took the elevator to the eighth floor and found her way back to the area where Dana had been sitting during her last visit. She was pleased to find the area empty; she wanted to give things a whirl with Vikram before she moved on to his support staff.

Vikram was seated in the same position, his back to the door, facing his computer screen. Fina knocked on the door and entered the room.

"Dr. Mehra?" she said, taking a seat in the chair in front of his desk.

"Yes?" He turned.

"We spoke on Thursday. I'm Fina Ludlow, the private investigator looking into the attack on Liz Barone."

"Miss, I have no more to say to you than I did in our last conversation."

"That's fine. I have more to say to you. Do you think Liz is the reason your lab wasn't awarded the grant from the pharmaceutical consortium?"

Vikram glared at her.

"Rumor has it that someone in the lab was to blame," she said, "and you had a conflict with Liz. I wondered if the grant was the source of that conflict."

"I'm not going to discuss this with you," Vikram said, studying some papers on his desk.

"That's your choice, but just because you choose not to discuss it doesn't mean I won't find out."

"To what end?" His voice got louder. "What does any of this have to do with your investigation?"

"Perhaps you haven't heard, but Liz died Saturday night, so my investigation has turned into a murder investigation. You had a problem with her, which makes you a suspect."

"You are wasting my time."

"Where were you the night she was attacked?"

"That is none of your business. Leave or I will call security."

"Actually, I wouldn't mind being hauled away by Louis," Fina said. "I've grown quite fond of him."

Vikram pointed at the door. "Out."

"I'll be in touch," Fina promised, walking into the hallway.

"If you come back, I will call the police!" Vikram hollered after her.

Fina strode over to the grouping of desks where Dana was now seated.

"Does he always yell at people like that?" Fina asked.

"Yes. It's charming, don't you think?"

"I'm investigating the attack on Liz Barone. Is there any way I could interest you in a cup of coffee?"

Dana glanced at her watch. "I can sneak out in twenty minutes," she said quietly, "if you don't mind waiting."

"I'm happy to wait. The place around the corner?"

Dana nodded.

Fina made herself scarce when Vikram started bellowing about something else.

Downstairs, she peeled off her visitor's sticker and stopped at Louis's desk.

"I spoke with Dr. Mehra, and Dana's going to meet me for coffee in a few. I think this will turn out to be a productive visit, and—bonus—I got to see you again, Louis."

"It's been a thrill for me, too," he said, not even looking up from his computer screen.

"See you soon," she said, pulling on her scarf and gloves.

"I sincerely hope not," he replied as Fina pushed open the exit and stepped out into the freezing conditions.

She jogged toward the coffee shop, but slowed her pace when a familiar-looking sedan pulled away from the curb. It looked like the one in the lot a few days earlier, so Fina stopped and turned toward the car. If the driver was interested in doing her harm, he would have done it already, which was why she started walking toward the car at a brisk pace. The car peeled away at her approach, and Fina knew it wasn't a coincidence. She didn't like being followed or receiving anonymous notes, but if she wanted tranquility, she should have been an actuary. She'd have to be more alert, since someone definitely had a beef with her.

Inside the café, she ordered a hot chocolate with whipped cream.

There were a couple of free seats near a gas fireplace, which she claimed with her butt and her belongings. Checking her e-mail kept her busy until the door opened and Dana arrived. She was wearing a heavy parka, her lab coat peeking out from underneath. She waved to Fina and ordered a drink before having a seat.

The young woman pulled off her parka and stuffed it down into the crevices of her chair. She straightened the lab coat. "I'm not trying to be pretentious by wearing this, but if I leave it behind, he knows I've left the building, which raises all kinds of questions."

"I'm Fina, by the way," Fina said, shaking Dana's hand. She offered her PI license for inspection.

"Dana Tompkins. I'm a postdoc in the lab."

A barista brought over Dana's coffee. She took a small sip of the steaming liquid, leaving a faint lipstick print on the rim of the cup. She looked like she'd been summoned from central casting to play an Irish lass, given the smattering of freckles across her nose, delicate features, and strawberry blond hair. Fina imagined she was in her late twenties, but the older Fina got, the more difficulty she had guessing other people's ages.

"Liz Barone's mother and husband hired me to find out who hurt her," Fina said. "I don't know how often you read the paper or check the news, but Liz died Saturday night."

"I know." Dana looked at the floor. "That's why I wanted to talk to you."

"Because you have some information that might be helpful?" Fina spooned up some whipped cream.

"Because Vikram was pissed at her," Dana said.

"Why was he pissed at her?"

"Look." Dana placed her mug on a side table. "I really liked Liz a lot, and I certainly don't want to disparage her in any way."

"I will treat whatever you tell me with sensitivity," Fina assured her.

"Vikram blamed her for the lab losing out on a grant. She had screwed some stuff up lately, but I don't think she should be blamed for the grant fiasco."

"Was it her fault?"

Dana picked up her mug again and took a sip. "I don't know. I'm not privy to all the details, but it seemed like she was forgetting stuff and letting things slide. Was it enough to torpedo the grant application? Vikram seemed to think so."

"Why didn't he fire her?" Fina asked.

"I think he would have, given the chance, but she had some leverage: I overheard him threaten her."

"What do you mean exactly?" Fina drank some hot chocolate. It was thick and creamy. Why did anyone drink coffee when this was an option?

"The day we found out about the grant, Vikram had a complete hissy fit. He was angry with all of us—nothing is ever his fault, of course—but later that day, he chewed Liz out in his office."

"You heard what he said?"

"How could I not? You've heard him. He's not familiar with the concept of discretion."

"So he chewed her out about the grant application?"

Dana nodded. "Yes. He said it was her fault the lab didn't get the funding, and she wouldn't get away with it. He said she would pay."

"Those are the exact words he used?"

"Yup."

"Did you interpret that as a threat of physical violence?"

"I didn't interpret it as anything," Dana said. "You don't want to get on his bad side, though. I've heard stories about how he's made life miserable for people who cross him."

"Have you ever known him to be violent?"

"I've seen him smash test tubes when he was angry, but I've never seen him hurt another person," she conceded.

"So why do you still work for him if he's such an ogre?"

Dana grasped her cup tightly. "Because there aren't a lot of labs doing this kind of work. I was lucky to get this spot."

"I understand," Fina said. "Anything else about Liz or Vikram that was unusual or noteworthy?"

Dana shook her head. "No, but if you ask around, you'll hear how much people dislike him."

Fina looked at the gas fireplace. It was attractive, but gave off little heat. "What happens to the lab without that grant?"

"I don't know. We'll have to scramble for other funding. We may have to let some lab techs go."

"The university can't make up the difference?"

Dana frowned. "We're not usually at the top of their list. Have you been by the new student center recently or the sports complex? It's pretty clear what NEU's priorities are."

"And what about the lawsuit that Liz was pursuing? Do you know anything about that?"

"Just what I've read in the paper. Professionally, it's not good if the university has to make a big payout, but personally? I thought it was great. They should be held accountable."

Fina reached into her bag and pulled out a card. "Will you contact me if you think of anything else?"

"Sure." Dana slipped the card into the pocket of her lab coat.

"Also, if you feel unsafe or threatened in any way by Vikram, let me know. I can help you with that."

Dana smiled. "Thanks. I appreciate it."

They brought their mugs over to the counter and pulled their jackets on. Dana headed back toward the lab, and Fina put her head down and picked her way around the snowbanks to return to the garage.

Fina had learned early in her career to take information with a grain of salt, particularly when that information was damning. However, having seen Vikram in action, she wouldn't underestimate what he was capable of doing.

13.

Haley had left a message on her voice mail. Fina dialed her niece's number while still parked in the garage.

"Hey," Haley answered.

"Hey. What's up?"

"Are you busy? You wanted to do something, right?" Haley asked.

"I would like to do something. I take it this is a good time for you?" Ah, to be a teenager, the sun in a universe where everyone else orbited you.

"Yeah, but I'm not home." Fina was glad to hear her referring to Scotty and Patty's house as "home." She seemed to be adjusting well to her new living arrangement.

"Okay. Where are you?"

"At Pap and Gammy's."

"What are you doing there?" she asked Haley.

"Gammy took me shopping. Can you pick me up?"

"Are you calling me because you want to spend some time together or because you need a ride?"

"Because you're one of my favorite aunts," Haley said.

"The other being Aunt Patty?"

"Well, you're in good company."

"Fine. Give me half an hour."

Unless Fina was truly unavailable, she wouldn't turn down a request from Haley that promised some interaction. Fina was happy to err on the side of being solicitous if it gave her niece a sense of security. Her mother's death, the fact that her father had sexually abused her, and the revelation of the abuse seemed like enough trauma for one lifetime, let alone fifteen years on the planet. It was having to see Elaine that gave Fina pause.

She pulled up to her parents' multimillion-dollar eyesore, hopeful that Haley would be waiting by the door, but no such luck. Fina parked and entered the house through the side entrance, still hopeful that she might be in and out like a cat burglar.

The maid was in the kitchen unloading the dishwasher, a telenovela on the TV nearby. Fina smiled and asked for Haley.

"*Señorita Haley está en la sala de familia,*" she said, gesturing toward the hallway.

Fina wanted to tell her that her days were numbered in the Ludlow house unless she buried her native tongue like a corpse. Elaine wanted to pay people like they were immigrants, desperate for a paycheck, but she didn't want to catch any trace of foreignness.

"*Gracias,*" Fina said, and left the kitchen.

She wound her way to the family room, where she found Haley and Elaine sitting on a couch, looking at the latest issue of *People* magazine. They were studying a photo of an up-and-coming starlet.

"She's got a bit of a tummy," Elaine said.

Fina leaned over the couch and examined the picture. "Mom, that girl has about ten percent body fat."

"I didn't know you were here, Fina."

"I am. You don't seriously think she's fat, do you?"

Haley pretended she wasn't interested in the conversation, but Fina knew better.

"I think she could tone up a bit," Elaine said.

The suggestion was absurd under any circumstances, but particularly from a woman who was easily twenty-five pounds overweight.

"Don't listen to her, Haley. If anything"—Fina gestured at the photo—"she should gain weight. You all set?"

"I just need to get my bags," Haley said, rising from the couch and leaving the room.

"Why do you do that, Fina?" her mother asked.

"Do what?"

"Undermine me in front of her?"

"Because you're being ridiculous. Do you want to give Haley an eating disorder on top of everything else?"

Elaine didn't know the whole story about Rand's crimes and Haley's brief time as an escort; Fina, Carl, and the other brothers had decided that telling her would only generate more grief in the family. But occasionally, Fina wondered if they'd made the right decision.

"I don't want her to get fat," Elaine insisted. "That's the last thing she needs."

"Mom, Haley is skinny! And even if she did get fat, so what? There are worse things in the world."

Elaine sniffed. "She'll want to look good in a bathing suit."

"When? What are you talking about?"

"Rand wants her to visit him in Miami for spring break."

Fina gripped the back of the couch to steady herself. "What? Why?"

"Because he's her father, and he has someone new in his life that he wants her to meet."

"Who?"

"A girlfriend. I don't know all the details, but he'd like her and Haley to get to know each other."

Fina wanted to declare that Haley would not be going to Miami to reconcile with her perverted father, but she knew that throwing down the gauntlet with Elaine would be a strategic error. It took every ounce of her strength to swallow her objections.

"Sounds interesting," Fina said, starting to leave the room.

"I think it will be good for Haley to spend time with her father. She doesn't have her mother, after all."

Which is partially his fault, Fina thought. She needed to leave before her head exploded all over the deep pile carpet.

"Bye, Gammy," Haley said from the doorway, laden with bags from their shopping spree.

"Good-bye, sweetheart. Don't listen too much to your aunt."

"Let's go, kiddo," Fina said, putting an arm around Haley and guiding her back to the kitchen. Once in the car, Fina let out a deep breath and rubbed her temples.

"Are you okay, Aunt Fina?" Haley asked.

"I'm fine. Little headache, but nothing that can't be cured with a snack."

"Umm. Frappes sound good."

"Haley, you want ice cream? It's twenty degrees out."

"But not inside the ice cream shop," Haley reminded her.

"Touché. Let's go."

C ristian called her as she was driving on Route 9 after dropping Haley home.

"Are you in the car?" he asked.

"Yes."

"You should pull over."

"Why?" Her stomach did a small flip-flop. "What's wrong?"

"Nothing's wrong. You shouldn't drive and talk on the phone at the same time."

"But I'm using Bluetooth," Fina insisted.

"It still isn't safe. Seriously, I'm not talking to you unless you pull over."

"How would you even know if I kept driving?"

"The intermittent swearing at your fellow drivers would be a dead giveaway."

"Fine." She turned onto a side street and pulled into a no-parking zone. "What can I do for you?"

"I'm returning your call," Cristian said.

"I did call you, didn't I?" Fina said. "I had an interesting conversation with Kevin Lafferty this morning."

"The NEU guy?"

"Yes, Mr. Booster. Have you spoken with him?" Fina asked.

"Yes, but why don't you tell me about your conversation with him."

"Okay. Maybe you heard something different, but when I first spoke with him, he told me that he hadn't been in contact with Liz for more than a year."

"Uh-huh."

"But it turns out that she went to see him at his office twice in the last six weeks."

"For what reason?" Cristian asked.

"Her husband thought they were having an affair," she said, "but I'm not sure I buy that."

"What reason did Kevin give?"

"He claims he was trying to dissuade Liz from pursuing the lawsuit against NEU. For her own good, of course."

"Of course. Do you think he's telling the truth?"

"I'm not sure, but if he was trying to dissuade her, it was for his own benefit. That guy is a complete NEU sports nut."

"But would the lawsuit really affect him? We're not talking about his job."

"No, but we are talking about his life, Cristian," Fina said. "His whole identity is wrapped up in being a booster. If he didn't have that, he'd have to redecorate his office, at the very least."

Cristian snorted. "How did you leave things with him?"

"He's not very happy with me."

"I'm shocked."

"And there's another angle related to him that I'm looking into."

"Which is?"

"I'm not ready to share yet. Not until I have something concrete."

"But when you do have something concrete, I'll be the first to know, right?" he asked.

"You'll certainly be the first law enforcement officer to know."

"Great."

"I knew that would make you happy," Fina said. "Now I'm going to hang up and put the car in drive. Okay?"

"Good-bye, Fina."

"Good-bye, Detective."

Pamela had been building up a head of steam all day, which she managed to contain, but barely. Bobbi Barone's announcement that Liz had donated her brain to the BU lab had set off a flurry of activity at NEU. Pamela had spent the day in a variety of emergency meetings discussing the donation and the lawsuit, which was now on everyone's radar screen.

When she finally left the office after eight, having missed a dinner date with Deb, she felt as if she'd been wrung out like a towel. She needed to unload on someone, which is why she called Fina on her way out of the office and insisted they meet at her favorite wine bar in Charlestown.

The Vintage Wine Bar was just around the corner from Pamela's condo and had been her "local" for more than ten years. The place was a nice mix of friendly atmosphere, outstanding wine list, and dark corners; it fit the bill whether Pamela was drowning her sorrows or having a romantic nightcap.

Located on the first floor of a brick town house, the bar boasted original dark wood beams and low ceilings. Unlike so many places that worked hard to be historic, the Vintage truly was, like much of Charlestown. Some nights, especially when it was rainy, Pamela imagined she'd stepped back in time walking the streets of her neighborhood.

Fina hadn't balked at Pamela's insistent invitation, and she showed up right on time. Pamela, who'd arrived early, had already downed a glass of wine.

Fina sat and looked Pamela in the eye.

"Hello, Pamela," she said. "What can I do for you?"

"Did you know about this?" Pamela demanded.

"About what?" Fina asked, glancing at the menu handed to her by the waiter. "Just a glass of Shiraz, please."

Pamela waited for the server to retreat.

"About the fact that Liz Barone was at death's door and was planning to donate her brain to BU?"

"Everyone knew she was at death's door, but no, I didn't know about the brain donation." Fina unwound the scarf from her neck. "A little ironic, isn't it? Yet another donation you're not getting."

Pamela flinched. "That's a horrendous thing to say."

Fina shrugged.

"You came into my office under false pretenses."

"How do you figure that?" Fina asked. "You knew exactly who I was and exactly why I was there."

"I didn't know this was going to turn into a fiasco!" Pamela's voice pitched up, and the two men at the next table over stared.

"Are you talking about the lawsuit or Liz's murder?"

The waiter gingerly placed a wineglass down in front of Fina. "Would you ladies like anything to eat?"

"No," Pamela responded before Fina could open her mouth. He retreated, and Fina sipped the wine. She knew nothing about wine, just that she liked some more than others.

"You didn't answer my question. Are you upset about the lawsuit or the murder?" Fina asked. She could feel the stares of the men at the next table. "Can I help you with something?" she asked them sweetly.

"No, no," one of them replied.

"Okay then, mind your own beeswax."

He pulled back, offended.

"I'm upset about all of it," Pamela explained, lowering her voice.

"I don't understand why," Fina said.

Pamela took a long drink from her wine. She placed the glass back on the table and wiped her mouth with her cocktail napkin.

"Here's my take on things," Fina said. "The lawsuit is messy for you because anything that has a negative financial impact on the university makes your life more complicated. It's going to get really messy if the BU lab finds that Liz's brain shows evidence of chronic traumatic encephalopathy, a nasty byproduct of her soccer playing, which I'm guessing it will. The murder is only a problem if you're a suspect."

"Why would I be a suspect?" Pamela tightened her grasp on the stem of her glass.

"Because you and Liz got into an argument about the lawsuit."

"I already told you we didn't."

"Or maybe there is some other reason that you're so testy," Fina said. "Where were you the night Liz was attacked?"

"What?" Pamela's eyes got wide. "You're asking me for an alibi?"

"It's a reasonable question," Fina said.

"I was home that evening—alone."

"Hmm," Fina mused. "I find your reaction to all of this puzzling. I don't get why you're so worked up."

Pamela tugged on her suit jacket. "I care deeply about my job and the university."

"Neither of which are at risk, from my perspective, so I have to wonder what else is going on."

"There is nothing else going on, but I shouldn't expect you to have a normal reaction to these circumstances," Pamela said. "You deal with these sorts of things every day, and you strike me as being insensitive."

Fina smiled. "Actually, I'm quite sensitive, which is what makes me good at my job. That and my wealth of experience have honed my antennae to know when things aren't quite right."

"And quite modest as well," Pamela said sarcastically. She finished her wine and signaled to the waiter for another.

"I'm not trying to be immodest, but I'm good at my job. If you're hiding something, I'm confident I'll find it."

"I'm not hiding anything."

"Right, just being a loyal employee," Fina said.

The waiter brought over another glass for Pamela and tipped his head toward Fina's half-empty one. She shook her head.

"I have to ask," Fina said. "If it turns out that Liz's brain was damaged, don't you think it's better to know that than not?"

"I never said it wasn't better," Pamela said. "I just don't think NEU should be held accountable for damage that nobody knew about twenty years ago."

"I'm not suggesting they should, either."

"But that's exactly the kind of thing your family does: holds innocent people responsible for things out of their control."

Fina tilted her head from side to side. "Occasionally, but more often than not, we hold people responsible for things they damn well could have stopped. You'd be surprised what people will do for money. Or maybe you wouldn't."

Pamela glared at her.

"This is bigger than you, and it's bigger than me," Fina said, sipping her wine. "It's going to run its course. It could be worse. At least we're not talking about a Penn State situation."

Pamela didn't respond.

"At least, I'm assuming it's not a Penn State situation." *Please God, no more pedophiles,* Fina thought.

"No, it isn't, and for God's sake, keep your voice down," Pamela hissed. "This isn't *Silkwood,* Fina. There's nothing to expose; there's no cover-up."

Fina reached into her bag and pulled out fifteen bucks, which she placed on the table. She drained her wine and grabbed her jacket before standing. "If there's anything else you'd like to discuss, you know where to reach me."

Fina scooted between the closely placed tables and pushed out the door.

Pamela didn't feel much better after their conversation, but she was feeling a little drunk, which was better than nothing.

Fina was tired when she got home. She'd kept an eye out for the dark sedan all day and other potential threats, and it had tuckered her out. Rather than head straight for bed, Fina made the mistake of flipping on the TV. She was having trouble peeling herself away from a show about a young man who smuggled drugs into some jungle nation and then was surprised to find himself locked up without due process. The show was supposed to make viewers thankful that they lived in a nation with a robust justice system, but it always made Fina wonder why the travelers were such nincompoops.

Her phone rang, and Fina answered without looking at the caller ID since she assumed it was one of the men in her life: Milloy, Cristian, or Carl.

"Yes?"

"Is this Fina?" a woman asked on the other end.

Fina muted the TV. "Yes, it is. I'm sorry. I was expecting someone else."

"This is Tasha Beemis-Jones. I was wondering if we could meet tomorrow. I have some things I'd like to discuss."

"Of course." Fina clicked off the TV so as not to be distracted by the image of the traveler befriending his cellmate, a large hairy rat. "Just tell me where and when."

"Our place. We're in Back Bay. Can you make it at six thirty?"

"Sure."

"Six thirty in the morning," Tasha clarified.

"Sure." Fina silently cursed her own can-do spirit. "What's your address?"

After hanging up, she went straight to bed, but it took some time for her brain to settle down and succumb to sleep. She was like a kid on Christmas Eve, wondering what goody Tasha was going to bring her.

14.

Fina did not feel refreshed when her alarm sounded the next morning, but she dragged herself out of bed with the promise of an afternoon nap if needed. She wasn't sure if this was truly the only time Tasha could talk or if she was pulling some power play, but it didn't matter; sometimes she had to kowtow to get what she needed. Fina showered, dressed, and scarfed down a few forkfuls of leftover lo mein that she found in the fridge before heading to the Beemis-Jones household.

The power couple and their two young children lived on Marlborough Street, a couple of blocks from the Public Garden. It was one of the most beautiful streets in the city, with its old brownstones and mature flowering trees that bloomed in the spring and summer. Residents were within walking distance of Copley Square and the Charles; all of the conveniences of the city combined with beautiful architecture and a sense of history.

Fina found a parking space a few blocks away on Commonwealth and played do-si-do on the narrow sidewalks with the other early risers. She rang the bell and was greeted a minute later by an exceedingly handsome man wearing dark gray suit pants, a dress shirt, and a tie.

"Fina Ludlow, right?" He offered his hand and beckoned her inside.

"Dr. Jones?"

"It's Dwayne, but everyone calls me D. Let me help you with your coat. Tasha will be out in a minute." He helped her pull off her jacket and hung it in the front hall closet.

"After you," he said, pointing up the stairs. Fina got the sense that the doctor's good manners were habitual and inbred. This was the kind of man that her mother wished she would date. Except for the fact that he was black. That would probably go over like a screen door on a submarine.

She climbed a stairway crowned with a skylight to the top floor of the brownstone. Upstairs, there were three spaces open to one another, but clearly delineated by the furniture and the use of strategic columns and coffered ceilings. The kitchen area had a substantial island and glass-fronted cabinets. Fina could see a dining room in one direction and, directly off the kitchen, a family room with two large couches. The TV was tuned to *Sesame Street*, and two young children were camped on the rug in front of it, both in footie pajamas. The girl looked to be five years old, and the baby boy, about one. Both were transfixed by Cookie Monster and his hijinks.

"I'm just finishing packing lunch for Lyla," D said, nodding toward the little girl.

Dwayne Jones was about six feet two inches with broad shoulders. He was making a peanut butter and jelly sandwich with a precision that attested to his profession. He swiftly removed the crusts from the bread and cut the remainder into four equally sized triangles.

"She hates crusts," he informed Fina with a broad smile.

"Who doesn't?" Fina asked, climbing onto one of the stools at the island. "You're a surgeon, right?"

"Cardiothoracic. Can I offer you some breakfast?"

"No, thank you."

"You sure? I've got some green power smoothie in the fridge."

"That's very kind, but I've already eaten." She spared him the details of her meal.

"That's good. You can't function without fuel," he said.

"I hear ya, but unlike you, no one's life is in my hands," Fina said.

He pointed at her and smiled. "Just your own."

Fina squinted at him. "Have you been talking to my mother?"

D chuckled. He pulled a package of Goldfish crackers out of a cabinet and poured a helping into a plastic Baggie. From a hot-pink backpack, he pulled out a My Little Pony lunch box and nestled the sandwich, crackers, juice box, and one Hershey's Kiss inside. Next to the pony-adorned container, his hands looked like catcher's mitts.

"If you don't mind my asking," Fina said, "how do you get your hands in anyone's chest cavity? They're substantial."

He grinned and lowered his voice. "If my hands are in your chest cavity, they're the least of your problems."

"Right."

Tasha crested the stairs with an older black woman in her wake. She introduced Fina to the nanny, who swooped the little boy up in her arms before taking him downstairs. D picked up Lyla in one arm, the pink lunch box under the other, and the threesome exchanged kisses.

"Nice to meet you, Fina," D said.

"You too." She listened as the girl chattered to her father as they descended the stairs.

"Where are the tears and tantrums?" Fina asked Tasha, who was pouring herself a cup of coffee from a high-end coffee machine embedded in the kitchen wall.

"Oh believe me, there are plenty, just not yet. But there are still outfits to be chosen and teeth to be brushed." Tasha was wearing a fitted dress in a deep plum knit. She wore black tights, but was shoeless. "Do you want some coffee?" she asked, adjusting a wide gold cuff on her wrist.

"Sure." Fina was awake; she might as well cement it with a heavy dose of caffeine. "I'm sorry about Liz," she said, taking a mug from Tasha.

Tasha grabbed the remote and turned off the TV, then walked into the dining room. They sat down across from each other at a Shaker-style table. The windows at one end of the room overlooked the treetops on Marlborough Street.

"Since the day she was hurt, I knew that it wasn't going to end well," Tasha said. "But I still can't believe it."

"Anticipating it and experiencing it are two different things," Fina said. "You probably won't be able to wrap your head around it for a while."

Tasha was silent.

"Any word on a funeral?" Fina asked.

"Not yet, but I'll let you know once Bobbi and Jamie make plans."

"So what did you want to talk to me about?" Fina picked up the mug and wrapped her hands around it. If nothing else, she appreciated the warmth.

Tasha adjusted so her posture was more upright. "It occurred to me that I hadn't been completely forthright with you."

"It occurred to you?" Fina asked, raising an eyebrow.

Tasha frowned. "Don't bust my chops, Fina. I'm telling you now."

"Go on."

"When we spoke at the gym, I told you that Liz and Gus Sibley were on good terms, but that wasn't actually the case."

"What do you mean?"

"Liz was upset with Gus."

"Did she tell you why?" Perhaps this was what prompted Gus to go running to Pitney. Maybe he did have something to hide.

"No, she wouldn't go into details, but I assumed it was about the lawsuit."

"What about the lawsuit?" Fina asked.

"I think that Liz wanted Gus to support her, give some medical credence to her claims."

"And he wouldn't?"

"I don't know. I think she assumed he would be an ally, and it wasn't turning out that way."

"You mentioned at the gym that you and your teammates played hard," Fina said, "and no one could have convinced you to take it easy. Were you pressured to play when you were injured?"

Tasha sat back and folded her hands on the table. "You have to remember, this was a different time. Nobody knew anything about the dangers of concussions."

"True, but you probably knew when you were hurt."

Tasha traced the floral pattern on the placemat with her finger. Her nails were short and painted a pale pink color. "I wouldn't say this in a court of law, but yes, we were pressured to play hurt, but everyone was back then. It was a badge of honor, proving how tough you were."

"So you think Liz wanted Gus to admit that?"

"It's the only reason I can imagine that she would be upset with him," Tasha said.

Fina took a sip of her coffee. She placed the mug down before speaking. "I don't mean to be cynical, but you're an attorney, so I imagine you can take it."

"Yes?" Tasha asked warily.

"Are you telling me this now because Liz died and you feel guilty or because her brain is going to BU?"

Tasha looked at Fina over her coffee cup. "That is cynical."

Fina shrugged. "If the lab finds evidence of brain trauma, then you're going to want to be on the right side of that issue come election time."

"I wish that politics were only a matter of telling the truth, but you and I both know that's bull," Tasha said. "As long as there isn't any definitive proof of brain trauma, I'd be foolish to jump on that bandwagon, but if there is . . ."

"You'd be foolish not to," Fina concluded.

"You know I'll deny this whole conversation if it ever comes out," Tasha said.

Fina shook her head. "I'm not interested in slamming you in the press or impeaching your leadership ability. In fact, I'll probably vote for you. I just want to find out who killed Liz. That's my only concern."

"I can't imagine that Gus would hurt her," Tasha said. "He's a decent guy."

"But? It sounded like there was a 'but' hanging there."

"*But* if he gets caught up in a lawsuit, he has a lot to lose."

"You just said that people didn't know better when you and Liz were playing for NEU," Fina said.

"Sure, but you of all people should know that lawsuits are career killers. Even if the final judgment goes your way, you still suffer."

"True." Fina had conflicted feelings about Ludlow and Associates when it came to the medical community. In many cases, they were the advocates wronged patients needed, but sometimes, innocent doctors got caught in the crossfire. Since she never knew the story until she investigated—unlike her brothers and father—she liked to reassure herself that she wasn't spinning things, just uncovering the facts. Sometimes this made her feel better, but sometimes it didn't.

"So what happens now?" Tasha asked.

"I'm going to speak with Gus again, and I'll let the police know that his relationship with Liz was more complicated than it appeared."

"Any way you could leave my name out of it?"

"I'll do my best. There's no reason Gus has to know you've told me this, but I don't want to lie to the police if they ask me for specifics."

Tasha exhaled deeply. "I suppose that's all I can ask for."

"But Tasha, if you are running for city council, you should be prepared for a lot worse than conjecture about your soccer career," Fina said.

"Believe me, I know. It's one of the things that gives me pause when I contemplate running for public office." She rose from her seat, indicating that her confession was over.

Fina followed her into the kitchen and handed Tasha her mug.

"Does Jamie know that Liz was having problems with Gus?"

Tasha shook her head. "I have no idea."

"What about Kelly? Is it something Liz might have mentioned to her?"

"She might have, but I don't know. You'd have to ask her."

She followed Tasha down to the foyer, where they retrieved her belongings from the closet. "I really appreciate your contacting me," Fina told her, zipping up her coat.

"I know you might question my motives, but Liz was my friend. I want you to find out who did this to her."

"I'm doing everything I can," Fina said. She pulled open the heavy wooden door and left Tasha standing on the threshold. She stood there with her regal posture, seemingly impervious to the cold, while Fina shivered and took off down the street.

Fina called Gus Sibley's office and was able to learn the broad strokes of his schedule. He was at the office seeing patients and would be at NEU later in the day for a soccer round robin. She'd have better access to him at the university, so she put Tasha's revelations on the back burner and turned her attention to Jamie.

Fina wasn't looking forward to stopping by Liz and Jamie's house so soon after Liz's death, but time was of the essence. What she lacked in sensitivity now, hopefully she would make up for in results later.

There were a number of cars parked outside the house in Hyde Park when she arrived. She noted that Kelly's minivan wasn't among them, but perhaps she was off on some errand. She didn't seem like someone who was able to stay put for very long.

The front door was opened by a woman in her thirties in black pants and a brown sweater—a casual version of mourning attire.

"Can I help you?" she asked Fina.

"I'm Fina Ludlow, and I'm here to see Jamie. Is he around?"

"This isn't a good time," the woman said.

"I know, but he and Liz's mom have hired me to do some work for them. I think he'll want to speak with me."

The woman frowned, but admitted Fina to the house. "One moment." She left Fina in the front hallway and opened a door that led down a flight of stairs to the basement. Fina craned her neck, but couldn't see much.

"He's in the basement," the woman said when she returned.

Fina thanked her and started down the carpeted stairs. The finished space consisted of a play area and a makeshift music studio where Jamie now sat, a guitar across his lap. A door was ajar at the other end of the room, and Fina caught sight of a washer and dryer. The only natural light in the space came from small windows in the foundation.

"Hi, Jamie. Mind if I sit?" she asked.

He looked at her and nodded at an old Barcalounger.

"I'm so sorry about Liz."

"Thanks." He plucked at the strings on his guitar. His hair looked unwashed, and his ripped jeans and navy blue T-shirt were rumpled, sweat stains darkening his underarms.

"I wanted to let you know that I'm investigating your suspicion that Liz and Kevin were having an affair," Fina said. "So far, there's no evidence to prove that."

He looked at her. "That doesn't mean it's not true."

"No, it doesn't, but it means there's a possibility it isn't true. I spoke with Kevin, and he vehemently denied it."

Jamie snorted. "And I'm supposed to believe him?"

"No. I'll do some more digging, but he claims he was only trying to dissuade Liz from filing the lawsuit."

"He may have been." He ran his fingers over the neck of the guitar. "But I'm not convinced that's the only thing he was doing."

"Why do you think he was opposed to the lawsuit?" Fina asked.

"Because he loves NEU sports more than life itself. He'd do anything to protect his teams." Jamie brushed his bangs out of his eyes, revealing a thin sheen of sweat on his forehead.

"Anything?" Fina asked.

Jamie looked at her, but was silent.

"I can't deal with this right now," Jamie said, his face anguished.

"I'm sorry. I don't mean to add to your grief. I just wanted to reassure you that I'm taking your concerns seriously."

"Fine." He brushed away a tear from his cheek. "Great."

"Do you want me to be in touch when I know more?"

"I want you to find out who did this to Liz."

"Of course." Fina stood and walked over to the stairs, where she rested her hand on the banister. He hadn't answered her question, but that was okay. Jamie couldn't give her what he didn't have, and he didn't seem to have the energy for much of anything.

He struck a chord, which she took to be her exit music.

She turned up the heat once in her car and rubbed her hands together vigorously.

She understood that Jamie was grieving, but she had to wonder why he seemed stuck on one thing: Why was he so committed to the idea that his wife was cheating on him with Kevin Lafferty?

Fina tracked down Cristian at a diner near police headquarters, where he was grabbing a bite with Pitney.

"What do you have for us, Fina?" the lieutenant asked before biting into a dripping tuna melt.

"I don't work for you, remember?"

"Oh. Is this a personal visit?" Pitney asked.

Cristian shifted in his seat.

"I'm not here on a personal matter," Fina clarified. "I'm here to give you some info, as a professional courtesy."

"What is it?" Pitney asked.

Fina looked at Cristian's plate before responding. He stuck to a healthy diet, which was great for his physique, but not so good for Fina when it came to mooching food from him. "Cristian, you're the only person I know who gets a salad in a diner."

"I have a sandwich, too," he said, pointing at a turkey sandwich on anemic-looking white bread.

"That's almost worse. You're eating a sandwich without chips or French fries." Fina eyed the golden brown fries on Pitney's plate, but thought better of it.

"What do you have to tell us, Fina?" Pitney asked again. A glob of mayonnaise threatened to drop onto her brightly striped sweater. She looked like she was wearing a foreign flag across her bosom.

"I know you spoke with Vikram Mehra at the Schaefer Lab," Fina said.

Pitney and Cristian nodded.

"Do you know about the grant they recently lost?" Fina asked.

"We've heard their funding is tight," Cristian said. Fina noted his noncommittal answer, but she decided to plow ahead anyway.

"Did you know that he believes it was Liz's fault? That they lost the grant because of her?"

"How so?" Pitney asked.

"Presumably, she screwed up some part of the application, thereby costing the lab a five-year grant."

"Because of her mild cognitive impairment?" Cristian asked.

"Undetermined if her MCI was the cause," she said. If she were being truly giving she would tell them about the source of the grant—the pharmaceutical consortium—but she wasn't feeling quite that generous.

"Do you have any proof that Vikram and Liz butted heads?" Pitney asked.

"The postdoc in the lab claims that Vikram threatened Liz."

"What's the postdoc's name?" Cristian asked, pulling out a small notebook.

"Dana Tompkins. I don't know what your experience with Vikram was like, but the guy seemed like a bully to me."

"Did he threaten to physically harm Liz?" Pitney asked.

"He said that she wouldn't get away with it and he would make her pay."

"Which could mean a lot of things," Cristian said.

"None of them good," Fina said.

"True," Cristian conceded.

"So, what?" Pitney asked. "He killed her because he was angry about a grant? It seems a little thin."

"Lieutenant, you're underestimating the cutthroat world of scientific research. There are a lot of people competing for very limited resources. And the attack wasn't premeditated. Whoever did this was pissed."

"What makes you so sure it wasn't premeditated?" Pitney asked, biting the end of a dill pickle.

"I think if you want to kill someone you usually bring your own weapon. You don't look around the room and think, 'Yes! That kitchen counter will be perfect!'"

Cristian chuckled.

"We appreciate the information," Pitney said, waving down the waitress for the check. It was dropped on the table within seconds.

"I should hope so. In the interest of quid pro quo," Fina said, "what's the story with Kevin Lafferty's alibi?"

"What about it?" Pitney asked.

"He told me he was at the Medical Society dinner at the Westin with hundreds of witnesses, but we all know that's not really an airtight alibi."

Cristian and Pitney exchanged a look.

"Yes, we know that," Pitney said. "That's why we're looking into it."

"My brother Matthew once went to a Bar Association dinner, rented a room to watch *Thursday Night Football*, and came back downstairs later when the event was winding down," Fina said.

Pitney looked annoyed. "Why does that not surprise me?"

"I'm just saying that unless you're the keynote speaker, those events are flimsy covers."

"Noted," Pitney said, examining the check before placing some bills on the table. "Anything else before we go?"

Fina briefly considered sharing Tasha's impressions of Gus, but only briefly. Pitney was always riding her for proof, and she didn't have any. She didn't know what she had when it came to Gus Sibley.

"Nope. You're all caught up," Fina said. "It's been fun."

"And you're staying away from Gus Sibley?" Pitney asked, maneuvering her way out of the booth.

"I haven't been near him."

"Good. Glad to hear it."

Fina sat at the table for another few minutes contemplating the situation. It was always a balancing act, deciding what to tell the cops and what to keep to herself. She'd gotten in trouble in the past for withholding information, but that was an occupational hazard.

If you were going to tell the cops everything, why bother being a PI?

15.

Fina did another search on Gus Sibley before heading to the NEU campus. This time, she focused on the fluffier items that came up. He'd been named to *Boston* magazine's Best Doctors list a few times and had also been featured in a couple of articles in the *Globe* sports section over the years. There were a number of photos of him at NEU sporting events and functions, and she stumbled onto the Facebook pages of two of his children. There was nothing remarkable about any of it.

She drove to the NEU field house, the location of the soccer round robin, and parked her car in yet a different lot. She'd spent more time in the past week on a college campus than she had in two decades, but it didn't make her feel the least bit nostalgic. Fina had enjoyed her college years, particularly with Milloy by her side, but she wasn't someone who pined for the good old days. She believed that the past was the past, and you should get your head in the game in the present. Occasionally, she heard people wax rhapsodic about high school; she could only imagine that their personal development had been arrested upon graduation.

The sports complex had a card scanner at the door, but Fina just tucked in behind a couple of guys and smiled when one of them held the door open for her. The world would never be a secure place until people worried less about offending strangers and instead insisted that they show proper ID.

Inside, she walked purposefully down the hallway. That was another trick that gained her access to more places than her lock picks: If you acted like you belonged someplace, most people assumed that you did. The first hallway led to a basketball court, which was crowded with large, sweaty men. One of them directed her to the field house at the opposite end of the vast complex.

Fina couldn't help but wonder what previous generations would make of the facilities. Aside from workout spaces and a plethora of equipment, there was a pool, tennis courts, a café, and locker rooms boasting saunas and steam rooms. There was no denying that exercise was crucial to good health, but there was something ironic about having to schedule in physical activity because you were too busy the rest of the day driving or sitting behind a desk.

The field house itself was huge, with delineated track lanes around the outer edge, separated by netting from the two turf fields in the center. A handful of young men were scrimmaging on one field, and a group of young women were on the other, running soccer drills. Fina found an opening in the netting and walked around to a grouping of benches. A couple of players were putting on shin guards and sneakers. One young woman was lying on her back, and Gus was grasping her leg, kneeling next to her. He manipulated it in different directions while they talked.

"Hey, Dr. Sibley," Fina said, striding over to him. She figured that approaching him in front of his players would perhaps keep him from kicking her out. Or at the very least delay it.

Gus looked at her for a moment before recognition washed over his face. He wasn't happy to see her.

"Ms. Ludlow. Hello."

"I just need a few minutes. Once you're done with that." She gestured at the young woman's leg.

Gus didn't say anything, and Fina took a seat on the metal bench a few feet away. She listened as he asked the player questions and then gave her suggestions regarding specific stretches. Fina knew that stretching was important, but she always felt she could spend her time doing something more productive—like eating or sleeping.

"I have nothing to say to you," Gus said when he came over to Fina. He was wearing a suit with an NEU-themed necktie.

"You don't have to say anything," Fina said. She wondered if he was going to mention his call to Pitney.

"Then why are you here?"

"You don't want to sit down?" Fina asked, gesturing toward the bench. "I know you're not thrilled to see me, but we could have a civilized conversation."

He glanced toward the players. The women had various body types, but all of them looked to be in terrific shape. Their calves and hamstrings were well defined, and their arms were lean. Most of them had long hair pulled back in ponytails.

Gus took a seat next to her, but was silent.

"These benches are so uncomfortable," Fina commented. "How does anyone sit on them for more than two minutes?"

"They don't, usually," Gus said. His gaze traveled up and down her body. "It would be more comfortable if you sat up straight. You're not doing your back muscles any favors."

"Well, thanks for that tip." She sat up a tiny bit straighter. "So, obviously, you know about Liz's death."

"Of course. I certainly hope you didn't come here to tell me that."

"No, no. What are your thoughts about Liz's brain being donated to BU?"

Gus paused for a moment. "I don't have any thoughts about it."

Fina studied him. "You were her team doctor. It's hard to believe you don't have *any* thoughts about the situation."

"If I have any thoughts," Gus said, "I'll share them if I'm deposed."

"Ahh, right. Why say anything until you have to say it under oath?"

"I thought you said you weren't here to ask me questions." An errant ball rolled in their direction. Gus stood and kicked it back to one of the players.

"I'm not," Fina said. "I just wanted to update you on my progress."

He studied her. "Why?"

"Because I thought you'd be interested. I know you've been in touch with the police."

He was quiet. Maybe he realized that going to the cops had been a miscalculation.

"I've heard that your relationship with Liz wasn't as good as you led me to believe," Fina said.

Gus remained silent.

"I wonder why you would suggest otherwise," Fina said, "and I wonder why you two were at odds."

He swallowed.

"Maybe it was because of the lawsuit," Fina ventured. "Maybe Liz wanted you to take her side, but it's hard to believe you would. After all, NEU still signs your paycheck."

Gus gave her a tight smile. "I assure you, I don't do this for the money."

"Which suggests you do it because you love it. That's an even more compelling reason to side with NEU. If you love this gig, you wouldn't want to jeopardize it."

"As I told you the last time we spoke," Gus said, "I followed the protocol for head injuries that was in place at the time. I didn't violate any regulations."

A whistle blew, and the players gathered in a circle near the goal before dispersing for another drill. Fina and Gus watched as they took shots on the goalie; her arms seemed to extend like Stretch Armstrong.

"But you did put players back in against your better judgment," Fina said.

"No, I did not," he insisted, "and I don't see how anyone could claim I did."

"So if not for the lawsuit, you and Liz would have been fine?"

There was a minor collision on the field, and it took a moment for the players involved to untangle themselves from one another. One of them started to limp off, signaling the end of the interview. Gus stood up and beckoned the young woman over.

"Things were fine," he said. "Friends occasionally disagree. There's nothing noteworthy about it."

"I think it's my Achilles," the player said, dropping down onto the bench. "Dammit!" She banged the metal bench with her open fist.

"Calm down, Colleen. We'll fix it."

"Thank you for your time, Dr. Sibley," Fina said, and started to walk back toward the opening in the net. She paused for a moment and watched him attend to the player. He had dropped down to his knee again and was examining her foot.

Before leaving the sports complex, Fina checked out the offerings at the café and ordered a peanut power smoothie, which promised a creamy mix of peanut butter, banana, yogurt, and protein powder to propel her through her day. Presumably, the concoction was geared toward people who had already exercised, or planned to, but she never knew what might lie ahead. Better to fuel up now, just in case.

As she pushed a straw into the thick liquid, Fina wondered about Gus and Liz's alleged falling out. She didn't doubt that a lawsuit could fracture or even decimate a long-standing friendship—she'd seen it happen before—but something about it didn't jibe. This lawsuit was going to be bigger than Liz and Gus. It was going to involve teams of lawyers and millions of dollars and probably years of legal wrangling.

Yes, Liz was injured and that was personal, but Gus was right: There hadn't been concussion protocols back then.

So did Liz blame Gus for not being a mind reader or did she blame him for something else?

Fina called Kelly and asked if she could stop by and ask her a few questions. She hesitated, which seemed to be the general reaction to Fina these days. Kelly ran down a list of pickups and drop-offs that boggled the mind, finally settling on ballet class. Fina could meet her at her daughter's ballet class in an hour.

The studio was in an old brick building in Roslindale Village—MISS

LETTY'S SCHOOL OF DANCE was etched on a glass door. Fina pulled it open and climbed the stairs to the second floor, piano music rising in volume as she did. She arrived at a scene that was like a whirling bowl of pink cotton candy come to life. Little girls, emerging from a room that had a curtain for its door, were chattering and shrieking, wearing pink tutus and matching tights, their hair pulled back in buns that were successful to varying degrees. They wandered around an area filled with small cubbies and wall hooks as a few mothers tended to flyaway hair and struggled to cram small feet in ballet slippers.

A woman appeared from behind another curtained doorway.

"Children," she announced sternly. "Please proceed to the studio." She was probably eighty years old, her face resembling that of a shar-pei. Her hair was pulled back in a tight bun, and her face was heavily made-up. Blue eye shadow, heavy black mascara, and ruby-red lips only accentuated her skin's lack of elasticity. To complete the look, she was dressed in a black leotard, black tights, and a small sheer skirt.

She looked at Fina with disapproval, her gaze lingering on Fina's shoulders. "Yes? Are you here about classes?" Little girls maneuvered around them toward the dance studio, like water around river rocks.

"God, no," Fina replied. "Are you Miss Letty?"

"I am."

"I'm meeting one of the moms, Kelly Wegner."

"Mrs. Wegner!" Miss Letty hollered above the din. "Someone is here for you." She stared at Fina. "Please be sure not to disturb the class," she warned before turning on her ballet slippers and striding down the hallway toward a line of folding chairs that provided a viewing area into the windowed studio.

Kelly ducked out from behind the curtain and shooed a small girl after the others.

"I don't think Miss Letty is happy I'm here," Fina said.

"Miss Letty isn't ever happy. Period," Kelly said. She didn't look as tired as she had on Saturday, but she certainly wasn't as perky as she'd been at their first meeting. "We can go watch, but we should try to be quiet."

Fina followed her to the chairs, and they claimed two that were separated from the other mothers. Inside the studio, an elderly man—Mr. Letty, perhaps—was plunking out a simple tune as Miss Letty led the little girls through warm-up exercises. The pupils looked to be about four years old, their bodies just growing out of the baby stage marked by smooth round tummies.

"Is that your daughter?" Fina asked, gesturing toward the small towhead who had pranced down the hall in front of them.

"Yes, that's Ruby."

"She's adorable," Fina commented. Ruby had her mother's fine hair and an impish grin.

"Miss Letty doesn't think she pays attention enough," Kelly said.

"How old is she?" Fina asked. "Four?"

"Almost." Kelly's gaze followed her daughter's movements.

"I'd be worried if she *did* pay attention," Fina said.

They watched as Ruby continued spinning in a circle long after her classmates had stopped. Miss Letty spoke to her, at which point she arrested her turning and listed to the side, grinning.

"Miss Letty thinks if I'm here watching, Ruby will be more focused."

"Well, even if she isn't focused, she looks like she's having fun," Fina noted.

The girls were paired off and started progressing down the length of the room, two at a time. Fina couldn't figure out what move they were supposed to be doing, there was such variation.

"So you wanted to talk to me?" Kelly asked.

"Yeah, thanks for making the time. I know your life is probably crazy right now."

"It sure is."

"How's Jamie doing?"

"As you would expect," Kelly said, focusing on the class. "I think he's in shock."

Fina nodded. "I'm not surprised. What do you think about the BU stuff?" she asked a moment later.

Kelly was quiet. "I think it's kind of creepy, to tell you the truth. I don't want anyone cutting up my brain after I die."

"The idea is unnerving, but I suppose that Liz thought it was worth it. Has Jamie talked to you about it?" Fina asked. "How does he feel about it?"

"I think he's okay with it."

Miss Letty was demonstrating something to the class, and Fina had to give her credit. Her posture was outstanding, but maybe that was from the stick up her butt.

"Did Liz ever mention that she had a problem with Gus Sibley, the team doctor?"

Kelly frowned. She opened her purse and dug around before pulling out an open roll of breath mints. "Do you want one?" she asked Fina.

"Sure." Fina thought time was being bought, and she wondered why that was.

"She never said anything about Gus to me. I didn't even know they were still in touch."

"Really? Tasha knew they were."

Kelly's lip curled slightly. "Well, I guess Liz and Tasha were better friends."

Fina wondered if she had stumbled onto some college resentment that had simmered over the years. Three was a difficult number when it came to relationships, which was why Fina thought that polyamory was never a good choice. The whole concept seemed fraught with peril, not to mention exhausting.

"Were the three of you friends in college?" Fina asked.

"Uh-huh." Kelly didn't elaborate. If she had been the odd man out, it wasn't surprising that she didn't want to share the details.

"So Liz never mentioned Gus or any disagreement they might have had?"

"I said she didn't," Kelly snapped.

"Right. Sorry," Fina said.

Kelly rubbed her temples. "Sorry. I'm just really tired."

"I'm the one who should be sorry. I don't mean to be a pest."

Ruby was waving her arms like a windmill; it was no classic ballet move that Fina had ever seen. Kelly shook her head in wonderment. "What is she doing?"

"Hey, at least she's getting her ya-yas out," Fina said. Patty was a big believer in running kids around so that they collapsed into bed each night, spent and satisfied. As far as Fina could tell, it was a successful strategy for happy, well-adjusted kids. "That's a good thing."

"Yeah, if only Miss Letty agreed," Kelly said.

Fina considered suggesting that she find a more age-appropriate class for energetic Ruby, but held her tongue. Funny, parents rarely appreciated getting parenting advice from the childless.

"Thanks for talking to me," Fina said, rising from her seat. "Any word on the funeral?"

"Friday. They haven't figured out the details yet."

"Got it. Thanks, Kelly. Let me know if I can do anything."

"Sure. Bye."

Fina trotted down the steps, happy to be free of the rigidity of Miss Letty's School of Dance. On the sidewalk, she slumped her shoulders and ambled to the car.

It was good to be an adult.

This is utter bullshit. That's what it is," said the trainer. "Giving her brain to BU. If anything, NEU should get it."

It was later that afternoon, and Kevin was leaning against the doorjamb in one of the athletic training rooms at the NEU sports center. The room, one of many in the complex, was where the student athletes came for rehab and fine-tuning.

Kevin didn't bother to explain that NEU had no use for Liz's brain; the young man wasn't the sharpest knife in the drawer, so Kevin didn't waste his breath.

The room was cramped with two padded tables and two hydrotherapy whirlpool baths. It wasn't the most attractive space, but the equipment was top-notch, and that's what mattered. Providing every possible advantage to the student athletes was one of the reasons Kevin worked so hard as a booster. If there was anything he could do to give an NEU team an edge, he'd do it.

The trainer was massaging the quadriceps muscle on one of their star basketball players, Paul Valmora. The kid lay on his back, his feet hanging well off the table. He was at least six feet five, with broad shoulders and well-defined arm muscles. Kevin liked to put in face time with Paul and other athletes off the field, and it was easy to do since they trained year-round, no matter which season they actually played. Those interactions helped build relationships and reassured the standouts that Kevin was available to them; whatever they needed, Kevin was the man for the job. He worked hard to be indispensable.

"Don't worry about it, Chad," Kevin assured the trainer. "It's going to be fine."

Chad shook his head. "And what does girls' soccer have to do with football?"

Another young man kneeled in front of a large metal cabinet, sorting through rolls of athletic tape. Kevin walked farther into the room and leaned against a counter.

"Nothing. That's why you don't need to worry about it." Kevin took his role as a booster seriously and felt a responsibility to rally the troops. This was true whether they were stuck in a losing streak or facing a PR nightmare.

Loud laughter echoed down the hall, and a moment later, three enormous young men wandered by the door to the training room.

"Yo, Laff!" one of them exclaimed.

Kevin's face brightened at the greeting, and he went out to the hallway, where he traded high fives and man hugs with the three football players. He'd been given the nickname years ago by some student athletes. The moniker had started as a joke, but over time, it had evolved into a term of affection.

Two of the kids—and they were kids to Kevin—were black and one white, but more divisive than their skin color were their physiques. The white guy and one of the black kids were clearly linemen; they were fat, not just muscular, their bellies flopping over their waistbands. Their rear ends were gelatinous masses that strained the seams of their tight football pants. The other one was tall, muscular, and lean. Even Kevin could appreciate his body—not that he was into that sort of thing. The torso exposed by his cutoff T-shirt was rippled and looked like sand after the tide had gone out: firmly packed and dense.

"You see the news, man?" one of them asked. "'Bout that dumbass lawsuit?"

Kevin nodded. "You guys shouldn't be thinking about that. You should be focusing on training."

"They better not pay out using our cash. We get beaten up for that money, man. We've earned it."

"And a soccer player?" the fat white kid piped up. "The girls' soccer team is going to tell us how to play football?"

"Don't worry about it, fellas," Kevin reassured them. "You just focus on the team. All the rest of it is bullshit."

"Later, Laff." They performed their awkward straight-man farewell ritual—physical contact, but not too much and not below the waist—and wandered off.

"Kevin?" A man poked his head out of an office down the hallway. "Do you have a minute?" Don Messinger was the assistant director of NEU's athletic program, and they'd known each other for more than twenty years. The men got along okay, but they were never really friends. Don always seemed too tightly wound. Kevin took competition just as seriously as Don, but believed that celebrations and fun should also be a part of the equation.

"Sure, Don. What can I do for you?" Kevin came into the office, which was small, but had a window overlooking the practice fields.

Don gestured for him to close the door. The motion should have made him feel important, but instead, it made him feel like a child called in to the principal's office. Rather than wait for a directive, Kevin chose to sit on the couch instead of the chair in front of Don's desk.

"I've been touching base with all the coaches and athletic staff in light of Liz Barone's death and this lawsuit," Don said, gazing at Kevin over his half-frame glasses. They made him look more like a professor than a jock.

"It's a hell of a thing," Kevin said, shaking his head. He spread his arms across the back of the couch.

"There's probably going to be a lot of press, and everybody needs to be on their best behavior. I need you to spread the word to the boosters," Don said.

"Of course. You don't need to worry about the club. I'll make sure people are behaving."

Don stared at him. "*Everybody* needs to behave."

Kevin didn't ask for specifics. Whatever Don knew or thought he knew, Kevin didn't want any details.

"Absolutely," Kevin said, rising from the couch. "Some of the guys mentioned the lawsuit just now. I tried to reassure them that it's nothing to worry about."

"Good. I don't want them to be distracted or mouthing off."

"You know I'll do whatever I can. Take care, Don." Kevin opened the door and walked back down the hallway to the training room.

The lawsuit angered him, but it also gave him a burst of energy. NEU athletics needed him now more than ever, and he was raring to go.

16.

Fina woke early and spent over an hour catching up on the news related to Liz's death and performing the administrative duties associated with being a business owner. Although most of her work came from Ludlow and Associates, she was technically self-employed and was in charge of keeping her own records. Frank had taught her that the only way to manage paperwork and other administrative tasks was to do them regularly. It always felt like it was taking her away from more pressing—and interesting—matters, but if the cops or the IRS ever came knocking, she would be ready.

Her work was interrupted by a summons from Carl.

"I could have given you an update over the phone," she told her father an hour later at the office. Carl looked dapper in a dark charcoal suit paired with a light blue shirt and a tie sporting blue and lavender stripes. "You look very nice, Dad." It couldn't hurt to start the morning with a kind word.

He eyed her suspiciously. "Thank you."

"So why am I here?"

"I do want an update, but that's not why I called you." Carl pointed a pen at her.

"What is it, then? I have work to do."

"I need you to babysit Scotty today."

"He's older than I am," Fina pointed out helpfully.

Carl ignored her. "He has a deposition in Lynn, and I want you to go with him."

"Why?" Fina asked. "Is he in danger?"

"No, but the client is jumpy, and your presence will reassure her," Carl said.

"Why didn't you tell me this sooner? I have things to do today. Let me call Dennis Kozlowski. He can do it, or one of his subs can." Dennis was a PI in Boston who Fina used when she needed an extra pair of hands. He was good at his job and well connected.

"Because I want you to do it," Carl said.

Fina looked at her father. "You know, you complain about my job performance pretty frequently, and yet you keep employing me."

"I don't have time for this, Josefina."

"Fine. Is the client here or are we meeting her?"

"She's here. Scotty's waiting for you."

"Great." Fina stood up. "What's this I hear about Rand having a new girlfriend and wanting Haley to visit?"

Carl looked at her, but didn't speak.

"What?" Fina asked. "You have nothing to say on the subject?"

"What do you want me to say?"

"That you're not going to let him get within a mile of her, given his past behavior."

"I don't think we can keep them separated forever, Fina."

"We can keep them separated until she's an adult and can make her own decisions," she said. "You've just ordered me to change my whole day. Why can't you order Mom to butt out of Haley's life?"

"It's a little more complicated than that." Carl's phone rang. "I have to take this."

"We're not done talking about this," Fina said, moving toward the door.

Carl rolled his eyes and reached for the phone. "Don't take your car," Carl called after her. "Take an SUV from the fleet."

"Fine."

Fina got a set of car keys from the head of security, then stopped by Scotty's office. The client was a small woman embroiled in a personal injury case with some mafioso types. Fina understood why she might want protection, but it still felt like a waste of her time.

Muscle was easy to hire, but the brains that solved cases like Liz's were harder to come by.

That wasn't so bad, was it?" Scotty asked. It was late afternoon, and they were at Bell Circle in Revere. The deposition had been completed without any physical violence, and the client had gotten a ride home with a muscular friend who looked like he could hold his own.

"It was fine," Fina said. "It just wasn't what I planned on doing today."

"You could have said no to Dad," Scotty ventured, smirking.

"Like you do?"

"It's different for me," he said. "We have a more complicated business arrangement."

"Uh-huh. Did you know that Rand has a new girlfriend?" she asked her brother.

Scotty turned and looked at her, his eyes wide. "What? Really?"

"Yes."

"Who told you that?"

"Who do you think?" Fina asked.

Scotty sighed. "Mom."

"Of course. And he wants Haley to visit him over spring break."

Scotty leaned over and adjusted the heat. "What did you say to that?" They were climbing the ramp toward the Tobin Bridge, the city coming into view before them.

"I haven't said anything yet, but you can be damn sure it's not going to happen."

Scotty tapped the window lightly with his finger, but was quiet.

"Yes? You'd like to say something?" Fina asked.

"I just don't know how much we're going to be able to manage Rand."

"I'm not suggesting we manage Rand. I'm suggesting we take care of his underage daughter."

"I *am* taking care of his underage daughter, Fina. Remember?" Scotty said.

"Yes, I know, and I can't tell you how much I appreciate that you and Patty have embraced her the way you have."

"I love Haley," he said, "but we weren't planning on having four kids. Certainly not one who was handed to us as a teenager with a lot of baggage."

"I know." She nodded. "You guys have been amazing. I'm just suggesting that all of that love and hard work will be undermined if we allow Rand back in her life. We can't let him do more damage than he already has."

"I don't disagree," Scotty said as they flew through the E-Z Pass lane. "You're supposed to slow down, you know."

"Only if you're a bad driver," Fina responded, smiling.

A moment later, her nose perked up. "Do you smell that?" she asked Scotty.

He took a whiff and looked at her. "I think that's smoke."

The gears were just starting to turn in Fina's head when a flame escaped from the hood of the car.

"Jesus Christ, Fina!" Scotty exclaimed.

"Shit!" She watched the fire escape from the hood and wend its way from the driver's side to the passenger's side. There was no place to pull over, no breakdown lane, so Fina put on the brakes and stopped, unleashing a tirade of angry horns and more screeching brakes. She grabbed the keys from the ignition. The hazard lights seemed unnecessary, given that the front of the SUV was fully engulfed.

"Get out, Scotty!" she yelled, flinging her door open.

"I can't! We're too close to the guardrail." His face was a mask of panic.

Fina hopped out of her seat and reached back inside the car for him.

She grabbed the collar of his coat and helped him scale the middle console between the seats. Scotty tumbled onto the pavement amid a cacophony of crackles, pops, and more honking horns. He started to run away from the car, but Fina ducked her head back in and grabbed his briefcase and her bag. She left her coat, which was just out of reach.

"What are you doing?" Scotty yelled at her when she caught up with him, twenty feet behind the engulfed SUV. "It's going to explode!"

"No, it's not," Fina said, leaning over with her hands on her knees. She took a couple of deep breaths. "You watch too much TV."

"I'm calling 911," Scotty said, pulling his phone from his pocket.

"I'm guessing somebody did already."

"That's what everyone assumes," he said.

"They've called because it's screwing up their commute," Fina said. "If for no other reason."

Scotty kept dialing.

"But knock yourself out," Fina said. "Are you okay?"

"My chest hurts a little."

"Probably from the smoke. Or you're having a heart attack," she said.

"Really, Fina?" He turned away from her. "Yes, hello, our car's on fire," he said into the phone.

A car moved by them at a fast clip, honking.

"Fuck you, too!" Fina called out after them. She started pacing in a small circle by the guardrail.

"You guys okay?" A worker from one of the tollbooths was jogging toward them, fire extinguisher in hand. Another motorist had stopped and also asked if they were hurt.

"We're fine. Here, let me." Fina took the red canister from the toll worker and approached the car. She had been driving, and she should assume the risk of putting out the fire, kind of like a captain going down with his ship. Not to mention, she was freezing. Getting close to the mini inferno was a welcome respite from the freezing temperature.

Scotty, the worker, and the Good Samaritan were engaged in conversation while Fina sprayed the white foam over the hood of the car. It had already migrated to the rest of the vehicle, and the extinguisher did little to quell the flames.

Two minutes later, sirens blared in the distance, and two fire engines squeezed through the tollbooths. They were followed by a fire department ambulance, two police cars, and a couple of fire department SUVs. The trucks' compression brakes made loud squeaking noises when they rolled to a halt, and the doors opened, disgorging a troop of men wearing bunker gear.

"Step away, ma'am," one of them instructed her, taking the fire extinguisher from her grip. "We've got it."

Another firefighter led her away from the blaze and started asking questions. Was there anyone else in the car? Was she hurt? What was her name? What had happened?

Fina answered the questions and pointed out Scotty so they could check him out. An EMT insisted she come to the ambulance, which Fina didn't feel was medically necessary, but she went anyway. In her experience—both as a PI and as the daughter of a highly litigious attorney—when health and safety experts offered their expertise, you took them up on it.

Fina sat down next to Scotty on the back of the rig.

"Are you okay?" he asked her.

"I'm fine, just freezing." One of the EMTs reached into a cabinet over the gurney and pulled out a scratchy wool blanket. Fina draped it around her shoulders while he started giving her a cursory once-over.

"Look at the car," Scotty said wistfully. "It's totaled."

"You sound like a teenager."

"I feel like one. Dad's going to go berserk."

"Did you call Patty?" Fina asked. "You don't want her to see this on the news."

"I texted her that we had car trouble, but that we're both fine."

"Ha!" Fina said.

"You're all set, sir," an EMT said to Scotty. He thanked the man and stood up slowly.

"I'm going to see if I can find anything out," Scotty said before wandering back to the nearly extinguished fire.

Fina took stock of the scene, which was a weird amalgamation of opposites: freezing temperatures and intense heat; cold water and severe dryness; the early dark of January and the blinding lights from the emergency vehicles. The people who worked in these conditions needed to be brave, certainly, but they also needed to be steady in an environment of contradictory stimuli. It was hard to know where to look or what to pay attention to, but obviously, those were skills well honed by these first responders.

The EMT checked her vital signs and responses. He examined her hands and applied some ointment to her right hand and wrist, which were red and starting to pucker.

"Did you reach back into the car?" he asked.

Fina looked sheepish. "Maybe."

He shook his head.

"Hey," Fina said. "Do you have any idea how difficult it is to cancel all your credit cards and get a new license?"

He shook his head. "Not as difficult as getting skin grafts."

Fina smiled at him. "Fine. You win. It wasn't my best moment."

"I think it's going to be okay." He uncapped a bottle of water and handed it to her. "You should have your doctor check it in twenty-four hours."

"I will. Thanks," Fina said as he climbed into the rig and started tidying things. Fina remained perched on the back and scanned the crowd for Scotty.

"Seriously?" a voice said.

She looked over to see Lieutenant Pitney coming toward her.

"Well, Lieutenant, it doesn't get more serious than your car erupting in flames on the Tobin Bridge, now, does it?"

"Are you hurt?" Pitney asked. She was bundled in a puffy silver parka. The look called to mind a disco ball.

"Some minor burns, but I'm fine. Thank you for asking."

"So, what happened?" Pitney pulled out a notebook and a pen.

"I'm thrilled to see you, as always," Fina said, "but why are you here exactly?"

"Because we're both investigating Liz Barone's death, and it looks like someone tried to blow up your car. That seems awfully coincidental."

The firefighters were rolling up hoses and loading gear back into their trucks.

"Are we sure this wasn't a mechanical failure?" Fina asked. "If it was, it's got lawsuit written all over it."

"The fire guys don't think so, but obviously, they'll know more once they take a closer look. For now, we're treating it as a crime scene."

"And you're assuming I was the target?" Fina asked. "Scotty was with me."

"I know," Pitney said. "That's why Cristian is talking to him." She pointed toward the two men engrossed in conversation. "We're covering our bases, but if I were a betting woman, my money would be on you."

"Great."

"So is this the car you usually drive?"

"No. It's a fleet car from the firm," Fina said.

"Why were you driving it today?" Pitney asked.

"My father asked me to accompany Scotty and a client to a deposition."

"What case?"

"Talk to Scotty about that. I'm sure there are all kinds of rules governing what we can say."

"Of course there are. We wouldn't want anyone's rights to be violated," Pitney said with a note of sarcasm.

"No, we wouldn't. I know you find it inconvenient, but I assume that in general, you're a fan of the Constitution," Fina said.

"I am, but you're right—it's highly inconvenient."

Fina sipped the water. Her throat hurt a little when she swallowed, but she didn't know if that was from the smoke or the hollering.

"So your father told you to drive this car?"

"Yes," Fina said, eyeing Pitney, "but my father did not try to kill me or my brother or—more importantly—a paying client."

"Did anyone else know you'd be using that car?"

"I don't think so. I only found out ten minutes before I picked up the keys, but it was parked close to my car in the garage."

"So if someone was watching you . . ."

"They'd know I changed cars," Fina acknowledged.

"Where did you go today?" Pitney asked.

"We were at a law firm in Lynn. Scotty can give you the particulars. We spent about three hours there this morning, then got some lunch and returned for another hour."

"Did you take the car to get lunch?"

"No," Fina said. "We walked."

Pitney tapped her pen against the notebook. "Anybody tail you or seem suspicious?"

Fina considered for a moment whether or not she should tell Pitney about her shadow and the note she'd found in her car. "Not today, and I was keeping an eye out."

"What do you mean 'not today'?"

Fina fiddled with the bottle cap. "I've been wondering if I have a tail."

"Since when?"

"The last week or so."

"Did you get a look at the guy?"

"No," Fina said, "and that's why I'm hesitant to tell you. It could have been a coincidence."

Pitney squinted at her. "You really believe that?"

Fina shrugged. "Not really," she admitted.

"Was this person on foot? In a car?"

"In a car," Fina said.

"What about the car? A plate or even a description?"

"A dark sedan with tinted windows. Not the least bit useful, I know."

Pitney sighed. "What else?"

"What do you mean?"

"Have there been any other threats or strange occurrences?"

Fina studied the gauze on her hand. "There was a note suggesting I mind my own business."

"Details, please," Pitney said, shaking her head.

Fina filled her in.

"And it didn't occur to you to tell me or Cristian?"

"Of course it occurred to me, but there was no point," Fina insisted. "You weren't going to find any prints on it. There aren't any cameras in the area, and as you always tell me, I piss off a lot of people. I didn't want to waste your time or cause Cristian to worry."

"How thoughtful of you." Pitney gestured toward the carcass of the SUV. "Where did you park the car today?"

"In a private garage attached to the building that houses the law firm. I'd have to look at a map to give you the address." Fina watched the cops directing traffic. "You really think this is related to Liz?"

Pitney shrugged. "You tell me. Who have you pissed off most recently?"

"Oh, Lieutenant. You know that's a long list."

"Well, who's at the top of the list?"

Fina thought for a moment. "I can tell you who I've spoken with recently, but no one jumps out as being especially annoyed."

"Go ahead."

"Jamie Gottlieb, Kevin Lafferty, Pamela Fordyce, Vikram Mehra, Tasha Beemis-Jones, Kelly Wegner, Dana Tompkins, Gus Sibley."

Pitney's pen paused over her notebook. "You haven't spoken with Dr. Sibley since I told you not to, correct?"

Fina squinted in concentration. "When was that exactly?"

"I specifically told you not to speak to him." Pitney glared at her.

"I know, but you know me: I'd rather ask for forgiveness later than permission ahead of time."

"I know, Fina, and it drives me crazy. When did you speak with Gus Sibley?"

Fina took a long drink, trying to put off the inevitable. She wiped her mouth with the blanket before speaking. "Yesterday."

"Yesterday?"

"That is correct."

"That's terrific," Pitney said. "Just great."

"I think he tattled on me because he has something to hide," Fina said.

"That may very well be, but if you annoy him and I have to clean up your mess, it takes me away from the investigation."

"Or," Fina protested, "it accelerates the investigation because I'm making him nervous, thereby prompting him to act and possibly make a mistake."

"Where do you get this stuff?" Pitney looked genuinely perplexed.

"Come on. Don't tell me that you don't use witness irritation as a barometer in your investigations. Innocent people generally don't mind answering questions, even multiple times."

Before Pitney could answer, Cristian wandered over. "You okay?"

"Yeah. I'm fine," Fina said. "How's Scotty holding up?"

Cristian glanced back in that direction. "I think he's shaken up."

"This is more excitement than he's used to," Fina said.

"She got a threatening note," Pitney said.

"When?" Concern flitted across his face.

"On Friday night. I didn't want to worry you needlessly," Fina said.

"It wouldn't have been needlessly," Cristian said, his voice rising.

"You two kids can fight about this later," Pitney said. Even though some of the emergency vehicles had left, the traffic was still bumper-to-bumper. The smoking heap of metal accounted for the curiosity factor, and Fina could feel the eyes of the Boston-bound commuters on her. A tow truck was backing up to the car to haul it away, which would ease the bottleneck.

"The arson bomb squad guys want to talk to you," Cristian said, his voice laced with a touch of irritation.

"Sure. Did Scotty tell you about his nefarious client and the people she's suing?"

Cristian gave her a weary smile. "Yes, and we'll look into them."

"Good. Everyone assumes the worst about me."

"You just told me you think someone's been following you," Pitney said. Cristian looked at Fina, his face scrunched into a question mark.

"I said it was a hunch, nothing more. You still need to look into Scotty's client. A thorough investigation and all that."

The EMT asked them to move away from the ambulance so he could go back to saving lives. Fina, Pitney, and Cristian wandered over to a police department SUV that had arrived on the scene. Scotty was talking with a couple of men, and they asked Fina a number of questions about the appearance and speed of the fire.

"I'm sure you hear this all the time, but it really did happen fast," she told them. "The whole thing is a bit of a blur."

"We understand," the one in command responded. "The physical evidence will tell us more, but we like to get as much information as possible."

"Of course," Fina said, and tried to fill in as many blanks as she could. Once they were done, she looked around, realizing she and Scotty were effectively stranded. "Can someone give us a ride downtown?" Fina asked.

"One of the uniforms will take you," Pitney said, gesturing to an officer. "We'll be in touch, and if you think of anything relevant, give your friend here a call."

"Call me regardless," Cristian said, giving her a meaningful stare that was supposed to convey both his concern and annoyance.

"Will do," Fina promised.

She and Scotty followed the cop to his patrol car. "Can I ride up front?" she asked him as Scotty rolled his eyes.

"Sure." The officer grinned at her. "You're not in trouble."

Scotty burst out laughing. "Not yet, but she will be soon."

17.

"You owe Dad an SUV," Matthew said when she and Scotty arrived in Carl's office twenty minutes later.

"Very funny. I need something to eat." Fina rummaged around in the minibar until she found a can of mixed nuts. She grabbed a soda and took both over to the couch. Matthew watched as she struggled to peel the vacuum seal off the nuts, finally taking pity on her and reaching for the can himself.

"Seriously. How do you manage that?" Matthew sat down on the couch next to her while Scotty grabbed a bottle of scotch and a glass from the bar. He took the chair across from the couch and poured himself a drink. "You borrow the car for one day, and it catches on fire." Matthew shook his head in amazement.

Fina chewed on a nut and swallowed. "I have no idea how *we*"—she gestured at Scotty—"managed it."

"You think it happened because of him?" Matthew asked, looking at their older brother.

"Why not? You guys have a ton of scummy clients."

"But we don't get in trouble like you do," Matthew said. "We associate with our less than desirable clients in an office setting. You're the one frequenting dens of iniquity."

Fina stared at him. "I'm sorry. What century are we in?"

Carl strode into the office. When he caught sight of Fina, he tossed some folders on his desk and faced her. "That's how you end the day? By torching the car?"

"This is like a bad game of Telephone," Fina said, throwing a handful of nuts into her mouth. She took a moment to chew. "I didn't torch the car. It erupted in flames, and you shouldn't discount Scotty as a target. He has plenty of enemies."

"We're still out an SUV," Carl said.

"Yes, but we're fine, thank you very much for asking, Dad."

Carl looked at Scotty, who was downing his drink.

"We're fine," Scotty agreed.

Carl nodded. "Who do you think is responsible?"

Fina looked at her watch, then glared at him. "It happened less than two hours ago! I haven't had time to investigate, but I assure you, I'm extremely motivated to find the perpetrator."

"You missed the six o'clock news, but maybe the local cable news has something on it." Carl picked up the TV remote from his desk and turned on the large flat-screen.

"This is going to create some major PR," Scotty commented. Fina gave him the hairy eyeball. "Not that that makes it worth it," he said.

"I'm tired," Fina said, closing the can of nuts. "I'm going."

"Do you need a ride home or anything?" Matthew asked, his concern on some kind of time delay.

"No, I'm good."

What she needed was a little sympathy, something she would never find in Carl's office.

Maybe her father and her brothers wouldn't provide much sympathy, but there were people farther west who would.

Frank was planted in his recliner, and Peg was on the couch when she arrived at 56 Wellspring Street.

"I saw you on the news," he announced.

"I need some ice cream before you grill me," Fina said. "No pun intended."

She fixed herself a large serving of Brigham's chocolate chip and liberally sprinkled it with jimmies. Her heart did a little pitter-patter when she saw the six-pack of diet soda in the fridge. Neither Frank nor Peg drank soda. It was all hers.

"Thank you for the soda, Peg, and the ice cream," she said as she settled on the couch next to Peg.

"You're welcome, sweetie." Peg patted her knee.

"Is this a first for you?" Frank asked.

"A fire?"

"An incendiary device, Fina. Let's call it what it is. Unless you know that it was only a glitch with the car."

"That's highly unlikely. So, yes. It is a first." She had a bite of ice cream.

"It's something else."

"It's good to have new experiences," she said. "It keeps you young."

"Unless it kills you," Frank commented.

"We're both fine. I think Scotty was unnerved by the whole thing, but he'll get over it."

"Is your hand okay?" Peg asked, eyeing the bandage.

"It's minor," Fina said. "Nothing to worry about."

"What did Carl say about your new experience?" Frank asked.

Fina ate a too-large spoonful of ice cream and paid the price. A cold headache gripped her forehead. "'What did you do to my car?' Blah, blah, blah."

"That's what insurance is for," Peg commented. "We're just glad that you're okay."

"Exactly," Frank agreed.

"Thank you." Fina took a sip of soda in hopes of moving the lump out of her throat. She knew her reaction was in part because she was tired and the afternoon's excitement was catching up with her. But it was also nice to have people articulate their pleasure that she was still walking the earth.

"Hey, how was Maine?" she asked.

"It was a little rough getting up there," Frank said. "They've got a lot more snow."

Fina nodded.

"But you were right about the town," he said. "It's a very friendly place."

"We've been invited back," Peg added.

"You made friends?" Fina asked.

"We pretended that we were considering buying a summer cottage," she said, "and we hit it off with the owner of the diner, who introduced us to a real estate agent."

"Oh, a little pretexting," Fina said, grinning. "How was that, Peg? You didn't feel too guilty?"

A small smile crept onto Peg's face. "At first, I felt a little bad, but honestly, it was kind of fun."

"Aha!"

"We didn't do any harm," Peg insisted. "We wasted an hour of people's time, but let's be honest: I don't think they had anything else to do."

Fina snorted.

"She was very good at it," Frank said, smiling at his wife. "I was impressed."

"Did you get any dirt?" Fina asked.

"As you can imagine, the real estate agent was a Chatty Cathy, born and raised in Rockford," Frank said. "She seemed to know everyone's business and was happy to share it."

"Uh-huh." Fina pressed her fingertip into the stray jimmies lining the bowl.

"We mentioned Greta Samuels and her sister Elizabeth, as if we were friends, and how concerned we were about Greta's health," Frank said.

"That was very nice of you."

"I said I was a nurse," Peg added, "and how difficult transplants could be, but the agent was very excited to report that Greta had found a donor."

"What? Since when?" Fina leaned forward on her chair.

"She talked about the donation like it was a done deal." Frank looked at her.

"Did the agent say who the donor was? Was she referring to Risa?"

Frank and Peg exchanged a glance. "She said the kidney was from a stranger through Maine's organ donor registry," he said.

Fina gaped. "You're kidding."

"No," Frank said.

"But she must be talking about Risa. There is no other kidney, as far as Risa or I know."

"I assumed she was talking about Risa," Frank said. "For whatever reason, she's pretending that she's definitely getting Risa's kidney, but that it's coming from a stranger."

"Why?" Fina asked.

Frank shrugged. "My best guess is that she doesn't want people to know about Risa."

"Great." Fina leaned back, deflated. "That's just terrific."

"But just because Greta is saying that doesn't mean she and Elizabeth never tried to find Risa," Peg said.

Fina and Frank looked at her with skepticism.

"It does make it seem pretty unlikely, though," Fina said.

"I suppose," Peg conceded.

Fina drank some soda. "Wow. I really don't know where to go with this."

"Not what you were hoping for, I imagine." Frank ran his hands down the armrests of his recliner.

"No, I was hoping that you guys would come back with a grand tale about how Risa's birth family spent their entire lives searching for her. That everyone in the town knew they were tortured by this chapter in their history and knew they wouldn't rest until she was found."

"Sorry, hon," Peg said.

"I can ask Greta more questions about this and so can Risa," Fina said, "but what's to stop her from lying about it? I can't exactly prove her inaction."

Frank looked at her. "I think you and Risa should sit down with the aunt and have a conversation. Ask her your questions—knowing what you know from our end—and see what she has to say. Your instincts are good. Your gut will tell you."

"I know, I just hate that Risa has to base a major decision on a gut feeling."

"Sweetie, we do it more often than you'd like to think," he said. "Just because you can't articulate the process doesn't mean it isn't a good one."

"True."

He glanced at the clock next to the TV. "It's getting late. Why don't you stay?"

Frank and Peg had a fully furnished basement and a spare room that was loosely designated as Fina's home away from home. She stayed over on occasion and pretended, if only in her own mind, that she was part of a functional family. Every once in a while, it was just what she needed, and it allowed Frank and Peg to play parents, a role that they missed since their two sons lived out of state.

"I'll have to get up early," Fina said. "Obviously, I have a lot of work to do."

"You can join us for our constitutional!" Frank said.

"What time is that?" Fina asked out of curiosity.

"Five thirty," Peg said.

"Good Lord. That won't be happening, under any circumstances. Can I stay anyway?"

"Anytime, you know that." Frank winked at her.

Fina sat with them as they watched the local cable news station. A report of her fiery SUV led the update.

"There's nothing halfway about your life, is there?" Frank asked.

"Go big or go home," Fina said. "It's the Ludlow way."

Bobbi Barone was at home in West Roxbury when Fina called her the next morning. Fina wanted to make a proper condolence call, but she also had a few questions that she preferred to ask in person; there was no substitute for seeing a person's facial expressions. That was one of the reasons she was highly suspicious of relationships that were conducted mostly online; people lied face-to-face, but it wasn't as easy.

Bobbi's house was off Washington Street, a few blocks from Stony Brook Reservation. Fina forgot sometimes about the green spaces dotted throughout the city. She was glad that somebody had the forethought to set aside land for uses other than development.

She wound through streets lined with center-entrance colonials and ranches before finding Bobbi's raised ranch. Dark gray with white shutters, it had a single-car garage under half of the house and a front door in the center of the facade. The dwelling was boxy and surrounded by denuded shrubs and a yard delineated by a chain-link fence. Fina could see an attached deck out back and a swing set that she imagined was utilized by Bobbi's grandchildren. She parked her car and noticed the long stare from the elderly neighbor who was clearing snow off his front path. The neighborhood watch signs she'd seen indicated it was a place where people looked out for one another, and visitors were suspect until proven otherwise.

Fina rang the bell and waited for a moment. Bobbi peeked out through a curtain covering the front door, her face relaxing when she saw the identity of her visitor.

"Is this an okay time?" Fina asked once Bobbi opened the door.

"Yes, come in. I'm glad to see you." Bobbi leaned out the door and waved to the nosy neighbor in reassurance.

"He was giving me the hairy eyeball," Fina said, leaving her belongings on a coatrack by the door.

"That's Barry. He's a grump, but he's just being protective," Bobbi said. "He doesn't want anyone bothering me."

"Have people been bothering you?" Fina asked.

Bobbi paused. "There's been a lot of press around, and there have been some e-mails."

"What kind of e-mails?"

"You know, 'You're ruining football, you bitch.' 'Don't piss on our sports.' That type of thing. I don't understand why they're angry with me."

"I think they're terrified that someone will draw an irrefutable line between concussions and long-term brain damage. God forbid their pleasure or income generation be curtailed by a small thing like dementia."

"It really is a ridiculous notion—that I'm a threat to the NCAA."

"But Bobbi, you should have contacted me right away. I'm going to get a security review for you and possibly some protection." The e-mails sounded like the work of typical Internet cranks, but she couldn't risk that her note writer also had an eye on Bobbi.

"That's not necessary, Fina."

"I insist. I don't think you're in actual danger, but you can't discount those threats."

Bobbi smiled. "Barry won't be happy if he's replaced."

"They can enlist him in the effort. He'll think he works for Blackwater or whatever they call themselves these days."

Fina followed her back to the kitchen overlooking the deck and the backyard. The cabinets were 1970s wood with fussy pulls, and the countertops were beige Formica. Linoleum covered the floor, and a country-style table dominated one corner. The counters were crowded with floral arrangements and Tupperware containers of food.

"I've had so much company," Bobbi said, pulling out a coffee mug and filling it from a pot on the counter. "I know they're just being supportive, but I'm ready to be left alone."

"And then I came over," Fina said, accepting the mug of steaming liquid.

"You're different. I don't think I have to make you feel better about everything that's happened."

"Hardly." Fina reached for the sugar bowl and poured in a heaping spoonful.

"What happened to your hand?" Bobbi asked.

Peg had examined her hand that morning and reapplied ointment and gauze. She thought it would heal on its own, but, like the EMT, suggested Fina see a doctor for a follow-up, which was never going to happen.

"I had a bit of an adventure yesterday," Fina said.

Bobbi gestured for her to continue.

"I don't know if you saw the news, but there was a car that caught fire on the Tobin."

"That was you?" Bobbi asked, wide-eyed.

"Yeah. I'm fine, though. My brother was with me, and he's okay, too. The car's a complete loss, but it's just a car."

"What happened?"

"We don't really know yet." Fina sipped her coffee.

"So the car just caught fire?" Bobbi asked.

"Well, I think it may have had a little help."

Bobbi slowed her coffee cup on the way to her mouth. "Someone did it on purpose? Because of Liz?" She looked alarmed.

"I don't know. Some of my brother's cases are contentious, to say the least, so maybe it had to do with him." Fina shrugged. "That isn't why I'm here, though, and like I said, I don't think you're in danger."

Bobbi took a sip from her cup. "I wish I could pretend that I care right now, but frankly, I'm finding it hard to care about much of anything."

"I don't blame you."

"You're not going to lecture me about my other children and my grandchildren? Everything I have to live for?"

Fina smiled. "I'm not big on lectures, maybe because other people are always giving them to me." She sipped her coffee. "Can you tell me how the decision to donate Liz's brain came about? Was it something she'd discussed with you?"

Bobbi picked a petal from a bouquet of flowers in front of her. The vase held white carnations and lilies. There was no mistaking their funereal theme.

"We did talk about it," she said finally. "And it's in her will."

"Where does Jamie fit into all of this? Usually it's the spouse who makes that kind of decision and announcement."

"Jamie doesn't object," Bobbi insisted.

"No, I know," Fina said. "He told me that the other day. I was just wondering why he wasn't more involved in the process."

"My daughter was very stubborn," Bobbi said, her eyes watering. "Once she accepted her diagnosis, she was determined to do everything she could to save herself and to stop it from happening to anyone else."

"So even if Jamie didn't agree, he wouldn't have been able to stop her."

Bobbi nodded. "She put it in her will, and Jamie's not the type to contest something like that, even if he disagreed."

"Who drew up her will?" Fina asked.

"Thatcher Kinney."

Ahh. The small-town legal eagle.

"Is there anything else of note in it?" Fina asked.

"No. She had a living will, which we followed, and she wanted to be an organ donor in addition to donating her brain to BU. Everything else goes to Jamie, but they don't have much. The house, their cars, and the kids, obviously."

"Did anyone else know that Liz was planning to donate her brain to the lab?"

"Not to my knowledge," Bobbi said. "That's not a conversation people are generally comfortable having. I don't mean Liz. I mean anyone who might have been on the receiving end."

Fina traced a circle on the tabletop with her finger. "Liz was very brave, Bobbi, and she obviously got that from you."

Tears rolled down Bobbi's cheeks. "I miss her so much."

"I know." Fina was silent for a moment. "I've talked to her boss, Vikram Mehra. He's a real peach."

"Do you think he had something to do with this?"

"I'm not sure, but he certainly had a motive," Fina said.

"What motive could he possibly have had?" she asked.

"The lab lost a big grant, and according to my sources, he blamed Liz."

"That's ridiculous," Bobbi said. She plucked another petal from the flowers. "When I think that she might have died for some stupid reason like that, my blood boils."

Fina fiddled with her coffee mug. "I'm sorry to say this, but every reason is going to be stupid. I've seen people hold out the hope that it will make sense once they know why their loved one was killed, and it never does."

Bobbi was silent.

"But obviously," Fina said, backtracking, "whatever gets you through the day."

"It's okay, Fina. I know you're just trying to give me the wisdom of your experience."

"But it would probably be more helpful if I just shut up," Fina said.

Bobbi gave her a weak smile. She looked tired. Her shoulders sagged, and she rested her elbows on the table.

"I'm going to go," Fina said, "unless you want me to stick around."

"No. It's okay. I think I'm going to lie down for a little while." Bobbi took their coffee mugs to the sink and rinsed them under the tap.

"How's Jamie holding up?" Fina asked as they walked to the front door.

"As well as can be expected. He's always been involved with the kids, but being both parents is all new to him."

"Sounds stressful and exhausting," Fina noted.

"And his knee has been acting up, which doesn't help." Bobbi handed Fina her coat and scarf.

"What happened to his knee?"

"When he stopped playing music," Bobbi said, "Liz got him training for a triathlon. It was going okay, but then he wiped out on his bike and blew out his knee."

Fina cringed. "That sounds brutal. Both parts: the triathlon and the knee."

"I thought so, too, but it was the kind of thing that Liz loved. I think she was hoping it would be something they could do together."

"Kelly said the funeral is tomorrow?" Fina asked, zipping up her jacket.

"Yes."

"Okay. Hang in there, and call me anytime. Day or night."

"Thank you." Bobbi gave her a hug and closed the door behind her.

Barry was still in his front yard, doing the world's most thorough job of snow removal. He and Frank had practically elevated the chore to an art form. Fina waved and got into her car.

She felt a wash of gratitude that she didn't have to stay in that sad house, but then she felt a wash of guilt for feeling that way.

18.

Fina called Risa and suggested they meet for an early lunch. They settled on a small Greek place in Newton Lower Falls. On the way to the restaurant, Fina kept a careful watch on the cars around her, wondering if her tail would make an appearance or if the car fire had been his way of reaching out to her. She didn't see anyone suspicious, but she didn't like having to be so vigilant; being on guard was exhausting.

She parked and called Dennis Kozlowski. Per Fina's request, he would send someone over to Bobbi's house to do a risk assessment and, if needed, assign her some protection. Fina hoped it wouldn't come to that, but personal security was not the place to cut corners.

The Greek restaurant was casual and dimly lit, calling to mind a grotto on the Mediterranean. An older gentleman, wizened and tan, greeted her at the door and led her to the table where Risa was already seated, sipping from a glass of seltzer. Fina took a seat in front of a mural depicting an olive grove and the Parthenon, outlined in the iconic blue of the Greek flag.

They perused the menu and caught up on various family members. Fina returned the menu to the host, who also appeared to be owner, maître d', and waiter. Once he'd relayed their orders to the kitchen, he sat down a few tables away and flipped through the pages of a Greek-language newspaper.

Risa spotted the gauze on Fina's hand. "What happened?" she asked.

"I had a spot of car trouble on the Tobin last night."

Risa forced the lime wedge in her glass down toward the bottom. She looked puzzled. "What kind of trouble? You don't mean that exploding car, do you?"

"Yes, that was me, but it wasn't an explosion."

"You're kidding me," Risa said.

Fina laughed. "No."

"What happened?"

"We don't know for sure, but it looks like someone placed an incendiary device on the car," Fina said.

"How did you discover it?" Risa asked.

"Ah, it was kind of hard to miss. The whole car erupted in flames," Fina said, accepting a glass brimming with ice and a can of cold diet soda from the waiter. "Scotty was with me. I think it was the most excitement he's had in a long time."

"Is your hand going to be okay?"

"Yeah. It's just a minor burn. I'm fine. The car is totaled, but what are you gonna do?"

Risa shook her head. "I'm just glad you two are okay."

The waiter brought over a mezze plate with olives, taramosalata, pita bread, and stuffed grape leaves. He returned to his table and his newspaper. It was on the early side, which Fina hoped accounted for the lack of diners.

"Enough about me," Fina said. "How are *you* doing?"

Risa sighed. "I'm fine. I'm supposed to have the next round of tests in a couple of days."

"That's why I wanted to talk to you," Fina said. "I saw Frank Gillis last night, and he told me about his trip to Rockford." Fina was conflicted about how much of Frank's report she should pass along. She'd decided to keep Greta's assertion that she was getting a stranger donation to herself. Other than upsetting Risa, there didn't seem much point in sharing the information.

Risa pulled an olive pit out of her mouth and deposited it on the plate. Somehow she made the gesture look dainty. "Okay."

"He made the trip with his wife, Peg."

Risa frowned. "I thought you weren't going to tell anyone but Frank."

"I don't consider Peg just anyone," Fina explained. "She's extremely discreet, and I knew that her presence would make their job easier. I made an executive decision on that."

Risa nodded. "Fine. Did it help? Having her there?"

"It did. People are generally less suspicious of women who ask questions, and an older couple is even better."

"No one expects them to be private investigators," Risa offered.

"Exactly."

"So what did they find out?"

"Keep in mind that none of this is set in stone. They were just fishing around for some gossip."

"You're stressing me out," Risa said as a Greek salad was set in front of her. Fina accepted a plate with a gyro and French fries. A thin trail of aromatic steam curled up from the sandwich.

"I'm sorry. I don't mean to," Fina said. "The gist is that they didn't find any suggestion that Greta or her sister ever made an effort to find you."

Risa picked up her fork and methodically cut a thick slice of cucumber in half. She didn't look at Fina.

"I'm sorry, Risa. I know that isn't what you wanted to hear."

"I'm not sure what I wanted to hear," Risa said, "if I'm being totally honest."

They ate in silence for a few minutes.

"Who did they talk to exactly?" Risa asked.

"Keep in mind that Rockford's pretty tiny," Fina said. "They started in the local diner and eventually hooked up with a real estate agent who showed them a few properties."

"Wow. They really put on a show."

"Sometimes it's the only way to get people to talk to you. They said they were old friends of your mother's."

"Was the agent familiar with her?"

Fina took a bite of gyro before answering. "Yes, and Greta. They didn't ask outright about Elizabeth's offspring, but there was no mention of blended families or that sort of thing. There was no sense that Greta or her family were interested in contacting you."

Risa speared a grape tomato. "So she just wants me for my kidney."

"I think we should do a little more digging before we decide that Greta is just in it for your organs."

Risa straightened the napkin on her lap. "Maybe it doesn't even matter."

"What do you mean?"

"Maybe she does just need my kidney, but maybe that's reason enough for me to give it to her."

"Uhh, that's not reason enough," Fina said.

"Why not? I have something that could save her life. Who am I to deny her that?"

"You're the owner of the kidney, that's who. You're not obligated to help someone at the expense of your health or your own family."

"No, but I should at least seriously consider it."

Fina swallowed some soda. "Clearly, you're a much better person than I am."

"Not necessarily." Risa fiddled with the straw in her drink. "I have my own reason for considering it."

"Which is?"

"Greta would have to be really cold to not want to know me once she's walking around with my kidney."

Fina raised an eyebrow. "So you want to guilt her into a relationship?"

"That's not how I would put it, but perhaps it would provide an added incentive."

"Why don't you throw in a cornea and a chunk of your liver? You two would be BFFs in a heartbeat."

Risa snorted.

"I think we should talk to Greta," Fina said. "Let's ask her if they ever tried to find you, and if not, why not?"

Risa put down her fork. Her face looked pinched. "But what makes you think she's going to tell the truth?"

"I have no expectation that she'll tell the truth," Fina admitted, "but we'll learn something, whatever she tells us."

"You think you'll be able to tell if she's lying?"

Fina bit into a chunk of feta. She held up a finger while she chewed.

"Probably," she said. "Regardless, she needs to make her case. The burden is on her, not you."

Risa sat for a moment, thinking. "Fine. When should we do it?" she asked.

"As soon as possible. I'll call her and try to set something up, but I think you should postpone your tests until after we've met with her."

"Where should we meet?"

"She is sick," Fina said, "so I don't want to make it impossible for her, but we probably shouldn't meet in Rockford if we want some privacy."

Risa sipped her drink. "Do you think Marty should be a part of the conversation?"

"What do you think?" Fina asked.

"Maybe not. I think he'd have a hard time listening and being objective. Not that I'll be objective, but I'd be worrying about him the whole time."

"Then he probably shouldn't join us," Fina said, "but I'll be there, and I'll steer the conversation. You know I don't have any problem asking tough questions."

"I know." Risa winced. "I almost feel a little sorry for Greta."

"Which is exactly why I'll be there," Fina said. "I'm sorry Greta is sick, but my concern is for you, not her."

"Thank you. I couldn't do this on my own."

They conferred about Risa's schedule and then moved on to other topics of conversation, including Haley. Fina didn't mention the proposed visit to Miami. Hopefully, she'd successfully derail that plan before anything came of it.

The waiter started to clear their plates, a process that took a considerable amount of time given his advanced age.

"I think this conversation warrants something really sweet and sinful," Fina said, ordering a slice of baklava for them to share.

"Sure, why not?"

Once the man had wandered off, Fina reached across the table and squeezed Risa's hand. "It's going to be okay. We're going to figure this out."

Risa nodded. "I know. I just never thought I'd be in this position."

A few minutes later, the old man deposited a gleaming, sticky piece of baklava in front of them. Fina picked up a fork and broke through the crunchy top layer of phyllo.

"There's nothing weirder in this world than family," she said, licking honey off her fork. "Or at least, that's been my experience."

A ccording to the desk sergeant at police headquarters, Cristian and Pitney were unavailable, but Fina was welcome to wait. She checked her e-mail and left a message for Hal while sitting on a straight-backed wooden bench across from the main desk. It was not a seating arrangement conducive to lingering, but Fina wasn't that easily dissuaded. As long as she could keep busy, she'd give them a half hour before giving up.

Sharing the bench with her was a young woman who had the curious combination of a young face with signs of age that suggested a hard life. Her skin—pocked with youthful acne—contrasted with the dark smudges under her eyes. Her hair was stringy and shoulder-length, a yellowish blond except for an inch of dark brown growth at her scalp. She'd parked a stroller next to the bench, and the toddler in it keened intermittently. The mom scolded him, which was highly effective, until he started up again thirty seconds later. Fina wondered who they were waiting for. The baby daddy, perhaps? A sibling or parent? They were all depressing options.

Cristian showed up a few minutes later with a laptop under his arm. Fina watched as the mother appraised him. He touched Fina's shoulder, and the young woman glanced at her. Her expression soured, but Fina couldn't tell if it was because Fina was consorting with the enemy or because the young woman deemed her unworthy of Cristian's attention.

"Sorry you had to wait," Cristian said, leading her upstairs to the squad room.

"Sorry I didn't call, but I thought I'd take a chance that you were in."

"How's the hand?"

"It's fine. Peg Gillis took a look at it this morning."

"How are Frank and Peg?" Cristian asked.

"They're good."

She followed him down a hallway, bypassing the interrogation rooms. Out of sight, a man was hollering, but nobody seemed to notice. Cristian directed her into one of the interview rooms that was used for victims' family members. The space was unthreatening with its couch, round table, and chairs. A bulletin board on the wall featured helpful posters about staying safe in the city and protecting your property. A couple of framed prints on the wall were clearly inspired by Monet. Fina wondered how Claude would feel about being the equivalent of the generic brand for the art world.

Fina sat down at the table, and Cristian took the chair next to her.

"Why didn't you tell me about that note?" he asked.

Fina shrugged. "What would you have done?"

He was silent.

"Exactly. There was nothing to do. You know I'm not shy about asking for favors, but there wasn't anything you could have done. I kept my eyes open after I got it."

He stared at her. "You were burned by an incendiary device."

Fina held up her hand. "Barely. I'm fine, and now you can help me. So, who tried to burn me to a crisp?" she asked.

Cristian grinned, despite his best efforts not to. "I don't know yet, but we're working on it. Your family isn't being helpful, by the way."

She widened her eyes. "Really? That doesn't sound like them at all."

"It's very frustrating," Cristian said.

"I hear ya. I'll see if I can get anything out of them," Fina said.

"I would appreciate it."

"I aim to please, Cristian. You know that."

He opened the laptop and tapped on a few buttons. "Here's what we have so far." The screen came to life, and he made the video player full-screen. "This is from one of the cameras in the parking garage."

"Did you check the tapes from Ludlow and Associates? I know we've got beefed-up security in the section we lease," Fina said.

"Yes, but there was nothing on them. I'm not surprised. The quality was good at least; your father springs for top-notch security."

"I think that's the nicest thing you've ever said about Carl." Fina moved her chair closer to him and adjusted the machine so she had a better view. Cristian hit the play button, and a grainy video started. It showed a segment of parking garage and the fleet SUV.

"Nothing happens for a while," he said, advancing the frames with his mouse. "Until . . . there."

He slowed the video down to real time so Fina could watch as a man entered the frame. He was wearing a baseball hat and a hoodie, which obscured his face. He kneeled down next to the car for a minute or so, then got back up and moved out of the frame toward the hood of the car. A minute later, he reappeared before walking away and not returning.

"Is it my imagination or was that guy really big?" she asked Cristian as he hit pause.

"That guy was really big," he agreed.

"Definitely over six feet, right?"

"We're guessing around six feet five inches."

"But not just tall," Fina said. "He also looks thick and broad, like he's carrying a lot of weight."

"Yup."

"Well, that narrows it down a little."

"It would if we had a registry by height and weight," Cristian said.

"Well, can't you search with those parameters?"

"Sure, but only if the guy's in the system."

"Hmm."

They watched the video a couple more times in silence.

"I think he's black. Do you agree?" Fina asked.

"Or possibly Hispanic."

Fina stared at the images. "I hate these useless security systems. What's the point?"

"To some extent, it's a deterrent."

"Not enough of one, obviously." Fina leaned toward the computer. "What's that?" She pointed at the area around one of his ankles.

"Part of his sock?" Cristian asked.

"An emblem or an insignia?"

He enlarged the image. "Can't tell. It could be a shadow or even dirt."

They were both studying the screen when Pitney walked into the room.

"Do you recognize him?" she asked Fina. She stood next to Fina's chair, her hands on her hips.

"No. There's not much to recognize beyond his size."

"Fina, what are we going to do about you and Gus Sibley?" Pitney asked.

"Is that a rhetorical question?" Fina asked.

Cristian shook his head and struggled to suppress a smile.

"Don't be a smart-ass," Pitney said.

"I'm not being a smart-ass. Has he contacted you about our most recent chat?"

Pitney folded her arms across her ample chest. She was wearing navy blue pants and a chevron-patterned turtleneck in shades of greens and purple. Fina wanted to look away, but couldn't, it was so hypnotizing.

"No," the lieutenant conceded.

"So what's the problem, Lieutenant? I know you find this hard to believe, but I don't purposefully defy you to make your job more difficult."

"I do find that hard to believe. I think you're playing out some parent-child issues."

"Well, of course I am, but not with you! I have Carl and Elaine for that." Fina sat back in her chair. "I think that Gus Sibley is hiding something, and he shouldn't be allowed to dictate if and how he's investigated just because he's rich and well known."

Pitney rolled her eyes. "Like your family doesn't play the rich and famous card all the time."

"Actually, I would argue that we're made an example of because we're rich and *infamous*, and most of our clients aren't rich and famous. At least not until we start working for them."

"Gus Sibley is not calling the shots," Pitney said. "We'll investigate him as much as we want to."

"Fine, and if he wants to sue me for harassment, he's welcome to," Fina said. "In the meantime, he's got us going around in circles instead of going after him. By the way—where was he the night that Liz was attacked?"

Pitney sighed.

"He was at home with his wife," Cristian said.

"Ah. An alibi from the one person who can't testify against him. That's awfully convenient."

"We're on top of it, Fina," Pitney insisted, "but you're wasting my time when I'm hauled into my captain's office and he chews me out because a citizen is complaining."

Fina held her hands up in a motion of surrender. "I get that, and I'm sorry, but I'm not going to stop doing my job because Gus or your boss doesn't like it."

Pitney stared at her. Cristian's gaze bounced between the two women.

"Do not piss him off unnecessarily," Pitney finally said.

Fina started to protest, but the lieutenant cut her off. "And don't pretend that you don't do that, because you do. Do your job, but try not to be a pain in the ass, at least not any more than usual."

"Fine. I will do my best to behave."

Pitney snorted.

Fina rose from her seat and started out the door. "Thanks for sharing the video with me. I'll see if I can get some info from Scotty."

"That would be a refreshing change," Pitney said.

"I look forward to seeing you guys at the funeral," Fina said.

She returned to her car and contemplated the video. Fina didn't recognize the man on the tape, and although she was happy it was a lead, she didn't find it particularly reassuring.

She was being followed by the Jolly Green Giant.

Her presence was requested at a family dinner, which was enough for Fina to lose her appetite. She had no interest in attending, but knew she would be the topic of conversation either way. A more mature person might have recognized the futility of showing up—Elaine and Carl, in particular, would think what they wanted to think—but Fina still clung to the idea that defending herself wasn't completely without merit.

Tonight's dinner was being hosted by Patty, and Fina always got a small thrill watching her mother be relegated to second-in-command. Patty gave Elaine tasks to do and let her do things her way, but it was clear that it was Patty's house, not Elaine's.

The two women were in the kitchen prepping dinner when Fina arrived. Her nephews were playing a game on the Xbox, and Haley was on the couch, flipping through a magazine.

"Where's everyone else?" Fina asked.

"Scotty is upstairs getting changed. Your dad and Matthew should be here any minute," Patty said, tending to a couple of large steaks under the broiler.

"Hi, Mom," Fina said. She pulled a diet soda from the refrigerator. "Anything I can do to help?" she asked Patty.

"I don't think so. Not unless Mom needs help with the salad," Patty said. Fina never got used to hearing Patty refer to Elaine as "Mom." Why would she claim the woman as her own if she wasn't legally obligated to do so?

"No," Elaine said. "You got here the moment I finished."

"Well, I didn't time it that way," Fina said.

Elaine didn't respond.

Haley wandered over to Fina and took hold of her arm. "Are you okay?"

"I'm fine." Fina rotated her wrist for her niece's inspection. "Just a minor burn."

"I wouldn't call that minor," Elaine muttered under her breath.

"She's talking about her arm, Gammy," Haley clarified.

"Right," Fina said. Her pulse quickened. "I wasn't talking about the fire."

Patty put the broiler pan on the stovetop with a bit more force than seemed necessary. Fina looked at her, but Patty avoided her gaze.

"Haley, have you shown Gammy that new outfit you got?" Fina asked.

Her niece looked perplexed. "Which outfit?"

"I thought you got a new dress that you wanted to show her." Fina gave her an imploring look. "Why don't you show her, and I'll finish helping Aunt Patty."

A glimmer of understanding crossed Haley's face. "Come on, Gammy. I have some stuff to show you in my room."

Elaine followed her granddaughter out of the kitchen, and Fina walked around the island toward Patty.

"Do you want to talk about it?" Fina asked. The boys were engrossed in their game across the room.

Patty took off her oven mitts and leaned her hip against the counter. "I can't deal with something happening to him, Fina."

"I know."

"Do you?" Patty asked. "I know we all laugh about the scrapes you get into, but it's different when Scotty's at risk, too."

"We don't know for sure that I was the target," Fina said, defensiveness creeping into her voice.

"Oh, come on, Fina."

"We don't! You guys are all acting like Scotty works for the Dalai Lama. He defends and sues all kinds of creeps."

"But they're not violent!" Patty insisted.

Fina stared at her. "The whole reason Dad had me go with him yesterday was because he was afraid of it getting violent! He wanted me to provide protection for Scotty's mafioso girlfriend client."

Patty transferred one of the steaks to a cutting board and pulled out an electric carving knife from a drawer.

"The last thing I want to do is put anyone else in danger," Fina said, "but I'm tired of this collective fantasy that I'm the only one involved with people of questionable character. We all work for the same firm."

Patty cut into the meat. The knife made a soft whirring sound as red juices flowed from the flesh.

"But Scotty said that your current case isn't for the firm," Patty said.

"No, but all the other times I've been hurt—when I've been run off the road, when I was jumped in my garage—those were Ludlow and Associates cases. I may be on the front lines, but Dad and Scotty and Matthew are right behind me."

"I just couldn't deal if something happened to him," Patty repeated.

Fina took a deep breath. "I understand that, and I'm sorry if he was in danger because of me."

Patty cleaved a strip of fat from the steak. "It just really freaked me out. I'm used to this stuff happening to you, and I know you can handle it, but Scotty isn't you."

"No, he's not, and I know that it was scary for him, and it was scary for you to hear about it." Fina wanted to say that it was scary for her, too, but nobody wanted to hear that. "But he's fine, and I'm fine. I spoke with Cristian and Lieutenant Pitney this afternoon, and there's a lead they're following."

"That's good," Patty said, covering the platter of meat with aluminum foil before handing Fina the bowl of salad. "Can you put this on the table?"

There was a large dining table off to the side of the room, which had been set with placemats and cutlery. Fina put the salad on the table as Scotty came into the room.

"Hey, Sis."

"Hey. Has your heart returned to its resting rate?" Fina asked.

"Barely," Scotty said.

"I talked to the cops this afternoon. They said you weren't giving them much to go on."

He shook his head. "I'm not going to just open up the files to them."

"I know. Can I look at them and see if anything looks hinky?"

"No," Scotty said. "You can't."

"Well, then, can *you* look at them in a more timely fashion?" Fina asked.

"I'm doing what I can," he said. "There are a lot of files, and I've got active cases I'm working on."

"Fine, but we may not figure out who's responsible until we dig into them."

"I don't know what you want me to do," Scotty said.

"Where are Dad and Matthew?" Patty asked, perhaps hoping to sidetrack the conversation.

"They should be here any minute," Scotty said, reaching into the refrigerator for a beer.

Elaine came back into the kitchen a moment later. Patty looked behind her. "Where's Haley? It's time to eat."

"She's having a teenage moment," Elaine said. She plopped down on the couch and folded her arms across her chest. Someone was having a teenage moment, that's for sure.

"What do you mean?" Patty asked.

"She was showing me some clothes, and I pointed out some things she should take to Florida, and she got upset."

"You told her about Florida?" Fina asked.

"Of course," Elaine said. "What did you think? I was going to put her on the plane blindfolded?"

Fina pressed her hands into the kitchen counter. "Mom, Haley doesn't want to visit Rand, and she doesn't have to if she doesn't want to."

"You're not her guardian, Fina. You don't make those decisions for her."

"Nor do you, unless I'm mistaken." Fina and Elaine looked at Scotty.

He held his cold beer bottle up to his forehead. "Can we not talk about this now? Not with the kids around?"

"Sure, 'cause there's nothing to talk about," Fina said. She started toward the kitchen door.

"Where are you going?" her mother asked. "It's dinnertime."

"I'm going to check on Haley."

She was in the front hall at the bottom of the stairs when Matthew and Carl came in the door. Fina started to climb the stairs, making no attempt to hide her anger.

"Oh no," Matthew said, shedding his coat. "I don't like that look."

"What now?" Carl asked.

"Mom announced to Haley that she has to visit Rand in Miami, and not surprisingly, Haley's upset." Fina didn't wait for him to respond. She continued on to Haley's room and knocked softly on the door.

"It's Aunt Fina," she said when her knock went unanswered.

"Come in."

Haley was curled up on her bed, plugged into earbuds. Her cheeks were wet, and her eyes red.

Fina took a seat next to her and gestured for Haley to pull out the earphones. "Hale, whatever Gammy said, ignore her."

"She said I have to visit Dad."

"You don't. I promise," Fina assured her.

Haley pulled at a string that was unraveling from the seam of her comforter. She wound it around her finger, trapping blood in the tip.

"Does she know about him?" she asked Fina.

Fina took a deep breath. "No. Do you want her to?"

"No!"

"I didn't think so."

"But if she doesn't know, she's going to make me see him."

Fina wished that were true, but she knew better. Even if Elaine knew the truth about Rand, her denial had no bounds, and she would believe whatever she wanted to. Ignorance or knowledge were beside the point.

"No, she can't make you do anything, regardless of what you do or don't tell her."

"You're sure?"

"I'm sure," Fina said, pushing a lock of hair away from Haley's face. "Do you feel up for dinner or do you want to hang out up here?"

"Are you going to stay? Now you and Gammy are mad at each other."

"We're usually mad at each other, so don't worry about that. I'm definitely staying." Fina wanted to flee the house and never speak to her mother again, but that wasn't very mature. And she wasn't going to leave Haley to fend for herself.

"Okay, but I don't want to talk about this stuff at dinner," Haley said.

"Of course not. Everyone will be too busy blaming me for the car fire."

Haley sat up and brushed the tears from her face. "True. That makes me feel better."

"Then it's worth it," Fina said.

Haley reached out and gently patted Fina's injured arm before climbing off the bed and heading for the door.

19.

Fina didn't really need to keep the bandage on her arm the next day, but decided it might be a useful prop at Liz's funeral. Visible injuries were conversation starters, and if the person responsible for the incendiary device was present, he or she might show some reaction to her wounds.

After showering, she added some extra gauze for good measure before pulling on a black dress, black tights and boots, and a jacket with a subtle pattern in shades of gray. Fina pulled her hair back into a low bun and lined her upper lids with a dark brown eyeliner. She dusted blush on her cheeks and rolled pale pink lipstick onto her lips. She wolfed down a Pop-Tart over the kitchen sink, then made her way down to her car. She'd been jumped in the garage during an earlier case and still didn't feel carefree when navigating her own building. In some respects this was a good thing—given her line of work, she should be attentive to her surroundings—but it was also discouraging to think she might not be safe in her own home.

At a large Presbyterian church in West Roxbury, Fina parked her car and dashed to the entrance. It was freezing, and she was dressed for the occasion, not the weather. Inside, an usher handed her a program featuring a smiling picture of Liz. An organist was playing, and the front of the church was adorned with muted flower arrangements. Fina scanned the crowd and found Cristian sitting by himself in a pew two-thirds of the way back.

"Hey," she said when she reached his row.

"Hey."

It was early, and there was only a smattering of other people seated.

"Can I sit with you?" Fina asked.

"You want to be seen with the cops?"

"I think as far as the murderer is concerned, we're on the same side. I realize your boss may not share that view."

Cristian slid over on the bench, and Fina sat down next to him. The program was rolled up in his hand.

"You look nice," he told her.

"Thanks. So do you."

He was wearing a dark suit and tie. Cristian was handsome under any circumstances, but he was one of those men who was downright dashing in a well-cut suit.

"You don't happen to have any water, do you?" she asked, digging around in her purse.

"You're in luck." He reached underneath the pew and produced a half-empty bottle, which he handed to her. Fina tossed a couple of aspirin into her mouth and washed them down with a swig.

"What's wrong?" Cristian asked.

"Nothing. I've had a headache since last night."

He looked at her, waiting for her to elaborate.

"I had dinner with the family, and it was actually physically painful."

"More so than usual?" he asked.

"Yes, actually. Everyone seems convinced that the car fire was my fault, and Rand has a new girlfriend in Miami and wants Haley to visit."

Cristian raised an eyebrow. Unlike Elaine, he knew about Rand's crimes against his daughter.

"I was trying to kill the whole idea before Haley even heard about it," Fina said, "but then big-mouth Elaine told her, and now Haley's freaked out."

"*I'm* getting a headache," Cristian said. A few people came down the aisle and took seats near the front of the church.

"Exactly."

"So what are you going to do about it?"

"She's not going to Miami, and don't even get me started on the new girlfriend thing."

"Who would find Rand attractive?" Cristian mused.

Fina looked at him. "Cristian, he's rich and handsome and a seemingly successful lawyer. I think a lot of women would find him attractive. He doesn't wear a scarlet *P* after all. Life would be easier if he did."

"That's what the sex offender registry is for," he said.

"You and I both know that's mostly for strangers who are predators, not the pedophiles on the family tree."

He squeezed her hand. "Sorry you have to deal with this."

"Me too."

"Sorry to interrupt your chat, but you should probably move." Lieutenant Pitney stood at the entrance of the pew, staring at Fina. "I'd like a little distance."

Fina stood and moved into the aisle. "I don't suppose we want Gus Sibley to see us being buddy-buddy."

Pitney sat down next to Cristian.

"You look very nice, Lieutenant," Fina said, eyeing her outfit. The somber occasion had prompted Pitney to dial down her usual level of clothing exuberance. She was wearing a navy pantsuit with a royal blue fitted top. It was a stretch for funeral wear, but Fina appreciated her attempt to blend in.

"I think it's terrible," Pitney said. "So boring, but I wanted to be respectful of the dead."

And everyone's eyeballs, Fina thought.

"All righty then," Fina said. "I'll catch up with you two later."

She walked forward a few rows and took a seat in the same pew as an older couple. Fina imagined they were friends of Bobbi's. The steady stream of arriving mourners ran the age gamut, and Fina alternated between checking them out and perusing the program.

The program was printed on cream-colored card stock and included a schedule of services and pictures of Liz. Some of the shots showed her as a young woman and college student—both alone and with Tasha, Kelly, and their soccer teammates. Other pictures were of Liz and Jamie and the kids, the ages of the kids highlighting Liz's relative youth. Everyone complained about getting older, but few would opt for the alternative.

The church was filling up, and Fina saw a couple of familiar faces. Dana Tompkins, the lab postdoc, was there, and heads turned when Tasha and D walked down the aisle toward the altar. They were an extremely attractive couple; people probably noticed whenever they walked into a room. Fina was checking her watch, antsy for the service to begin, when Gus Sibley took a seat a couple of rows in front of her.

The organ stopped for a brief interlude during which the only sounds in the church were rustling programs, whispers, and the occasional cough. Fina turned to see Liz's family milling around at the back of the church. Jamie was standing near the front door, wearing sunglasses, his daughter gripping his hand. Bobbi stood with two women who Fina assumed were Liz's sisters. Liz's son held on to Bobbi. The music started up again a few minutes later, prompting Jamie to straighten his tie and tuck his sunglasses into his pocket. The family proceeded to the front of the church, their faces a combination of sadness and confusion.

Fina took a deep breath.

A car fire was nothing compared to this.

People always talk about funeral services being "lovely," but Fina didn't understand what that meant. That the deceased was remembered fondly? One would hope that would be the case. That the readings and music were pleasing? She found it hard to focus on those elements with bereaved family members in attendance.

She supposed that Liz's funeral was lovely, but was still relieved when it was over. Fina followed the flow of mourners out to their cars while the immediate family continued on to the cemetery for the interment. The guests were told to meet for a reception at the local community center.

Fina drove the five minutes to the center and was directed into a parking space by a young man in a dark suit. Inside the building, she was sent down a hallway to a function room that probably hosted everything from funerals to parties to Mommy and Me classes. Tables were pushed to the side of the room, laden with food and drink. Flower arrangements flanked a smaller table that held framed photos of Liz and her family. Fina scoured the crowd for a familiar face and saw Kelly emerging from a set of swinging doors, carrying a tray of little sandwiches.

"Kelly," Fina said, meeting her at the refreshments.

"Hi, Fina."

"How are you holding up?"

Kelly brushed her hair back from her eyes. She was wearing a black skirt suit that could have been an interview suit in another life. Fina couldn't help but notice that the attire for funerals and corporate America were interchangeable.

"I'm okay," Kelly said.

"I didn't see you at the service," Fina noted.

"I offered to take care of things here. The last thing Jamie or Bobbi needed was to be worrying about this." She gestured toward the food.

"That was nice of you."

"I'm just trying to help out. Speaking of which, I should check on some things."

"Of course. Take care."

Kelly left, and Fina got a cup of punch before wandering over to the table of photographs. A few of them had been featured in the program, but others were unfamiliar. Fina examined them while keeping an eye on the rest of the room. Cristian and Pitney were speaking to an older couple she didn't know, and Gus Sibley was deep in conversation with a couple of younger men. Tasha and D walked in her direction from the bar area, each with a plastic cup in hand.

"How are you two?" Fina asked, meeting them halfway. The three of them drifted over to a bank of windows overlooking the woods.

"We're okay," Tasha said, "given the circumstances."

"I just saw Kelly," Fina said.

Tasha looked around. "I haven't seen her."

"She organized this; she's been in and out."

Tasha made a face, but Fina couldn't identify it. Amusement? Irritation?

"What?" Fina asked.

"I'm just not surprised that she organized it. She's big on organizing stuff."

"Well, I suppose somebody had to do it," Fina said.

"It's probably a big help to Jamie," D commented.

"I know," Tasha said. "I don't mean to downplay her support."

"Were the three of you close in college?" Fina asked, sipping her punch.

"Liz and me and Kelly?" Tasha asked.

"Yeah."

"We were. Liz and I lived in the same dorm, so that made our relationship a little bit different, but we were all friends."

There was a murmur near the door as Bobbi, Jamie, and the rest of the family came into the room. They didn't make much progress before well-wishers approached them to offer hugs and words of condolence.

"I can't imagine losing my wife," D commented, watching someone embrace Jamie.

"Good," Tasha said, and gave him a smile.

"And with little kids to raise? I guess maybe that helps you get through the day, knowing you have to take care of them," he said.

"Jamie's going to need help, that's for sure," Tasha said. "He looks exhausted."

Fina watched him. He looked disengaged, but he was probably just trying to hold it together. "Bobbi told me the other day that his knee's been acting up," Fina said.

Tasha nodded. "I did the same thing to mine a few years out of college. It still bothers me once in a while."

"His injury's a little different," D said, sipping his drink. "You tore your meniscus, but he fractured his knee."

Fina looked at D, surprised at his familiarity with Jamie's injury.

"I checked it out for him when he wiped out," D explained, sensing the question on her face.

"Ah. It's always good having a doctor for a friend."

"It is, if you don't mind people wanting free consults all the time," Tasha said, rolling her eyes.

"It's not that bad," D insisted. "If I can take a quick look and save someone a trip to the ER, I'm happy to do it."

"So you were able to fix him up?" Fina asked.

"I took a look, but he needed to see an orthopedist. There's only so much I can do in our living room, particularly when it's not my specialty."

"I wonder who he saw," Fina mused.

"I assume he saw Gus Sibley, or someone at his practice. Speaking of injuries," D said, gesturing to her hand, "what happened to you?"

"I was in that car fire on the Tobin the other day. I'm fine."

"You live quite an exciting life, Fina," Tasha said, with perhaps a touch of disapproval.

Fina smiled. "Not really. Do *you* know if Jamie saw Gus for his knee?" Fina looked at Tasha, who held up her hands.

"I have no idea who he saw," Tasha said. "Does it matter?"

"Nope," Fina said. "Just curious."

Tasha gave her a sidelong look, but Fina ignored it. There was no blueprint for an investigation, and Fina had learned that being curious was her best guide.

Fina spent another forty-five minutes making small talk with other mourners in the hopes of uncovering some nugget of information that would blow the case wide open. Instead, she heard stories of Liz's childhood and descriptions of the associations that linked the attendees to the Barone family.

Now she stood listening to an elderly gentleman give her a blow-by-blow description of his knee replacement. Fina did her best to nod and murmur in the appropriate spots, but her attention was drawn across the room to where Jamie and Gus were standing a few feet apart, steadfastly ignoring each other. Although both were speaking to other people, their body language betrayed their true intentions. Rather than coexisting in the same space casually, they stood stiffly, angled away from each other. Fina had seen it before and had practiced this kind of body language herself, especially if Elaine was nearby.

Jamie's conversation wrapped up, and he stole a glance at Gus. A woman spoke to Jamie, but he brushed her off and, giving Gus a wide berth, made his way out of the room.

The old man was threatening to roll up his pant leg and give Fina a gander at his new knee, but she had better things to do. She wished him luck with his orthopedic endeavors and set her empty plastic cup on a table, then left through the same door Jamie had.

The hallway was empty, so Fina retraced her steps to the entry of the community center, but its only occupants were a few preschoolers dragging backpacks across the tiled floor. She popped outside and thought she caught a flash of him turning the corner of the building.

When Fina caught up with him a minute later, he was hunched over a cigarette, trying to strike a match in the stiff, frigid wind.

"Here," Fina said, standing in front of him and cupping her hands above his.

Jamie touched the flame to the end of the cigarette and inhaled deeply. Taking a step toward the building, he pulled his sunglasses out of his jacket with his free hand and placed them on his face.

Fina fished her gloves out of her pockets and pulled them on. "I don't know how people deal in places where it's really cold," she commented, "like Alaska."

Jamie held out the package of cigarettes in her direction. "Want one?"

She shook her head.

"It's my wife's funeral," Jamie said after a minute of silence. "I'm thirty-eight, and it's my wife's funeral. There's something seriously wrong with that."

"I agree." Fina kicked at a small hillock of ice. "Anyone you're surprised to see here today? Or not, for that matter?"

"What do you mean?" He tapped loose ash onto the ground.

"Just that. Is there anyone that you thought would show up who hasn't?"

He shook his head. "No."

"Anyone you weren't expecting?"

"What? Like her attacker?"

Fina shrugged. "It's more common than you might think."

"Like arsonists who return to the scene?"

"Essentially."

Jamie inhaled again and held the smoke in his lungs for a moment before exhaling. "Nope. I haven't noticed either way."

Fina nodded. She wasn't going to ask him about Gus. It would be easy for him to shrug it off or claim she was mistaken about them purposely ignoring each other. She was going to hold on to that little tidbit for the time being.

"I'm going to say good-bye to Bobbi," Fina said, backing away from him.

Jamie made an approximation of a wave and turned his focus to his cigarette.

Inside, Fina sought out Bobbi and they exchanged a tight hug. The grief and exhaustion etched on Bobbi's face were just the impetus Fina needed to get back to work.

Is this supposed to be symbolic, Pamela? Meeting the day of Liz Barone's funeral?" Kevin slid onto a bar stool next to her. They were at a restaurant and bar near his office, just before the lunch hour.

"No. There's nothing symbolic about it." She took a long drink from the tumbler in her hand.

"Are you drinking at this hour? You need to calm down and stop worrying."

"It's club soda, Kevin. Don't be a moron."

He made a face of mock offense and gestured to the bartender. Kevin ordered a soda, and his attention drifted to the TV over the bar. A basketball game was on. It took him a few seconds to identify the teams and would only take a minute more for him to become thoroughly engrossed.

"Focus, Kevin," Pamela said, tapping the bar in front of him. The bartender put a tall glass down. Some tiny bubbles leapt off the surface, but Kevin was willing to bet it would taste flat and slightly metallic.

"What's the emergency?" he asked, taking a sip that confirmed his suspicions.

"I spoke with Fina Ludlow a few days ago. She's not going to stop nosing around."

"She'll stop eventually."

"I want her to stop now," Pamela said, nudging her empty glass away.

Kevin shrugged, feeling irritated. "No one cares about minor transgressions when there are more serious matters at hand."

"So you say."

"What do you want me to do? We've already had this conversation. Stop worrying and just do your job."

"Right." Pamela reached into her bag and pulled out some cash.

"That's it? You dragged me out of my office for this?"

She stopped and looked at him. "How's your girlfriend, Kevin?"

"I don't have a girlfriend, and idle gossip is beneath you, Pamela."

"I just want to make sure that you understand the seriousness of the situation," she said.

"Oh, I understand, but it seems to me that you're causing more problems by freaking out."

"I am not freaking out."

Kevin leaned toward her and lowered his voice. "Then calm down, for Christ's sake."

She exhaled loudly. "Just remember that you have something to lose, too. It's not just me."

He glared at her. "That sounds like a threat."

"Of course it's not a threat. Don't be so touchy." Pamela slid off the high stool and picked up her coat and bag. "I thought you were good at getting your way and fixing things. I'm not seeing much evidence of that."

Kevin watched as she crossed the room.

That woman could be such a cow.

20.

Fina stopped by a drive-thru and got a burger and fries to take home. There had been finger food at the reception, but she'd been too focused on the guests to make a dent in her hunger.

Once home, she kicked off her heels and padded into the living room. She grabbed a diet soda from the fridge—carbonated drinks from a fountain machine were a crime against humanity—and unwrapped the food on the coffee table. It felt good to sit back and ingest some calories.

As she chewed, Fina replayed the funeral in her mind. There hadn't been any earth-shattering revelations, but there were morsels here and there that warranted a second look. Not that deep reflection was at the top of her list at the moment; she was due a nap.

Fina was heading to the bedroom to change when there was a knock at her door. When she'd first moved into Nanny's, she'd provided the concierge with a list of visitors who should always be granted access, including her brothers, Cristian, Milloy, Frank, Patty, and Risa. She'd also added Hal and Emma to the list given their frequent visits, so she wasn't surprised to see Hal on the other side of the peephole.

She opened the door and ushered him inside. "Hey, Hal."

"Is this a bad time?" he asked. "I thought I'd take a chance and see if you were in."

"This is a good time."

He followed her into the living room, Fina gazing longingly in the direction of the bedroom. Alas, her nap was not to be.

"You look so nice, Fina," Hal said, placing a computer bag on the floor and struggling out of his parka. "I'm not used to seeing you so dressed up."

"I had to go to a funeral. Have a seat." She wandered into the kitchen and returned a minute later with a glass of ice water, which she handed to him. Given his corpulent nature and perpetual signs of exertion, Fina was always a tad worried Hal would keel over in her home. Not that a glass of water would stave off the inevitable, but it seemed like a good first step.

"Thanks," Hal said, taking a long drink. "Was it Liz Barone's funeral?"

"It was," Fina said. "No one likes funerals, but there's something about little kids at their parent's funeral that's particularly depressing."

Hal shook his head. "I can't imagine if I died or my ex did. Sarah would be devastated."

"Don't even contemplate it," Fina said. "I mean, contemplate it to the extent that you have your affairs in order, but then put it out of your mind." Fina was well acquainted with estate planning; the Ludlow men might have been personal injury lawyers, but they acted like estate attorneys in their insistence of "having your affairs in order." But they were also greedy control freaks, which might explain their diligence in that area.

"Don't worry," Hal said. "I'm very careful about that sort of thing."

"Good." Fina raised herself off the couch and tucked her feet underneath her. Hal averted his gaze, as if not wanting to catch her in a compromising position. "So do you have info about Liz?" Fina asked.

"What happened to your hand?" Hal asked.

Fina looked at the gauze. "Just a minor mishap."

"You wouldn't have it bandaged if it were minor," Hal said seriously.

"You worry too much," Fina insisted. "It's really okay."

Hal was one of the few people in her life who seemed genuinely distressed by the injuries she sustained. If she told him about the car fire, he'd probably get worked up and have trouble focusing. It was a story for another day.

"So, Liz?"

He glanced at her hand before continuing. "Right. Liz. A couple of things. First of all, I haven't found any signs that she was having an affair, at least none of the telltale ones."

"Like what? Hotel receipts, fancy restaurants?" Fina asked.

"Right. Victoria's Secret."

"I know people do that, but it's such a cliché."

"Most clichés have some truth to them," Hal said. "Both men and women rack up those bills. Hundreds of dollars' worth sometimes."

Fina always thought that if novelty was your goal, you should buy new lingerie and model it for your current partner rather than finding a new partner. Granted, it wasn't as exciting an option, but it was less expensive in the long run.

"So her expenses were pretty routine," Fina said.

"Yes, and you know, I always say that it's about the patterns." Hal sipped his water.

"If the patterns change, that's a red flag, but everybody has their own weird bugaboos when it comes to money."

"Exactly. I don't understand women who spend thousands of dollars on shoes, but that's beside the point. It's only noteworthy if that spending habit changes over time. Does she stop buying shoes? Does she buy even more or from a new place?"

"So Liz's patterns hadn't changed recently?" Fina asked.

"No. She was very consistent."

"What about her husband, Jamie?"

"He's consistent, too, but I did find one thing that piqued my curiosity."

"Oh, goody." Fina pulled Nanny's afghan over her legs, as if settling in for a juicy story.

"Starting a few months ago, Jamie started withdrawing cash from a particular ATM in Central Square."

"Okay."

"So that's a change in the pattern. Normally, he only took money out near their house or his office."

"Neither of which is near Central Square," Fina said.

"Correct, and the withdrawals have become more frequent over time."

"How much is he taking out?"

"Initially it was a hundred dollars a pop, but more recently, up to three hundred," Hal said.

"Did you find any receipts from purchases in the area? Any credit card charges?"

"The occasional purchase at CVS."

"So the only thing that shows up in that neighborhood is the withdrawals and those small purchases?" Fina asked.

"That's right."

"When did this start?"

Hal reached into his computer bag and pulled out a slim laptop. He flipped open the top and tapped on some keys. "Mid-October. I can send you the exact dates."

"Thanks. That would be helpful." Fina thought about it for a moment. "Did you find any signs of significant debt?"

"No. They have a big mortgage, but so does everyone these days. No student loans."

"Liz went to NEU on at least a partial soccer scholarship, so I'm not surprised by that," Fina said.

"They did recently upgrade their insurance," Hal noted.

"Life insurance?"

"And disability and long-term care."

"That could just be good planning," Fina said. "Liz, at least, was planning for a less than rosy future."

"Her husband, of course, is the main beneficiary of her life insurance. Five hundred thousand is nothing to sneeze at."

"But is it enough to kill someone for?" Fina asked. "Half a million doesn't get you very far these days."

"That's a sad commentary, but maybe true. It depends how high off the hog you live, and I don't get the sense that either Liz or Jamie had expensive tastes. Five hundred thousand could certainly make life easier," Hal said. His fingers flew over the keyboard. "I just sent you my report. Read and destroy, as always." He tucked his computer back into his bag.

"Of course. I never hang on to anything that I don't want the cops to read."

Hal shuddered. "God forbid." He placed his nearly empty glass on the coffee table and struggled to a standing position. Fina handed him his coat and walked him to the door.

"Don't be a stranger, Hal," she said.

"Always a pleasure, Fina."

She watched him walk to the elevator before closing her door and taking a seat in front of her computer at the dining room table. Hal's e-mail was sitting in her inbox. She clicked it open and perused the details they had just discussed, not learning anything new.

Unfortunately, it was too late to nap; by the time she woke up, Fina would want to get ready for bed, so she decided to do a little work and touch base with Milloy instead. She left him a message wondering if he was available for dinner, then dialed Cristian.

"Menendez."

"Hey," Fina said.

"I'm guessing you want something from me," Cristian said. Fina could hear a child in the background and a singsong sound track that would garner better results than waterboarding.

"Is that Matteo?" she asked.

"Yes."

"What's that awful music?"

"It's one of his train videos," Cristian said.

"Sounds horrible."

"I don't even notice."

"Parental deafness," Fina said. "I've heard it's a vital skill."

"We were talking about what you want."

"Right. Could you send me a copy of the videotape from the parking garage?" Fina asked.

"Not necessarily."

"Well, then, how about some still photos of the guy?"

"Maybe," Cristian said. "You're going to try to identify him?"

"That's the plan."

"We're working on it, you know."

"I'm not questioning your competency, Cristian, just the allocation of resources. I'm guessing that Liz's murder and my car situation are not the only things you have to solve."

"That's true."

"So let me help."

"I'll see what I can do."

"Thank you. See how painless that was?"

He snorted.

"I'll talk to you soon then," Fina said.

"Do you want to have dinner one of these nights?" Cristian said in a rush before she could hang up.

"Sure," Fina responded, a slight question mark in her voice.

"You're right; we haven't seen much of each other outside of work," he said. "I thought we should remedy that."

"I'd love that, but there's a reason we haven't seen each other, and that reason is named Cindy."

There was a long pause. "Yeah, she's not really a reason anymore," he said.

"You broke up?"

"Something like that."

"I'm sorry, Cristian. I thought things were going well."

"They were. It's just . . ." He trailed off.

"Dinner would be nice," Fina said, no more anxious than he was to do a postmortem on his relationship. "Just let me know when, and I look forward to getting that videotape and maybe the inventory from the crime scene at Liz's house."

"Photos, wisenheimer, and I didn't make any promises."

"You never do," she said, hanging up.

She sat on the couch, pondering the turn of events. She wanted Cristian to be happy, but she was glad to hear that Cindy the speech pathologist wasn't the woman of his dreams. Before she could contemplate it further, Fina's phone rang, and she hatched a dinner plan with Milloy. He'd be over in about an hour, which gave her time for one more call.

Fina scrolled through the numbers on her phone and pressed the button for Greta Samuels. She was on the brink of hanging up when Risa's aunt answered.

"Hello?" Greta always answered the phone with a question instead of a declaration of greeting.

"Greta? It's Fina Ludlow, Risa's friend."

"I'm sorry, who?"

"Fina Ludlow. Risa's friend." Unlike Risa, Fina had met Greta in person. Their brief interaction had been contentious, leaving neither woman with warm, fuzzy feelings. Fina's ire had only grown since hearing about Greta's claim that her kidney donor was a selfless stranger. She considered asking her about it, but really, what was the point?

"How are things with you?" Fina asked.

"Not very good."

"I'm sorry to hear that."

Greta sniffed, and Fina rolled her eyes.

"Risa would like to meet with you," Fina said.

"I thought she didn't want to meet me." Greta sounded hopeful, but skeptical.

"She wasn't ready to, but now she is."

"That would be wonderful."

"Good. I know travel isn't easy for you, but I'm wondering if you could meet us someplace other than Rockford."

There was a pause. "Us?"

"Yes, I would be joining you," Fina said.

"You mean you're going to drive her to the meeting?" Greta asked.

"And join you as you get acquainted."

"My health is a family matter, Fina," she said. "It's really not your business."

Fina rubbed her temple, feeling a headache coming on.

"Here's the thing, Greta. Risa is practically part of my family, and she's asked me to participate. Secondly, you're not in a position to dictate terms."

"You make it sound like a business meeting," Greta said disparagingly.

"You may be biologically connected, but you and Risa don't actually know each other. For all intents and purposes, you're strangers, which does make this a business meeting of sorts."

"Fine. If that's how you want to do it."

"It's not how I want to do it," Fina clarified. "It's how Risa wants to do it."

"That's fine." Greta sounded annoyed, and Fina didn't give a shit. Organ beggars didn't get to be choosers.

"How about Tuesday? Do you have dialysis or are you available?" Fina asked.

"I'm available."

"Do you still have the same e-mail address?"

"Yes."

"Good. I'll send you the particulars and the location once I figure it out."

"How is Risa?" Greta asked before she could hang up.

"She's well." Fina didn't elaborate.

"And her tests are going okay?"

"As far as I know, the tests are going okay."

"Well, that's good," Greta said.

"Good night." Fina hung up and scowled at the phone.

She hadn't walked in Greta's shoes—didn't know what it was like to need something so desperately that only one person could provide—but regardless, the woman rubbed her the wrong way. Risa had her own family, and Greta never asked after them or seemed curious about things that weren't directly connected to her own experience. Maybe her circumstances created blinders, or maybe Greta just didn't care about her niece.

21.

Fina woke the next day feeling rested and ready to pound the pavement. Dinner with Milloy had banished any lingering annoyance with Greta Samuels, and she'd slept well. Fina wondered if the funeral having come and gone also contributed to her good mood. Even though she hadn't known Liz personally, the anticipation of her death and burial had cast a certain pall over Fina's days. Liz's life was officially over, but Fina felt like her investigation was just getting started.

Cristian had relented and sent her stills from the surveillance photos and even thrown in a copy of the crime scene inventory. Fina reviewed the list, but nothing struck her as unusual. The items the police found in Liz's kitchen were exactly what you'd expect to find: mail, bills, a sweatshirt, a pair of kid's soccer cleats, an empty laundry basket, and the typical eating and cooking detritus. Fina tucked the information away for the time being.

Her enthusiasm about the case waned when she retrieved a message from her father. Fina had learned at a young age that it was best to suck it up and deal with Carl head-on. Avoiding him was a fruitless endeavor, so you might as well just call him back—sooner rather than later.

"I'm working on it if you're calling about the car fire," she told him.

"Good, but that's not why I'm calling."

"Oh! Are you just calling to wish me a good morning? Perhaps inquire after my health and well-being?"

"Are you on something, Josefina?" he asked. "You sound high."

Fina sighed. "If only. What's up, Dad?"

"I want to meet with Bobbi Barone as soon as possible."

"For any particular reason?"

"Yes. I want in on this lawsuit. Do I need to remind you that's the whole reason you're working this case?"

"To fill your coffers and get justice for Liz—in that order. No, you don't need to remind me," she said.

"Just set it up. It's in her best interest to jettison the Podunk lawyer. The stronger she goes into this, the better off she'll be."

"I'll call her, Dad, but it's Saturday, and her daughter's funeral was yesterday. She may not want to talk to anyone."

"If that's the case, schedule it for Monday, but today would be preferable."

"Fine. I'll call her." Fina wanted to add that she couldn't make any promises, but that was the sort of statement that only annoyed Carl. He didn't want promises or excuses. He wanted action. *Stat.*

"Good. I have some time later this afternoon, or I can make time tonight. Talk to Shari."

"It would be my pleasure," Fina said, but he'd already hung up.

She called Bobbi and asked if she'd be willing to stop by the Ludlow and Associates offices later in the day. Fina wanted to update her on the case, and Carl was interested in discussing the lawsuit with her.

"I completely understand if the last thing you want to do today is discuss the lawsuit."

"It beats the alternative, which is lying in bed with the covers pulled over my head."

"I don't know," Fina said. "That seems like a reasonable response to recent events."

"If I crawl into bed," Bobbi said, "I may never crawl out. I need something to focus on, and the lawsuit seems like a good option."

"I want to be up front, Bobbi," Fina told her. "My father wants to represent you, but I'll still investigate Liz's death regardless of your legal representation."

"I appreciate your honesty, Fina, but I'm not opposed to the idea of changing lawyers. Thatcher Kinney may be a friend, but I'm not convinced he's a legal dynamo."

Fina *knew* he wasn't a legal dynamo, but kept that to herself. They made a plan to meet at five at Ludlow and Associates. After Fina confirmed it with Carl, she showered, ate breakfast, and got on with her day.

She drove over to the North End and shoehorned her car into a questionably legal space on a side street. Before getting out, Fina took a survey of the scene to see if she had any company. She'd been vigilant since the fire, but no one seemed to be on her tail.

She walked a couple of blocks to a small dry cleaner, where she asked for the owner and waited by the counter for a few moments. The middle-aged woman at the register seemed to be doing some paperwork while listening to talk radio. Fina hated talk radio. If she wanted to hear people heatedly bitch about things of which they knew nothing, she'd have dinner with her parents.

"Fina!" A man came out from behind a set of curtains with his arms spread wide. "My dear, you look wonderful!"

"Thank you, Angelo," Fina said, leaning in for matching kisses on both cheeks.

"Come in. I was just finishing something."

She followed him into the back room, which was a mess of bolts of fabric, a large folding table, a small changing area, and a pedestal in front of a three-way mirror, as well as a couple of file cabinets and an old wooden desk. Angelo took a seat in an easy chair and gestured for Fina to take the folding chair beside it.

"To what do I owe the pleasure?" he asked.

Angelo Capriasano was in his late seventies and had been making the Ludlow men's suits for more than three decades. He was an Italian immigrant—rumored to be connected to organized crime, though not actively involved—and a whiz with a needle and thread.

"My father sends his regards," Fina told him. Carl didn't even know she was there, but it was the polite thing to say.

"And send mine to him. I just did a suit for him a couple of months ago."

"He always looks good thanks to you."

Angelo beamed.

"I'm actually here to pick your brain," Fina said.

"I'm all yours."

"I'm trying to locate a guy, and I have very little to go on."

Angelo nodded. "Okay."

"Here's a picture of him." Fina handed him a printout of the photo that Cristian had finally sent her the night before. "His defining feature is that he's probably six feet five, so I'm thinking he can't buy clothes just anywhere."

Angelo reached into his shirt pocket and pulled out a pair of glasses. He studied the photo. "He looks big, but how do you know how tall he is?"

"There are other photos of him, and the cops were able to come up with measurements relative to the location."

"And the cops can't find him?" Angelo asked.

"Probably, but I'd like to find him first." She smiled. "And I have to be a little more creative in my methods."

He nodded. "He's not just tall," Angelo noted. "He looks broad to me, too."

"Right. Can you buy clothes that big off the rack?"

"Sure, but there aren't that many racks to choose from. There are only a handful of places that sell that kind of stuff."

"We think he's black and young," Fina said. "Are there any places that come to mind?"

Angelo returned his glasses to his pocket and got up from the chair. He was of average height, an inch or two lost in the stoop of his posture. His hairline had steadily receded over the years, and now a pillowy tuft of white stood up from his pate. He went to a file cabinet on one side of the room and started rooting around in the drawers.

"Hmm," Angelo said before moving his search to a box of paperwork on one of the shelving units. Fina looked around at the crowded space and wondered how he ever found anything.

"Here we go." He held up a slip of paper and returned to his chair. Fina glanced at it, but couldn't make sense of the chicken scratches covering it at various angles in both pen and pencil.

"It's in Italian, *cara mia*," Angelo told her, grinning.

"That explains it," Fina said.

"I have some big customers, but mostly I do their suits," he explained. "The young guys—the more urban ones—go to these places for other stuff."

Fina didn't know if "urban" was code for "black" or "gangster," but she wasn't going to give Angelo a lecture on political correctness.

He dictated the names and addresses of four shops, which Fina typed into her phone. Before putting the photo away, she asked him to look at it once more.

"What does that look like to you?" she asked, pointing at the man's ankle.

Angelo pulled his glasses out again and studied the image. "It looks like a logo of some sort, but I can't make it out."

"Neither can I," Fina said.

"You know, a guy this tall has feet to match. He definitely can't buy his socks at Lord and Taylor."

"So they were also bought at a specialty store," Fina mused, "or online."

Angelo made a small disapproving noise and waved his hand in front of his face.

"Not a fan of online shopping, Angelo?" she asked.

"Craziest thing ever. You need something, you go to the store or the person who makes it. Not out there," he said, gesturing into the ether.

"Good luck with that approach," Fina said, leaning over to kiss him good-bye. "And thanks for the suggestions. I owe you."

"You kidding? Ludlows are my best customers. Your father understands. You have to be loyal."

"He certainly values loyalty," Fina said. *As long as you're loyal to him,* she added in her head. "See you soon."

She went back through the curtains and returned to her car, where she scrolled through the list she'd just compiled.

God, she hated clothes shopping.

How'd she end up with this task?

Fina pulled into the parking lot of the first store on Angelo's list, which was in Medford. The store didn't open for twenty minutes, so she called Risa and confirmed that her schedule could accommodate the tentative date with Greta. She hopped on a nearby Starbucks Wi-Fi and searched for a good meeting spot. Kittery, Maine, was just over the New Hampshire border and offered a host of meeting options, given the outlet mall and all the hungry shoppers who needed to be fed. It also provided some distance from the prying eyes of Rockford.

Fina wanted something more conducive to conversation than a fast food joint, so she settled on the Popover Place, which promised "bread, butter, and Yankee hospitality," whatever that was. She wrote a quick e-mail to Greta with the details and asked for confirmation that she could make it. If Greta was a no-show, there was no amount of Yankee hospitality that would appease Fina.

The clothing store was like being inside a room full of fun house mirrors. Everything was taller, longer, and wider than seemed humanly possible. Fina couldn't imagine having to wear such clothes, let alone launder them. One outfit would be half a load. And the shoes took the carnival theme even further; they were enormous, like something only clowns or performers in sideshow attractions would wear.

A couple of young men were browsing among the racks. She walked over to the counter, behind which stood an associate who looked to be a customer, too. He was upwards of six feet four inches with a head of curly black hair. Unlike the man on the video, his height wasn't matched by his weight. He was thin, almost reedy, like a stiff breeze might take him airborne. He was wearing a suit with a name tag reading JOE and was making a note on a pad of paper.

"One moment, ma'am. I'll be right with you," he said.

Ugh. The "ma'am" was like a dagger through Fina's young heart.

The phone behind the register rang. "Stuart? Can you answer that?" Joe said to another clerk who popped up from behind a display of sweat suits. Stuart was tall, but not much more than six feet. He was slightly overweight and looked to be in his fifties. He ambled over and, much to Joe's chagrin, answered the phone on the fifth ring.

"How can I help you?" Joe asked Fina as Stuart looked something up in the computer for the caller.

Fina smiled and leaned on the counter. "I'm trying to locate a man who might be a customer of yours." She pulled the picture out of her bag.

Joe took the photo and examined it carefully. "Can I ask why you're trying to locate him?"

"I found something—something of value—next to my car." She pointed at the photo. "And I'm trying to locate the item's owner, but I can't really see his face."

"What makes you think he might be one of our customers?" Joe asked.

"His size, which I know seems silly, but I didn't know where else to start."

"I don't know him," Joe said, folding his hands and resting them on the counter, "but even if I did, we like to protect our customers' privacy."

"I completely understand," Fina said, thinking it was one of the dumbest things she'd ever heard. "The thing is, a few years ago I lost a piece of jewelry that my grandmother had given me. She died and then I lost it in a movie theater. I was so upset."

"I can imagine."

"But there's a happy ending," Fina said. "A week later, a man contacted me, and he'd found my ring! I was so relieved."

Joe sighed. "I still don't think I can help."

"I hate to think that I have something of value that belongs to some-one else," Fina said.

Stuart hung up the phone and peered over Joe's shoulder. "What did he lose?" he asked.

Joe adjusted his body so his colleague was forced to take a step back.

Fina smiled. "I don't think I should say what the item is. That way, only the rightful owner can claim it."

"Of course," Joe said.

Stuart craned his neck to get another look at the photo.

"I wish we could be of assistance, but I'm afraid we can't." Joe handed the photo back to her.

"I knew it was a long shot, but I thought I'd try," Fina said, folding the picture and slipping it into her bag. "Would you mind if I left my number in case he happens to come into the store?"

"That would be fine," Joe said, reaching for paper and pen. Fina dic-tated her number to him rather than handing over her card. They didn't need to know her true line of work.

Fina watched Stuart out of the corner of her eye. She wondered if he was governed by the same sense of propriety Joe was.

"Perhaps the police could be of assistance," Joe suggested.

"I went to them first," Fina said, "but they've got more serious issues to deal with. I know it seems silly, like a wild-goose chase, but someone else did it for me once."

"It seems very decent of you," Joe said, and smiled. He was cute if you didn't mind snuggling up to a beanpole.

"Thanks for your time," Fina said, heading for the door.

Sometimes she wished for a job where she could cross things off her list with confidence, but that was rarely the case. At least in the initial stages of an investigation, Fina had to listen to what people had to say without any assurance that they were telling the truth. Maybe Joe and Stuart didn't recognize the man in the photo, or maybe they needed a little time to contemplate what was in it for them.

W ho's Fina Ludlow?" the young woman asked from the bed.

"What?" Kevin asked, his hand frozen on the refrigerator.

"Fina Ludlow."

He pulled open the door and grabbed a beer. He took his time popping off the top before wandering back to the bed and climbing in next to her.

She was on her back, the sheet around her belly button, a business card pinched between two fingers.

"Where'd you get that?" Kevin asked, plucking it from her grasp.

"Your wallet."

He saw his wallet lying open on the duvet cover.

"Why are you going through my wallet?" Kevin snapped it closed and tossed it on the bedside table, a white melamine number from IKEA that looked like it could be destroyed in less time than it took to assemble.

"I needed a tip for the pizza guy," she said, stretching her hands overhead.

"What? You don't have any money?" He tried to make it sound like he was teasing, but even to his own ears it sounded accusatory.

"Don't be cheap, Kevin. Just give me a few bucks."

He pulled out some ones and held them out to her.

She put the singles on her bedside table and reached for his beer. "You didn't answer my question," she said, taking the bottle from him and having a long swig.

"She's no one you have to worry about." He reached out and grazed his fingertips across her flat, hard belly.

His companion took another long drink and held his gaze. She handed the bottle back to him. "Don't treat me like a child, Kevin."

As he looked around the studio apartment, it was no wonder that Kevin felt like the grown-up of the pair. The room was a tiny amalgamation of bedroom, kitchen, dining room, and living room all in one, with the bathroom the only area separated by a door. Her books were stacked on the table that doubled as a desk, and posters were tacked on the walls. The only reason he'd agreed to meet her here was that she was getting impatient and moody, which made him nervous. He needed to keep her happy, at least for the time being.

"I'm not treating you like a child," he insisted.

"Then tell me who she is, and what kind of a name is Fina?"

"I couldn't tell you. I've only met her a couple of times. At the office," he added hastily when she raised an eyebrow. "It was university business."

There was a buzz at the door. She got up and pulled on a silk robe he had bought her. It looked sexier when she wore it in hotel rooms. She paid the delivery man and got plates and napkins from the kitchen area. Kevin took the box from her outstretched hands and started to place it on the duvet cover.

"Wait! You're going to get grease on the duvet." She pulled a ratty-looking towel from an open shelving unit and spread it out. Kevin put down the box and sat up, adjusting the pillows behind his back. The young woman tossed the robe onto a pile of unfolded laundry and reclaimed her spot next to him.

Kevin pulled a steaming slice of pepperoni out of the box.

"What kind of university business?" she asked, biting into her slice.

"Stuff related to the lawsuit. That's why I told you we had to cool it, because people would be asking questions."

She chewed. "I don't like it," she commented after a moment.

"Which part?"

"Having to cool it and people asking questions, especially women."

"Would it make you feel better if I told you she was a troll?" He grinned.

"I'm not sure I'd believe you." She nibbled on the crust. "How much longer until we can go back to the way things were? Go back to our regular routine?"

"I don't know, but this isn't so bad, is it?" Kevin asked. "I know we're not seeing as much of each other, but distance makes the heart grow fonder."

She glared at him. "Some people say it makes the heart wander."

It occurred to Kevin that somehow, over these past few months, she'd gotten the idea that she was in control of the relationship—that what she said or did or even felt would determine their future. He wasn't sure how she'd gotten that idea. Maybe he'd given it to her, and maybe it wasn't such a bad thing. Or maybe he was just kidding himself, and he wasn't in control, either.

Fina spent the rest of the day working her way down the list of stores that Angelo had provided. No one she spoke with recognized the man or admitted to recognizing him. She hadn't really expected a positive ID right away, but she'd hoped for one nonetheless. Fina wasn't sure what her next move was, and she had a little time to kill before her meeting at Ludlow and Associates.

Traffic over the Charles was slow. On the Cambridge side, Fina took a few shortcuts and drove into Central Square. Once a poor cousin to Harvard Square up the road, Central Square had cleaned up, boasting hipper restaurants and nicer housing options. It was symbolic of the age-old arguments for and against gentrification: The area felt safer, but less diverse. There were more things to do, but fewer people could afford to do them.

A brief walk from her car brought her to the ATM that Jamie frequented. Immediately across the street from her vantage point was a CVS, a real estate office, a liquor store, and what looked to be some kind of nonprofit. A couple of bars and restaurants were visible, and a dental office that, with its neon sign, looked more like a fast food restaurant. Fina made a note of the businesses that she could easily identify and then checked her watch.

The businesses that shared the sidewalk with the ATM were varied: a coffee shop, a dry cleaner, two bars, another restaurant, a law office, and a hardware store. Fina jotted these down with the others and tucked her notebook into her bag. A few of them were worth investigating, but that would have to wait if she was going to be on time for her meeting.

And she wanted to be on time. Not because she couldn't deal with the wrath of Carl, but because she didn't want Bobbi to have to face him on her own.

Fina didn't wish that on her worst enemy, let alone someone she liked.

22.

Bobbi was sitting in the waiting area outside Carl's office when Fina arrived at Ludlow and Associates. Fina gave her a hug, and they were ushered in to see her father.

Carl stood and came around to the front of the desk to shake Bobbi's hand. He looked handsome and prosperous in his Angelo-designed suit. He and Bobbi were probably close in age, but Carl's edges were smoother than hers, from a lack of grief, but also, Fina imagined, from the relative ease of his life.

"Mrs. Barone, or should I call you Bobbi?" Carl asked, gently guiding her to a chair, his hand on her back.

"Bobbi is fine."

Carl went around his desk and sat down. "First, let me say how sorry I am about the loss of your daughter. We lost a family member not too long ago, one of my daughters-in-law. I know it's not the same thing, but there's something unnatural about the younger generation predeceasing us."

Bobbi nodded and gave him a tight smile. Fina thought it was interesting that her father didn't reference the loss of his own daughter. Perhaps you couldn't compare the death of a young child to that of a fully grown one, or maybe he didn't care to share this personal information with a stranger. Fina imagined it was the latter.

"Did Shari offer you something to drink?" Carl asked. Fina had taken off her coat and settled in the chair next to Bobbi.

"Yes, but I've had enough tea and coffee to last a lifetime."

"How about something stronger?" Carl asked, gesturing toward the minibar.

Bobbi's eyes wandered in that direction. "If you've got it, I'm game," she said after a moment.

Carl nodded at Fina, who retrieved two tumblers, a bottle of scotch, and a diet soda from the bar. She placed the glasses and scotch in front of her father, who poured a generous amount for himself and Bobbi. Fina sat back down and popped open her soda.

Bobbi took a sip of her drink and exhaled deeply. "This is good stuff," she said.

"Only the best for our clients," Carl offered.

"Aren't your clients footing the bill?" Bobbi asked. She raised her glass with a slight smile on her face.

"No. The insurance companies and manufacturers and corporate America—they're footing the bill." He took a sip from his glass. "Fina, why don't you start by giving Bobbi an update on your progress?"

"Oookay," she said, not expecting to be first up. "I have to warn you, though, I'm at a stage in the case where I don't have much to update, but I'm making progress."

Carl gave her a look. It wasn't the kind of update he wanted, but Fina wasn't going to sugarcoat it. It was like the tectonic plates shifting deep below the earth: Lots of stuff was happening, but it wouldn't be obvious until the earthquake hit.

"Okay," Bobbi said. "Is there anything you can tell me?"

"I have a lead on the man who planted the incendiary device in my car."

"So you think that was related to Liz?" she asked.

"I won't know for sure until I find the guy, but I'm making progress on that front."

Carl waggled the bottle of scotch at Bobbi. She hesitated, so he leaned over and poured some more.

"You deserve it," Carl said. Her father was like the devil on your shoulder who told you exactly what you wanted to hear, giving you permission to indulge your basest desires.

Bobbi picked up the glass and took a sip before carefully placing it back down on the desk. "It's so frustrating. I feel like no one has any real information for me."

"I'm sorry," Fina said. "I wish I could give you something concrete."

"Fina is excellent at her job," Carl said. "She'll find whoever did this to your daughter."

Fina looked at Carl. She was surprised by his vote of confidence, but also troubled by his promise. He shouldn't make any guarantees on her behalf.

"I know," Bobbi said. "It's just that the police aren't telling me anything, either."

"They have to protect their case. I know it's maddening, but just try to hang in there." Fina took a drink before continuing. "Do you know if Jamie saw Gus Sibley for his knee injury?" she asked, hoping to get her questions answered before Bobbi got another refill.

"I don't think so, but I don't know. Is that relevant?"

"It might be." Fina adjusted in her seat. "I know this is a delicate subject, and I've asked you before, but do you think Liz was involved with someone outside her marriage?"

Bobbi looked surprised. "An affair? I doubt it."

"What makes you so sure?" Fina asked. Carl watched them intently.

"First of all," Bobbi said, "she didn't have time, and secondly, I don't think she had the inclination."

"Parents don't always know what their kids are up to," Carl offered.

"And some of them choose to ignore what's going on," Fina said, looking at him.

"I don't think she was involved with anyone," Bobbi said, shaking her head.

"Okay," Fina said. "Just covering all the bases."

Bobbi looked weary, so Fina gave her father a pointed look. *Get on with your spiel,* she tried to wordlessly communicate to him.

"Bobbi," Carl said, leaning forward. "I know it probably seems indelicate to discuss the lawsuit against NEU at this time, but time is of the essence."

"Mr. Ludlow—Carl—discussing the lawsuit doesn't even register when you think about the two weeks I've had. My child was attacked, hooked up to every conceivable machine, her organs were harvested, and we're donating her brain to science, per her wishes. I don't see how you can live through that and still care about politeness or sensitivity."

Carl nodded. "I understand. Who is the executor of Liz's estate?"

"I am, although her husband is the main beneficiary." Carl and Fina exchanged a brief glance.

"And he supports the lawsuit?" he asked.

"He'll support whatever Liz wanted to do, but he has no interest in meetings like this one."

"So he's on board, but he's not leading the charge," Carl clarified.

"Correct."

"I'm going to get right to the point, Bobbi. Your current attorney isn't providing good representation. I can do better. In fact, we're the best, and we'll get you the biggest settlement possible."

"If he does say so himself," Fina murmured, toying with the tab on her soda can.

Bobbi gave her a weary smile. "What would you do differently from Thatcher Kinney?"

"Everything," Carl said. "First of all, lots of lawsuits are won or lost in the court of public opinion. Mr. Kinney hasn't taken advantage of that, and it's costing you."

Bobbi cradled the heavy tumbler in the palm of her hand and listened.

"I will make sure that NEU is held responsible for the damage they inflicted on your daughter," Carl said.

"And it won't cost me anything unless you get money?" Bobbi asked.

"That's right," Carl said. "You won't incur any out-of-pocket expenses, and if Fina's investigation proves that Liz's death was connected to NEU in any way, you won't be responsible for that cost, either."

Bobbi placed her glass on the desk. "I'd like to learn more about your other cases."

"Absolutely. I'll have information messengered over to your house."

"When news of the suit went public, Bobbi got some threats," Fina told Carl. "I hired Dennis Kozlowski to run a security check, and he put some things in place. I think we should continue with that for the time being."

Carl looked at her. He knew it was Fina's way of firmly transferring the bill to him.

"Of course. Your safety is paramount, Bobbi. You just let Fina know if you need anything else."

"Thank you. I need to go," Bobbi said, rising from her chair. "I told Jamie I'd help get the kids dinner and ready for bed."

Carl and Bobbi exchanged good-byes, and Fina walked her to the office lobby. When she returned to Carl's office, he was sitting behind his desk, reading something on his computer.

"What do you think?" he asked Fina.

"About her signing on? I think she will."

"Good."

"Nice touch, pulling out the good booze."

"Her kid died," he said. "I figured she could use a stiff drink."

"That's surprisingly sensitive of you, Dad."

Carl raised an eyebrow. "Don't start with me."

"I was complimenting you. Jeez." Fina looped her bag over her shoulder and started for the door.

"I don't like what happened the other night at dinner," he said before she could make her exit.

"Meaning?" Fina asked, turning in his direction.

"You went upstairs and then came down with Haley, who looked upset. Your mother was hurt."

Fina opened her mouth in disbelief. "My mother was hurt? Are you shitting me?"

"Jesus, Fina."

"I don't know who's crazier; her for thinking the way she does, or you for taking her side."

"Fine," Carl said. "Forget it."

"With pleasure," Fina replied, and strode out of the office.

Fina called Cristian from the car. Her conversation with Carl had soured her mood, and she thought a crumb of encouraging news might turn it around.

"Do you have any news for me?" she asked. "Any good news about this case?"

"Hello to you, too. Are you in your car?"

"Yes."

"Pull over if you want to talk," he said.

"Cristian, you can't be the boss of everyone."

"That's rich coming from you. Why are you in such a bad mood?"

"The usual reasons. Hey, did you ask Vikram about threatening Liz?" she asked.

"It's a dead end," Cristian said. "He claims he never threatened her, and it's Dana's word against his."

"And you believe him?"

"I didn't say that, but there's no proof supporting either claim, which makes it useless from an evidentiary standpoint."

"Great," Fina said.

"We're still looking at him."

"What about the bomber?"

"What about him?" Cristian asked.

"Anything new?" she asked.

"You first."

"I'm making progress," Fina said, "but nothing concrete yet."

"That about sums things up."

"Ugh. This is so frustrating," she said before laying on her horn. An SUV with a BABY ON BOARD sign had cut her off. If the driver was that concerned about her precious cargo, she shouldn't be crossing three lanes of traffic to make her exit.

"Fina!" Cristian exclaimed. "Either get off the phone or get off the road!"

"Fine. I'll call you later."

"Fine, but eat something before you do. You sound hangry," Cristian said, and hung up.

He was right, of course, which only made her feel worse.

Fina spent most of Sunday stewing and reviewing the case. Her family was a constant source of frustration, but usually she was able to distract herself with her work. But when a case was also frustrating her, it was like a double whammy. Fina knew she just had to push through it, which was why she spent the day poring over the notes and materials she had and trying to figure out her next steps. She broke up the day with an intense workout, and when she climbed into bed, Fina had assembled a plan of sorts.

Her review of the case kept bringing her back to Jamie and the unanswered questions that related to him. So in the shower the next morning, Fina pondered those questions and the best way to get answers. Once dressed and fed, she put in a call to Matthew.

"Do you still have those vouchers from the maid service?" she asked when he came on the line.

"Can you be more vague?"

"The maid service? The one you represented against the cleaning chemical people?"

"Oh, you mean the Cheerful Cleaners? Yeah." Matthew had represented a small cleaning company in their fight against a fluid supplier and the alleged toxicity of their products. He'd won a handsome settlement for Cheerful Cleaners and a seemingly endless supply of house-cleaning vouchers. "Why?" he asked. "Have you decided to have your home cleaned? Are you feeling okay?"

"I have a housecleaner come in a couple times a month, thanks very much." Fina eyed her space; it wasn't exactly ready for a spread in *House Beautiful*.

"So why does it always look like a pigsty?" he asked.

"It's messy, but that's different from being unclean."

Matthew snorted.

"Anyhoo," Fina continued, "I need some of those vouchers if you still have them."

"Sure. You want Sue to pop some in the mail?" he asked.

"No, I need them now. If I swing by can she run them out to me?"

"She has better things to do, Fina."

"Come on," Fina said. "You must have an intern or somebody who can take five minutes to run down to the lobby. It's for a case."

"You always say that," Matthew said.

"'Cause it's always true."

"Fine. Give Sue a call when you get here, and she'll send someone out."

"Thanks. Hey, I don't know if Scotty clued you in, but Mom has been campaigning for Haley to visit Rand in Florida."

Matthew sighed. "Great."

"Exactly. She doesn't want to go, and we need to back her up on this."

"Fine."

Fina knew that his support was given grudgingly. Matthew relished conflict in the courtroom, but preferred to stay out of things on the family front. Not getting involved, as far as Fina was concerned, was a luxury she and her siblings didn't have.

"Thank you. I appreciate the support," she said.

"Anything else?" he asked.

"Just one question: When are you going to settle down and make some girl very happy?" It was Elaine's constant refrain to Matthew.

"Piss off," he said to his sister.

"Love you, too," Fina said before disconnecting the call.

Their mother was a pain in the ass, but she did provide moments of comic relief.

Fina didn't call ahead so she wasn't sure who she'd find at Liz and Jamie's house when she arrived two hours later. The minivan and the Passat were in the driveway, but there were no additional cars out front as there had been on previous visits. Fina knew that once the funeral was over, most of the mourners returned to their normal routines, while the immediate family and closest friends were left in a grief-filled limbo. It was a lonely place to be, and even though she had an ulterior motive for stopping by, Fina was sensitive to the fact that a show of support might be appreciated.

Or maybe not, Fina thought when Jamie opened the door a minute later. He looked exhausted, with dark smudges under his eyes, the whites of which were bloodshot. He was wearing baggy jeans and a long-sleeved waffle-weave top. His feet were bare.

"I'm sorry to stop by unannounced," Fina lied, "but I was in the neighborhood. Do you have a minute?"

Jamie stepped back and opened the door wide. Fina came in and slipped off her boots and coat. The living room was reverting to its original state, with piles of clutter on most of the flat surfaces.

She followed Jamie into the kitchen. As she took a seat at the table, a loud bang rang out overhead.

"The kids are home," he said in explanation. "I couldn't deal with getting them to school."

Fina nodded. "I imagine it's hard doing the morning routine with only one grown-up."

"Liz handled it most days," Jamie admitted. "I'm not very good at it."

Fina was amused by the idea that Liz or anyone else was inherently good at the morning routine. Yes, some people were more organized than others, but really, it was a skill like any other. You just figured out the steps and practiced them, and if you couldn't master the routine, chances were either you didn't have to or didn't want to.

"I'm sure you'll get the hang of it," she assured him.

"Did you want coffee?" he asked.

Fina nodded and reached into her bag. She took out her phone and slipped it into her pocket. Jamie placed a mug in front of her, and she slid an envelope over to him when he took a seat across from her.

"I thought this might be more useful than another casserole." Fina dipped a spoon into the sugar bowl and stirred a generous helping into her coffee.

Jamie opened the envelope and pulled out the vouchers for free housecleaning. "Huh. Thanks." He seemed appreciative, but perplexed.

"I know it seems like a weird gift, but there's nothing like having someone bring order to chaos. Those will give you a few months of relief."

"Thanks. I appreciate it," Jamie said. "Kelly has been doing a lot around here, but I feel bad."

"I wouldn't feel too bad," Fina said. "From what I can tell, she enjoys getting things whipped into shape."

"That's true."

"But she probably has responsibilities she needs to get back to," she said. "Cheerful Cleaners will at least give you a bridge until you figure out a new routine." Fina sipped the coffee and had to stop herself from grimacing. It was dark and strong, even with the sugar. "When you schedule the first appointment, you should mention that you were referred by Matthew Ludlow. He's my brother, and he represented them in a lawsuit. They love him."

"So people either love you guys or hate you," Jamie mused, taking a sip of his black coffee.

Fina tipped her head. "I suppose. We tend to generate strong feelings in people." She wrapped her hands around her mug. "Bobbi mentioned that your knee had been acting up. How's it feeling?"

"It's been pretty bad lately. The cold doesn't help," he said.

"How'd you hurt it?" Fina asked, trying to stomach another sip of coffee.

"I was riding my bike and wiped out. I was going to do a triathlon—not a full one, just a sprint one to start—but obviously, that's not going to happen."

"That's a bummer."

"Yup. So much for taking up a healthy hobby."

"Did you see Gus Sibley about it?" Fina asked.

Jamie studied her. "Why would you ask that?"

"I was just curious. My nephews are always breaking things and in need of recommendations."

Jamie shook his head. "No. I saw a guy in Burlington."

"I guess I assumed you'd seen him since he and Liz were friends." Fina patted her pocket and pulled out her phone. "It's on vibrate. Sorry, I need to check this," she said, tapping on some buttons.

Jamie drank more coffee and tugged at a cuticle on his finger.

"Do you know Cambridge well?" Fina asked. "I'm supposed to meet someone at a restaurant in Central Square, but I don't go there very often." She pretended to send a text before putting the phone in her bag.

"I don't spend much time over there," Jamie said. "I did when I used to play music, but now I probably wouldn't even recognize the place. All the businesses have changed and have been taken over by chains."

"I hear ya. When I go to Harvard Square, I still expect to find the Wursthaus," Fina said, referring to an old German bar and restaurant that used to anchor the Square and had closed nearly twenty years before.

"I loved that place," Jamie said, a smile overtaking his features.

"You and me both," Fina said, bringing her mug to the sink. "Well, I'm sure my GPS will get me where I need to go in Central Square."

"Sorry I can't help," he said, following her to the door.

"I'll figure it out," Fina said. "I'm good at that."

"Thanks for the vouchers," Jamie said when she was starting down the front steps.

"Happy to help, and don't hesitate to call if you need some other practical assistance. You'd be surprised the contacts I have."

Jamie closed the door, and Fina returned to her car, where she set the heater to high.

It irritated her when people lied to her, but once she put that aside, she was able to focus on the crux of the issue.

There was clearly something that Jamie didn't want her to know.

23.

Pamela sat behind her desk and tried to focus on the document on her computer screen. She was drafting a letter to soothe the Astral Donors— people who gave more than fifty thousand dollars a year—who were already expressing concerns about the lawsuit. Like it wasn't difficult enough getting people to give money these days; now she'd have to spend her time reassuring skittish supporters.

Deb was cooking dinner for her tonight, and Pamela toyed with the idea of canceling. She wasn't in the mood to socialize, and she wondered if her hesitation was a reflection of her or Deb. If they had a better relationship, would Pamela seek out her company? Or was the inclination to share her troubles just not in her wiring?

Her assistant came to the door and hovered. Pamela knew she had been short with the young woman in recent days, but the hovering was more irritating than solicitous.

"Yes, Jill?"

"I have some documents from the San Diego conference organizers."

Pamela was confused. "Which conference is that?"

"The higher ed development officers meeting? You're giving one of the keynotes."

Pamela's back stiffened. "Since when?"

"Since a few weeks ago. Paul was supposed to, but he has a conflict. He said you would do it instead." Paul was senior to Pamela in the development office, much to her annoyance.

"Well, nobody asked me," Pamela said. "I don't even know if I'm available."

"You are," Jill said. "I checked your schedule."

Pamela looked at her. "You shouldn't have done that."

The young woman looked confused. "I shouldn't have checked your schedule? I assumed since Paul was asking that you knew about it."

"You shouldn't have put it on my schedule without asking me," Pamela said.

"I'm sorry." Jill stood there, the papers hanging loosely by her side.

Pamela wiggled in her chair. Her panty hose were digging into her upper thighs, but there was no polite way to ease the pressure.

"So what should I do?" Jill asked.

"Let me see it." Pamela held out her hand.

Jill crossed the room and offered the papers as if they were radioactive. Pamela smoothed them down on her blotter and scanned them. They were a draft of the highlights of the conference, including a speech by Pamela. There was an entry with her name and photo, a brief description of the talk, and a list of her credentials.

Pamela pressed her palm against the documents. "I can't do this talk. You need to tell the organizers that my schedule has changed and I'm unavailable."

"But it's only a month away."

"That means they have a month to find someone else. You know I don't like these kinds of events," Pamela said. "They take me away from my real work."

Jill chewed on her lip. "What do you want me to tell Paul?"

"Tell him that I'm not available. Tell him to find a replacement." Pamela looked at the document on her screen and clicked her mouse.

Her assistant remained in front of her desk.

"Was there something else?" Pamela asked her without looking up.

"No. Sorry." Jill left the room, pulling the door closed behind her.

Pamela hadn't asked her to close the door, but perhaps her assistant's instincts were right; she wasn't in the mood for human inter-action.

Cristian asked Fina to meet him at the courthouse, where he was tes-tifying in another case. She was eager to get an update, but she didn't feel good about the way their phone call had ended the other night. She knew it was largely her fault, but as much as she liked to eat, Fina hated humble pie.

She found him seated on a bench in the hallway, which was empty aside from a handful of people on their phones.

"Hi," Fina said, taking a seat next to him.

"Hey."

She took a deep breath. "Let me start by apologizing for my attitude on Saturday night," she said. "It wasn't my finest moment."

Cristian looked at her. "Maybe I should take you down to the im-pound lot and show you the wrecks from people who insist on talking and texting while they drive."

"Cristian, I never text while I drive," she insisted.

"Fine. The ones who talk. It's just as dangerous as driving drunk."

"I understand that this is your thing, but I'm an adult, Cristian. I don't know why I should be held to a stricter standard than the rest of the commonwealth."

"I don't care about the rest of the commonwealth," he said, tugging at his tie.

"That's sweet," she said, touching his arm lightly, "but annoying."

The doors next to them swung open, and a woman in a suit walked out at a clip.

"Do you have time for some lunch?" Fina asked.

He shook his head. "Nah. They told me to stay in the building."

"Are there any vending machines? I'm hungry."

Cristian led her down the hallway to an alcove that housed three vending machines. One offered drinks, another candy and snacks, and the third featured shelves on a turnstile apparatus. That machine contained sandwiches in triangular plastic containers, under-ripe fruit, and yogurt.

"Who eats that stuff?" Fina asked, studying the sandwiches. "Who knows how long they've been in there?"

"They must have expiration dates," Cristian said, fishing in his pocket for change. He dropped coins into the drink machine and selected a bottle of thick-looking green juice.

"What about that?" Fina asked, eyeing his choice. "Does that have an expiration date? It looks like medical waste."

"Thanks for sharing." He dropped more change into the machine and selected a dark red smoothie.

"Who's that for?" Fina asked.

He handed her the bottle. "It's sweet. Give it a try."

"Really?"

"Humor me."

Fina took the proffered bottle reluctantly.

"Listen," Cristian said as they returned to the bench, "we got some information about the device that was planted on your car."

"What's the deal?" she asked.

"Our techs think it was a mid-range device in terms of sophistication."

Fina uncapped the drink and nodded.

"If it had been built by a pro, you and Scotty would be dead," Cristian continued.

"I'd never live that down," Fina said.

Cristian rolled his eyes. "But it definitely required some chemical know-how. I'm not an expert, but apparently the fire was caused by an incendiary metal that was made into beads and covered in wax. The bomber put the beads in some kind of a mesh bag in the radiator, and when the radiator heated up, the wax melted and then something about metal and water making hydrogen and fire."

Fina looked at him blankly. "Cristian, I failed high school chemistry. Gimme a break."

He grinned.

"What about the components?" Fina asked. "Anything that will help you track down our guy, assuming it is a guy?"

Cristian took a swig of the green liquid. "I think it's a safe assumption we're looking for a man; for whatever reason, they enjoy blowing things up more than women. The main ingredient was lithium metal; that's what the beads were made of. You might be able to order it online, but it's generally found in labs."

Fina asked. "What kind of labs?"

"The kind of lab where Liz Barone worked," Cristian said.

"Or the kind of lab run by Barnes Kaufcan?"

"Yes," Cristian said. "That kind of lab."

Fina sipped the berry-flavored smoothie. "So Vikram Mehra and Kevin Lafferty are still in the frame?"

"Yes, but so are half of your brother's clients," Cristian added. "He's sued a lot of doctors and other people who might have access to these materials."

"I suppose it doesn't narrow things down," Fina said, "but it does give me a reason to follow up with some people."

Cristian eyed her. "Remember that Pitney isn't happy with you. I suggest you tread lightly."

"Pitney is never happy with me." She looked at the label on her drink. Oh good Lord, it contained beets. "I assume you guys are going to talk to Vikram and Kevin."

"Of course."

"Sloppy seconds, as usual," Fina said.

"If you wanted first dibs, you should have been a cop," Cristian responded.

"No, thanks. I'm good. Any word on Kevin Lafferty's alibi?"

"He was at the Westin that night, but there's a chunk of time for which his movements are unaccounted for. So far, we aren't getting anywhere."

"That's annoying," Fina said. She squeezed his arm. "Thanks for the update."

"Sure." Cristian drained his bottle and screwed the top back on. "That wasn't so bad, was it?" he asked, gesturing at her half-empty bottle.

"I have to admit that it was rather tasty."

He grinned. "Wonders never cease. When are we doing dinner?"

"Whenever you want," Fina said. She turned on the bench and looked at him. "Is this dinner going to be a date?"

Cristian squirmed on the bench. "No, it's what it always is with us."

"Which is?"

"We like to hang out."

"Okay. How about tonight?"

Cristian tossed his bottle in the recycling bin. "Not tonight. Maybe tomorrow."

"Sure." Fina knew that a detective's schedule was unpredictable. If you were someone who needed things set in stone and plans kept, you shouldn't spend time with a cop. The uncertainty was enough to drive some people—like Cristian's ex—batty. "Keep in touch, and I appreciate the info."

"And you'll let me know if you come up with something on your end?" he asked.

"Of course." Fina smiled and started down the hallway.

She wasn't sure if Cristian's recent dalliance with monogamy had made him long for the days of their casual relationship. Fina was pleased with the notion that he'd become more available, but a little frustrated, too. She'd just gotten used to his absence.

Hal called while Fina sat in traffic on Mass Ave.

"How's your hand?" he asked.

"Practically healed," she told him. "You'd never know it happened."

"Except you won't soon forget a car fire."

"How'd you know it was a car fire?" Fina asked, allowing a car to merge in front of her. Sometimes she liked to throw off her fellow Boston drivers by being civil and benevolent.

"You were injured, and the fire was on the news. I put two and two together."

"I'm practically as good as new, Hal. What do you have for me?"

"You know that grant that we discussed? The one that the Schaefer Lab wasn't awarded?"

"Yes," Fina said, blocking a different car from cutting in front of her. She didn't want anyone to get used to her generosity. "Vikram Mehra blamed Liz for that."

"Right. Well, you asked me to research the pharmaceutical companies who sponsor the grant. I've got the names."

"Great. Let me hear 'em."

Fina tapped her thumbs on the steering wheel as Hal recited a roll call that included Pfizer, Merck, Bristol-Myers Squibb, and a few companies she didn't recognize. He concluded the list with the one she'd been hoping to hear.

"Did you say Barnes Kaufcan?" Fina asked.

"Yup. They're smaller than the others in terms of sales, but they're sponsors just like the big ones," Hal said.

"Who was awarded the grant this year? Someone local?"

"Nope. A lab at Rice University. Do you want me to get more information about that particular lab?"

"No, thanks. This is great. Thanks, Hal."

"Anytime. Be careful, Fina. Are you checking your car before you get into it?"

Fina rolled her eyes. "I'm perfectly safe, Hal. No need to worry."

She disconnected the call before he could continue his train of thought. She didn't need Cristian's lectures about her driving habits or Hal's warnings about her safety. She wasn't a fan of unsolicited advice.

She parked her car a few streets away from Central Square and headed to the restaurant on her list of businesses near Jamie's ATM that afforded a closer look. Unfortunately, the staff in the French bistro didn't recognize a photo of Jamie, so Fina moved on.

Back outside she contemplated the two bars that had caught her eye the other night. The first was a seedy dive with a smattering of patrons who could best be described as affectless, wan, and rumpled. No one claimed to know Jamie, and Fina was happy to make a quick exit and take a deep breath of fresh air. It was freezing out, but at least it was sunny. The people inside the bar were like moles, burrowing in the earth, limiting their stimuli. It couldn't be good for their eyesight and mood, let alone their livers.

Her last stop was another bar, not yet open for business. Fina peeked through a window and saw a man righting chairs from the tabletops. She knocked, but he ignored her and continued with the task at hand. Fina banged a second time and engaged in a muted discussion with him until he finally relented and opened the door.

"We're closed," he said when he popped his head out the door.

"I know. I just have a quick question. Can I come in for a sec?" She hugged her arms tight. He pulled the door open wider, and Fina stepped past him into the bar. He locked the door behind her.

This establishment was light-years away from its neighbor in terms of ambience and, presumably, clientele. Four-top tables dominated the space, and exposed lightbulbs in mason jars hung from the pressed-tin ceiling. A large mirror behind the bar sat in an ornate wooden frame, reflecting back the room. A quick glance at the chalkboard menu revealed gourmet and unconventional takes on the usual bar fare, like pork belly sliders and carrot fritters. At the far end of the room, there was a stage raised a couple of steps off the floor.

"Do you guys have live music?" Fina asked as the man pulled another overturned chair from a tabletop.

"Yeah. Wednesday through Sunday. Was that your question?" He looked to be in his midthirties, with a bushy beard and mustache. He was wearing black jeans and a flannel shirt over a T-shirt. He looked like an indie rocker lumberjack.

"No," Fina said, "but I think I've come to the right place."

He nodded for her to continue.

"This is going to sound crazy, but I'm planning a birthday party for my friend, and I'm trying to include all of her favorite things." Fina followed him to the next table. "There's a local band that used to be really popular, and I'm trying to figure out if they still perform."

"Did you try looking on the Internet?" he asked, smirking.

"Obviously, but I didn't find anything. But this seems to be the go-to place for good live music." Lie, lie, lie. It may have been true, but if so, her mentioning it was merely a coincidental collision with the truth. She was so going to hell.

"Which band?"

"Wells Missionary. The lead singer was Jamie Gottlieb."

He paused, resting his hands on the back of a chair. "I know Jamie, but those guys don't play together anymore."

"That's what I was afraid of," Fina said, feigning disappointment.

"Sorry. They might be available—for a price."

Fina winced. "I'm kind of on a tight budget."

He set the final chair down on the floor and pushed it under the table. Behind the bar, the man washed his hands at the sink.

"Jamie still comes in and jams, though," he said, drying his hands on a bar towel.

"Really? It's not the same as the band, but it would still be cool to see him," Fina mused. "Is he here on a regular basis?"

"Pretty often, but he's got a regular job and a family now," he said with a withering look.

"Do you know if he'll be in this week?" Fina asked.

"When's the party exactly?"

"Not for a couple of weeks," Fina said, "but I'd love to stop by and hear him."

"You should drop by. Even if Jamie isn't here, our other bands are awesome."

"Okay. I'll do that. Thanks for the info," Fina said, walking to the front. He followed and unlocked the door.

"What did you say your name was?" he asked.

"Amy, and you're . . . ?" She smiled at him.

"Marshall."

Fina offered her hand. "Nice to meet you, Marshall. Maybe I'll see you one of these nights."

"I'll buy you a drink," he said.

Fina kept smiling and nodded before stepping out onto the sidewalk.

Marshall seemed like a lovely fellow, but he was a little too hirsute for her taste. Fina liked her male companions to look as if they had some familiarity with shaving cream and a razor.

Kevin Lafferty had left the office for the day, but could be found at NEU attending a volleyball match. Fina learned this from his extremely helpful assistant, Colin, after she adopted a slight accent and claimed she was calling about one of Kevin's children. She routinely took advantage of people's naïveté and goodwill, but honestly, someone had to teach them to be more guarded.

She drove back across the river to the university and parked near the sports complex. She used the same trick to gain access as before—sneaking in behind a crew of flirtatious undergraduate boys—and asked at the front desk for the location of the volleyball game. The directions took her down a hallway that opened up to a small atrium with a couple of couches and a smattering of tables. Large doors were propped open, beyond which Fina could see what appeared to be volleyball warm-ups. A group of women on each side of the net was engaged in drills, punching at the ball and diving at the unforgiving wooden floor. Just watching made Fina's knees and wrists hurt.

Before venturing into the echo chamber of the gym, she scanned the lounge area, which had a small snack bar. Kevin Lafferty was at the counter, talking to an older man who was clutching a tub of popcorn.

Fina fell into line behind them. She listened as Kevin ordered a lemonade and the two men debated the strengths of the opposing teams. As they stepped away from the counter, Fina interrupted.

"Kevin! What a nice surprise!"

He hid his distaste with a wide smile. "How are you?" he asked jovially.

"I'm great. I'm so glad I bumped into you. I need a minute to catch up."

Kevin glanced at the man next to him, who was busy dipping his hand into his buttered snack.

"You don't mind if I steal him for a moment, do you?" Fina asked the man. She touched his shoulder lightly when she asked.

"Of course not. He's all yours." Kevin's companion wandered over to the gym entrance and found someone else to jabber with.

"So you're a volleyball fan?" Kevin asked her before taking a long suck from his straw.

"I do admire the players' athleticism, but it's almost painful to watch. Don't you think?"

He glared at her. "Why are you here?"

"I just wanted to keep you in the loop regarding the Liz Barone situation."

Kevin shook his head. "This is beginning to feel like harassment."

"This?" Fina looked around innocently. "*This* feels like harassment? Oh, Kevin, I'm just getting warmed up."

A whistle blew in the gym, and the players vacated the court and gathered around their respective benches.

"Say what you have to say," Kevin said.

"Did you know that your company is one of the sponsors of a grant that Liz's lab tried to win?" Fina asked.

"So what? So is every lab in the area."

"True, but it just seems a little weird that she would be having cognitive issues, is blamed for losing the grant, and—what a coincidence—your company sponsors the grant."

"I think your job has made you paranoid," Kevin said, leaning toward her. "I have nothing to do with the grant process."

"What about lithium metal?"

"What about it?" he asked.

"I assume you have it in your labs."

"As does every academic and commercial chemistry lab in the greater Boston area."

"Right, but not every lab has a connection to a murder victim."

"What does any of this have to do with Liz?" Kevin asked, fiddling with the straw in his drink.

"I don't know if you heard," Fina said, "but I had a little mishap on the Tobin Bridge recently."

"It doesn't surprise me that you're a terrible driver," he said, with a hint of pleasure.

"It wasn't my fault. Someone planted an incendiary device on my car. A device made from a chemical found in your lab."

Kevin chuckled. "And you think I had something to do with that? Do I seem like the sort of man who would plant an incendiary device?"

"The sort of man who would do that is the guilty, threatened sort, and I've yet to rule you out of that category."

"I think you're nuts," he said.

"Thank you," Fina said. "That's very kind."

Kevin shook his head and sucked on his lemonade.

"I'm not giving up," Fina said. "Fair warning, I'm like a dog with a bone when it comes to my cases."

"Well, then, I wish you the best of luck."

"I'm sure we'll see each other soon," Fina said, and retraced her steps to the sports complex entrance.

She hadn't learned anything, but she'd put Kevin on notice, which was something.

You put enough people on edge and eventually someone would jump off.

Fina retrieved a phone message from Greta agreeing to meet the next day. She called Risa and updated her, then dialed Milloy. He was finishing up with a client and suggested she come to his place.

Milloy lived in a high-rise building a block away from the Common on the edge of the Theater District. Fina parked and rode the elevator up to the seventeenth floor. The hallway was carpeted and dimly lit by contemporary wall sconces. She was reaching up to knock on his door when it opened and an older woman stepped out.

"Hi," Fina said, more to Milloy than the woman.

"Hey," he said to her. "I'll see you next week, Connie."

Connie, who was definitely a card-carrying member of AARP, grinned like the Cheshire cat. "I look forward to it, Milloy," she said, winking. She threw her scarf over her shoulder and sashayed toward the elevator.

"Somebody looks like she got a happy ending," Fina said, following him into the condo.

Milloy made a face. "Gross." He started to disassemble the massage table in the middle of the living room. "How's your hand?"

"It's fine." Fina flopped down on the couch. Milloy's one-bedroom was neat and tastefully decorated. It wasn't a large space, but his attentive housekeeping made it feel roomy. "What's for dinner?"

"You tell me."

"Do you have any interest in going to a bar in Cambridge?"

Milloy disappeared with the folded table and returned a moment later. "I assume you have a particular bar in mind."

"I do, and it's not greasy bar food. They have things like octopus and roasted Brussels sprouts."

"This is for a case?" he asked.

"Yes, and I introduced myself as someone else, so I need to keep a low profile."

Milloy sighed. "Of course you do."

24.

Fina and Milloy's evening out netted nothing more than tasty snacks and sore throats from hollering at each other over the music. It was wishful thinking that Jamie would turn up at the bar that very night, but she'd never find him there if she never went.

Her alarm the next morning was a rude awakening, and she had a lingering headache, but once she hopped in the shower and swallowed a couple of aspirin, Fina felt ready to get down to business. She was picking Risa up at eleven A.M. to head to Kittery, but first she wanted to speak with Vikram Mehra about the chemicals in his lab. Getting access to Vikram was the challenge. Louis, her favorite security guard, probably wouldn't fall for her usual tricks, and Vikram wouldn't agree to see her.

Fina did a quick online search and found his home address. It was in Hyde Park, just a few streets away from the homes of Liz Barone and Kelly Wegner. The police must have known that, but Fina's antennae started to vibrate anyway.

On the drive over, Fina contemplated her approach. Vikram seemed like enough of a control freak that family members wouldn't invite a stranger into the house without his consent, and he certainly wouldn't welcome Fina with open arms. The best she could hope for was a brief conversation outside.

Vikram's house looked to be one of the pricier ones on his street, but it wasn't particularly attractive. A newly built colonial, it had fake siding and a twin on the neighboring lot. The landscaping was immature, and a few pathetic-looking saplings dotted the grass. Fina never understood why builders couldn't leave some of the trees in place rather than make a pathetic attempt at planting new ones. Was it *that* time-consuming or expensive to steer clear of a few old oaks and maples?

It was nearly seven thirty A.M. when she arrived. She was relieved to find two cars in the driveway, suggesting that he hadn't already left for the lab. Fina parked across the street and kept one eye on the front door and the other on a game of solitaire on her phone. Surveillance was one of the more boring tasks performed by PIs. You actually had to pay attention, and you always felt like you had to pee, if only because you couldn't.

Luckily, she didn't have to wait long. At five minutes before eight, the front door opened and Vikram emerged. He was wearing a parka over his suit and a stocking cap on his head. It really was hard to look fashionable in twenty degrees, which is perhaps why there was little haute couture originating from Siberia.

Fina turned off the car and jumped out. She jogged across the street and came to a stop at Vikram's driver's-side door a moment before he did.

"Move or I will call the police!" he announced.

"For Pete's sake, take it down a notch," Fina said. "I just want a minute of your time."

"I have nothing to say to you." He extended his key toward the door handle, but Fina maneuvered her body to block his access.

"Do you have lithium metal in your lab?" she asked.

"My lab is not your concern."

"I'm guessing the cops asked you the same question."

"Get out of my way," he said.

"Unless you say otherwise, I'm going to assume you have lithium metal. I hope you can account for all of it."

Vikram threw up his hands. "Of course! Because I am dark-skinned and not named Michael or Joseph, you assume I'm a terrorist. Just because I'm from the other side of the world does not mean I aim to murder people!"

"I assume you're from India and a Hindu," Fina replied. "Am I incorrect in that assumption?"

Vikram closed his mouth abruptly.

Fina looked annoyed. "Yeah, some of us do actually know the difference, so why don't you put away your race and religion card."

Vikram stood up straighter, but remained silent.

"I'm asking *you*, Dr. Mehra, because you have access to lithium metal, the main component used in the incendiary device that was planted on my car, a device that could have killed me and my brother. And I'm asking *you* because I'm investigating Liz Barone's death, a death in which you had a stake."

He shoved the key into the door lock. "That's preposterous."

"And I didn't realize how close you live to Liz Fina said, surveying the street. "I can't say I'm surprised you didn't mention it, but it does seem like a salient fact."

Vikram climbed into the car, and Fina saw the lock pop down. He started the car and rolled down the window.

"That woman has been nothing but trouble," he said. "Even in death, she is causing problems for me."

Fina made a sad face. "Well, poor you, Vikram."

He rolled up the window and backed out of the driveway. She looked back at the house and caught a small motion in one of the windows. Maybe Mrs. Mehra was just as mean as her husband, but Fina thought it was more likely that he bullied her, too. Fina could knock on the door, but she didn't want to risk getting the wife in trouble.

Contrary to what some people believed, she wasn't interested in gaining information at any cost.

F ina's phone rang as she navigated a rotary.
   "Fina, it's Bobbi Barone."

"Hi, Bobbi. How are you?"

"Well, I have to admit that I'm feeling mighty pissed off at the moment."

"What's going on?" Fina pulled into a mini-mall parking lot so she could give Bobbi her full attention.

"You talked with someone from the fund-raising office at NEU, didn't you?" Bobbi asked. "Before Liz died."

"Uh-huh. A woman named Pamela Fordyce."

"She's the one who Liz was so angry with?"

"That's right," Fina said. "Her office kept sending out annual fund solicitations."

"Well, I'm going through the mail at Liz's house—Jamie has let it stack up—and there's another letter from her," Bobbi exclaimed.

"From Pamela Fordyce?" Fina asked.

"Yes. I mean, are you kidding me? Don't they know she's dead?"

It was the first time that Fina had heard a hint of unhinging in Bobbi's voice, but it didn't surprise her. People could be very good at holding things together in high-stress moments, but when the dust settled, the littlest thing could send them over the edge.

"Is it a form letter?" Fina asked, gripping the steering wheel tightly, "or a personal letter?"

"Form, and the reason I called you is so that I don't call this woman and give her a piece of my mind. Your father said I wasn't to speak with anyone from NEU."

"He's right, and you were right to call me. I promise you, I will give Pamela Fordyce a piece of my mind."

Bobbi exhaled deeply. "That makes me feel better. I bet you're scarier than I am."

Fina laughed. "Don't sell yourself short, Bobbi. You've got plenty of fire in the belly. I'll give you a call once I get this straightened out."

"Thank you. I know it's a little thing, but it's making my blood boil."

"It's not a little thing," Fina argued. "It's insensitive and tasteless. Your indignation is completely reasonable. Don't worry. I'll take care of it."

They ended the call, and Fina glanced at the clock. She had a little time before she had to get Risa.

She took a few deep breaths and counted to ten.

Nope.

Still pissed.

Fina didn't give Pamela the benefit of advance notice before arriving at her office half an hour later. She informed the assistant that she didn't have an appointment, but it was regarding a lawsuit. Jill fluttered around her desk and made a quick phone call.

Fina wondered if an armed escort was on the way to relocate her, but decided to plant herself on the couch and wait anyway.

Five minutes later, a handsome young man in khakis and a button-down sauntered into the office and perched on the edge of the assistant's desk.

"Jill, any word on the replacement speaker?" he asked.

Fina imagined that his good looks granted him privileges he wouldn't enjoy if he were unattractive—privileges like claiming so much real estate of the young woman's work space. He was just the sort of charming bully that made Fina's skin crawl. Given her current mood, she felt like leaning over and shoving his ass off the desk.

"I'm working on it, Darryl," Jill said, tapping away at her keyboard.

"Pamela left Paul in the lurch. If she won't give the talk, she'd better find someone who will."

"Here's an idea," Jill said tartly. "Why don't you help me find a re-placement instead of breathing down my neck?"

"'Cause I work for Paul, not you or Pamela. She can't make commitments and then just blow them off."

Jill's cheeks were turning red.

"You should get your ass off her desk," Fina said innocuously, as if she were commenting on the weather.

Darryl glared at her. "What?"

Jill looked astounded.

"I said, you should get your ass off her desk. You're encroaching upon her physical space," Fina said. "It's very aggressive behavior, Darryl. If I were Jill, I'd call security."

"Who the hell are you?" he asked, rising up and stepping in Fina's direction.

"I'm a private investigator who's in a very bad mood, so move along, young man."

He sneered at her, but didn't approach.

"And don't blame Jill for my little outburst," Fina added. "She doesn't even know who I am."

He left the office, and Fina turned her attention back to the alumni magazine on her lap. She could feel Jill staring at her.

"That was crazy," the young woman said finally.

Fina met her gaze. "I'm sorry. I shouldn't have interfered."

"No." Jill looked around. "It was crazy good. I hate that guy. He's a douche."

Fina shrugged. "I can be a bit heavy-handed, but you know, Jill, you're allowed to tell someone to back off. You can even do it politely, although that takes the fun out of it, in my opinion."

Jill shook her head and fiddled with some papers on the desk. "I get sick of being blamed for everything. She's mad I put it on her calendar. They're mad I took it off. These weren't my decisions!" she said more to herself than Fina.

"Pamela doesn't like giving speeches?" Fina asked.

"Nope. Most of these people love hearing their voices projected across a banquet hall," she fumed. "Do you want some water while you wait?" she asked Fina, rising from her desk.

"Yes, please."

Jill left and returned with a cold bottle of water.

Pamela strode into the office ten minutes later. Her color was high, and her hair looked out of place. She was wearing a skirt suit similar to the others Fina had seen her in. It was charcoal gray and tight around her middle.

"What's going on?" Pamela asked her.

"Why don't we speak in your office?" Fina suggested. Pamela was lucky that Darryl had crossed her path. Confronting him had taken the edge off Fina's anger.

Pamela closed the door behind Fina before taking a seat behind her desk. "I'm very busy, Fina."

"So am I. I just got a call from Bobbi Barone. She was extremely upset."

"I don't think we should be discussing the lawsuit without counsel present," Pamela said, picking up a pen and rolling it between her fingers.

"This isn't going to be a discussion. You have got to take Liz Barone off your mailing list."

Pamela put the pen back down. "We did take her off."

"No, you didn't. Her mother just found a letter sent after Liz died."

Pamela laced her fingers together, kneading them gently. "I'm very sorry, but it's just an administrative error. It doesn't mean anything."

Fina sat down in the chair in front of the desk. "Do you really not understand why this is so upsetting to Bobbi Barone?"

Pamela looked at her before her gaze skipped to the window. "Of course I understand. I'm not heartless."

"Then fix it."

"I really thought I had, Fina."

"Yeah, yeah, but you didn't, so do it now."

Pamela looked tired. "I suppose you're going to leak it to the press: 'Cold NEU hounds grief-stricken mother.'"

"I'm hoping it doesn't come to that," Fina said, starting toward the door. "I had a chat yesterday with your friend Kevin Lafferty."

Pamela's hands stilled on her blotter. "I wouldn't characterize us as friends."

"Acquaintances, colleagues, whatever. I didn't realize how many ties he has to this case."

"What do you mean?"

"Well, there's his connection to the NEU athletic program, and he'd seen Liz in recent months—not that he admitted that, but I found out. His company was one of the sponsors of a grant that Liz's lab didn't get, and then there are the chemicals."

Pamela squinted. "What chemicals?"

"Someone tried to blow up my car with a device that uses lithium metal, which Barnes Kaufcan has in their labs. It totaled the car."

Pamela's face relaxed. "I'm sure there are numerous places to acquire that chemical or metal, whichever it is. That's the problem with home-made devices. Anyone can make them at home."

"And yet," Fina said, "most people aren't cooking up IEDs in their kitchens."

Pamela shook her head. "I have little contact with Kevin, so I don't see how I can help."

"Right," Fina said. "Please don't make me come back here about another fund-raising letter."

"You made your point."

"Glad to hear it."

Fina left and returned to her car.

Pamela had made an interesting point. Lots of people had access to lithium metal and could cook up some trouble at home. Maybe even she did.

Fina picked up Risa and they headed to Kittery. They chitchatted at first, but as the miles and minutes ticked by, they fell into a companionable silence. Risa was undoubtedly thinking about her aunt, and Fina mulled over the morning's conversations.

The farther north they traveled, the more snow blanketed the landscape. Unlike the drifts in the city, most of the snow at the side of the highway was white and pristine, throwing off an intense glare in the sunlight.

The Popover Place was just off the exit for the outlet mall, the parking lot practically full. As Fina maneuvered into a space, Risa pulled down the visor and flipped open the mirror. She applied a fresh coat of lipstick and examined her face. She futzed with her hair before snapping the mirror closed and pushing the visor back into place.

"Ready?" Fina asked.

"No, but let's go."

The restaurant had a small entryway that was divided from the rest of the space by rows of wooden spindles. The young woman who greeted them was wearing a brown dress with a white apron, her hair tucked into a fabric bonnet. The getup fell somewhere between Florence Nightingale and Goody Proctor of Salem witch trial infamy.

Greta was already seated at a booth next to the window overlooking one of the busy thoroughfares leading to the mall. She looked healthier than she had when Fina met her a few months earlier. Her skin was less jaundiced and less puffy, and her eyes looked brighter.

When she caught sight of them, Greta squirmed out of the booth and moved as if to hug Risa. Panic washed over Risa's face, and she offered Greta her hand. The weak handshake communicated Greta's displeasure.

"I ordered some coffee," Greta said once Fina and Risa were seated across from her.

"I wonder if the popovers are any good?" Fina mused.

"They're excellent," Greta said.

Risa glanced at the menu before squaring it with the edge of the table. Fina nodded to the waitress, who had just delivered two large stacks of pancakes to the table across the aisle.

"Risa, go ahead," Fina urged as the waitress stood poised with her order book and pen.

"I'm not that hungry. Just coffee, please."

Greta shook her head when it was her turn, but Fina wasn't suffering from the same anxiety-fueled loss of appetite.

"Could I please have a hot chocolate, and how about some popovers for the table? You two might change your minds," Fina said.

Once the waitress left, a thick silence claimed the table. Greta looked at Risa while Risa studied her manicure. Fina took a sip of water and cleared her throat before speaking.

"Thanks for meeting with us, Greta. You look much better than the last time I saw you."

"I'm on dialysis now. I have more energy."

"That's great," Fina said.

"You look wonderful, Risa," Greta said, gazing at her niece. "You look like Elizabeth did when she was your age."

"Do I?" Risa asked. "I've always wondered if I look like my birth mother." Fina sensed the chill under the words, but Greta didn't seem to notice.

"That's why we wanted to meet," Fina said. "Risa would like to hear more about her mother and her birth father, if you have any information about him."

The waitress brought a coffeepot to the table and topped off Greta's cup before filling Risa's. Her other hand gripped a mug brimming with hot chocolate and whipped cream, which she set down in front of Fina.

Greta added some creamer to her coffee and stirred it slowly. "Elizabeth never told me who the father was, which means she didn't tell anyone. If she wanted to talk about it, I'm the one she would have told. We were best friends."

"Rockford is a small town, though," Fina said. "I can't imagine there were too many candidates."

"I had my suspicions," Greta conceded, "but that's all they were."

"I'd still like to hear them," Risa said, looking at Greta over her raised mug.

Greta shrugged. "If it's important."

"It's important," Risa said, shooting Fina a look.

Greta spent ten minutes describing the two men—boys, at the time—who she suspected might be Risa's biological father. They sounded like average American boys from the northeast who liked being outdoors, playing sports, and going to the movies. Fina took notes while Greta spoke, in case Risa wanted her to track down either of the men. Greta might not have known the identity of Risa's father, but that didn't mean that *he* didn't know he was the father.

"I don't think you should bother those men, Fina," Greta said, glancing at the notebook.

"No need to worry, Greta. I'll be discreet."

Greta frowned, but didn't argue.

A steaming basket of popovers—each the size of a softball—was dropped off at the table by a different waitress. Fina pulled aside the napkin in which they were wrapped and let more steam escape. After a moment, she dropped one onto her plate and reached for a pat of butter.

"I understand why Elizabeth went through with the pregnancy, but did she ever consider keeping me?" Risa asked.

Greta's hand went to her head, her fingertips grazing her gray curls. "Well, no. Our father wouldn't have allowed it."

"Ah," Risa said. She grasped her coffee cup and raised it to her lips.

"Because he didn't approve?" Fina asked.

"Of course," Greta said. "It wasn't respectable to have a baby out of wedlock. It wasn't like today, when young girls have babies left and right."

Fina fought the urge to roll her eyes. Everything was better in the good old days.

"But when did your father—my grandfather—die?" Risa asked.

"When we were in our forties," Greta said.

Fina pulled open the popover and spread a generous chunk of butter into it, then tore off a piece and put it in her mouth.

"So he died more than twenty years ago?" Risa asked, doing the math.

"Yes."

"But why didn't Elizabeth try to contact me after he died?"

Greta sipped her coffee. "Well, she had a child by that time. A son."

Fina cringed inwardly. Fina wanted to give Greta the benefit of the doubt, but man, was it hard. Greta's sensitivity meter—if she had one—always seemed to be on the fritz.

"Actually, she had two children at that point," Risa said.

"Well, you know what I mean," Greta said.

"So he was my replacement?" Risa asked.

Fina had another bite of popover. Greta looked flummoxed. Risa was asking her tough questions, but they were fair questions.

"No, he wasn't a replacement," Greta insisted, "but she had to take care of him. She was busy with him."

"Did she marry his father?" Fina asked.

"Yes, they were together for thirty-three years before William died."

"And when did her son die?" Fina asked, drinking from her mug.

Greta swallowed and stared into her coffee cup. "When he was nineteen."

"I'm sorry," Fina said. "That must have been very difficult."

"It was," Greta said, dabbing at her eyes with her paper napkin.

Risa sat back in the booth. Fina could see a faint tremor in Risa's hands, which she slipped into her lap.

"Elizabeth's son predeceased her by how many years?" Fina asked. Until Risa gave her a sign to back off, she'd forge ahead.

"Twenty-two, no, twenty-three years," Greta said. "I think that's right."

"More coffee?" The waitress appeared at the table. Risa put her hand over her mug, but Greta pushed hers forward.

"I know you're curious about your mother," Greta said after the waitress had left, "but I'm not sure how all this information is helpful."

Risa looked at Fina, who tilted her head in question. Risa gave the tiniest nod.

"Greta," Fina said, "did your sister ever make any effort to find Risa?"

"I . . . I don't know."

"All those years—especially after her son died—she never expressed an interest in finding her firstborn?"

"She didn't to me," Greta said, "but that doesn't mean she didn't *ever*."

"But you said you were best friends," Fina reminded her. "Who else would she have discussed it with?"

"I don't know. This was all a long time ago."

Fina frowned. "But it wasn't really. Your sister died eleven months ago. She had forty-five years to reach out to Risa, and she didn't."

"But that's not my fault!" Greta said. "That was her decision."

"Absolutely," Fina said, pulling off more popover. "But did *you* ever broach the subject with your sister or do some searching of your own?"

Greta pulled her cardigan sweater tight across her chest. The top two buttons were undone, and she struggled to do them up. "Not really, but you have to understand, it was a different time."

"I know it was different forty-five years ago," Fina said, "but it wasn't so different one year ago."

Greta shook her head. "She didn't want to be reminded of it. Elizabeth didn't want to talk about it, so we didn't."

"She wanted to forget about it," Risa said quietly, "about me. That's what you're really saying."

Fina reached down and squeezed Risa's knee. For once, Greta was quiet.

They sat for a moment in silence. Fina stirred the lumped chocolate from the bottom of her mug into the remaining liquid.

"If you didn't need a kidney," Risa asked suddenly, "would you have found me?"

Greta's eyes widened. "I . . . Of course I would have."

"But you never tried to before," Risa insisted.

"Because Elizabeth was alive and didn't want me to, but I always planned to find you."

Fina studied Greta's face. It was hard to read, but if Fina had to wager a guess, she'd guess that Greta was lying. She might have even been lying to herself, but Fina found it hard to believe she would have reached out to Risa if her health were good. In Fina's experience, people did amazingly hard things when they were spurred on by a deep-seated drive. Some projects—like finding one's birth parents or single parenthood—were only undertaken with a strong dose of commitment and fortitude. Fina didn't think Greta possessed either quality in any great quantity.

"So you were going to contact me?" Risa asked again. "Even if you had remained healthy?"

"Yes. Yes, I was."

"What kind of relationship do you want to have moving forward?" Fina asked Greta. "What are your expectations, aside from a kidney?"

"Whatever Risa wants," Greta insisted. "It's up to her."

On the face of it that sounded respectful, but to Fina it also sounded like a cop-out. Greta should have been anxious to meet her great-nephews. She should have been planning for the events and milestones that were part of having an extended family. Fina had no aspirations for a white picket fence or 2.3 children, but she loved participating in her niece's and nephews' lives. School plays, soccer games, graduations—sure, they were boring, but Haley, Ryan, Teddy, and Chandler never were. She relished her time with them and took pleasure in the facets that parenthood added to her relationship with Scotty. You saw your siblings differently when they were also someone's parent.

Fina glanced at her watch. It had been almost an hour, and Risa looked tired.

"Was there anything else, Risa?" she asked her friend.

Risa shook her head. "Not right now."

"Is there anything you want to ask Risa?" Fina asked Greta.

Greta touched her hair near her temple. "I just want to say that I'm so happy to meet you, Risa, and I hope we can get to know each other even better."

In the transplant ward, Fina added silently.

Goodness, she was cynical.

25.

The drive back to Boston was as quiet as the drive to Kittery had been. Risa didn't want to talk, and Fina respected that. When they pulled up in front of Risa's house, Fina put the car in park and looked at her.

"When or if you want to talk, I'm here," Fina said.

"I know. I need a little time to digest it."

"Of course."

"I'm guessing you have an opinion?" Risa asked.

"I always have an opinion, but I'm going to digest, as well," Fina said. "I don't think either of us should dismiss our first impressions, but we also don't have to act on them, whatever they might be."

"Okay." Risa reached over and gave her a hug. "Thanks, Fina."

"I know this feels out of control, but you get to decide what's right for you."

"That's what's so scary; I feel like I'm deciding someone else's fate in addition to my own."

Fina shook her head. "You're not, and you're not deciding your fate, just one piece of your life. You could be hit by a bus tomorrow and this whole discussion would be moot."

"Thanks, I guess," Risa said.

Fina grinned. "Keep in touch."

She watched Risa climb the front stairs and disappear into the house.

Fina needed to switch gears and turn her attention back to Liz Barone, not an easy task. All this talk of siblings and family actually made her feel a little sentimental, but she didn't get paid to navel-gaze. She pulled out the list of stores that Angelo had provided and noted that one was nearby.

Men's Universe was on Route 9 in Natick and featured more athletic gear and casual clothes than business attire. Fina found a woman of average size behind the counter, and she seemed generally interested in helping Fina identify her mystery man. Mary, the saleswoman, was studying the photo.

"Do you think that's an insignia or just a smudge?" Fina asked her, pointing at the area on the man's ankle.

Mary brought the picture close to her face and examined the image. Fina wondered if she had a big 'n' tall fella in her life or if this was just a job to Mary. She couldn't have been more than five feet three inches, and Fina was trying to imagine life—okay, sex—with a tall man. She knew the mechanics would still work, but what would it be like gazing at your lover's rib cage?

"I can't tell for sure," Mary said, "but I think we used to carry those socks. Hold on a second."

She disappeared into a back room and came out a moment later struggling under the weight of a stack of thick binders. Fina grabbed a couple to lessen the load while Mary cleared a space on the counter. She flipped open the first binder and started thumbing through the pages.

"So you don't carry them anymore?" Fina asked.

"Nah. We didn't sell enough. They were expensive." Mary brushed back a lock of her hair and scanned the pages. Fina watched as she traced her finger down columns of data, her bright pink nail serving as a pointer.

The bell at the front door jangled as a customer entered, and Mary looked in that direction. "Let me know if you need help finding any-thing," she called out across the space.

The man nodded and started perusing a rack of sale items.

"It's not in there," Mary said, closing the first binder and moving on to a second.

Fina didn't want to breathe down her neck, so she wandered away from the counter and checked out a display of pajamas. Did men even wear pajamas these days? Men who weren't her father's age? As far as she knew, her brothers slept in boxers or sweat shorts, and Milloy and Cristian slept in nothing when she had the pleasure of their company. She picked up a pajama top on a hanger and held it up to her body. It reached from her shoulders to her knees. For a brief instant, Fina felt delicate.

"I think this might be it," Mary said, summoning Fina back to the counter. She rotated the binder so Fina could get a good look at a picture showing a pair of athletic socks with an insignia near the ankle. The photo of the mystery man was too blurry to provide a positive match, but it looked promising.

"Does any place around here carry these socks?" Fina asked.

"I wouldn't know. I can give you the manufacturer's info, and you could ask them."

"That would be great," Fina said.

"It's so nice of you to go to such trouble to find this man," Mary said, jotting the name of the company and the sock details on a Post-it note. "Just when I start to feel bad about my fellow man, I meet someone doing something good, and it makes me feel so much better."

"Well," Fina said, "I'm just doing what I can."

Back in her car she felt a brief surge of guilt for misleading Mary, but she got over it when she reminded herself that the man in the picture had tried to barbecue her on the Tobin Bridge. Fina wasn't doing the exact good deed that Mary credited to her, but she was doing a good deed by getting a dangerous man off the street. One less creep made Mary's world a little bit safer, even if she didn't know it.

It was close to dinnertime when Fina swung by Patty and Scotty's house. Patty was in the kitchen on the phone, the family calendar on her laptop. Fina climbed onto one of the stools at the island.

"Hi," Patty said a few minutes later, once the date of the rummage sale meeting had been confirmed.

"Hey. Is this a bad time? I was in the neighborhood."

"No, it's good. I'm just catching up on all the crap that I need to keep track of."

"Where are the kids?"

"Chandler is upstairs playing in his room, Teddy is at a friend's, and Ryan should be home any minute from soccer practice. Haley is having dinner at a friend's house."

"It's quiet," Fina said.

"I know. Isn't it glorious?"

Fina didn't respond.

"You okay?" Patty asked, a concerned look on her face.

"Yeah, I'm fine."

"Is it something about the car fire?"

"No, no," Fina said. "I'm making progress on that."

Patty walked over to the built-in desk and gathered a small stack of paper. She brought it over to the island and began sorting it into different piles.

"If you ever need a kidney," Fina said a minute later, "I would give you one of mine."

Patty looked at her, bemused. "Okay. Is there something you're trying to tell me?"

"Nope. Just that I love you and am lucky to have you for a sister-in-law."

"I love you, too, Fina, and I'd give you a kidney, although Scotty would probably be a better match."

"Maybe, but could you imagine the whining? 'It hurts! Am I going to have a scar? When can I eat again?'"

Patty laughed. "Good point." She tidied up one of the piles and grabbed a manila envelope from a cubbyhole above the desk. "You're sure you're okay?" she asked Fina again.

"Absolutely. I *am* a little concerned that my expression of affection makes you so worried, but I suppose it's out of character."

"Actually, you express your affection quite frequently," Patty said. "I just know that everyone relies on you, and I'm not sure who you rely on."

Fina smiled. "I have people, don't worry. You're one of them, even if it's not obvious."

"Are you staying for dinner?" Patty asked, stowing the manila folder back on the desk and pulling open the refrigerator door.

"No, I'm good, thanks. I'm still dreaming about the popover I had a few hours ago."

"Where did you have a popover? They're hard to find these days."

"The Popover Place in Kittery, Maine."

Patty raised an eyebrow in question.

"No, I wasn't shopping."

"Glad to hear it," Patty said. "That would really be cause for concern."

Fina slid off the bar stool and gave Patty a hug. "I'm off like a prom dress. First I'll pop up and say hi to Chandler."

Fina found her nephew in his bedroom, which was an example of controlled chaos. Unlike Elaine, who routinely invaded her children's privacy, Patty and Scotty tried to respect their kids' space, with some caveats. Food wasn't allowed upstairs, and their belongings, if not organized and tidy, had to at least be contained. Chandler's room was full of fancy canvas bins holding books, toys, sporting equipment, and even socks. If Fina ever adopted an organizational system, it might look something like this.

She spent a few minutes visiting with her nephew, then ventured back downstairs and bumped into her brother at the front door.

"Hey," Scotty said, dropping his briefcase.

"Hey. What's up?"

"You here for dinner?" Scotty asked.

"Nah, I have plans. I just wanted to stop by and say hi."

"Ah. Found our bomber yet?"

"I don't think it was a bomb," Fina said, "technically speaking."

"Right," Scotty responded. "Now's the time to split hairs."

"I'm making progress," Fina assured him.

He started toward the kitchen.

"Scotty, wait a sec. We need to talk about Haley and this Florida trip that Mom keeps pushing for."

Scotty sighed. "I'm not going to make Haley do anything she doesn't want to do, Fina."

"Of course not, but I don't think we should be acting like it's her decision. We're the adults; we should be actively protecting her; you know, keeping her away from sexual predators."

Scotty winced. "I hate it when you say things like that."

"The truth, you mean," Fina said. "You hate it when I speak the truth."

His shoulders sagged. "So what are you suggesting?"

"I'm suggesting that we tell Mom that Haley will not be seeing her father in Florida because we are concerned for her safety and well-being."

"If she's not going to go anyway, why antagonize Mom?"

"It's not about antagonizing Mom—although that is an added bonus. It's about demonstrating to Haley that we have her best interests at heart and that we'll protect her even when things get messy."

"I'm not getting in between you and Mom," Scotty said. "How about if we make Haley unavailable for the visit, and you do whatever you want."

"Fine."

Scotty started toward the kitchen again, but stopped just short of the hallway. "Mom just has this fantasy of Rand and Haley and Karla and her kids. Like one big happy family."

"Wait. Is Karla the girlfriend?" Fina asked.

Scotty nodded.

"And she has kids?" Fina closed the gap between them. "Girls or boys?"

Scotty paused. A moment later, recognition spread across his face. "I think they're girls."

"So our brother"—Fina leaned closer to Scotty—"the pedophile, is dating a woman with daughters?"

Scotty nodded slowly.

"Oh my God," Fina said, grasping her head in her hands.

"You don't know what's actually happening, Fina," Scotty cautioned her.

"I feel like throwing up," she said.

"Go to the bathroom if you're going to puke."

"Thanks for the tip," Fina said, rubbing her temples. "This is worse than I thought."

"But it was bound to happen," he said. "Did you think he was going to remain single forever?"

Fina threw up her hands. "I guess I didn't think. I didn't want to contemplate Rand's future."

Scotty reached out and rubbed her shoulder. "Trust me, I'm not happy about this, either, but there's nothing we can do."

"But we can't do nothing."

"Fina, you can't fix everything, and you can't protect everyone."

She squeezed his hand and left, not trusting herself to respond.

Pamela sat on the couch, her phone in hand. She'd just finished a call with Deb, who'd been none too pleased about the last-minute cancellation of their dinner date, but it couldn't be helped. Pamela did not have the energy to make small talk, and she definitely didn't want to discuss her feelings with Deb.

It was becoming clear that Deb was a big sharer who believed the road to intimacy was paved with confessions and the dissection of personal interactions. This had never been Pamela's approach, and she didn't believe that she would change her tune if only the right person came along. She was fifty-four years old; she was who she was going to be. It wasn't that change wasn't possible, but after half a century, you didn't change unless there was an enormous benefit to doing so. So far, Pamela couldn't see one. She wanted to keep things casual, but doubted that such an arrangement would suit Deb. She wanted happily ever after, whereas Pamela would be fine with happily right now.

She'd spent the better part of the day ensuring that Liz Barone's name was scrubbed from every mailing list and database associated with her office. The recent fund-raising plea sent to Liz had been a genuine mistake, but it still looked bad, like she had ignored a sick woman's wishes. Her fears that she and NEU were under a microscope were being realized; this was abundantly clear given Fina Ludlow's comments about Kevin.

Over the years, Kevin and Pamela had had an alliance. They'd had each other's backs and tried to keep the other's interests in mind. But now she was having doubts. Kevin had always seemed loyal, but she didn't find his reaction to recent events reassuring. His easygoing demeanor was either an impressive acting job or he truly didn't appreciate how much was at risk.

Pamela padded into the kitchen and pulled an open bottle of wine from the fridge. She poured a generous glass and went back to the couch. Her phone beeped, and Pamela clicked open a text from Deb. Sorry dinner hadn't happened. Sorry she got upset with Pamela. Maybe they could reschedule for tomorrow?

Pamela placed the phone facedown on the coffee table without responding. She felt irritated, a relationship death knell if ever there was one.

She needed to start taking action. Waiting for other people to act wasn't getting her anywhere. Pamela had been clear with Kevin that she was worried, and he had dismissed her concerns. And now she'd found out that things were even worse than she thought.

From here on out, it was every woman for herself.

I assume you know that Vikram Mehra lives a few streets away from Liz Barone?" Fina asked Cristian the next morning. She was leaving soon to meet Pamela Fordyce for breakfast—an unexpected and intriguing invitation extended the night before.

"Yes, I assumed you knew, too."

"I didn't."

"Maybe you're losing your edge," Cristian said on the other end of the line.

"I doubt it, but I am only human. Mistakes are made." She swapped the phone and the mascara wand between hands. "So was he in the neighborhood when she was attacked?"

"Presumably, but there's no way to prove it either way."

"Hmm."

"Is that the only reason you called?" Cristian asked.

"That and to say hi." Fina knew she should tell him about the sock insignia research, but something made her hold back. She had a few more avenues she wanted to explore before handing that nugget over to the police. It wasn't actual evidence yet, she rationalized, just a lead. It could be a dead end, and she didn't want to waste the cops' time. Neither Cristian nor Pitney would buy that explanation for a second, but it worked in her head.

"Okay," he said. "Hi."

"That's it. Hi. When are we having dinner?" Fina asked.

"Tonight?"

"Is that a question for me or you?"

"Both of us, I guess."

"Why don't we touch base later?" Fina said, applying a coat of lip gloss.

"Sounds good. Talk to you later."

She hung up and grabbed her bag and coat.

Fina was hungry—for food and information.

———————

amela had suggested they meet at a hotel situated in the middle of NEU's urban campus. The building—constructed from yellow brick and limestone—dated from the mid-1800s. At ten stories, it was one of the taller structures in the neighborhood, which was probably helpful to visiting parents trying to navigate the area for the first time.

Fina left her car with the valet and pushed through the revolving door into the lobby. It was an ornate space with dark coffered ceilings and crystal sconces. There were oversized canvases on the walls— paintings of oceanscapes and historical gatherings. It was the kind of place that attracted a certain wedding reception clientele: people who wanted to imagine they were stepping back in time and up the social ladder in one quick move.

Pamela was already seated in the dining room with a cup of tea in front of her.

"Good morning," Fina said, and waved off the coffee-wielding waiter.

"I waited to get some food until you got here," Pamela said.

"Thanks. I'm hungry."

"After you," Pamela said, pointing Fina in the direction of the buffet.

Fina took a warm plate from a tall stack and scanned her options. Pamela was doing the same, and after five minutes, they reconvened at the table. Pamela had selected yogurt and fruit plus two strips of bacon. Fina had opted for French toast, bacon, a few cubes of cantaloupe, and two small cinnamon rolls.

Pamela examined Fina's plate. "How do you eat like that and stay thin?" she asked.

"I've been blessed with a very fast metabolism," Fina said, sipping a glass of orange juice. "I also don't eat a ton at any one time."

"Must be nice," Pamela murmured.

"It is, although you'd be surprised how many people want to weigh in on my diet. It gets annoying after a while."

"I wish I could eat like that," Pamela said, spearing a chunk of pine-apple with her fork.

"I'm sure you're blessed with other talents," Fina said. She nibbled on a piece of bacon and waited. Pamela had called this meeting; Fina would let her dive in when she was ready.

"I wanted to let you know," Pamela started, "that I spent a great deal of time yesterday making sure that Liz Barone's name has been deleted from the development office's rolls."

"Good. Glad to hear it."

Pamela picked up her teacup and sipped from its delicate lip. Fina doubted that bit of information was the reason she'd been sum-moned.

"Also, I was thinking about the things you said about Kevin Lafferty."

"Oh?" Fina asked casually.

"Well, I wouldn't want to cast aspersions on anyone," Pamela said, gearing up to cast aspersions, "but this is an unusual situation."

"Which part of the situation are you referring to?" Fina asked.

"Liz's death and the lawsuit, of course."

"Right." Fina cut off a bite of French toast.

"You can't repeat what I'm saying to anyone," Pamela insisted.

"Then what's the point of telling me?" Fina wondered.

"Because I think you should know. I'm trying to be helpful." People often wanted credit for coming forward with information they shared only when it was in their best interest.

"And I appreciate that," Fina said.

Pamela frowned and dipped her spoon into the ramekin of yogurt. She swallowed a mouthful before speaking. "Nobody can know that I told you."

"Pamela." Fina looked at her. "If the police ask me for information and the source of that information, I have to comply. If I don't cooper-ate, I could be charged with obstruction."

"I understand that," she said.

"In terms of people other than the police, I will do everything I can to keep your name out of it. It's the best I can do."

Pamela poured more tea from the small pot into her cup and stirred in some sugar.

"Well, I guess I can live with that."

"Good," Fina said, biting into a cinnamon roll. "You wanted to tell me something about Kevin Lafferty?"

"Yes."

A party of six was led to the table next to them. Pamela didn't continue until they had deposited their bags, cameras, and maps and headed for the buffet.

"Kevin has done many wonderful things for NEU," she said. "He's been a tremendous booster, raised lots of money, and has always pitched in when asked."

Fina looked at her. "I get it. He has many good qualities. Blah, blah, blah. I'll bear those in mind, but I'm not terribly interested in that at the moment."

Pamela sat back. "You don't mince words."

"No, I don't. I'm not a development officer, remember? I can piss off whomever I like."

"What that must be like," Pamela mused.

"It's delightful," Fina said, "but back to Kevin. I assume you want to tell me about his less-than-stellar traits."

Pamela smoothed the napkin on her lap. "Rumor has it that he plays around."

"So do half of all married men, if we're to believe the statistics," Fina said.

"He plays around with students," Pamela said in a hushed tone.

Fina considered that for a moment. "Okay, that's slimy, but is it against school policy? He isn't an employee, and if the students are of age, it's not against the law."

"It's frowned upon, particularly when the man is in a position of influence."

"You'll have to be more specific, Pamela," Fina said. "Are we talking about female students? Male students?"

"We're talking about female student athletes." She sat back. The tourists reappeared at that moment. Finding room for their multiple plates was a noisy and extended production that served to temporarily quell Fina and Pamela's conversation.

"You're saying that Kevin has affairs with young women who are currently athletes at NEU?" Fina asked.

"Yes."

"Do you have any proof of this?"

"No."

Fina chewed on some bacon. "If this is true, why is he allowed to remain as a booster?"

"Because he's practically an institution himself," Pamela said. "If he stopped doing what he does, people would ask questions. There would probably be a scandal, which would hurt him and NEU."

"So they're looking at mutually assured destruction?" Fina asked.

"Something like that."

"But in terms of the position of influence, does he have enough sway to impact the athletes' lives? What's in it for the players?"

"He has a lot of influence," Pamela insisted. "Booster money might get routed one way and not another. Or if a player has a problem with the coach, Kevin is tight with the athletic director. There are lots of ears he can whisper into to make certain things happen."

"How long has he been doing this?" Fina asked.

Pamela shook her head. "I have no idea."

"Does he currently have a girlfriend?"

"I would bet he does, but I don't know for sure. He does have a wife, though, I can tell you that."

Fina shrugged. "For all we know, they've worked out an arrangement. Who knows what goes on in other people's marriages?" She popped the remainder of a cinnamon roll in her mouth. "I'm not sure what this has to do with Liz."

"I don't have all the answers, Fina, but I thought you should know."

"Why now?" Fina drained her juice.

"What do you mean?" Pamela asked, busying herself with a piece of pineapple.

"This is the fourth time we've spoken since the start of this investigation. Why are you only telling me this now?"

Pamela patted her lips with her napkin. "It didn't seem relevant before, but when we spoke yesterday, I realized that I wasn't in a position to judge relevancy."

"Have you shared your suspicions with the police?" Fina asked.

"Not yet."

"Are you planning to?"

"I haven't decided yet." Pamela grasped the handle of her teacup. "I assume you're going to urge me to tell them."

Fina sighed. "I think people should tell the police the truth when asked, particularly if one's statement can be either proven or disproven, but I can't be your conscience."

"Would you tell them if you were me?"

Fina looked at the tourists, who were debating the city map in a language that sounded like fingernails on a chalkboard.

"I suggest you do whatever will ensure a good night's sleep."

Pamela signaled the waiter for the check. She reached into her purse and pulled out some cash, which she slipped into the folio.

"Do you think Liz Barone knew about Kevin's affairs?" Fina asked, rising from her chair.

Pamela tilted her head side to side. "I have no idea."

Fina waited in the vestibule for her car, turning the conversation over in her head. There was a lot that Pamela claimed she didn't know. But she certainly knew enough to shine a bright, unflattering spotlight on Kevin Lafferty.

26.

Fina's questions for Kevin were piling up, but she needed to do more digging before confronting him with them. Tasha and Gus might shed some light on the rumors, but given their professional responsibilities, they were hard to track down. Fina was able to get Kelly on the line, but she had a packed schedule of her own.

"I don't have time to meet with you today. I'm sorry," Kelly said. She sounded like she was on speakerphone in the car.

"I'm happy to meet you at one of the kids' activities or tag along while you do errands," Fina said.

"What is this about exactly?" Kelly asked.

"I have some questions about Kevin Lafferty."

There was a long pause. "I suppose you could join me at Costco."

"Great," Fina said, wondering if Kelly's change of heart could be solely attributed to the proposed topic of conversation. "Just tell me where and when."

They met an hour later in the parking lot of the Dedham store. Fina pushed a cart that was the size of a small flatbed truck as Kelly deposited oversized items into it. She'd wrapped her hand in fresh gauze that morning, and it was healing nicely, but it still hurt when she tried to maneuver the cart.

"This must last you a while," Fina commented as Kelly struggled with a box of thirty granola bars.

"I come every couple of weeks," Kelly said, her hair escaping from a loose ponytail. There were dark circles under her eyes. "The kids go through the basics like you wouldn't believe: bread, milk, yogurt, cereal. If I got standard sizes, I'd be at the grocery store every other day."

"And here, you can get new tires and underwear at the same time," Fina noted.

"Hey, don't knock it," Kelly said. "Aren't you from a big family?"

The Ludlows had a high enough profile that people often knew general information about them, even if they weren't personally acquainted. It had always been this way, so Fina didn't think much of it.

"I'm one of four," she said.

"So your mother really had it bad. Did she shop in bulk when you were growing up?" Kelly asked.

Fina rested her forearms on the cart handle and followed Kelly down an aisle of canned fruit and vegetables. She didn't have many memories of Elaine performing household tasks. Her mother hired someone to take care of those sorts of things so she would have plenty of time for playing tennis and gossiping.

"My mother wasn't very hands-on," Fina said.

Kelly gave her a funny look, but didn't comment. They passed a family of several generations who were nibbling from small paper cups. There seemed to be food samples available at the end of every other aisle. You could make a meal of it, if you didn't mind chasing canned salmon with cinnamon swirl tea loaf.

"So what did you want to ask me about Kevin?" Kelly asked. "I don't really know him."

"Did you ever get the sense that he fooled around with some of the soccer players or any other students at NEU?"

Kelly didn't respond. She pulled a twenty-pack of single-serving fruit cocktail off the shelf and heaved it into the cart. "He had a bit of a reputation," she finally answered.

"A reputation for?"

"For being a flirt. He loved hanging around the sports complex, but he seemed to like hanging with the guys just as much as the girls."

"So as far as you know, he wasn't having a fling with anyone?" Fina asked.

"Well, he might have been. I don't really know." She sounded annoyed.

"Oookay," Fina said, tamping down her frustration. "Did you see any evidence that he was having an affair with a player or a student during that time?"

Kelly pushed some hair behind her ear. "I didn't see any evidence, but that doesn't mean something wasn't going on."

"Right, but why assume that something was going on if you didn't have evidence of it? Do you suspect that something was happening?"

Kelly shoved an enormous package of toilet paper onto the bottom shelf of the cart. "I don't want to bad-mouth anyone."

"Of course not. I'll keep that in mind," Fina said, thinking of Pamela's similar protestations. Fina always took that sort of comment with a grain of salt. The people who really didn't want to bad-mouth anyone just didn't.

"He seemed pretty chummy with a few girls on the team, but I never saw him do anything. He's a good-looking guy; I'm not surprised the girls found him attractive."

"But you didn't? Find him attractive, I mean?" Fina asked.

Kelly shrugged. "He was cute, but I didn't go out with him, if that's what you're asking."

She ducked into the refrigerated room and came back carting two gallons of milk. In the alcohol section, Kelly chose a few bottles of white wine that she dropped in the cart. She hesitated over the reds and walked away, then turned back and plucked two from the wooden display crates.

"When you were in college, Kevin was, what, ten years older?" Fina asked. "Nowadays there's quite an age difference between him and the undergrads."

"Sure, but some women like older men," Kelly commented.

Fina had sometimes wondered if her father ever cheated on Elaine.

She imagined that he would be quite a catch for certain women. He was handsome, rich, and powerful. He was also bossy, domineering, and uncommunicative, but some women went for those qualities, too.

"Did you know that Liz's boss, Vikram, lives in your neighborhood?" Fina asked.

"Liz had mentioned it. She hated seeing him outside of the office."

"Did they have any run-ins close to home?"

Kelly shook her head. "Not that I know of, but I know she dreaded bumping into him at the neighborhood store. She would have been thrilled if he'd moved."

They made their way toward the checkout lines, Kelly adding various items to the cart. At the end of one aisle, a display of vending machines caught Fina's eye. One was on sale for $5,900. She examined it.

"You're in the market for a vending machine?" Kelly asked.

Fina put her hand on it. "You don't understand. This is the answer to all my prayers. I never realized you could just buy one."

"For your house?" Kelly asked with wide eyes.

"I know, it's crazy, but then I could use my kitchen for something else, like storage."

Kelly kept walking, and Fina worked to steer the heavy cart around other shoppers.

"Anyone you think I should talk to about this?" Fina asked as they took a spot in the checkout line. Even at only half full, the cart held enough food to feed a small army.

"You could ask Tasha," Kelly said, "but she can be a tough nut to crack."

"What do you mean?"

"Sometimes she'll talk about things, and sometimes she won't."

"What about Gus Sibley?"

"What about him?" Kelly asked, unloading a packet of gym socks onto the conveyor belt.

"He's been around as long as Kevin has. Presumably, their paths cross pretty often. Gus might have something to say about it."

Kelly shook her head. "I doubt it. He was always really focused on our injuries and the games. But I could be wrong."

In the parking lot, Kelly rummaged through her purse for her keys, cursing under her breath when the innards tumbled to the pavement. Fina helped her gather the items, locate the keys, and load her purchases into the back of her minivan.

"Thanks for letting me tag along," Fina said.

"I don't think I was very helpful," Kelly said. "Thanks for helping with my shopping."

"I don't think *I* was very helpful, but you're welcome."

Fina brought the empty cart over to the corral in the middle of the lot and watched Kelly pull out.

Either Kevin really had been up to no good or at least two people didn't mind suggesting that he had. Either scenario warranted a closer examination.

Fina needed to make some calls, a task that didn't lend itself to setting up shop in a Starbucks. She could have done it in her car, but she felt like her corneas might peel off her eyeballs soon in the dry heat of the enclosed space. If Fina were closer to the city, she would have gone to Ludlow and Associates and claimed an empty office or conference room, but she didn't want to drive there only to have to return to the MetroWest area later. Instead, she decided to drop in at her home away from home.

"Hiya, sweetie," Frank greeted her when he opened the front door.

"Are you in the middle of something?" Fina asked. "I wanted to say hi, and also camp out and make a few calls."

"We're just a pit stop to you, is that right?" he asked, chuckling.

"Basically, and the food's good."

Fina left her boots and jacket in the front hall and joined Frank in the living room. "Peg should be home in an hour or so," Frank said.

"How goes it?"

"Terrific. This semiretirement thing is really working out. I'm getting to all those things I never had a chance to do earlier."

"Like what?" Fina asked. "Bungee jumping? Snowboarding? Please don't say golf. It will ruin my image of you."

"No golf or extreme sports, but I'm sprucing up my workshop in the basement, and I have more time to read, one of life's great pleasures."

"What are you working on now?" Fina asked, gesturing at the book on the small table next to Frank's recliner.

"It's a biography of Winston Churchill. Fascinating stuff."

Fina feigned a yawn. "I'll take your word for it."

"What's going on with Risa's situation?" Frank asked.

"That's why I wanted to stop by; we met Greta Samuels yesterday in Kittery."

"And?"

Fina tapped her fingers on the arm of the couch. "I told Risa that I was going to withhold judgment until I had time to think about the meeting."

"I'm guessing you already have a judgment in mind," Frank said.

"Honestly, Frank, I think the only reason she contacted Risa was for her kidney," Fina said. "I don't think Greta would have made any effort to find Risa if her life didn't depend on it."

Frank frowned. "Do you think Risa thinks the same thing?"

"I don't know, but I didn't want to influence her before she had a chance to give it some thought."

"You don't think she should give her the kidney?" he asked.

"I'm not saying that, but I don't think Risa should give her a kidney believing that this is going to be the start of some beautiful friendship. It wouldn't surprise me if Greta drifted away after getting the organ."

Frank shook his head. "Sounds like a real pickle."

"Indeed." Fina rose from the couch. "How about if I go make my calls in the kitchen and let you get back to your reading?"

"Sounds good. Help yourself to a snack if you're hungry."

Fina grabbed a diet soda from the fridge and settled down at the kitchen table with her phone and laptop. She typed in the name of the sock manufacturer that Mary had provided the day before, but the website wasn't helpful. Tekmark only sold their products directly to retail stores, and when Fina tried to use their search tool to find retailers in Massachusetts, she got an error message.

She dialed the 800 number for the company, and after being passed around to a couple of people, she was connected with a woman whose lilting accent led Fina to believe she was in Mumbai or Delhi at that very moment, but that didn't stop her from giving Fina the names of three stores in the state that sold Tekmark products. One store was in Worcester, another in Quincy, and the third in Medford. Fina smiled when she heard the name of the Medford store where Joe and Stuart worked. A return visit was definitely in order, and she gave them a quick call and asked if Joe or Stuart was there. Joe'd be there until five, the helpful associate told her, at which point Stuart would be in. *Perfect,* Fina thought.

She caught up on some administrative tasks before closing her machine, draining her drink, and pitching the can in the recycling bin.

Frank was engrossed in his book when Fina returned to the living room.

"All done?" he asked.

"Yup. Think I might have a lead."

"You still working on that NEU case?"

"Yeah," Fina said. "Liz Barone."

"Good luck with that, and let me know what happens with Risa."

"Will do. Thanks, Frank." She leaned over and kissed his whiskered cheek. "Give Peg my love."

Fina sat in her car for a moment, contemplating her next step. She had time to kill before heading to Medford. She dialed the number for Gus Sibley's office and was told he had left for the day. When she reached someone in the athletic department at NEU, she was informed that Dr. Sibley was at an off-season training event in western Massachusetts for the women's soccer team.

She mentally ran down the list of people related to the case and stopped at Kevin. She still wasn't ready to confront him about the cheating rumors, but maybe it was time to have a chat with Mrs. Lafferty.

In general, Fina tried to steer clear of any potentially volatile domestic situations. Her arrangement with Ludlow and Associates meant she rarely had to take on domestic cheating cases, which were boring and fraught at the same time. Calling out adulterous spouses or getting mixed up in their drama was at the bottom of her to-do list, but sometimes it couldn't be avoided.

She pulled up to the Lafferty home, which was on the Newton-Wellesley line. One of the more modest houses in the neighborhood, it was a yellow colonial with a small farmer's porch on the front. The original structure was dwarfed by a newer-looking two-car garage and the bonus space above it.

The driveway was empty, but that didn't mean no one was home. A lot of people parked their cars in the garage when it was freezing or there was a chance of snow. Fina had never understood people who filled their garages with crap and kept their cars outside in the winter. Why would anyone choose to dig out their car if they didn't have to? But perhaps the woman who moved into a dead woman's apartment and kept it exactly as it was wasn't in a position to comment on the sentimentality of objects.

Fina rang the bell and looked through the pane of glass embedded in the door. The more modest staircase one would expect in a traditional colonial had been replaced with a two-story entryway and a wide stairway. A woman appeared, and Fina took a step back. She didn't want to seem rude or nosy.

"Yes?" the woman asked after opening the door.

"Are you Mrs. Lafferty?"

"Yes. Who's asking?"

Fina pulled a business card from her bag and handed it to Sheila Lafferty.

"A private investigator? What's this about?" she asked.

"Could I come in and ask you a few questions? I won't take long."

Sheila glanced at her wristwatch. She was wearing scrubs with teddy bears and rainbows on them, her feet in athletic socks.

"I'm getting ready for work, so I don't have much time. You didn't say what this is about."

"I've spoken with your husband already," Fina said. "It's regarding a lawsuit and NEU."

Sheila studied her feet for a moment. "I'm not the right person to talk to; I don't have much involvement with NEU." She had wavy brown hair cut in layers, the longest pieces just reaching her shoulders. She was pretty, but not beautiful, and the scrubs didn't do much for her figure.

"That's actually why I'd like to speak with you. I wanted to get an outsider's perspective," Fina said. She really would say just about anything to get in the door.

Sheila stepped back, opening the door wider. To the immediate right was a living room with a large-screen TV and two couches, a cream-colored shag area rug, and a ficus tree in the corner.

"You can leave your boots by the door," Sheila said.

Fina took off her boots, coat, and scarf and piled them near the front door. She followed Sheila into the living room and sat at the opposite end of one of the couches.

"I'm guessing you're a nurse," Fina said, trying to break the ice. Sheila had invited her in, but there was something cool about her demeanor. Most people offered Fina coffee or water, but there was no attempt on this hostess's part to make Fina feel particularly welcome.

"At Children's."

"Right. Hence the teddy bears."

"When did you talk to my husband?" Sheila asked.

"I've spoken with him a couple of times, actually," Fina said. "Both at his office and at the NEU sports complex."

"What does he have to do with this case?"

"I don't know how much you know about it," Fina said. Sheila shook her head, which only confused Fina. She knew? She didn't know? Fina decided to dive in. "I'm working for the family of Liz Barone. She was a soccer player at NEU about twenty years ago. Her estate is suing NEU for damages because she suffered cognitive disabilities from playing soccer."

"Allegedly suffered, isn't that right?" Sheila asked.

"Correct," Fina conceded. "Her attorneys are alleging that she suffered the damage as a direct result of playing soccer at NEU."

"And NEU should have known better?" Sheila asked, raising her eyebrow in skepticism. "Twenty years ago?"

Fina held up her hands in a conciliatory gesture. "That's for the attorneys to figure out. I'm just trying to learn more about the soccer program."

"And about her death," Sheila suggested.

Fina nodded. "Yes. I'm also trying to determine who killed Liz."

Sheila picked at a pill on her scrubs. The teddy bears were drawn to look as if they were flying around the rainbows. How was that reassuring to anyone? Fina wondered.

"I can't tell you more than my husband did," Sheila said. "He's the expert on NEU sports."

"That's what I've gathered," Fina said. "He seems to be incredibly popular at the university."

"He is." Her expression didn't give anything away.

"How does he find the time for everything?" Fina wondered. "Work, family, NEU? Does he ever sleep?"

Sheila gave her a tight smile. "He's very organized and very productive. He'd be bored if he didn't have a lot going on."

"I know the type," Fina said. "Do you ever go to any NEU events?"

"Sometimes we take our boys." Sheila looked out the window. "I imagine they'll want to go more often the older they get." Fina thought perhaps there was some wistfulness in her tone.

"It's fun to do as a family," Fina said. "When I was growing up, we went to a lot of ball games together. We still do sometimes. Come to think of it, it's the only place we all get along."

"Good thing our boys love sports," Sheila said, shaking her head. "Imagine if they wanted to play the flute or visit museums?"

Who's to say they didn't? Lots of interests and preferences were determined by wiring, but parental influence couldn't be underestimated. Were the Ludlow children born competitive or did they rise to the occasion when it became clear that Carl wouldn't have it any other way? Would Matthew have been an opera lover in another clan, or Fina a fan of the ballet?

"Is there anyone at NEU who has a bone to pick with your husband?" Fina asked.

"Why are you asking me that?"

"Like I said, I'm just trying to learn about the sports programs and the different relationships at play."

"My husband gets along with most everyone," Sheila said. "It's one of the reasons he's good at his job and a successful booster."

"Right." Fina nodded.

It was clear that asking Sheila about her husband's alleged infidelities would be fruitless. Whether or not the rumors were true and whether or not Sheila knew about them, Fina couldn't imagine she would discuss it with a virtual stranger. Some people wanted nothing more than to spill their guts and tell their sad stories, but Sheila Lafferty was not one of those people.

"Are you worried what might happen if the lawsuit goes against NEU?" Fina asked. "In terms of the athletic program?"

"I can't imagine it will," Sheila said, "and even if it does, there's no way the school will let the athletic program suffer. It's too important."

"But if Kevin weren't as involved," Fina mused, "that would be quite an adjustment."

"Why wouldn't he be as involved?" Sheila fiddled with the rings on her left hand. She was wearing a modest-sized diamond engagement ring and a thicker gold wedding band.

"Oh, I don't know. Maybe if there were some shake-up with the program?"

Sheila looked at her watch again. "Look, I don't think there's any-thing else I can tell you, and I've got to leave for work."

She rose from the couch and headed toward the front door. Fina fol-lowed her and pulled on her boots and coat.

"Did you go to the Medical Society benefit dinner with Kevin?" Fina asked.

"That's a random question."

"I'm just covering all the bases."

"What does the benefit dinner have to do with anything?" Sheila asked, and then the answer dawned on her. "I wasn't at that dinner, but I can assure you my husband was. There are a lot of people who can vouch for him." She pulled open the front door. "He had nothing to do with that woman's death."

"Well, people saw him at the beginning of the evening and the end, but nobody's really sure where he was in the middle."

"Good-bye," Sheila said, putting her hand on Fina's shoulder in a not-so-friendly way.

"Thanks for talking to me, Sheila."

"I wish I hadn't," she said, slamming the door after her.

Another satisfied customer, Fina thought, returning to her car.

27.

Fina got to Medford a little after five and sat in her car outside the clothing store for ten minutes. She wanted to make sure that Joe and Stuart had plenty of time for the changing of the guard, and it gave her a chance to reflect on her conversation with Sheila Lafferty. There were various possible outcomes from their little chat, but Fina thought two were most likely. The first was that Sheila would tell Kevin and he would go ballistic. The second was that Sheila wouldn't tell him anything. Fina couldn't predict which way it would go, but she wouldn't be surprised if Kevin left her an angry voice mail before day's end.

Inside the clothing store, an extremely tall man stood in front of a three-way mirror as another man wielded a tape measure around his treelike limbs. The customer was on a small raised platform, rendering him even more giant. Fina found Stuart behind the counter, staring at a computer screen.

"Hi there," Fina said. She'd fluffed her hair in the car and reapplied her lip gloss. She wasn't opposed to using her feminine wiles for the greater good.

Stuart looked up briefly. "Hi." His head bobbed back up to study her more closely.

"I was here the other day," Fina said. "I spoke with you and Joe about the man I was trying to locate." She held up the photo.

"Right. I remember," he said. "Joe isn't here. You can try back tomorrow."

"Actually," Fina said, leaning against the counter, "I was kind of hoping to talk to you instead."

"Yeah?"

Fina smoothed the photo down. "I know he's a customer," Fina said, "because of his socks."

Stuart looked at the man's ankle. "What do you mean?"

"His socks. He got them from this store." Fina didn't know that for sure, but there was no harm in bluffing. Either Stuart was going to give her some info or he wasn't. Lying about the guy's sock purchases didn't hurt anyone.

Stuart scratched his belly. He was wearing a mustard-colored sweater that made him look like an oversized jar of Grey Poupon. It wasn't a good look.

"I don't know the guy," he finally said.

"But you have an idea?" Fina rummaged around in her bag and pulled out a small packet of tissues. Before she'd left the car, she'd positioned a couple of twenties so they were peeking out of the plastic sleeve. Stuart's gaze was drawn to the cash.

He glanced around the store. The giant customer and the tailor were talking, and a couple of other shoppers were eyeing the merchandise.

"I don't know who he is," he admitted quietly, "but I've seen him."

"You don't have a name or an address?" Fina asked.

Stuart shook his head. Fina looked around the space and noticed two security cameras in opposite corners. If they were working—and that was a big *if*—they might provide evidence that the mystery man was a customer, but it still wouldn't tell her who he was.

"Do you think Joe knows his name?" Fina asked.

"He pretends to know all the customers, but I doubt it. This isn't Brooks Brothers, after all," Stuart said, his mouth veering off into a sneer.

Fina suddenly felt wearied by the whole task. Maybe she should just call Cristian and share this new development, but that might lead to even greater frustration. He would investigate the same avenues she would, but in a less timely fashion, and he'd get all the credit.

"Do you have a mailing list or some other system for keeping track of your customers?" she asked.

He rested his hand on the edge of the counter as if he were sidling up to the saloon in a western. "Maybe."

Fina put the tissues and the money back into her bag and started to turn away. Stuart was completely out of his league when it came to bluffing, and even if he let her walk away, Fina could live with that. A willingness to walk away was the key to successful negotiating.

"Wait," he said, raising his hand. "I didn't say no."

"Yeah, but I really don't have time for maybe," she said, taking another step toward the door.

"You don't want to talk to this guy because he lost something, do you?" Stuart asked.

Fina didn't respond. If her calculations were correct, Stuart would be more motivated to help if he believed it was part of a cloak-and-dagger operation, not the recovery of lost property.

"I'll give you a list," he said, his eyes trained on her bag. "I don't know what good it's going to do you."

"Don't worry about that," Fina said. She wasn't sure what she'd do with it, either, but she'd learned never to dismiss any piece of information, no matter how useless it seemed in the moment.

Stuart clicked the mouse, and a printer under the counter started humming. Fina reached into her bag and pulled out the cash. The risk when paying for information was that people told you what they thought you wanted to hear, which was not necessarily the truth. But it was a risk that she was willing to take. More often than not, the recipients of Fina's bribes weren't interested in repeat visits from her.

He handed her a few sheets of paper with names, e-mail addresses, and mailing addresses.

"We send out a lot of coupons," Stuart said.

Fina took the list and scanned it. There were about three hundred names listed. Tracking these people down would be a huge task, assuming her theory wasn't completely off base to begin with, but she couldn't spend time worrying about that. She had started down this road, and when it came to detecting, it was always better to keep moving than to stand still.

F ina dreaded tackling the list of customers, nor did she have a plan for how to do it, so she decided to put the information aside for the moment. She was getting hungry and called Cristian, but he was tied up at work and dinner wasn't an option. In the interest of killing two birds with one stone, she called Matthew at the office.

"Are you free for dinner?" she asked him.

"What's the catch?"

"You're so cynical."

"Sorry. I'll be free in a couple of hours," Matthew said. "Why don't you meet me here?"

"Actually, I have a place in mind in Cambridge."

"So there is a catch!"

"I'm trying to cross paths with a certain someone, and he frequents this particular place," Fina said.

"Does 'cross paths' mean you want to talk to the guy?"

"Probably not, but I'll play it by ear."

"Well . . ." Matthew trailed off.

"The food is good, there's live music," Fina said, "and they make lots of fancy cocktails. It'll be fun."

"Is it dangerous?"

"No. I wouldn't invite you to something that was going to be dangerous."

He hooted. "I'll tell Scotty you said that."

"I didn't invite him that day. He invited me, remember?" Fina really wished the car bomb culprit could be found so she could clarify the target. If she was going to be given a lot of grief, at least it should be earned.

"Okay," Matthew said. "Where is it?"

Fina gave him the address. "And take off your tie," she said. "We don't want to stick out like sore thumbs."

"Jeez. Any more rules?"

"Nope. That's it. See you soon!"

She smiled in anticipation. Good booze and a good brother were a winning combination.

Two hours later, Matthew ordered a Manhattan and Fina opted for a glass of red wine at the bar. Technically she was on the clock, so hard alcohol seemed like a bad idea. Not long after they sat down at a table tucked into the corner, the man she'd spoken with two days earlier made his way over to their table.

"Hey, I saw you a couple of nights ago, but you left before I could stop by," he said to Fina.

"Sorry about that. My friend needed to get going."

"Amy, right?" he asked, smiling.

"That's right."

Matthew looked at her askance and studied the menu.

"And you're Marshall?" Fina asked.

"Right." He extended his hand.

"This is my friend Matthew," Fina said as the men shook hands.

They chatted for a few more minutes, then Marshall was summoned to the bar.

"Amy?" Matthew asked once they were alone.

"You know I use different names sometimes."

"Why are you using one here?"

"Because I couldn't risk having Marshall mention me to the guy I'm looking for. Have you ever met another Fina?"

"No, thankfully," her brother said. "But if the guy's here, isn't he going to see you?"

"Possibly, but it's getting pretty crowded. Even if he does, I can explain it away."

"Of that, I have no doubt," Matthew said, holding up the rocks glass of his newly arrived drink.

Fina clinked her glass against his and took a sip. She didn't know anything about wine, but her rule of thumb was to choose the second least expensive option. Unless Carl was paying, in which case she would opt for the second most expensive option. It still wasn't clear who was footing the bill for this investigation, so she erred on the side of frugality.

Fina had decided before Matthew arrived that she wasn't going to bring up the Haley situation. Something had to be done, but until she had a plan, she'd keep her mouth shut. Harping on the issue might just annoy Scotty and Matthew, and she needed their support. The information about Karla's kids was creating a slow burn in her stomach, like an ulcer, but Fina knew that she needed to be strategic and clever. She didn't want to be the next Ludlow exiled from the family fold.

It was a welcome respite to spend time with Matthew and not discuss family drama. He got a second drink, and they sampled a variety of foods, including pork belly sliders, oysters, roasted Brussels sprouts, and sweet potato fries.

"This is a weird combination of food," Fina noted, pushing at a piece of octopus with her fork.

"But it's all delicious," Matthew said.

There was movement at the end of the room with the stage. Fina turned her chair so she could see better and swiped a couple of fries from a serving dish. After a few minutes, three guys took the stage and kicked off a thirty-minute set. It was a mix of folk, country, and rockabilly, and though she wouldn't download the album, it was pleasing enough to listen to. Not that Fina was really listening; she was mostly scanning the crowd and keeping her eye on the door in hopes that Jamie would show.

She and Matthew took turns hitting the bathroom during the band's break. As Fina weaved her way through the crowd, she noticed Marshall checking her out. Fina pretended that she didn't notice and hoped his seeming interest wouldn't put a damper on her investigation.

Back at the table, Matthew had ordered coconut macaroons and a rhubarb tart.

"No chocolate?" Fina asked.

"'Thank you' would be nice, but I forgot who I'm with," he said, flagging down the waitress. "Do you have anything chocolate for my sister?" he asked the woman. She left, promising to return with milk chocolate panna cotta.

Fina leaned over toward Matthew. "I'm not your sister tonight, remember?"

Matthew rolled his eyes.

"You would suck at undercover work," she said, grinning.

Before he could respond, the band returned and launched into another set.

The panna cotta arrived and was quickly consumed. Fina and Matthew were contemplating calling it a night when something caught Fina's eye at the side of the stage. There were two men, their heads bent in conversation. The hair on one of them looked familiar, and when he raised his head, Fina could see that it was Jamie.

"Yes," she said, but not so quietly that Matthew didn't hear her.

"Your guy?" he asked directly into her ear.

She nodded and watched the conversation for another minute. The second guy abruptly walked toward the door leading to the restrooms and disappeared. Thirty seconds later, Jamie followed him.

"I need you to go see what they're doing," Fina said to Matthew.

"What?" he asked over the din.

"Those guys. I'm interested in the one with longer hair. I need you to go see what they're doing."

Matthew looked annoyed. "You said this wasn't dangerous."

"It's not. For all I know, they're just peeing."

"Oh, come on." Matthew shifted in his seat.

"Now, Matthew," Fina insisted. "It's important."

He tossed his napkin onto the table and pushed back his chair. "People are going to think I have bladder control issues," he said.

"Well, you are nearing that age," Fina said, then ducked from his swatting hand.

She watched him thread his way through the crowd and pass through the same doorway as Jamie and the mystery man.

Fina watched the door and finished her wine.

Five minutes after he'd left, Matthew made his way back to her. He pulled out his wallet and threw a wad of cash on the table.

"Let's go," Matthew said.

"That bad?" Fina asked, grabbing her coat and standing.

He started to push her in the direction of the door.

"Did you leave enough money?" she asked. "Wait, I need a receipt!"

"For Christ's sake, Fina. Come on." He glanced toward the door to the restrooms, and Fina followed his gaze. The mystery man was scanning the room, an angry expression contorting his face.

Fina picked up the pace and ducked through the velvet curtain hanging between the room and the front door. Presumably, it tempered the frigid air that blew in with every entry and exit, but it also provided an abracadabra feel to the moment. She pushed the door open, and Matthew followed on her heels. He took hold of Fina's elbow and steered her around the corner toward the parking lot.

"What did you do?" Fina asked. "Am I going to have to shoot somebody?"

"Just get in," her brother said, unlocking his car with a tweet of his keys.

He started up the luxury sedan, and Fina flipped the switch to turn on the seat warmers. Everyone's priorities were different.

"Unless someone is actually coming after us," Fina said, "you should take a deep breath and calm down."

Matthew rotated in his seat and looked behind the car. "I don't see anyone."

"I'd say you and Scotty are like a pair of little girls, but that would be an insult to little girls," Fina said. "They're braver than you two are."

"Those two guys didn't go into the bathroom," Matthew said.

"Okay."

"They went down the hall to a back room and were doing a drug deal."

"So why'd we have to flee?" Fina asked.

"Because I walked in, and the guy got pissed. He threatened me."

Fina considered the scenario for a moment. "Who was the buyer and who was the seller?"

"Your guy was the buyer."

"Did you see what was for sale?" she asked. "Weed? Pills? Powder?"

"Pills. A little plastic Baggie of white pills. What do you think it was?"

Fina thought for a moment. "I don't know: ecstasy, amphetamine, oxy. Did you get a good look at the pills?"

Matthew shook his head. "No. At that point the guy was already threatening me. I can hold my own in a fight, but I'm an officer of the court. I can't be anywhere near a drug deal."

"You were right to hightail it out of there," Fina said. "I honestly didn't know that's what was going on."

Matthew looked at her dubiously. "What were the other options?"

"I don't know. Maybe he was hooking up with the guy or buying a gun. Maybe they're in a book club together and were exchanging this month's selection."

"I'm glad you never lose your sense of humor," Matthew said sarcastically.

"Come on," Fina said, punching him in the upper arm. "It's kinda funny, and you've got to admit, a little exciting." She grinned at him.

A hint of a smile appeared on Matthew's face. "I'm not going to admit that."

"Think what boring, sheltered lives you and Scotty would lead if not for me."

He snorted and put the car into drive. "Where are you parked?"

Fina directed him to a nearby side street, where he stopped next to her car. She reached into her wallet and started to pull out some money.

"You don't need to do that," Matthew said.

"I don't want to hear that I stiffed you on the bill in addition to putting you in danger," Fina said.

"I'm not going to take your money. You're my little sister. Until you find a man to take you off our hands, I'll do my part."

Fina made a gagging motion, then reached over and hugged him. "Thanks for dinner and the company. I had fun."

"Let's do it again," Matthew said, "minus the dramatic exit."

"Sounds good."

Fina climbed out of his car and into her own. He waited until she gave him a thumbs-up, and then he took off down the street, most definitely exceeding the speed limit. Fina's tactics allowed the rest of the Ludlows to pretend that they were simple, law-abiding folk, but that was a bunch of bull. Compared to your average family, they were a band of outlaws. Fina just offered a dramatic point of contrast.

She turned the heat up and glanced at the clock. It had been a long day, but it wasn't over yet.

Jamie had some explaining to do.

Fina sat in her car, her boots slipped off in the foot well. She pressed her feet close to the heater, hopeful that her running car wouldn't raise any red flags. She was parked outside Liz and Jamie's house, and it was late. A nosy neighbor might approach her or call the police, asking them to check out the unfamiliar car in front of the house where the neighbor was attacked. It would be an inconvenience having to explain herself, but Fina was willing to risk it.

She'd been sitting there for forty-five minutes when the Passat pulled into the driveway. Fina scrambled to pull her boots back on and get out of her car before he closed the front door behind him.

"Jamie," she called out across the front yard. "We need to talk."

He was startled to see her. "What are you doing here? It's late."

"I know, but it's important."

"I'm tired, Fina. Let's talk tomorrow."

She climbed the front stairs and stood next to him on the stoop. Fina reached into her pocket and pulled out her phone. She tapped on the flashlight app and shined the phone in his face.

"What the hell are you doing?"

"I'm confirming that your pupils are dilated. Do you realize that if you'd been pulled over, you would be in deep shit?"

Jamie was putting his key in the lock when the door opened. Mrs. Sandraham stood there, her face a mask of disapproval.

"You'll wake up the children," she said.

"Sorry," Jamie said meekly.

The woman pulled on her coat and walked cautiously down the dark path. She crossed the street to her own house and disappeared inside, the front light winking off.

Fina followed Jamie inside.

"Seriously, Jamie. One look at your pupils and a cop would haul you in for being under the influence."

He took off his coat and shoes and deposited them on the floor. Fina trailed after him as he dropped onto the couch, rubbing his eyes.

"If you're going to lecture me, please leave. I can't deal with it," he said.

Fina stared at him, incredulous. "I don't even know where to start."

He got back up as quickly as he'd sat down. "I'm heading to bed. You can let yourself out."

"I should have realized it sooner," she said. "The dizziness, the sweating. Wearing your sunglasses at inopportune times. I thought you were self-conscious about having bloodshot eyes from your grief."

"My eyes were bloodshot from my grief," he argued.

"Sure, and from your pill habit." Fina took a deep breath. "I'm not trying to judge you. Addiction is a horrible disease, but you've got two little kids to think about. Have you considered going to rehab?"

"I don't need to go to rehab," Jamie said.

She tilted her head. "Given the frequency with which you're buying drugs, I would disagree."

"I only do it occasionally, to get me through the rough spots."

"That's not true. You're buying every few days."

"How do you know that?" he asked.

"I'm an investigator," Fina said. "I find stuff out." People always seemed surprised that she uncovered information. Was that because they assumed their secrets were safe or that she was completely incompetent?

Jamie started toward the stairs.

"Is this a long-standing issue or is it because of your knee?" Fina asked. It wasn't uncommon for addicts to be introduced to pain pills for legitimate reasons, only to have their dependency spiral into full-on addiction.

"It's my goddamn knee," he said. "I stopped playing in clubs and ended up taking pills because my wife wanted me to be a triathlete. How's that for irony?"

"It's not unusual, if that makes you feel any better," Fina said. "Lots of people who wouldn't think of touching drugs under normal circumstances get sucked in trying to manage pain."

"Well, my wife didn't really understand that. Liz always played through her pain and expected everyone else to do the same."

Fina looked down at her feet. She'd met people who suffered from chronic pain and knew that it could be unbearable. Pain pills offered relief, but introduced their own hazards.

"Maybe we could get together tomorrow and talk about this once you've had some sleep," Fina suggested.

"There's no point. I'm fine."

"I can help. I have access to a lot of resources."

"Don't worry about it," he muttered.

Fina watched him disappear upstairs before she left through the front door.

Back in her car, she got on the road and tried to process this new piece of information. She'd made little progress by the time she pulled into her parking space at home.

Maybe a good night's sleep would provide some clarity. Even if it didn't, there was nothing more she could do tonight.

28.

Fina took a chance and showed up at Tasha and D's house at six thirty the next morning. She was tired, but the diet soda in her drink holder would undoubtedly kick in before too long and she'd be raring to go.

The door was opened by the nanny Fina had met during her last visit. She brought Fina upstairs to the family room, where D was sitting on the couch, the baby on his lap with a bottle. The little girl, Lyla, was putting together a large wooden puzzle at her father's feet.

"Fina," D said. "Were we expecting you?"

"No. I'm dropping by completely uninvited with no warning. I apologize, but I really need to speak with Tasha, and I thought this was the best way to do that."

"Your timing's not great," D said.

"I know, but I wouldn't be here if it weren't important."

D glanced at his watch. "Tasha should be up in about ten minutes. She's getting dressed. Have a seat."

Fina sat down on the couch across from him and watched the baby drink greedily from his bottle. After a moment, the child pulled the nipple from his mouth and let out a burp that would have been at home in a frat house.

"Good Lord," Fina said.

"That's my boy," D said, laughing.

"You must be very proud."

"I am. There's coffee if you want some," he said, nodding in the direction of the fancy coffeemaker in the open kitchen.

"I'm good. Thanks."

Lyla started chattering about her puzzle, and Fina listened as D responded to his daughter's questions. This was the part of parenting that Fina found most heroic: the endless conversations about nothing. She knew the interaction was vital to child development and all that, but she didn't know how parents didn't lose their minds in the infinite conversation loop of early childhood. It could certainly be utilized as a torture device by the CIA.

Fina asked D about work, and they chatted until Tasha came into the room dressed for the office with the exception of shoes. She placed her cell phone on the counter and did a double take when she caught sight of Fina.

"I'm surprised to see you this early, Fina," Tasha said, like the smooth politician she would undoubtedly be. "I got the feeling you aren't a morning person."

"I'm not, but you seem to be, so I thought I would be this morning."

Tasha pulled out a coffee cup and pressed various buttons on the machine. It whirred and deposited dark steaming liquid into the cup.

"I don't have much time," Tasha said, taking a tentative sip of her coffee.

"I only need a few minutes."

"We're heading downstairs," D said, hoisting the baby onto his shoulder and depositing the empty bottle in the sink. "Let's go, Lyla."

The girl squeezed her mother around the knees before following her father out of the room.

Tasha took D's place on the couch across from Fina. "What's going on?" she asked.

"I've heard that Kevin Lafferty gets his girlfriends from the pool of NEU female athletes. Is that true?"

Tasha placed her cup on the coffee table and picked a piece of imaginary lint off her dress. She was wearing a fitted sheath that complemented her physique.

"Where did you hear that?" she asked.

"Does it matter?"

"Maybe."

"I don't think it does." Fina leaned forward, her hands clasped. "This is the second time you've left out an important piece of information."

"You're not the police, Fina," Tasha said. "I'm not legally obligated to tell you things."

"But you were Liz's friend, right? I'm trying to figure out who killed her, Tasha. I'm sorry you don't find that a compelling enough reason to share information with me."

Tasha sighed. "I don't like spreading rumors."

"I don't, either, but I'm good at my job, and I know how to separate fact from fiction."

"I'm not sure how Kevin's relationships are relevant."

"Nor am I, but I can't figure it out if I don't know about it," Fina said.

"I don't have any definitive information."

"I understand that. I still want to hear what you suspect."

After studying her manicure for a moment, Tasha looked at her. "I think Kevin Lafferty has been fooling around with students since he was a student at NEU. He's aged, but his demographic of choice hasn't."

"So when he worked for the university, he was involved with students?"

"I think so."

"Is that why he stopped working there?" Fina asked. "Frankly, I was surprised he ever left NEU's employ."

"I don't know the answer to that," Tasha said. "Really," she reiterated when Fina raised an eyebrow. "He went to NEU, then worked there briefly, and then became a booster."

"And do you think he's had NEU girlfriends the whole time?"

Tasha nodded. "I don't know that for sure, but serial adulterers don't usually change their ways."

"Why hasn't the university put an end to it? They must know about it."

"I assume somebody does," Tasha said, "but it's complicated. I'm sure he chooses students who are of age. Technically, he isn't employed by the university, and the university benefits from his involvement in the sports program. They don't want him to go any more than he would want to."

"It seems so sleazy," Fina said. "Like having the fox guard the hen-house."

Tasha nodded and drank her coffee. "I agree."

"If you were a parent of a soccer player, would you want Kevin around your daughter?"

"No, but if she were over eighteen, there wouldn't be much I could do about it."

The cell phone on the counter rang, and Tasha got up to answer it. "I have to take this," she said, looking at the screen.

Tasha wandered into the dining room for her conversation, and Fina was left on the couch. She knew that open secrets in communities were commonplace, and some of them were harmless, but what about ones that weren't? Kevin might not have been doing anything illegal, but it was still an abuse of power as far as Fina was concerned. Was that really less important than his role as a booster?

Tasha returned a minute later.

"I have about two minutes," she told Fina, "and then I really have to go."

"No problem," Fina said, rising from the couch. "Just one more question: Who was Kevin's girlfriend when you were on the team?"

Tasha's head dipped down and she gripped her phone more tightly. "I don't want to answer that."

Fina crossed her arms in front of her. "That suggests to me that it was you or Liz. I'm not going to judge either one of you, but I need to know, Tasha. If it has nothing to do with her death, I promise to bury the information."

"Again," Tasha said, "I'm not certain."

Fina looked at her own watch pointedly.

"Liz," Tasha said. "I'm pretty sure that Liz was involved with Kevin when we were students."

"She never told you?" Fina asked.

"No, but I know she was involved with someone she didn't want to discuss—someone that her friends wouldn't approve of."

"So you assumed it was him?"

"I assumed it was an older guy or a married guy or both. Kevin flirted with all of us, but there was a vibe between them that was different."

"Did you ever ask her outright?" Fina asked.

"No, but I warned her that getting involved with him or anyone else in the 'inappropriate' category was asking for trouble," Tasha said.

"Did anyone else know they were involved?"

"Not as far as I knew, but people may have suspected it just like I did." Tasha looked at her watch. "Now I really do have to go."

"Of course," Fina said. "I can let myself out. Thanks for telling me."

"Sure."

Fina was annoyed that Tasha had held back this information, but as someone who often held things back, she could appreciate the inclination. If Cristian punished her every time she wasn't forthcoming, they wouldn't have much of a relationship—personal or professional.

Outside, Fina wound her scarf around her neck more tightly to try to stave off the frigid wind. The tide of information seemed to be flowing at a steady pace, but she didn't know how to harness it yet. Jamie had wondered early on about Liz and Kevin's relationship, and although Fina hadn't found any evidence to support that, she had to wonder if he'd been onto something.

Kevin was content. He was drinking a strong cup of coffee, the boys had been picked up for school, ESPN was on, and the sports page was open in front of him. He could almost pretend that all the other garbage—the lawsuit, the relationship, the investigations—wasn't happening.

He was chortling at the sports blooper reel when he heard the garage door open. Sheila was home from her shift at the hospital. Kevin did a visual inventory of the kitchen, spied the boys' cereal bowls in the sink, and popped up to load them into the dishwasher. His wife was tired when she got off the overnight shift, and little things could turn into big things. He'd learned early on that if he toed the line in certain areas, he could obliterate it in others.

"Hi, hon," Kevin said, reaching for a mug to pour Sheila a cup of coffee.

Her face had that peculiar cast to it that Kevin always attributed to a night shift spent in alternating darkness and bright light. Sheila was in and out of patient rooms, armed with a flashlight, but the hallways and nurses' station were illuminated like the Citgo sign.

He didn't envy her schedule, but in recent years, it had served them well. These days, when they were together, Sheila seemed less patient and more easily irritated—or maybe Kevin was growing tired of keeping all the balls in the air.

"Bad night?" he asked.

She sank down into a chair and waved off the mug of coffee that Kevin offered. "That little boy with the tumor got much worse."

"That's awful."

Sheila sighed. "It makes me want to come home and hug my boys."

"You can give them an extra-big squeeze tonight," Kevin said, sitting down across from her.

Sheila reached over and clicked off the TV.

He knew she had a tough job, but it irked him that her desires superseded his own. He'd never be able to trump a dying child, but did that mean he couldn't watch *SportsCenter* while enjoying his coffee?

"I was watching that," he said, reaching for the remote.

She glared at him and laid her hand over the device. "I was getting ready for work yesterday and a woman stopped by, a private investigator."

Kevin felt his muscles tense. He forced a smile and nodded his head. "I know who she is: Fina Ludlow. I can't believe she bothered you."

"Apparently, she's been bothering you a lot," Sheila said. "Why didn't you mention that?"

"Because I didn't want to involve you," Kevin said. "It's just more of this nonsense with the university. You've got enough on your plate." He reached out and clasped her hand. She didn't brush him off, but nor did she reciprocate his affection.

"You're sure that's the reason?" Sheila asked, studying him.

It was hard to take Sheila seriously in those ridiculous teddy bear scrubs. "Absolutely," he assured her.

She stood up and reached for a glass in the cabinet. She grabbed the carton of orange juice out of the refrigerator and shook it vigorously before pouring a glassful.

"She asked me about the night of the Medical Society benefit. Does she think you killed Liz Barone?" Her back was toward him; Kevin didn't know if that was for his benefit or hers.

"Of course not. She's a troublemaker. I don't want you to give it another thought."

Sheila drained the glass and rinsed it. She put it in the dishwasher and closed the door, then leaned her hip against the counter. "She also made it sound like your role at the university might be in jeopardy."

Kevin rose from the table and came over to her. He pulled her into an embrace, knowing that after a moment she would relax into his grip.

"She's just stirring things up. It's what she does, but she doesn't have any real authority. Fina Ludlow is just a loose cannon making money off other people's tragedies."

For a moment, Sheila rested her head on his shoulder before pulling away. "I'm going to sleep," she said, padding out of the kitchen.

Kevin dumped his now cold coffee into the sink and tossed the sports section into the recycling bin.

Nobody could ruin a day like Fina Ludlow.

B ack at Nanny's, Fina stripped off her clothes and climbed into bed. She had work to do, but was feeling fuzzy. Sometimes, when her brain got overloaded, it was better to take a break than force things.

She woke up two hours later craving a fluffernutter and made a bee-line for the kitchen. Fina got a grocery delivery every couple of weeks, and she rarely altered the list. It included her idea of staples: diet soda, peanut butter, Pop-Tarts, cookies, ice cream, and toilet paper. It also included other people's—mainly Milloy's—version of staples. He insisted that she have eggs, milk, bread, chicken breasts, and frozen vegetables in the house and dipped into those supplies as needed. Even though she unpacked the groceries, Fina was always startled when Milloy emerged from her kitchen sipping a green smoothie or eating a chicken and broccoli stir-fry. Really? That came from her kitchen?

Today all she wanted was two pieces of white bread slathered with peanut butter and Marshmallow Fluff, washed down with a glass of cold milk. Growing up, she and her brothers had often snacked on fluffer-nutters in those hungry hours between school dismissal and dinner. It was one of her few fond memories from childhood.

Fina took the sandwich and her milk to the dining room table and set them next to her laptop. She retrieved the clothing store customer list from her bag and steeled herself for the monotony that people rarely associate with detective work. Fina felt sorry for the cops, given the public's expectations of them. Thanks to the success of popular crime procedurals on TV, everyone assumed that crimes were solved by lab tests and computers, but that wasn't the case. *People* solved crimes with hard work and tenacity.

She started plugging the customer names into the image tool of a search engine in the hope that her bomber would magically appear. Given the poor quality of the surveillance footage, she didn't expect to ID him from another photo, but hoped to narrow down the list of potential subjects. Fina doubted that she'd find photos of all the customers or be able to verify that the name on the list was the same person online, but it was a place to start. She also knew that the mystery man might not be on the customer list at all, but she couldn't linger on that possibility. This was what she had to go on right now, and it was better than waiting for the ideal approach that would never come.

It took her a couple of hours to make a first pass through the list, which left Fina with 123 names. The other 184 didn't fit the bill because they were white, old, or skinny. Fina got up and stretched and got a diet soda from the fridge.

Back at the table, she brought up Facebook and started plugging in the 123 candidates. She was able to rule out fifty-two of the bunch based on their profile photos. Thirty-three didn't appear to have profiles, so that left thirty-eight potential bombers on social media, way too many to track down individually. Instead, she opened up a new browser and went to work creating a fake Facebook account. She chose the name Jennifer Mitchell for her alter ego and found a stock photo of a brunette with big boobs. Fina filled in the bio questions, making her profile as generic as possible. Under "Interests" she put Boston sports teams and travel. Reality competition shows and action movies filled out Jennifer's page, as did an interest in Jay-Z and Kanye.

Satisfied with her imaginary friend, Fina saved the page and then sent friend requests to her thirty-eight mystery men. Some people accepted every friend request they got, assuming that they knew the friend from somewhere, even if they couldn't remember where. Other people were more discerning about accepting requests. Fina hoped her amateur bomber fell into the former category.

Before closing her laptop, Fina did a search for Pamela Fordyce. She didn't know what she was looking for, but there was something nagging at her. A quick perusal of links didn't turn up anything new or particularly enlightening.

The phone rang, and Fina put aside her questions regarding Pamela.

"You'll never believe what was just delivered," Bobbi said.

Fina held her breath. She hoped it was nothing recently dead. "What?"

"An enormous gift basket and a handwritten note of apology from Pamela Fordyce. Whatever you said, it worked."

"Good. I'm glad to hear it." Fina walked over to the window and looked out at Logan and the harbor. She never tired of watching the boat and plane activity. There was something comforting about the idea that life was going on all around her, no matter what was happening in her own little universe. "I was just about to call you," Fina said.

"Do you have an update?"

"I have some questions, and it would be easier to go over them in person."

"What about a coffee in a couple of hours?" Bobbi asked.

"That would work."

"Can you meet me at the mall in Braintree? I'll be done with my walk by then."

"Are you one of those women who cruise by, weaving in and out of shoppers?" Fina smiled at the thought.

"Yes, I am, and let me tell you, it's a lifesaver. Not only does it keep my cholesterol in check, it gives me somewhere to go every day. I haven't felt like doing much of anything since Liz died, but my friends expect me, so I go."

"I'm not knocking it," Fina said. "I think it's great. I was just trying to picture it."

"Get there early and you can see for yourself."

"Any new threats I should know about?" Fina asked.

"No," Bobbi said. "Dennis has been very attentive."

"Good. Let me know if you need anything else."

They decided on a rendezvous point in the mall and ended the call. Fina was not looking forward to asking Bobbi about Liz's alleged relationship with Kevin Lafferty. She also was struggling with how much information—if any—to reveal about Jamie's pill problem.

Fina spent most of her waking hours trying to learn more, but occasionally, she wished she knew less.

Jamie worked for an interactive agency near Downtown Crossing, and since she had a little time to kill, Fina thought she'd revisit last night's conversation.

The company occupied one floor of a mid-rise building that had previously been some kind of factory. Inside, the office looked like a vestige of the late 1990s with its open plan, whiteboard walls, and sculptural sofas in primary colors.

Fina took a seat and waited for the receptionist to summon Jamie. The employees she could see were all young and casually dressed. They were parked in front of multiple computer monitors, with headphones hermetically sealing them off from the office hubbub.

Jamie walked into the reception area a few minutes later and scowled when he saw Fina.

"I'll be quick," she insisted, rising to her feet. "Is there somewhere private we can talk?"

He led her down the hall to a glass-walled conference room. The meeting table was glossy white surrounded by black leather and metal chairs. Jamie closed the door behind her and remained standing.

"Are you here to threaten me?" Jamie asked.

"What? Of course not. What are you talking about?" Fina took a seat at the table. A woman walked by the room, glancing in at them. Jamie pulled out a chair and lowered himself into it, perhaps realizing the tableau was a little curious.

"You have all these ideas about me," he said, "and you work for Bobbi. Are you going to tell her what you think you've discovered?"

"No," Fina said. "I came here to discuss it with you. I get no pleasure from your problems, Jamie."

He tapped his fingertips on the shiny tabletop.

Fina looked at him. "I'm concerned about your health and well-being. Would you consider speaking to someone about your pill usage?"

He stopped tapping and brushed his hand across the tabletop as if clearing away a layer of crumbs. "Like who?"

"I don't have a specific person in mind, but my family is well connected in the medical field. I'm sure I could get you in to see someone very quickly."

He was quiet for a moment. "My wife just died. I don't think it's unreasonable that I'm feeling stressed."

"Of course not," Fina said, "but opiates are highly addictive. It's not about willpower. You need support from people who know what they're doing."

Jamie shook his head slowly. "I can stop if I want to. It takes off the edge, that's all."

Fina didn't respond. You could argue with an addict all day, but it was fruitless until he decided that's what he was.

"What about the doctor who prescribed the pills initially?" she asked. "Have you spoken to him or her about this?"

"It has nothing to do with the doctor," he insisted.

"Does your doctor know that you're addicted?" Fina asked.

"Give it a rest, Fina. I'm fine."

She pushed her chair back from the table. "Okay. Just remember that buying and using prescription drugs without a prescription is illegal. You may not think you have a problem, but you will if the cops catch you." Fina paused at the door. "If you decide you want some help, call me. Anytime, day or night."

"Thanks, but it's not necessary," Jamie insisted.

She looked at him. "I know. It's never necessary until it is."

29.

Cristian had left her a message, but she decided to hold off returning his call. If she did things by the book, Fina would tell him about last night's drug deal and her subsequent conversations with Jamie. Luckily for Jamie, doing things by the book was never her strong suit; she decided to sit on the information for the time being. Once she identified Liz's killer, she could extricate herself from Jamie's personal drama, but, unfortunately, that wasn't going to happen in the next eight hours.

At the mall, Fina ordered a hot chocolate and took a seat at a table in the central courtyard. The space was an echo chamber with the laughter of tweens and the crying of babies spilling down over the railing from the second floor. She watched as young mothers pushed strollers and teenage couples held hands. There was a seating area next to a fountain that was a holding pen for older men. They sat on the comfortable couches flipping through the newspaper, except for the one whose head was tipped back, mouth open and eyes closed.

Bobbi arrived five minutes later. She purchased a bottle of water from a nearby kiosk, then took the seat next to Fina.

"How was your workout?" Fina asked.

Bobbi was wearing a sweat suit, and a thin sheen of sweat covered her face. "It was good. It's good to get some exercise, especially with the weather being what it is." Given the season's snowfall, many sidewalks were impassable, and the frigid temperatures certainly weren't conducive to outdoor activities.

"I have a rather sensitive topic to discuss with you," Fina said. "Are you sure you wouldn't like to go somewhere more private?"

Bobbi looked at the people toting shopping bags and the children throwing coins in the fountain before shaking her head. "I'd rather stay here, if you don't mind."

"It's fine with me," Fina said. Perhaps the distractions made it easier—reminders that there was life outside the confines of Bobbi's current personal hell.

"I've heard that Liz was involved with Kevin Lafferty when she was a student at NEU," Fina ventured.

"Is he the booster guy?"

"Yes."

Bobbi looked perplexed. "How old would he have been at the time?"

"Early thirties, I think. Were you aware they were involved?"

Bobbi shook her head. "No, I didn't know. She had boyfriends, and I thought there might have been one or two that she didn't want us to meet, but I didn't know anything about Kevin."

Fina stirred her drink, submerging the last bits of whipped cream into the liquid. "Jamie wondered if they were involved more recently."

Bobbi frowned. "I don't think so, but obviously, I didn't know everything that was going on with Liz. Is that important?"

"I'm not sure," Fina said. "He just keeps popping up in the investigation, which is always a red flag."

"Do you think Kevin would have hurt Liz?" Bobbi asked.

"I don't know," Fina admitted.

Bobbi took a long pull from her water and screwed the cap back on. She tapped her fingernail on the top.

"Why do you think Liz named you as the executor of her estate?" Fina asked.

Bobbi looked surprised at the shift in topic. She pulled a napkin from the metal tabletop dispenser and wiped off the condensation gathering on the bottle. "She never said why. She just asked me if I'd be willing to."

"You didn't wonder why?"

"Jamie isn't the most organized person," Bobbi said. "I just assumed that was the reason. Why?"

"It's a little unusual, so I wanted to ask." Generally, people didn't name a parent as executor if they had an able-bodied spouse. Fina was beginning to wonder if Liz had known that her spouse wasn't, in fact, able-bodied.

They watched as a woman struggled to get a double stroller between two nearby tables. Fina got up and moved some chairs out of the way. That was part of what made motherhood unappealing to her: You became so damn unwieldy. Fina liked to move quickly, in and out, with as little baggage as possible, pretty much the antithesis of parenthood.

The mom offered her thanks, and Fina reclaimed her seat next to Bobbi.

"Did Liz keep any memorabilia or keepsakes from NEU?" Fina asked.

Bobbi thought about it. "I know she kept some soccer-related stuff. I think I have a couple of boxes."

"Would you mind if I borrowed them?" Fina took another drink from her cup and replaced the plastic lid.

"I don't mind. You think they might be useful?"

"I'm not sure, but I want to take a look."

Bobbi stared at the fountain and the teenagers who were threatening to push one another into the shallow pool. "If she had died in a car wreck or something like that, it wouldn't matter what happened twenty years ago. If she'd fooled around with that Kevin man, it would have remained a secret."

"You're absolutely right," Fina said. When someone died under suspicious circumstances, her whole life was cracked wide open, exposed to the world. Any scrap of privacy or dignity was stripped away. The only bright spot was that the deceased wasn't around to witness the dismantling of her life.

"I'm doing everything I can to solve this," Fina said. "I know I'm probably not doing it fast enough for your taste, but I'm doing everything in my power."

"I know, Fina. You've been straight with me from the start." Bobbi stood up and grasped her water bottle in one hand. "Life never gets easier. You think as you get older that you'll have figured more stuff out or your kids won't need you anymore, but that's not what happens. They need you just the same, just in different ways. They need you even after they're gone."

Fina rose and gave Bobbi a hug. "I'll call you later and figure out a time to pick up those boxes. Hang in there."

Bobbi tugged on her sweat suit jacket. "I wish Liz could have met you, Fina. I think you would have liked each other."

"I would have liked that. At least I got to meet you," Fina said, "despite the crummy circumstances."

Bobbi gave her a weak smile and walked away.

Fina had to solve this case soon. Any more bad news and she might just break Bobbi Barone's heart.

G us Sibley was in his office seeing patients and would be busy the rest of the afternoon, according to his office manager. Like the general population, the gatekeepers that Fina encountered in her job ran the gamut from dumb as doorknobs to national treasures the NSA should have hired. Fina got the sense that this particular woman fell into the second category. There was no way Fina would be able to waltz in and refuse to leave until Gus saw her. She was certain that security would be called, and she'd be escorted off the property. She decided to wait in the parking lot instead, which was borderline stalkerish, but she'd done worse.

Gus's private practice was in a nondescript two-story building in Chestnut Hill. There was nothing unique about the space, although Fina imagined that the rent was pricey given the location.

She drove a slow circuit around the lot; there was a section designated for the patients of each medical practice in the building, as well as
reserved spots for the physicians. Fina found a visitor's spot a couple of
cars away from the space marked DR. SIBLEY in which a black Mercedes
sedan was parked. Fina wasn't as jumpy as some of her colleagues
were—some of whom were downright paranoid—but some things were
just common sense. Don't put your name on your parking space, front
door, child's backpack, or license plate. You probably didn't want a personal relationship with most of your fellow citizens, so why treat them
like friends?

Fina called Scotty while she sat waiting and watching a parade of
gimpy, casted patients make the trek from the parking lot to the entrance.

"I heard you had quite the adventure last night," he said.

"What did he tell you?" Fina asked.

"He said that you made him go undercover and then you guys were
pursued by a drug dealer," Scotty said.

Fina laughed. "That's not exactly what happened."

"I'm trying to decide which of us got the better deal, Matthew with
the drug dealer or me with the car bomb."

"You two have such a flair for the dramatic."

"And you're the queen of nonchalance and understatement," Scotty
said. "If I remember correctly, not too long ago, you shot a man and
then stopped for a frappe afterward."

"I was hungry!" Fina insisted. "I knew I had a long night ahead of
me, and I needed sustenance."

"Uh-huh," Scotty said. "So, what's going on?"

"Do you know the last name of Rand's girlfriend?"

"Karla's last name? Why?"

"I'm just curious."

"What are you up to, Fina?"

"I'm not up to anything. I just need her name."

Scotty was silent.

"You know I'm going to get it eventually," Fina said, "so you might as well tell me now."

"That's faulty logic."

"Oh, it's fine. Really. What's her name?"

"You can't do anything illegal," he insisted.

"*Moi?*" Fina asked.

He exhaled loudly. "This is exactly why I don't want to give it to you."

"Think of it this way: If I started dating some random guy, wouldn't you want to know as much about him as possible? We vet our business partners. Why not our companions?"

"Because most people don't," Scotty said. "Normal people don't run background checks on acquaintances."

"You're still clinging to the notion that we're normal people?" Fina asked. "Hello? Have you met our parents?"

"Fine, but you didn't get it from me."

She could hear him on the computer. Snowflakes were starting to fall and stick to the windshield. Fina turned on her wipers, not wanting to miss Gus Sibley in the increasing darkness.

"Her name is Karla Hewett."

"Address?"

"I don't have her address. We're not pen pals."

"Easy, killer. I was just asking."

Fina asked after Patty and the kids and promised to stop by soon for a visit. She ended the call and stretched her arms over her head and decided that Milloy's ministrations were in order. She left him a voice mail requesting time with his magic hands.

Gus still hadn't emerged, his car slowly turning more white than black with a thin layer of snow. Fina pulled out her tablet and hopped on the free Wi-Fi from the medical building. She typed in "Karla Hewett" and "Miami" and waited as the slow connection chugged like the Little Engine That Could. The first link that popped up was Karla's Facebook page, but unfortunately for Fina, she had opted to employ the most stringent privacy settings. Fina scrolled through the other search results and found a listing for a mortgage company. Clicking on the address for Horizon Mortgage East brought up an information page all about Karla Hewett.

Fina scanned it. "You have got to be kidding me."

The profile featured a photo of Karla, who had long, smooth blond hair and breasts the size of Florida grapefruits. These were on display in a deep V-neck dress that skimmed her waist and hips. Her teeth were bright white, her nails manicured in a deep coral shade. Fina studied the picture more closely. Karla looked to be in her late twenties. She was probably closer in age to Haley than she was to Rand. Rand's choice in girlfriend was incredibly predictable, but it was her striking resemblance to his late wife, Melanie, that gave Fina pause.

Her train of thought was interrupted when a small group emerged from the building and dispersed in different directions in the parking lot. One of them walked in Fina's direction, and as he got closer, Fina recognized him as Gus. She jumped out of her car and jogged over, nearly wiping out on the now slick pavement.

"Dr. Sibley!"

He looked up, his face wearing a friendly expression until he caught sight of Fina.

"I have nothing to say to you. If you keep following me, I'm going to call the police."

"I haven't been following you."

"You're in my parking lot!"

"Sure, but I purposely came here to see you. I didn't follow you here."

Gus pulled open the car door and started to duck down.

"Did you know that Kevin Lafferty beds NEU student athletes?" Fina asked.

Gus unfolded his frame and slammed the door shut. He faced her.

"What of it?"

"It seems like it might be important."

"Kevin's 'interests' have nothing to do with my job."

"But Liz Barone was one of his 'interests,' and she was your friend."

"I wasn't involved in Liz's personal life, certainly not when she was an undergrad."

Fina brushed a snowflake off her cheek. "Fair enough, but what about Jamie? You two went to great pains to ignore each other at the funeral."

"We didn't visit with each other, that's true," Gus said, "but we weren't ignoring each other."

"Hmm," Fina said. "I don't buy it."

Gus turned back to his door and pulled on the handle.

"What about his knee?" Fina asked.

"I don't discuss my patients."

Fina took a step closer to him. "But he's not your patient."

"What I meant is that I don't discuss anyone's medical issues with anyone else. I don't speculate on conditions even if someone isn't a patient."

"Ah. So you practice discretion," Fina said.

"Yes." He climbed in the car and slammed the door shut. A moment later, the sleek mass of metal purred to life. Fina moved out of the way as he backed out of the space and left the parking lot.

Most of the time, Fina could get people to talk. If they clammed up or referred her to their attorney she attributed it to one of two possibilities. Either the person truly valued his privacy or he was hiding something.

She wasn't sure which option applied to Gus Sibley, but she needed to find out.

Cristian invited Fina to dinner in his neighborhood, and she accepted with a touch of reluctance. She was pulling together seemingly disparate pieces of information related to the case, and one could argue she should share them with Cristian. But she wasn't ready to do that; she needed a little more time to investigate before handing the fruits of her labor over to the cops.

"Are you feeling okay?" Cristian asked halfway through their meal of sushi and sake.

"Sure. Why do you ask?"

"You're not pumping me for information about the case."

"I thought this was purely social—celebrating your status as a single man."

He nodded. "Yeah, but I worry when you're too well behaved."

"Oh, no need to worry on that front," Fina said, smearing some wasabi on a thin slice of tuna.

"That worries me just as much," Cristian said, signaling the waiter for more sake.

"Clearly, you worry too much. Let's talk about something else, like your recent romantic adventures."

He shrugged. "There's not much to say."

"I doubt Cindy would agree," Fina said.

The waiter brought over a small ceramic flask and poured more liquid into their cups. Cristian took a sip before speaking. "She wanted to move to the next step."

"Which step are we talking about? Moving in together? Marriage?"

"Moving in together," Cristian said, dipping a piece of spicy tuna roll in soy sauce.

"And you weren't interested?"

"I'm not going to live with anyone unless we're married. It's not a moral thing, but I don't want Matteo to get attached to someone unless it's permanent."

"That's very responsible of you," Fina said, "but it definitely narrows the options: get married, break up, or date indefinitely."

"Right. I'm not interested in marriage, so breaking up was the way to go."

"Cindy wasn't interested in dating indefinitely?" Fina grinned. She was the only woman she knew who preferred to date indefinitely.

"She was, but she's in her late twenties. I couldn't make her any promises, and she wants kids. She should find someone who's on the same page."

Fina dredged a piece of tempura shrimp through the accompanying sauce. "Well, I'm sorry if you're sorry."

Cristian chewed slowly. "I'm good."

Fina wasn't sure what that meant, but she'd had enough relationship talk for one night.

"Is Matteo excited for the Disney ice thing?" she asked, changing the conversational trajectory.

"Yeah, I showed him some video clips the other day. You know there's a royal Valentine's ball featuring the princesses?"

"Oh, barf. And the whole thing's on ice? What's the ice have to do with anything?"

"Don't overthink it," Cristian counseled.

They drank more sake and huddled together in the bitter wind on the way back to Cristian's apartment. There was no discussion about Fina coming up; it just happened. Which could also describe the rest of the evening.

They were wrestling out of their clothes in the bedroom when Cristian grasped her face with his hands.

"I've missed you," he said.

"I bet you have." Fina smirked and gently tugged his earlobe between her teeth.

30.

Fina lay in bed, curled on her side. She was warm and naked, listening to Cristian shower in the bathroom. With closed eyes, she allowed herself to replay the preceding night's events in her mind. Fina smiled. Still delightful, even in the reimagining.

But there was work to be done. She reached for her phone and scrolled through her voice mails and e-mails. Nothing demanded her immediate attention. Fina dialed Dennis Kozlowski's number, and after they exchanged pleasantries, they got down to business.

"Everything okay with Bobbi Barone?" Fina asked.

"Yup. She's a nice lady."

"She is," Fina said, her mind flipping through her mental file on Dennis. "She's a widow."

"What? You're a yenta now, in addition to all your other talents?" Dennis asked. He'd been divorced for over a decade and, as far as Fina knew, was currently single.

"No, but when I meet two single, likable people, my mind can't help but consider the possibilities."

"Uh-huh." Dennis wasn't buying it.

"But I actually called you with more work," Fina said.

"I'm all ears."

Fina gave him the scoop on Gus Sibley, and they discussed the parameters of surveillance.

"I want someone on him 24/7 for the foreseeable future," Fina said a few minutes later, as Cristian emerged from the bathroom, bare-chested with a towel around his waist. She wrapped up the call and tossed her phone on the bed.

"What's that about?" Cristian asked, opening a drawer in the bureau. He pulled out a pair of boxer briefs and dropped his towel. Fina gazed at his perfect ass.

"Fina?" he asked.

"Huh? Sorry. I was distracted by your butt."

"Who are you following?"

"I can't tell you that." She pushed back the covers and crawled to the end of the bed. "Come back," she said.

"No time."

"Oh, come on. I'm sure you can be quick," she teased.

"Was that call about the Liz Barone case?" Cristian asked, removing her hand from his hip.

"I can't tell you," she insisted, climbing off the bed. "As soon as I have something relevant to share, I will."

She pulled on her bra and thong. When her phone rang, it took her a moment to find it under the mound of blankets.

"Yes, Father," Fina said, rolling her eyes. Cristian smirked as he pulled on his pants.

"There's some asshole here who is ranting about you," Carl said.

"Does this asshole have a name?" Fina struggled into her jeans with one hand.

"Kevin Lafferty. I'm going to have security throw him out unless you have some use for him."

"Stick him in a conference room," Fina said. "I'm on my way."

"Does this have to do with a case?"

"Of course. What do you think, I'm dating the guy?"

"I have no idea what you do in your free time," Carl said.

"Dad, I bake and knit in my free time. You know that."

Fina smiled when Cristian let out a loud bark of laughter.

"Who's that?" her father asked.

"It's a cop."

"I don't want to know. Get over here." He hung up.

"Is Daddy pissed?" Cristian asked.

"Daddy's always pissed," Fina said, pulling on the rest of her clothes and tying her hair into a knot at the back of her head. She grabbed Cristian and planted a long kiss on his plump lips. "It was a pleasure."

He smiled. "Good. I look forward to doing it again soon."

"As do I."

Fina left the apartment and skipped down the front steps.

She really was a fan of law enforcement.

Fina watched from the hallway as Kevin Lafferty paced in a Ludlow and Associates conference room, his phone to his ear. He did not look happy.

On her way in she'd made a detour to the office kitchen and grabbed a diet soda, which she was sipping when she walked into the room.

Kevin glared at her and ended his call abruptly. "I'm going to sue you," he declared.

Fina took a seat at the table. "Okay."

"For harassment."

"Good luck with that."

"You went to my home and talked to my wife." Kevin put his hands on the table and leaned over Fina, his face just inches from hers.

"You smell good," she said. "What cologne are you wearing?"

Kevin sneered at her. "Everything's a joke to you."

"No, actually, it's not. There's nothing funny about a woman being killed or losing her cognitive function for a game of soccer. I find both of those situations extremely serious, and as for speaking to your wife, you are one lucky bastard."

"What?" He pushed his hands off the table and leaned against the wall. Fina couldn't tell if it was a pose of practiced nonchalance or if he needed the support.

"Well, I didn't ask her about your extracurricular activities," Fina said. "A less discreet investigator would have spilled the beans."

He glared at her. "What are you talking about?"

"Let's cut to the chase, Kevin. Can you just admit that you have affairs with NEU student athletes? That you've been having affairs for years?"

He walked around the table and stood opposite her. "I don't know where you're getting your information."

"From various reliable sources."

Kevin snorted. "So, rumors? You treat rumors as evidence? And what do those rumors have to do with Liz Barone's death?"

"That's what I'm figuring out. It seems to me that you have a lot to lose if your affairs become public knowledge—your role as a booster, your reputation . . ."

"I didn't hurt Liz, and I'm not having any affairs," he insisted.

"Of course not," Fina said. She took a long drink of soda. "You know what I've found during my years as an investigator?" she asked.

"What?"

"That it's the guilty who are the most righteous. The guilty are the indignant ones; the innocent feel no need to herald their innocence. They're confident that right is on their side."

"That's bullshit. The righteous are the wrongly accused."

"Not in my experience. Shakespeare was onto something—'the lady doth protest too much, methinks.' That whole business."

"You're crazy," he said.

"Well, thank you very much. I appreciate the feedback." Fina rose from her chair. "In the meantime, good luck with your proposed lawsuit against me. Criminal harassment is definitely a nonstarter, but maybe you'll have luck with a civil complaint." Fina scrunched up her face in concentration. "Probably not, the more I think about it, but I can get you in to see someone for a consult." She gestured toward the hallway.

"Stay away from my family," Kevin said, shaking his finger at her.

"Start telling the truth, and I will."

He stomped out of the room.

Fina watched him recede down the hallway. Perhaps Kevin's good looks and charming personality had provided a cocoon that had buffered him throughout his life. He was used to getting his way. He wasn't used to being questioned or doubted. No wonder Fina was sending him into orbit.

Fina went by Carl's office to let him know that she'd dealt with Kevin, but her father was in a meeting. She was heading out when her phone rang. Risa's number lit up the screen.

"Hey," Fina answered. "How's it going?"

"Good. Is there any way you could stop by today?"

"Sure. What works for you?"

"In a few hours?" Risa suggested. "I'll feed you."

Fina glanced at her watch. "Yum. Something to look forward to. I'll see you then."

Rather than go home and then head out to Newton, Fina decided to take advantage of the firm's Wi-Fi and free supply of diet sodas. She reclaimed her place in the conference room and pulled out her computer, then logged on to Facebook, pleased to see that twenty-four of her friend requests had been accepted. Who were these people who accepted a friend request from a complete stranger? She eliminated the new friends who didn't resemble the photo of the car bomber; men who were old, white, skinny, Asian, or lived outside of Massachusetts were dismissed with a click of her mouse.

That left Fina with five candidates. The five men were all black, in their twenties, and big. Fina scrolled through their profiles and immediately ruled out two of them based on their photos. The remaining three had few photos posted, none of them of particularly good quality, so Fina couldn't rule them in or out. She typed a private message to each man asking if he was available to catch up. Fina hoped they would respond, and she hoped that one of them was her guy. That was a lot of hoping—not her preferred method of private investigation—but it was the best she could do. She'd worry about her next step when she had to take one.

Fina rang Risa's doorbell and opened the door simultaneously.

"Risa!" she hollered toward the back of the house.

"I'm back here!"

Fina stripped off her jacket and padded back to the kitchen. "You shouldn't leave your door unlocked," she scolded.

Risa was pulling a pie pan out of the oven. She set it on the stovetop and dropped the pot holders onto the counter. "Has there been an uptick in crime I don't know about?"

"No," Fina said, climbing onto a stool at the island, "but if you lock up, you never have to be the doofus on the news who was robbed when a thief walked in the front door."

"Not that you're judging the victims," Risa said, smiling.

Fina shrugged. "Trust Allah, but tie up your camel."

Risa made plates for both of them.

"How are the kids?" Fina asked, filling two glasses with seltzer.

"They're good. Jordan has his first dance in a couple of weeks."

"Please tell me you're chaperoning."

"I've threatened to, but he's been on his best behavior to safeguard against that possibility. Let's sit at the table," Risa said, directing Fina toward the large farm table in the family room area.

"This looks delicious," Fina commented. "What is it?"

"You're my guinea pig. It's pistachio and arugula quiche. I'm thinking of making it for a committee luncheon that I have to host."

"I love being your guinea pig," Fina said, cutting off a piece of the quiche, which shared the plate with a green salad.

"I have to serve something that's easy to eat from a plate in your lap and won't scare anybody off in terms of fat and calories."

Fina rolled her eyes and put a forkful in her mouth. "Delicious," she declared after swallowing the bite.

"Obviously," Risa said after a moment, "I didn't just invite you here for quiche." She fiddled with the napkin on her lap.

"Obviously," Fina said.

Risa took a deep breath. "I've given it a lot of thought."

Fina nodded.

"Marty and I have had a lot of conversations," Risa continued, "and I've also met with a social worker who specializes in organ transplants." She looked away.

Fina put down her fork and squeezed Risa's hand. "Whatever you've decided is okay. There is no wrong answer."

Risa swallowed and a tear rolled down her cheek. "I can't do it, Fina. I can't give her my kidney."

"It's okay." Fina moved her hand to Risa's shoulder and rubbed it. "Really."

Risa blotted her eyes with her napkin. "It's the right decision, but that doesn't make it any easier." She gestured to her tear-streaked face.

"There's nothing easy about it," Fina said. "You must be exhausted from the whole process."

Risa took a long drink. "I am."

"Well, now you can put it behind you." Fina picked up her fork and pressed it into the golden crust of the quiche.

"I know I didn't want your opinion right after we met with Greta," Risa said.

Fina nodded. "And that made sense. You needed to figure this out on your own with Marty."

"But now that I've made my decision, I'd like to hear what you think."

Fina held up a finger while she finished chewing a mouthful. "I don't think you should give her your kidney," she said.

"You're not just saying that because I've decided the same thing?" Risa asked.

"No. Getting someone else's organ isn't a right, it's a privilege, and the recipient needs to earn it. Greta hasn't."

"What do you mean exactly?"

"Well, first of all, you have kids, and they should get first dibs on your spare parts."

Risa chuckled. "Like you have dibs on Elaine's."

"Oh, God. Let's not use my family as an example," Fina said, loading her fork with greens. She didn't encounter much produce, so she tried to take advantage when she did. "So your kids get dibs on your organs. Also, I wish I believed otherwise, but I think Greta's primary interest in you is your kidney."

Risa exhaled loudly. "I know. That's what I think."

"I really wish that weren't the case, but she never made any effort to find you or find out about you, even after her sister died." Fina tried to make her delivery gentle, but it was a difficult statement to soften. "I'm not convinced she would have sought you out if not for her declining health, and I'm not convinced she wants to foster a real relationship with you."

"But shouldn't I be the better person?" Risa asked. "Shouldn't I be more generous than she's being?"

"Why?" Fina asked. "Your body belongs to you. If you decide to give a piece to someone because that's truly what you want to do, that's one thing, but you shouldn't feel coerced into that decision. It's not your job to fix Greta."

"I feel like it is."

"Why? Who gave you that job?" Fina captured a pistachio between the tines of her fork.

Risa shrugged. "Because we're blood relatives, I guess."

"But if that creates an obligation, doesn't that obligation apply to Greta, too? An obligation to find you *before* she needed an organ?"

Risa considered the statement for a moment. "I suppose. It just feels like I'm being selfish."

"You're being thoughtful and responsible, and you're putting your own well-being and that of your family first. Maybe a transplant would go smoothly, but if it didn't and you suffered a setback either now or in the future, how would your kids feel?"

"They'd be upset."

Fina blinked. "That's an understatement. Did the social worker suggest you were selfish for not giving Greta your kidney?"

"No," Risa admitted. "She thought it made sense given the circumstances."

"Good. Now you just need to believe it." Fina ate another bite of quiche. Risa moved the food around on her plate.

"Another thing to keep in mind," Fina said, "is that you may not have been a match. Or you may have been a match, but the transplant wouldn't have worked. The choice isn't save Greta or let her die. The choice is whether or not you should set off down a long and difficult path with no guarantees. I think you're making the right choice by stepping off the path."

Risa smiled weakly. "Thanks. I appreciate what you're saying." She put down her fork and picked up her glass. "In the meantime, how am I supposed to tell her?"

"I'll tell her," Fina offered.

"I can't let you tell her."

"Why not? I know her as well as you do."

"That would feel like chickening out," Risa said.

"Why? Because you don't want to give her the opportunity to manipulate you and make you feel guilty?"

Risa was silent.

"How about this? You write her a letter explaining your decision, and

I'll call her once you've sent it to warn her about the contents," Fina offered.

"That might work," Risa said. "That way I can say what I have to say, but not actually have a conversation with her."

"Exactly. So write the letter and let me know when you're ready to send it."

They had a few more bites of food, both of their appetites dampened by the conversation. Fina helped Risa do the dishes and tidy up the kitchen.

"You've been a lifesaver during this whole thing, Fina," Risa said when she walked her to the front door.

"I'm flattered that you included me." Fina pulled on her boots and jacket. "I'm always here to talk."

"Thank you." Risa hugged her.

"Thanks for lunch," Fina said, walking out the door.

She got into her car and leaned back against the seat. Now that Risa had made her decision, Fina felt relieved that Risa wasn't going to volunteer to climb onto the operating table. Fina wanted the people she loved to stay intact as long as they possibly could.

A re you out of your goddamn mind?"

Pamela looked up to see Kevin in the doorway of her office. Jill stood behind him, distress etched across her face.

"Nice to see you, Kevin, as always," Pamela said, and gestured for him to come in. "Jill, could you close the door and hold my calls, please?"

Kevin planted himself in front of Pamela's desk, and Jill pulled the door closed behind her.

"Have a seat," Pamela said.

"I don't want to sit down," he said. "This isn't a social call." His cheeks were red, and his neck seemed to be straining against his collar and tie.

"So what is it, then?"

"What did you say to that private investigator, Fina Ludlow?"

Pamela leaned back in her chair and rotated slowly from side to side. "What makes you think I said anything?"

"She went to my house, Pamela. She questioned my wife."

"About what?"

"About where I was the night that Liz Barone was attacked," Kevin sputtered.

Pamela's shoulders relaxed ever so slightly. "That has nothing to do with me."

"And what about the claim that I fool around with NEU students? Does that have something to do with you?"

Pamela glared at him and gripped the armrests of her chair. "Everybody knows you can't keep it in your pants, Kevin. It isn't exactly a secret."

"So what? You told her?"

"This conversation is over," she said, reaching for her mouse. "I have work to do."

"Was she getting a little too close to the truth?" Kevin asked. "You wanted to distract her with some juicy gossip?"

"Gossip? Have you really convinced yourself that you're innocent in all this?"

"Have you?" He glared at her, and she tried to hold his gaze, but failed.

"You need to leave," Pamela said. "We have nothing more to discuss."

"That's always been your problem, Pamela. You don't think things through. You make rash decisions that you end up regretting."

"Don't threaten me, Kevin."

"Too late. You should have thought about the consequences before you threw me under the bus."

Pamela tugged on the sleeve of her jacket. "What difference does it make if Fina knows about your affairs?"

"If I lose my standing with the university, I'm going to hold you personally responsible."

Pamela picked up the phone. "I'm calling security."

"No need. I'm leaving." Kevin flung open the door and left.

Pamela kneaded her hands together.

Goddamnit. What had she done?

D inner at Carl and Elaine's was the last thing that Fina wanted, but she worried that if she didn't attend, some Rand-related plan would be hatched. She arrived at her parents' house exactly at the appointed hour, hopeful that her appearance would resemble a well-executed military plan—in and out, quickly and quietly, with minimal bloodshed.

Fina found Patty, Elaine, Haley, and the little boys in the media room.

"Where are Scotty and Matthew?" she asked.

"They're in with your dad," Patty told her.

Fina hated when family gatherings were split down gender lines. It was a practice from another century, or another decade, at the very least. Just what were the men discussing that was too coarse for her feminine ears? Money? Sports? Politics?

"Where are you going?" Elaine asked as Fina turned to leave the room.

"I'll be right back," she said.

In Carl's office, Scotty and Matthew were sitting on the couch, with Carl behind his desk.

"Hey," Fina said, sitting down on the couch across from her brothers.

They greeted her and returned to their conversation about the Bruins.

"Did you take care of that man this morning?" Carl asked her a few minutes later. This was one of the things that made him so good in court. He lulled you down one conversational path only to veer off into a ravine. Luckily, Fina was inured to his tactics.

"Yeah. I stopped by your office to tell you, but you were in a meeting," Fina said. "Shari was supposed to give you the message."

"What man?" Matthew asked.

"Kevin Lafferty. He's involved in the NEU case."

"He was running his mouth about suing you," her father said.

"I know," Fina said. "He's clueless."

"Well, he was certainly distracting."

"Ranting and raving distracted you, Dad?" Fina asked. "You're losing your edge."

Carl grunted in disagreement.

"You should be encouraged," she said. "Agitated people are a sign I'm about to crack the case."

"Uh-huh."

"Did you talk to your drug addict?" Matthew asked.

"I did," Fina said. "It wasn't a very satisfying conversation. He thinks he can stop anytime."

Her brothers nodded in understanding. They had dealt with addicts at various times in their professional lives and knew that the disease was pernicious. Money and status had little sway when it came to addiction.

They had returned to debating the Bruins' season when Elaine appeared in the doorway.

"It's time for dinner," she announced.

Carl rose from behind his desk.

"Wait, Carl. Bring up that picture on your computer," Elaine commanded.

He tapped a few keys without comment. Fina used to think that her father tolerated her mother, but she'd realized that what he actually did was ignore her. He would listen to the content of her speech and choose to act on the parts of it he deemed worthy of his attention. He let the rest of it—her tone and any requests in which he had no interest—roll off his back.

Fina started to follow Carl and her brothers out of the room, but was summoned back by Elaine.

"Fina, I want to show you something."

Fina looked at Matthew, a raised eyebrow indicating her confusion. He shrugged his shoulders and made his escape.

"What is it, Mom?"

"Look at this picture." She pointed at Carl's computer screen.

Fina came around the desk and looked at the screen. The photo showed Rand with his arm around a woman—Karla—and two young children posed in front of them. Rand's free hand was placed on the shoulder of the older girl, who looked to be about nine years old.

Fina took a step back and closed her eyes for a moment.

"Look at how pretty she is," Elaine said. "And her children are, too. I don't understand why you don't want Haley to spend time with them."

"I know you don't," Fina said, starting toward the door.

"That's it? That's all you have to say?"

"Trust me, Mom. You don't want me to say any more."

"You always think you know best, Josefina."

She looked at her mother. "I guess that's a trait we have in common."

Fina left the room and tried to calm down before arriving at the dining room table, where she claimed a seat between Teddy and Chandler.

There was nothing like an armpit farting contest to take her mind off her troubles.

Fina checked her e-mail before climbing into bed and was pleased to see that two of the three bomber candidates had responded. Darren Segretti wanted to meet her for coffee the following afternoon, and the other man, Zack Lawrence, invited her for a drink. She put the dates on her calendar and got under the covers.

Fina felt tired. Not the good tired she might expect after a night with Cristian, but the bad tired she got from spending time with her parents. The picture that Elaine had been so eager to show her erased any doubt Fina might have had about involving herself in Rand's life.

She had to—and quickly.

31.

Dennis sent over a batch of Gus Sibley surveillance photos first thing Saturday morning, and Fina's doorman brought them upstairs. She could have reviewed them via e-mail, but she was old-school about some things. Fina liked to hold things in her hands and examine them from all angles.

After showering and dressing, Fina examined the images while nibbling on a Pop-Tart. She hadn't slept well, and the mental image of Rand touching his girlfriend's daughter was even putting a damper on her appetite. He really did ruin everything he touched.

According to the investigator's notes, the previous day Gus had spent six hours at his office, never venturing outside. When he emerged later in the day, he drove to NEU and spent three and a half hours in the field house. Before returning to his home, he stopped at a shopping area on Route 9 and ducked into a coffee shop for about five minutes. Once home, Gus stayed in the entire night.

All of the shots were exteriors; there was no way to photograph Gus inside without his noticing. He may have been up to no good in the confines of his office or the field house, but determining that would prove more difficult. At the coffee shop, the tail had snapped Gus carrying in an NEU travel mug before emerging with it and returning to his car. It seemed a little late for a refill at seven thirty P.M., but some people mainlined coffee all day.

Fina pulled a magnifying glass out of a drawer and examined the pictures more closely. There were shots of Gus parking his car, walking to various buildings, walking from various buildings, and even some of him driving. Fina didn't find anything unusual or odd about the photos, but she couldn't shake the niggling feeling that she was missing something. Or maybe she was so anxious to find something that her mind was playing tricks on her.

Sometimes, taking a break was actually the best way to get work done. In Fina's experience, if she forced her mind to wrestle with a particular puzzle, her progress tended to slow, but if she focused on a different aspect of the investigation, her subconscious might do the difficult work for her. With that in mind, she called Bobbi Barone and arranged to go over to her house to look through Liz's memorabilia.

Bobbi's kitchen was free of the floral arrangements and casseroles that had threatened to overrun it nearly two weeks earlier. The table now looked to be command central for her thank-you note writing operation.

"It never seems right that the bereaved have to write thank-you notes," Fina commented.

"I agree."

"You could just not write them," Fina said.

"No, I couldn't," Bobbi insisted, and gave her a scolding look. "People have been wonderful, and I want to show them my appreciation. Anyway, it gives me a task to focus on each day and then cross off my to-do list."

"I suppose," Fina said, not sounding convinced.

"Do you want some coffee?" Bobbi asked.

"No, thanks," she said, following Bobbi out of the kitchen. "How do you want to do this? I can take the stuff with me or sort through it here; whatever is most convenient for you."

Bobbi thought about it for a moment. "Why don't you take a look at the boxes and decide. I told you there were only a couple, but I was wrong. It might be too much work to haul them out of here."

"Okay. Lead the way."

They climbed the stairs to the second floor. A bathroom and three other open doors greeted them at the top. Fina assumed the room with the queen-sized bed was Bobbi's. A second had a couch and a table with a sewing machine. Fabric was draped over the edge of the table, and tissue-paper patterns were stacked in a basket.

Bobbi stepped into the last room, which had two twin beds with a small dresser between them. There were sliding closet doors opposite the beds.

"This is where I keep the girls' things," Bobbi said, sliding open the closet doors. One side of the closet was filled with clothes, most of which seemed to be for warmer months. The other side was stacked with bankers boxes.

"Yikes," Fina said.

"I know, and they're not labeled," Bobbi said sheepishly. "It was one of those projects I always meant to get the girls to do, but it never happened." She brushed her hand along one box. "I don't think I can bear to go through them right now."

"Of course not," Fina said. "Just leave me to it."

"You sure you don't want any coffee?" Bobbi asked as Fina maneuvered the first box off the stack.

"No, thanks. I'll let you know if I need anything."

Bobbi left, and a minute later Fina heard the dulcet tones of the local classical radio station drifting up from the kitchen.

Sitting on the floor, the boxes arrayed around her, Fina was able to make quick work of the first few, which dated from the girls' high school years. The Barone girls were involved in a range of activities, including soccer, softball, the honor society, the school newspaper, and the international relations club. There were programs and certificates and stacks of photos from games and events.

Fina dug into a box of correspondence next. There were birthday cards and letters from summer camp and a sampling of romantic missives. Fina put aside Liz's sisters' items as soon as she identified them as such; no need for Fina to be a witness to Dawn's and Nicole's awkward years. But she took her time reading Liz's letters. From what Fina could tell, she'd had a couple of particularly close friends in high school and maintained limited correspondence with them in college. There was one boy with whom she traded notes in high school, but he was no longer in the picture once freshman year of college arrived.

When her phone rang, Fina pulled it from her bag and pushed herself up to one of the beds.

"Hello," she answered, stretching her back.

"Fina? It's Greta Samuels."

"Oh, hi, Greta." Fina owed Greta a phone call since she'd volunteered to break the bad news to her, but Fina didn't want to have that conversation now. She also didn't want to have that conversation until Risa sent the letter detailing her reasons for not donating her kidney.

"I need to be in touch with Risa."

"Really?" Fina asked, and stood. She shook out her legs to get some blood flowing and wandered over to the window that overlooked the backyard. Since Bobbi's property bordered a state park, all she could see were snowdrifts and bare trees.

"It's an emergency." Greta's voice sounded strained.

"What's going on?"

"I'm in the hospital."

"I'm sorry to hear that. What happened?"

"I woke up yesterday not feeling well, and it's just gotten worse. They're running some tests, but I need to talk to Risa."

"About what exactly?" Fina asked.

"That's none of your business!"

Fina sighed. "Does this have an impact on your transplant?"

"I don't know, but I'd like to discuss it with her."

"Greta, I'm sorry that things aren't going well, but there's nothing

Risa can do for you at the moment. She's still trying to figure out her next steps in this process."

"But things have changed," Greta said.

"Why don't you have your doctor call me, and then I can give Risa his update."

"You're just trying to keep me from her," Greta said.

"I'm trying to protect her."

"From me?"

Fina was quiet for a moment. "I suppose so."

"But I would never do anything to hurt her."

"You already have, Greta. It drives me crazy that you don't get that!"

"If I die, it's going to be your fault!"

"No, it's not, and comments like that only make me more reluctant to put you in touch with her. Your illness is nobody's fault; it just sucks."

"You've never liked me," Greta said bitterly.

"Initially, I didn't have any feelings about you, but you're right—I'm not your biggest fan now." Fina looked at her watch. "Give your doctor my number. Tell him I'm your niece if you have to, and I'll pass his information on to Risa."

"I don't understand why we have to involve him."

Fina was quiet for a moment. "Because I don't trust you, Greta. It's not that hard to understand. He can call—"

A dial tone buzzed over the line. Fina pulled the phone away from her ear and stared at it. "Seriously?" She'd been starting to feel a twinge of guilt about not telling the truth, but when Greta hung up on her like a tween, it offset any misgivings Fina was having.

She plopped back down onto the floor and picked up where she had left off. She tried not to think too much about Greta as she sorted through piles of yellowed notebook paper. Liz and her friends were in college just as the computer revolution was getting under way, so letters and cards hadn't yet been replaced by e-mails and texts. She flipped through ticket stubs from concerts and team photographs. Fina found receipts from a trip to Fort Lauderdale and a few dried flowers tied with a faded ribbon.

She was halfway through the boxes when Bobbi hollered up the stairs to offer her a turkey sandwich. Fina joined her downstairs for lunch and asked questions about the materials she'd just sorted through.

"If it's too painful to talk about Liz, I understand," Fina said.

"I want to talk about her. That's one of the things I'm afraid of," Bobbi said, brushing potato chip crumbs from her hands. "That no one's going to talk about her anymore."

"If you talk about her, I imagine people will follow your lead," Fina said. "They're probably just trying to be sensitive even if they're misguided."

Bobbi told Fina more stories, and half an hour later, they reluctantly decided to return to their respective tasks. Fina climbed the stairs back to the past, and Bobbi cleared the dishes and contemplated the future without Liz as she composed more thank-you notes.

Two hours later, Fina was ready to accept defeat when she came upon a small bundle of letters held together with an elastic band. She started with the oldest one and read through the stack, shocked and vindicated by what she read. They were love letters, of a sort. Liz's missives were urgent and optimistic in tone, but her boyfriend's responses were more measured. She seemed to be pushing for more, and he was pulling back, tempering his feelings with caution. Since letters from both were included in the stack, Fina assumed the ones Liz had written had been returned to her at the end of the relationship, or perhaps she'd claimed them rather than leave them in her boyfriend's possession.

But it was the last letter that Liz had written to Kevin Lafferty that gave Fina pause.

No wonder she wanted her letters back.

Senior year of college, when she was the leading scorer on the NEU women's soccer team, Liz Barone got pregnant.

F ina wanted nothing more than to jump in her car and track down Kevin, but she had a coffee date with a possible felon; she'd be a fool to miss that.

Her meeting with Darren Segretti was at a Dunkin' Donuts in Chelsea, a curious choice for a potential date, but an excellent choice in Fina's book. It was a public place that was frequented by cops, and it had delicious snacks. All blind dates should work that way.

She opted for a space at the far corner of the lot and retrieved a bag from the trunk before ducking into her car once more. Fina couldn't see anyone nearby, so she took a dirty-blond wig out of the bag and pulled it over her own hair. The wig had cost a fortune, but it was worth every penny. No one could tell that it wasn't her own hair, and it completely masked Fina's real identity. She was a little creeped out that it was made of human hair, but she did all kinds of creepy things in the line of duty. A quick glance in her visor mirror ensured that her new mane was securely in place.

A moment after stepping into the sweet-smelling shop, Fina spotted him, which wasn't hard since he was the largest and only black man in the place. He was sitting at a table near the window, his legs splayed. She kept an eye on him while waiting in line, and by the time she put in her order for a glazed donut and a hot chocolate, she was convinced it was Darren Segretti, but not her bomber.

Just to be sure, Fina borrowed the key to the ladies' room, the route to which led right by Darren. Up close, his nose looked different from the surveillance photo, and though he was tall, he wasn't broad like the man she was looking for. He gave her the once-over on her way by, but he wasn't expecting a dark blond with respectably sized breasts. He was waiting for a brunette with huge boobs, like the fake picture she'd posted, and she certainly didn't fit the bill.

Back in her car, Fina felt a little guilty for standing the guy up, but got over it quickly. Darren had friended a stranger and had arranged to meet her the next day at Dunkin' Donuts for a date. There was no way the guy had wholesome fun in mind.

After a moderate crawl on Route 16, Fina picked up 1A at Bell Circle and drove north to Lynn. It was twenty minutes of gas stations, more Dunkin' Donuts, car dealerships, and defunct racetracks before Fina pulled into a large lot on the water. It was on the early side for dinner, but there were already two dozen cars parked there. The neon sign for the Galley was festooned with garlands and a large wreath, and an illuminated Santa stood guard next to the entrance despite it being mid-January. Fina had been here before—twice for a case and the other times for the outstanding fried clams. She did another quick check on her hair before making the cold trek to the entrance.

Inside, the space consisted of a large square bar and two separate dining areas, one of which was sunken down a few steps. Lobster traps and buoys hung from the ceiling, and the plastic placemats featured a glossary of nautical flags. It was kitschy, but it was also real. There were still people in the area who made their living from the sea.

Fina climbed onto a bar stool and took stock. There was a smattering of patrons, including some older guys on the other side of the bar, a young couple a few seats away, and a few solitary drinkers. There were no black guys, but that didn't mean Zack Lawrence wasn't going to show.

Fina had worked out her approach on the ride up and decided that she wouldn't identify herself as the man's Facebook friend. She suspected that her bait-and-switch with the photos might annoy him, which was no way to start a relationship. Instead, she would try to make him feel better about being stood up—if he showed.

"Bud Light, please. In a bottle," Fina told the bartender, a woman who'd seen better days. Her straw-colored hair was pulled back in a messy ponytail, and her mouth bore the telltale wrinkles of a smoker.

The lighting wasn't very forgiving, but even if she were lit like Elizabeth Taylor, the woman would look sallow.

A couple of minutes later, a young black man Fina recognized as her Facebook friend Zack walked into the bar. She examined him out of the corner of her eye, which wasn't hard to do since he was a giant. Fina guessed he was about six feet five inches and 260 pounds. He was wearing jeans and a baggy sweatshirt, which didn't do much to hide his belly. Fina couldn't be 100 percent sure, but she felt confident this was the man who had incinerated her car. A frisson of excitement ran up her spine.

Fina pulled out her phone and scrolled through her messages rather than strike up any conversations. She was certain that one of her bar mates would do the honors before too long, providing her an opening for approaching Zack. That was one of the odd things about local watering holes during non-prime hours; they were often a curious mix of people who didn't want to talk to anyone and people who wanted nothing more than a friendly ear. They made for odd bedfellows.

Two stools away from Fina, in the opposite direction from Zack, was a skinny young man with a mustache wearing a hooded sweatshirt and a down vest. He was talking, but it was unclear if he was addressing his fellow patrons or the TV tuned to ESPN.

The bartender deposited Fina's beer on the bar. "Do you want to see a menu?"

"Don't need to. Fried clam platter with half onion rings, half fries, please." She'd only had a few bites of her donut, and it was practically dinnertime.

The older woman submitted the order on her computer and walked back over to the men who were sitting on the opposite side of the bar. Their easy conversation suggested they were regulars. Fina turned her attention to one of the large TVs and watched a countdown of the previous weekend's sports highlights. She glanced at Zack, whose eyes moved between the screen and the front door.

Ten minutes later, her clam platter emerged from the kitchen. Fina tipped her head down and inhaled the deep-fried scent. She smacked the ketchup bottle to dispense a pool next to her fries, then dipped a clam into the cardboard cup of tartar sauce. Zack looked at his watch and ordered a second beer. He seemed to know that he'd been stood up and was going to console himself with booze.

A few minutes after Fina started eating, the skinny man eased himself off his bar stool and tottered to the bathroom. When he returned, he approached Fina's stool and studied her.

"Can I buy you a drinks?" he asked, slurring and stinking all at once.

"That's a nice offer, but I don't think so." She wiped some grease off her fingers before picking up an onion ring.

"Why not?"

Fina looked at him. "Really? You really want to have that conversation?"

"I'm just offering to treat you right," he said, his volume climbing. The whiskers on his chin and cheeks were patchy, suggesting a prolonged adolescence or lack of skill with a razor.

"Jimmy, leave her alone," the bartender hollered from her spot on the other side of the bar.

Jimmy wiped his mouth with his shirtsleeve. "I blame this on women's lib."

"As you should," Fina said. "Another time, another era, I'd feel obligated to accept your offer."

Zack guffawed from her other side.

"That's not even why that should be that way so. If it was different, maybe then that would make no sense," Jimmy declared, leaning toward her, giving Fina an unwelcome view of his pores.

"Jimmy," Fina said firmly, "go away before I make you, and I can make you, believe me."

"Maybe I will," he said, stomping his feet, digging into the worn carpet.

Fina chewed a clam, preparing herself for battle, but then Zack heaved his large frame off his stool. He grabbed Jimmy from behind in a bear hug and deposited him on the other side of the bar. Jimmy made a weak verbal protest, but quickly settled into his new home. It was no wonder his protestations were weak; surrender was the only reasonable response to a man the size of a mountain.

"Thanks," Fina said when Zack reclaimed his seat.

"No problem." He picked up his beer and took a sip.

The bartender wandered over and asked Fina if she wanted another beer. She asked for a diet soda instead to wash the saturated fat through her arteries. The woman filled a glass from the soda dispenser and left a sad, flat specimen in front of Fina before returning to her cronies.

"I'm guessing Jimmy's a regular," Fina said, trailing a French fry through the ketchup.

"He'd sleep here if they let him," Zack said, studying the TV screen.

Fina reached up to her ear lobe and surreptitiously tugged off her hoop earring and slipped it into her pocket. She let a few minutes go by before brushing the hair back from her face.

"Shoot," she said at half volume. She glanced around the bar top and hopped off her stool.

"You okay?" Zack asked.

"I lost my earring."

"What's it look like?" he asked.

Fina showed the one still hanging from her other ear. "It's a silver hoop. It shouldn't be hard to see."

He looked around by his feet. Fina retraced her steps toward the door, bent over, studying the floor. On her way back, she circled near Zack's feet.

"This is so annoying. I just got them." She walked a few stools beyond him and then back toward her own seat, her eyes trained on the floor. On the way past, she stole a glance at his feet. He was wearing white tube socks with a distinctive logo on the ankle.

Fina's pulse quickened. She climbed back onto her stool and

reached up to pull off the other earring. "I must have lost it some-place else."

"That's too bad," Zack said.

Fina picked through the remaining French fries. She was on a life-long quest to find the perfect fry: crispy and oily on the outside, but soft on the inside.

"You know," she said to him, "you look familiar. Have we met before?"

Zack looked at her before shaking his head. "I don't think so."

"I'm Amy, by the way."

"Zack."

"Nice to meet you. Maybe I've seen you in here before," Fina mused.

"Maybe."

"Do you live here? In Lynn?"

"Yeah," he said. "What about you?"

"Salem, but I work in Lynn. You know the building on the corner of Maple and Wexford? That's where I work," she said, naming the location of Scotty's deposition. "It's got a garage out back."

Zack shook his head slowly. He picked up his beer and took a long swig. "I don't know it."

"Oh, well. I thought maybe that's where I've seen you before."

"I've never been there." He drained his beer and stood up, reaching into his pocket for his wallet. Fina watched as he pulled out a few bills and left them on the bar.

"It was nice meeting you," she said. "Maybe I'll see you again one of these days."

"Maybe," he said, and grabbed his jacket. He lumbered up the stairs and pushed open the door, revealing the dark winter sky.

Fina gestured for her check and pressed her finger against the plate to capture the last crumbs of fried batter. Check in hand, she pulled out her wallet and placed fifty bucks on the counter. It was a generous tip, but it was important to leave a positive, memorable impression when-ever possible.

It hadn't been positive, but hopefully she'd made a memorable impression on Zack Lawrence.

I'm in my car, but I'm not driving," Fina insisted when Cristian came on the line. She'd pulled off the wig and was scratching her scalp with her free hand.

"Happy to hear it, but you didn't need to call me to report that."

"That's the least of what I have to tell you," Fina said. She was sitting in the parking lot of the Galley. "You ready?"

He sighed. "Just tell me."

"I found the car bomber." She beamed even though he couldn't see her expression through the phone.

"Really?"

"Really. Get out a pen and paper, 'cause you're going to want to write this down."

There was some noise in the background. Fina imagined that Cristian was tucking the receiver into the crook of his neck, poised to take notes.

"Go ahead," he said.

"His name is Zack Lawrence, and he lives in Lynn. He's about six feet five inches and two hundred and sixty pounds. Somewhere around there."

"Car? License plate?" Cristian asked.

"Jeez, you want it all. There can't be more than one Zack Lawrence matching that description in Lynn, for goodness' sakes!"

"How'd you find him, and what makes you so sure it's him?"

"I found him by investigating, and I'm sure he's the one who planted the bomb for a variety of reasons," Fina said. She redirected the air vent away from her face.

"Such as?" Cristian asked a moment later. "I can't pick the guy up based on your gut feelings."

"He's wearing the same socks that are in the photo, and those socks are only sold at three places in the state. He shops at one of those places, and when I mentioned the garage, he got jumpy."

"When you mentioned the garage?" Cristian's voice went up a notch. "You talked to the guy?"

"Of course I talked to the guy. I wanted to be sure before giving you his name. I wouldn't want anyone to be falsely accused," Fina said. "You know I take civil rights very seriously."

"Where did you talk to him?"

"At the Galley in Lynn. It was a perfectly pleasant conversation, but he did hightail it out of here when I mentioned the garage."

"So he's gone?"

"Yes. I thought about following him, but I didn't want to spook him too much."

"That was very restrained of you."

"I thought so, too."

"You said 'planted.' You don't think he built the device?"

"I'm not convinced he's the sharpest knife in the drawer, but I know he's the guy from the garage."

"You heading home now?" Cristian asked.

"That's the plan," she said.

"Want some company later?" he asked.

Fina looked toward the far corner of the parking lot, which ended abruptly at the water's edge. The ocean looked inky. "Actually, tonight's not a good night."

"No problem. We'll figure something else out."

"Sure. Let me know as soon as you have something on this guy," Fina implored.

"Right. Like you did?"

"You're a better person than I am, Cristian. Everyone knows that."

Fina hung up and sat for a moment, contemplating Cristian's offer of company. She loved spending time with him, but she was surprised by the follow-up invitation so soon after their night together. She hoped

Cindy hadn't instilled in him a level of attentiveness that she'd have to undo.

Fina had enough on her plate.

She invited Milloy over for dinner, but he had a late appointment and then a dinner date with some guy friends. Fina wasn't very hungry and decided that the Ben & Jerry's in the freezer qualified as a balanced meal, particularly since she had eaten arugula and other greens at Risa's the day before.

She ate while watching an episode of Haley's favorite reality TV show, which combined blind dates and home renovation projects. Afterward, Fina wandered over to the dining room table and grabbed the stack of surveillance photos from Dennis. She turned on the table lamp and examined them again with the magnifying glass, first in chronological order and then in reverse. Next, Fina numbered the backs of the photos to preserve their original order before shuffling them on the coffee table and gathering them into a random stack. Sometimes when you performed a task in a practiced order or mode, your mind skipped over details that you should be scrutinizing.

She started through them again and kept getting tripped up on one particular photo. It showed Gus in the background walking into the coffee shop at the end of his day. In the foreground, his black Mercedes-Benz was parked next to a minivan. Fina didn't recognize the car's license plate, but something about it was bothering her.

Grabbing her phone, she punched in Dennis's number and waited for him to answer.

"Hey, it's Fina. Could you send me an electronic version of one of those photos?"

"Which one?" he asked.

Fina described the photo in question and clicked on the send and receive button half a dozen times before the file arrived.

"What do you got?" Dennis asked.

"The minivan," Fina said. "I recognize it."

"Really?" He sounded skeptical. "There are thousands of those around."

"I know, but I'm sure I've seen it before. I'll call you if I figure it out," she said, hanging up the phone.

Fina opened the file and zoomed in on the photograph. It was still blurry, but she was right; she had seen the window decal before. It was a stick-figure family, complete with pets.

"Those goddamn liars," she said, slumping back against the couch cushions.

32.

Fina rolled around all night, her mind racing with possibilities. She finally climbed out of bed at six A.M., an ungodly hour in her book, but there was no point in lying there, staring at the ceiling.

She'd called Dennis back the night before and arranged for a second surveillance gig on a different person. Surveillance involved waiting—even if you weren't the person doing the actual surveillance—and it was one of the hardest parts of the job. Fina would much prefer an angry confrontation to sitting by the phone, anxious for an update. But waiting was often the best strategy; it was always better to catch someone in the act even when you weren't sure what that act would be.

Keeping busy was critical if she didn't want to go nuts, so she spent most of Sunday cheering on her nephews at their indoor soccer games. Ryan, Teddy, and their teammates demonstrated some actual skill, but Chandler's game was by far the most entertaining. The younger boys ran around the enclosed playing field like mice in a maze, the ball bouncing off the walls at a rapid pace. Fina wasn't convinced that the ball made contact with their feet, and yet it was constantly in motion. It was the perfect distraction and kept both her anxiety about the case and her untapped energy at bay.

On Monday, Fina prepped for the day and arrived at Kevin Lafferty's office at nine A.M. She brought a bag of bagels and used them as a prop when the receptionist tried to flag her down.

"Delivery for Kevin Lafferty!" Fina called out, and continued down the hall toward Kevin's office. His assistant, Colin, was in the doorway talking to Kevin when Fina arrived.

"I brought you bagels," Fina said, gently pushing the bag into the young man's chest.

"I don't think . . ." he stammered as Kevin got up and came out from behind his desk.

"There's nothing to think about," Fina assured him. "I got a variety of flavors, cream cheese, the works."

Colin looked at his boss, and Kevin waved him away from the door. "I can handle this, Colin. Why don't you share Fina's largesse with everyone else?"

Fina walked into the office and sat down in front of his desk. "I think you'll want to close the door," she said.

Kevin closed it and returned to the chair behind his desk. "I don't think it's very smart talking to me without your lawyer. It's not in your best interest to be off the record with me," he said with a smirk.

"Yeah, I'm not the least bit worried," Fina said. She reached over and took a bottled water from the credenza.

"I'm a busy man, so get to it," Kevin said.

Fina unscrewed the top and took a long drink. "I want to know what happened to the baby."

He gave her a blank stare. "You really are nuts," he said finally.

"So you've told me," Fina said wearily, "multiple times."

"Well, I've got no idea what you're talking about."

"When you got Liz Barone pregnant? What happened to the baby?" Fina enunciated her words as if talking to a foreign language speaker.

Kevin gripped his armrests. "Liz and I weren't having an affair. I told you that already."

"Not now, dummy. I meant when she was a student at NEU. What happened to that baby?"

"I don't know who told you that, but it's a lie," he said, gaining momentum. "We were never involved, and there certainly wasn't any child."

"You want to know who told me? Liz told me." Fina reached into her bag and pulled out the bundle of letters she'd found amongst Liz's memorabilia.

"What are those?"

"Love letters," Fina said. "Well, yours aren't exactly love letters, they're more like 'I care about you, but don't get your hopes up' letters." She handed them across the desk.

Kevin pulled off the elastic band holding the envelopes together.

"The one on the bottom is the really juicy one," Fina advised.

He took the letter from the bottom of the pile and opened it. He skimmed it before slipping it back into its envelope.

Kevin sagged back into his chair. The color that had been rising in his cheeks began to fade.

"What is it that you want exactly?" he finally asked Fina.

"You know what I want. I want to know the truth."

Kevin glared at her. "It's none of your business."

"That's how you want to play it?" Fina asked.

"My personal life is none of your concern."

Fina shook her head. "You had an affair with a student while you were an employee of the university, and you got her pregnant." She reached out and retrieved the stack of letters. "You still have affairs with students. It may not be my concern, but the university can't keep ignoring it."

"Get out," he said.

"Thought you'd never ask," Fina said, rising from her chair.

At the door, she turned back to look at him. "It's all going to come out. If I were you, I'd get out in front of it while you still have the chance."

Fina sat in her car and thought about Kevin and Liz and wondered just how far he'd go to protect his secrets. Sometimes people killed to protect secrets, but she didn't know if Kevin was one of those people.

———————

Rather than going home and pacing the living room, Fina crossed Fort Point Channel and pulled into an alley to make some calls.

First, she left a message for Cristian requesting an update on Zack Lawrence. Next, she dialed Pamela Fordyce's office and was put on hold by the eternally grateful Jill.

"This is Pamela," the authoritative voice answered after a couple of minutes.

"It's Fina Ludlow, Pamela. How are you?"

"Busy, actually."

"Well, this will only take a minute. I wanted to let you know that I followed up on your tip and found some interesting information."

There was a long pause. "Did you tell Kevin that I said those things about him?"

"No, of course not. Why?"

"He came storming into my office on Friday and accused me of telling you things."

"I never mentioned your name," Fina said, "but apparently he figured it out on his own." Fina watched as a man shuffled into the alley. He looked like the Michelin Man with his layers of ill-fitting and inappropriate clothing. His feet were clad in men's dress shoes that were held together with duct tape. Fina hated the cold, but she had plenty of ways to keep warm. Other people weren't so lucky.

"I shouldn't have told you," Pamela said.

"I would have figured it out eventually," Fina said.

"I should have let you."

Fina reached into her purse and pulled out a couple of twenties. When she tapped the horn, the man came over to her open window and accepted her offering.

"What are you so afraid of?" Fina asked.

"Nothing, but I didn't want to be involved, remember?"

"Pamela, you wanted to take the guy down, and believe me, that's the direction he's headed. You're getting what you wanted."

"It's more complicated than that," Pamela said.

"I'm sure, but I called you for another reason. I need you to look up someone in the NEU system."

"I can't do that," Pamela said. "It's against school policy."

Fina let the comment hang in the air for a moment. "Kind of like sleeping with students is? I'm sure you can overlook one more small violation before your moral compass kicks in." Honestly. Now was not the time for Pamela to get a conscience.

"What's the name?" Pamela asked quietly.

"Zack Lawrence." Fina spelled it out for her. "I don't know if it's short for Zachary. I think he's early to midtwenties, and he lives in Lynn. He's black, if that makes any difference."

"It shouldn't. What am I looking for?"

"Any connection he might have to NEU. As a student, employee, anything like that."

"Fine. I'll be in touch," Pamela said, ending the call.

Something hinky was going on with that woman, but before Fina could take that thought any further, her phone rang.

"How close are you to NEU?" Dennis asked.

"Close enough. Why?"

"It looks like your two subjects are meeting again."

"Where?" Fina asked as she put the car in drive and pulled out of the alley, nearly colliding with a cab. She exchanged horn blasts with the cabbie and made a U-turn in the middle of the street. Dennis gave her the address, and Fina dropped the phone on the passenger seat so she could be completely focused on exceeding the speed limit and cutting off her fellow drivers. It was like a Best of Boston driving sample. She just hoped she wouldn't catch the attention of any cops or kill anyone in the process.

She pulled into the parking lot of a Peet's Coffee shop seven minutes later and found a space in the back corner of the lot. Once out of her car, she scanned the area until she found Gus's Mercedes. One row away, she spotted the minivan. Fina crept forward until she got to an SUV that gave her a good view of the coffee shop and the two cars, but still provided some coverage.

"Come on, come on," Fina urged quietly. She looked at her watch. She didn't doubt the surveillance guy's report, but she wanted to see it with her own eyes.

Which she did, a minute later.

Gus Sibley came out of Peet's carrying his NEU travel coffee mug and strode to his car.

He was pulling out of the lot a minute later when the front door of the shop swung open and a woman walked out.

Kelly Wegner carried an NEU travel coffee mug to her minivan and climbed behind the wheel.

Fina returned to her car and called Dennis. She asked him to keep the tail on Kelly but pull off Gus.

"I was wondering how long we were going to do that. You're racking up quite the bill," he commented.

"I think Carl will be paying for this," Fina said. "Can your guy be in touch in a few hours? I don't want to wait until the end of the day for an update."

"Of course."

Fina was thrilled to discover a link between Kelly and Gus, but she still didn't know what their actual connection was, and she couldn't just ask them. They'd claim it was a coincidence, so she had to keep waiting.

Rather than ruminate, Fina drove to Newton, happy for the distraction. Frank's car was in the driveway outside 56 Wellspring Street, and he looked pleased to see her when he opened the door.

"I'm taking you to lunch," Fina declared. "Unless you already have plans, of course."

"To what do I owe the pleasure?" Frank beckoned her inside while he got his coat from the closet and slipped on his boots.

"I'm happy because I'm on the brink of solving this case, and I thought, who would I like to share this with? You came to mind."

Frank patted her cheek with his rough hand. "That's so nice, sweetie. I'm happy that you're happy. Where are you taking me?"

"Your choice," Fina said, and rattled off a list of local establishments.

Frank paused in concentration. "I have had a hankering for baked Boston scrod recently."

"Well, by all means, let me make that dream come true," Fina said. "Legal Sea Foods it is."

O ver lunch, Fina updated Frank on her progress.

"Do you still think the case has something to do with the lawsuit?" he asked once their entrées had been served.

"I don't know," she admitted. "But everything keeps coming back to the university. Whatever's going on, the university plays some role in it."

"So what are you going to do?"

"I'm going to wait to hear what the tail has to report about Kelly's activities," Fina said, scooping up a buttered scallop from her seafood casserole.

"Ah, waiting." Frank grinned. "Your strong suit."

Fina narrowed her gaze. "Very funny. I'm also waiting to hear from Cristian about the bomber."

"What's going on with Risa?" Frank asked.

"She's decided not to give her kidney to Greta Samuels."

Frank nodded, sipping his coffee.

"Speaking of Greta," Fina said, "she called me on Saturday. She's in the hospital and wanted me to put her in touch with Risa."

"But you're not going to?"

"No. I think she's just going to lay a guilt trip on her," Fina said. She pushed the lime wedge in her drink down to the bottom with her straw. "Do you think it's wrong of me not to tell Risa?"

Frank shrugged. "No. I think you're trying to protect your friend."

Fina nodded. "For all I know, Greta isn't really in the hospital. I wouldn't put it past her—cooking up some story to gain sympathy."

"You're very cynical," Frank said.

"Kind of comes with the job, don't you think?"

"I suppose. Regardless, I think you're making the right decision."

"Glad to hear it," Fina said. "That makes me feel better."

Frank proceeded to tell her about an ambitious woodworking project he was planning, and soon after, the waiter came by with dessert menus.

"What do you think?" Frank asked, eyeing Fina over the menu.

"You know how I feel about dessert," she said.

"Haven't met one you didn't like?"

"You got it, except for sorbet and fruit." She pointed at that entry on the menu. "What's that all about?"

"That's Peg's version of dessert."

Fina perused the options. "I won't tell if you won't."

Frank smiled. "I think sharing a slice of Boston cream pie would be very reasonable, don't you think?"

"It's so light and airy," Fina said. "It doesn't even count."

Frank winked at her. "I couldn't agree more."

Fina dropped Frank back home and was on the Pike when her phone lit up with Pamela's number.

"Hello," Fina said, speeding through the E-Z Pass booth.

"It's Pamela. I have some information about Zack Lawrence."

"Great. What is it?"

"Well, he never graduated from NEU, but he was a student for three semesters."

"So he dropped out?"

"It looks like it was a mutually agreed-upon decision. His grades were abominable."

"What else?"

"I've had other things to do, Fina. I'm not your assistant."

"I know, Pamela, and I appreciate your help. I wouldn't ask if it weren't important."

Pamela sighed. "He hadn't yet declared a major, and he had a job on campus for one semester."

"What kind of job?" Fina asked. She heard papers being shuffled on the other end of the line.

"He worked in janitorial services for the science department," Pamela said.

"Like in a lab?" Fina asked, her attention sharpening.

"It looks like it, but I'm not sure. Remember, this was about five years ago."

"Does it say who his boss was?"

"No. He worked through the student employment department. Kids go there to find a job and get assigned to various places around campus."

"Anything else that might be helpful?" Fina asked.

"I don't think so." There was muffled conversation on the other end. "I need to go. I hope this is what you were looking for," Pamela added before hanging up.

Fina took the next exit and pulled over at the bottom of the ramp. She scrolled through the contact list on her phone and dialed the number for Dana Tompkins, the postdoc in the Schaefer Lab.

"Dana, it's Fina Ludlow, the private investigator," Fina said when Dana answered.

"Hi, Fina. How are you?"

"I'm good, and I don't mean to be rude, but I need some information, and I need it fast."

"Okay. What do you need?"

"Can you tell me if a guy named Zack Lawrence ever worked in the lab? It would have been about five years ago, and it would have been a janitorial-type job."

"Let me look," Dana said. Fina could hear keys tapping in the background. "Sorry. The system is really slow."

"No problem. I appreciate the favor."

"Okay. Let's see. There was a guy named Zack Lawrence here, but only for one semester."

Fina banged her fist on the steering wheel in excitement. "Does it say what kind of job he did?"

"No, just after-hours janitorial stuff. Nothing technical."

"That's fantastic. I wonder—" But before Fina could finish her sentence there was a loud bang at the other end of the phone and raised voices. "Dana? Are you okay?"

An argument ensued in the background, and Fina heard her name in the mix.

A man's voice came on the line. "You are a menace!"

"Dr. Mehra! How nice to hear your voice!"

"Are you trying to get her fired?" Vikram yelled. "She is violating school policy assisting you!"

"If you even think about firing her," Fina said, "I'll make sure she has the best legal representation, and I will make your life hell."

"Why are you asking about this Zack Lawrence?"

"Why don't you tell me? It's about the bomb that was placed on my car."

"I know nothing about this!" Vikram exclaimed.

"The alleged bomber once worked for you!"

A man pulled up in the lane next to Fina, and they made brief eye contact. He was cute and gave her a look that was more like an invitation. Really? Did people really make dates at the bottom of Mass Pike exit ramps?

"So? The student workers change constantly. Many people have worked for me," Vikram said. "I don't remember them."

"I'm not surprised, given your stellar interpersonal skills," Fina said, "but Zack's kind of hard to forget. He's black and about six feet five inches tall."

"Him? You think I hired him to set a bomb?"

"So *now* you remember who he is?"

"I remember because he was a useless employee," Vikram said. "He was very clumsy and broke everything. And he stopped working here after one semester."

"You fired him?"

"No! He stopped showing up. I would have fired him, but I didn't get the chance. Do not call here again!"

"Do not fire Dana!" Fina said. "Not unless you want me to put you on speed dial."

Vikram hung up the phone, and Fina just sat there, wondering what the hell had just happened. Was Vikram angry because Zack was a lousy janitor or a lousy bomber?

Fina tried to reach Cristian, but had to leave a voice mail saying she would stop by. She would have loved to put all the pieces together on her own—present Cristian and Pitney with a solved case, wrapped up in a bow—but that wasn't realistic. The cops were better equipped to chase down some leads, particularly those that might call for search warrants.

Kelly's tail had left a message summarizing her day, which sounded like a page from the diary of most suburban moms. It was routine and boring, but certainly gave Fina an appreciation for the demands of being a stay-at-home mother, which didn't entail much staying at home, if Kelly's day was any indication.

At police headquarters, the desk sergeant told her that Cristian was unavailable, but that Pitney would speak with her instead.

"I can come back when Detective Menendez is available," Fina said, retreating.

"I suggest you have a seat, young lady," the cop said, peering at her.

"Fine," Fina said, parking herself on the torturous wooden bench.

A uniformed cop appeared a few minutes later and led her upstairs. Fina expected to be shown to an interview room, but instead was granted access to an observation room. Lieutenant Pitney was there, looking through the one-way mirror at Cristian and Zack Lawrence in the interview room next door.

"Lieutenant," Fina said. The uniformed cop pulled the door closed, and they were alone in the dimly lit room.

"Fina." Pitney was wearing a cherry-red sweater and what looked like houndstooth-patterned pants. The large black-and-white print made her lower half look pixelated.

"Have you gotten anything from him yet?" Fina asked.

"Not yet. He hasn't asked for a lawyer, but he hasn't said much, either."

Fina took a step closer to the glass. "It looks like him, don't you think?"

"Seeing a resemblance isn't going to be enough for the DA."

"Well, of course not," Fina said, feeling her defenses rise, "but it's something."

"I assume there's a reason you're here?" Pitney asked.

Fina rested her hands on the frame of the mirror and looked at the two men on the other side. Cristian wasn't exactly small, but compared with Zack, he looked downright petite.

"Did you know that Zack worked in Vikram Mehra's lab, otherwise known as Liz Barone's lab?" she asked.

Pitney looked at Fina, her expression impassive.

"That lab has the chemicals that were used in the bomb, and he and Vikram had contact. You see where I'm going with this."

"I do." Pitney leaned forward and tapped on the window. Cristian and Zack both looked up. Cristian rose from his chair and left the room. A moment later, he stepped into the observation room.

"Hey," he said to Fina.

"Hey."

"Fina has some info for us," Pitney said. "Tell him what you just told me."

She filled Cristian in on Zack's link to the lab, and he jotted something down in his small notebook.

"Great. I'll see what I can do," Cristian said.

"When did you find this out?" Pitney asked Fina.

"Less than an hour ago!" Fina exclaimed. "Wow! You always assume the worst about me."

Cristian dipped his chin down in an effort to hide his grin.

"It's not funny," Fina said to him. "It's annoying."

"Well, I'm sorry if my question offended you," Pitney said, brushing a lock of curly hair away from her face.

"No, you're not," Fina said. "Why do I even bother?"

"Because it's against the law to withhold information," Pitney responded, at a slightly higher volume than the small space required. She gestured toward the mirror. "Go back in there, Menendez."

"Talk to you later," he said to Fina, and left, reappearing a moment later in the interview room.

"Can I stay and watch?" Fina asked Pitney.

"No, you cannot."

Fina walked to the door and was turning the knob when Pitney spoke. "So you and Cristian are back together?"

Fina turned to look at her. "Huh? That question has to be some kind of workplace violation."

"I'm asking as his friend, not as his boss."

Fina looked at Cristian in the next room. "We've never been together in the traditional sense, so we certainly can't be back together."

"But he's not with Cindy anymore," Pitney said. She tapped her tomato-colored nails on top of the room's lone file cabinet.

"Correct," Fina said. "This relates to you how?"

"He's a great guy."

"I know. That's why I spend time with him."

"I know everything is a big free-for-all with you, Fina," Pitney said, "but that's not always a great approach."

"Hmmm. I really don't want your advice about . . . anything. And I can't imagine that Cristian would be happy knowing that you're poking around his personal life."

"I'm just looking out for him."

"He's a grown man with a gun, Lieutenant," Fina said. "He can take care of himself."

She pulled the door closed behind her and threaded her way through the squad room and back downstairs.

Fina had gone into the station with a slight inclination that she should share her Gus and Kelly sighting with Pitney.

She was leaving with no such impulse.

Fina went home and ran every possible search she could on Vikram and Zack. She didn't really think she'd uncover something the cops wouldn't, but she needed to occupy her brain somehow. She found an old photo of Zack from high school and an announcement in the local paper that he'd been accepted into the NEU Local Scholars program, whatever that was. She left a message for Pamela asking for information about it.

Milloy arrived bearing take-out Vietnamese food, and they settled on the couch to watch a basketball game. Fina kept checking her phone and adjusting her position on the couch.

"What's up with you?" Milloy asked. "You keep squirming."

"Sorry. I'm just antsy about this case. I'm this close," she said, pinching two fingers close together.

"Which is usually when you start climbing the walls," he noted. Milloy had been around long enough to recognize the life cycle of a case.

They kept watching the game.

"Do you want to stay over?" Fina asked five minutes later. She welcomed a distraction, and there were few things more distracting than Milloy.

"Wish I could, but I'm not feeling great, and I've got an early morning."

"Are you seriously telling me 'Not tonight, dear, I have a headache'?" she asked.

Milloy grinned. "Kind of, but don't take it personally. I'm sure I'll feel better in no time."

He left right after the final buzzer, and Fina popped an over-the-counter sleeping pill and climbed into bed.

The tiny tablet was a poor substitute for Milloy's broad chest, but it would have to do.

33.

Fina awoke feeling slightly groggy, so she threw on some workout clothes and took the elevator down to the fourth floor. She ran a few miles on the treadmill and lifted some free weights in an effort to clear the cobwebs from her head.

Upstairs in the condo, she stripped off her sweaty clothes and showered. After dressing, she poured herself a glass of milk, rather proud that she was starting the day with a workout and a full serving of calcium.

Kelly's tail had sent Fina an e-mail detailing her whereabouts the day before. The list included the elementary school, a local pizza place, and a stop by Jamie and Liz's house. Fina changed gears and turned her attention to Pamela, who had yet to reply to Fina's message. Fina called her office and left another message with Jill. She knew that she didn't have any right to be irritated—Pamela had a job and didn't owe her anything—but she still felt irked by the lack of update.

That might have been what prompted Fina to open a browser window and run another search on Pamela, even though she'd done one a couple of weeks before.

This time, Fina took a page from Ronald Reagan's playbook: She decided to trust, but verify.

And when she couldn't verify, it all started to make sense.

At the beginning of a case, Fina would take hold of any potential lead and follow it. This usually led to dead ends, but it was the only way to gain traction at the outset. Toward the end of a case, there were often too many leads to follow, and she had to pick just one. She decided Jamie was due a chat, particularly in light of Kelly's visit to him the night before.

With a quick call to his office, Fina learned that he was working at home for the day. She stopped by a gourmet grocery store on the way to Hyde Park and picked up a frozen container of macaroni and cheese, a green salad, and a loaf of bread. Fina knew that the mac 'n' cheese was a gamble; her nephews only ate the kind with white cheese and macaroni of a certain diameter, but she figured it had a greater chance of appealing to Jamie's kids than poached salmon with saffron sauce.

Fina climbed the front steps with her peace offering and rang the bell. Jamie peered out from the front window a moment later and shook his head. "It's not a good time," he said.

"Jamie, come on," Fina said. "I've come bearing gifts. I just want to ask you a few questions. I'm not going to give you a hard time."

She waited on the front step, freezing her butt off, confident that she could outlast him in a test of wills. A minute later the door swung open and Jamie let her into the house.

"I brought you some food. You can freeze it if you don't need it now."

"Thanks," he said, and took the bag from her.

"Do you have a few minutes?" she asked.

"Fine," Jamie said. It was more like a surrender than an invitation.

Fina took off her coat and followed him into the kitchen, where a mug of coffee sat on the table.

"Do you want some?" he asked, gesturing to his cup.

"Water would be great."

Jamie reached into an upper cabinet and took down a glass, which he filled at the tap. He put it down on the table, and Fina took a seat. He sat down across from her and raised his coffee cup to his mouth. Fina noted a slight tremor in his hand.

"How are things going?" Fina asked.

He put down his cup and spread his hands open. "They're hunky-dory."

Fina took a sip of water. "Have you seen Kelly recently?" she asked.

"She was here last night. My daughter stayed late at school for a project, and she's in the same class as Kelly's son. Kelly picked them up and took them out to dinner, then dropped my daughter off. Why?"

"I've been trying to be in touch with her, and we keep playing phone tag." Fina waited while he drank some coffee. "Do you know what's going on with her and Gus Sibley?"

Jamie put the mug down a little too hard, and some drops dribbled over the side. "What do you mean?"

"I know they've seen each other recently, even though they both claimed they weren't in touch. I'm always curious when people lie to me."

Jamie stood up and got a paper towel from the dispenser hanging under one of the cabinets. Fina knew he was buying time, which was fine by her. It was always interesting to see what baloney people came up with instead of the truth.

"I have no idea," he finally said. "I didn't know they were in touch." He came back to the table and cleaned up the spilled coffee before tossing the paper towel into the trash.

"Hmm," Fina said, rotating her glass on the tabletop. "You sure about that?"

"I thought you weren't going to give me a hard time."

"I'm not. I haven't mentioned your drug habit."

Jamie opened his mouth to speak, but was interrupted by a ringing phone. He grabbed his cell off the counter and glanced at the screen. "I need to take this," he said, slipping out of the room.

Fina tried to listen, but he had moved to the living room and was speaking in hushed tones. Maybe the phone call was innocent, but people didn't tend to lower their voices when confirming a dental appointment.

She got up from the table and brought her glass to the sink, guessing that she had worn out her welcome. There were breakfast dishes piled up and what looked to be stacks of mail on the counter. Fina was placing her glass in the drying rack when something caught her eye. Next to the refrigerator, tucked behind a tall jar holding cooking utensils, she saw the familiar NEU colors. It was an NEU travel coffee mug, and it looked very similar to the ones toted by Gus and Kelly the day before.

Fina reached out and picked it up. It was light—too light to contain liquid. She shook it lightly, and the sound it made resembled a baby's rattle. Fina quickly pulled off the top and looked inside. The travel mug contained white pills, the same sort of pills that Matthew had described Jamie purchasing at the club in Central Square.

She did a quick mental calculation and put the top back on the mug and returned it to its spot next to the fridge. Fina grabbed her glass, squirted some liquid soap into it, and turned on the faucet. When Jamie came into the kitchen a minute later, she was busy washing her glass and placing it in the drying rack.

"I was just washing my glass," she said, noticing his eyes glance toward the counter and the travel mug. "I brought mac 'n' cheese and salad and bread. Like I said, you can freeze the mac 'n' cheese. I hope it's the kind your kids like."

Jamie avoided her gaze.

"Sorry for bugging you about Gus and Kelly," Fina said. "I'm just really frustrated."

"Me too," Jamie said, his posture relaxing.

Fina started toward the front door. "If you think of anything, let me know."

"Sure. I will."

"I'm not frustrated because I'm not making progress; I'm frustrated because I'm about to crack the case and I'm impatient," Fina said, pulling on her coat.

"I'm glad to hear it," Jamie said, looking anything but glad.

"I'll be in touch." She squeezed his arm before starting down the front steps. Jamie closed the front door, disappearing from view.

Fina could have asked him about the pills, but that would have meant blowing the element of surprise, and she needed every possible advantage.

The last thing she wanted was for Jamie to warn his dealer and his drug mule that she was onto them.

Fina pulled into a McDonald's drive-thru and ordered large fries, a diet soda, and an apple pie. She needed a plan, and she developed her best plans on a full stomach. When her phone rang she'd made no progress on a plan, but was halfway through her fries. The number was marked "unavailable," but private investigators don't have the luxury of sending calls to voice mail.

"Hello?" she said, licking salt off her fingers.

"Could I speak with Ms. Ludlow, please?" a man asked.

"This is she. Who is this?"

"This is Dr. Morrison at the Portland Medical Center."

"Oh, right," Fina said, trying to cover her surprise. "What can I do for you, Dr. Morrison?"

"Well, I'm sorry to have to tell you over the phone, but Greta Samuels passed away this morning."

Fina dropped the French fry she was holding back into the bag. "What? She did?"

"Yes. Your name was listed on the next-of-kin form. She was your aunt?"

"Actually, we're not related, but I'm close friends with her niece."

"Could you share the information with her niece?" he asked.

"Of course. Can I ask what happened? I just spoke with Greta a few days ago." Fina could hear someone being paged in the background.

"It was an opportunistic infection. Unfortunately, these things happen, especially with patients who are older and not in generally good health."

"I know she was waiting for a transplant," Fina said. "Would that have made a difference?"

He paused for a moment. "It's difficult to say."

"Her niece was in the early stages of possibly becoming a donor."

"If she was in the early stages, it wouldn't have helped. The infection was very fast-moving, and obviously lethal."

"I appreciate the information, and I'll be sure to tell Greta's niece."

"Like I said, I'm sorry to deliver news via the phone," Dr. Morrison said, "but there you have it."

"Thank you," Fina said, and pressed the end key on her phone.

She sat for a moment and stared out the windshield. She replayed her last conversation with Greta in her head and contemplated the conversation she needed to have with Risa.

Of all the outcomes Fina had imagined, this wasn't one of them.

N o sooner had Fina pulled out of the McDonald's parking lot than her phone rang again. She pressed the speaker button and kept driving.

"Hello," Fina said, sipping from her now flat diet soda.

"Fina, it's Pamela Fordyce."

"I was hoping I would hear from you," Fina said. "What can you tell me about the Local Scholars program?"

"It's a scholarship program that offers financial aid to local students who might not qualify for a scholarship otherwise. I didn't realize Zack Lawrence was enrolled until I looked at the file again."

"Why wouldn't the participants qualify for a scholarship otherwise? Because they don't have enough financial need or they don't have the grades?"

"Mostly because they don't have the grades to compete with needy students from other locations."

"So what's the point of the program? Why give aid to less-qualified candidates?"

"It's a win-win for everyone," Pamela said. "The university gives a leg up to local underprivileged students, and those students then return to their communities and are good PR for NEU."

Fina was in a backed-up left-turn lane and for once wasn't annoyed by the delay. Sitting through a few light cycles let her focus completely on the call. She was practically parked.

"Okay. I appreciate the information," she said. Fina wanted to know as much as she could about Zack, but she wasn't sure how this piece was relevant to her investigation.

"Why don't you ask Kevin about him?" Pamela said.

"What? Why would I ask Kevin?"

"Because Kevin was on the scholarship committee when Zack Lawrence was admitted."

Fina was glad she wasn't moving; she would have slammed on her brakes. "So they know each other? Kevin Lafferty and Zack Lawrence?"

"I don't know if they know each other now, but they did at some point. Local Scholars is a small program. They must have had some contact."

"Jesus," Fina said, the wheels in her head turning.

"What's this about? How is this related to the Liz Barone case?" Pamela asked.

"I'm not sure that it is, but I need to cover all the bases."

"Does this implicate Kevin somehow?"

"Not necessarily. Is there anything else you wanted to tell me?" Fina asked, wondering how long Pamela would maintain her own claim to innocence.

"No. That's it."

"Okay. Thanks for the update," Fina said. "Gotta run."

Fina pulled over into a strip mall parking lot. She took a deep breath and considered her options. She wanted to hightail it to Kevin Lafferty's house and accuse him of orchestrating the car bomb, but just as she valued the element of surprise, so did the police. If she tipped Kevin off, he could cover his tracks and derail the whole investigation. She knew better than to jeopardize a potential court case.

She sighed and picked up her phone. Cristian answered after a couple of rings.

"It pains me to make this call," she said.

"You really know how to get a conversation started," he said.

"I just want you to understand how hard this is for me."

"I understand." Cristian sounded distracted. "What is it?"

"Did you know that Kevin Lafferty was a committee member for an NEU scholarship program that Zack Lawrence was enrolled in? If you did, then my angst is for naught."

She heard what sounded like a file drawer slamming shut on the other end of the line.

"I did not know that," he said.

"Cristian, that's a pretty solid connection, and I can imagine Kevin getting someone to do his dirty work for him."

"Okay, I can see that, but why go after you?"

"Because Kevin doesn't want his dirty secrets to come out," Fina said, "and I kept pushing."

"What? You think he killed Liz Barone?" he asked.

"I don't know, but he has a colorful history of sleeping with NEU students and got at least one of them pregnant. If that becomes public knowledge, his role as a booster is going to be seriously jeopardized."

"How do you know he got someone pregnant?"

"I read about it in Liz Barone's correspondence. He had an affair with her back in the day."

"He really has been keeping secrets," Cristian said.

"Yes," Fina agreed. "I haven't mentioned it to her mother or husband, so mum's the word. Ha!"

"And why does it pain you to tell me all this? You don't like the guy."

"Exactly, and I would like nothing more than to go over to Kevin's house right now and tell him that I know about the scholarship program and his connection to Zack Lawrence."

"Which you absolutely cannot do," Cristian said.

"I know, hence the pain."

"Don't go anywhere near him, Fina."

"I won't. I promise."

"Good. I'll call you later," he said.

Fina hung up the phone. It felt good coming clean to Cristian. Not as good as confronting Kevin would have, but good enough.

Fina pulled up to Risa's house and emerged from her car only to be hit with a snowball. Jordan, Risa's eldest, looked momentarily stricken until Fina reached down for a handful of snow and took off after him.

"You're a dead man, Jordan," she called out.

He ran around the yard as his friends laughed and cheered Fina on. She caught him and smooshed the snow down onto his bare head.

"It's going down my back!" he yelped, grinning. He reached down and batted a scoop of snow toward Fina's face.

She grabbed his shoulders and wrestled him to the ground. "Seriously? You want to do this with me?" she asked, laughing.

"I give up! I give up!"

Fina stood up, and he rolled onto his back. His friends gathered around him.

"You got beaten by a girl, Jordan," one of them said.

"That's right," Fina agreed. "Don't you forget it." She climbed the front stairs, rang the doorbell, and opened the door. "Risa! It's Fina!"

Risa appeared a minute later. "What happened to you?" she asked, taking in Fina's slightly disheveled appearance. "Are you okay?"

"Jordan tried to ambush me, but I showed him who's boss."

"Are your clothes wet?"

Her clothes were damp, but Fina was hoping the visit would be brief and then she could head home and get in her cozies.

"I'm fine. I'm sorry to drop by unannounced," Fina said, putting her boots in the boot tray by the door and hanging her coat on the coatrack. "Do you have a minute? There's something we need to discuss."

"I haven't written the letter yet," Risa said, heading toward the kitchen.

"That's what I want to talk to you about."

"Okay. Do you want something to eat or drink? I can make some tea or hot chocolate."

"No, thanks. Can we sit down?"

Risa gave her a funny look and sat on the couch in the TV area. Fina joined her.

"I have some news," Fina said. "Greta died this morning."

Risa's face went slack. "What?"

"It was very sudden. I spoke with her doctor, and he said it was an opportunistic infection. There wasn't anything they could do."

"I don't understand. We just saw her a week ago, and she seemed okay." Risa reached for a toss pillow and began pulling on the braided seam.

"I know. She was admitted to the hospital a few days ago, but when I spoke with her, she seemed fine."

"You spoke with her?" Risa asked.

"She called me."

"Why?"

"She wanted to speak with you," Fina said, "but she wouldn't tell me what about, specifically, nor did I tell her that you had decided against the donation. I was waiting until you wrote to her."

"Why didn't you tell me she called?" Risa asked.

"Because I didn't trust her. I told her to have her doctor contact me, and if her situation was legitimate, I would pass the message on to you," Fina said. "I wasn't sure she was really in the hospital, and I didn't want her to try to coerce you."

"But maybe I should have spoken with her."

"Why? There was absolutely nothing you could have done. I asked the doctor and he said that even if you were going to give her your kidney, she wouldn't have gotten the transplant in time." Fina touched Risa's hand. "He also said that these types of infections can kill patients even after they've had a transplant. There's just no way to know."

Risa sat back against the cushions and braced the toss pillow against her chest. "Maybe I could have comforted her."

"She didn't want your comfort, Risa," Fina said. "I'm not trying to be harsh, but what she wanted was your kidney."

They were silent for a moment. "So that's it?" Risa asked. "All of that, and it's a moot point?"

"I'm sorry," Fina said. "It's a lot to wrap your head around."

Risa swallowed. "I'm sorry that she died, but I didn't really know her. Am I supposed to feel sad?"

"Not necessarily. If I were you, I'd be pissed."

"Fina!"

"What? You went through all this rigmarole and then she drops dead? I'd be angry and relieved."

"I'm not relieved," Risa insisted.

"Of course not," Fina said. "You're too nice for that, but don't feel bad if those feelings creep in. You wouldn't be the first person to feel conflicted about a blood relative's death."

They sat on the couch. The refrigerator started humming, and ice clanked around in the ice maker.

"Is Marty going to be home soon?" Fina asked. "I feel bad dumping this on you and taking off."

"He should be home before too long. He's—"

"Mom!" The front door banged open, and a hubbub ensued in the hallway.

"I'll be plenty distracted," Risa said. "You don't need to worry about me."

Jordan and his friends poured into the room, and Fina rose from the couch. "Call me if you need anything," she said. Fina started walking out of the room, but feinted in Jordan's direction. He started and grinned. Fina laughed and retrieved her belongings at the front door.

She was sorry that Greta had died, but she couldn't deny that a small part of her was relieved that this chapter was closed, once and for all.

Fina swung by Scotty and Patty's house since she was in the general neighborhood. Their door was locked, and rather than use her spare key, Fina rang the bell and waited. Haley appeared a minute later.

"Hi, pumpkin," Fina said, giving her a hug.

"Hey. Aunt Patty isn't here right now."

"That's okay. You'll do," Fina said, grinning.

"I'm taking care of Chandler, and I'm getting his dinner."

They walked into the kitchen, where Chandler was lying on the couch, transfixed by the TV.

"Hey, dude," Fina said, and gave him a juicy kiss on the cheek. He giggled, but kept his eyes glued to his show.

She pulled out one of the bar stools and took a seat. Haley was on the other side of the island, attending to the dinner preparation. She grabbed some pot holders and pulled a cookie sheet of chicken nuggets out of the oven. Once she'd arranged them on a plate, she popped a small dish of broccoli into the microwave and poured a glass of milk while the vegetables heated.

Fina looked at her and felt a small tug of pride in her chest. It wasn't that Haley was doing anything most kids her age couldn't do, but given her situation nine months ago, it was reassuring to see her behave like a normal teenager. In addition to the Shakespearean dysfunction of Rand and Melanie's household, Haley had had few responsibilities and wasn't expected to pull her weight in any way. Fina knew that Patty and Scotty's kids were privileged, but they weren't spoiled. They were being taught life skills and a concern and respect for one another that filled Fina with hope for the next generation of Ludlows.

The microwave beeped. "Chandler," Haley said. "Your dinner's ready."

"This is almost over," he said from the corner of the couch.

"You can pause it, but you have to eat now," his cousin insisted.

"Aww."

"That's what Aunt Patty said," Haley said.

The boy pushed himself off the couch and took the stool next to Fina. Haley slid the plate and cup across the island to him. She took two diet sodas out of the fridge and gave one to Fina before opening her own.

"Aunt Fina," Chandler said, after shoving a chicken nugget into his mouth. "Do you think that if you put a frog in a cardboard box and he tried to jump that he would get out or would he get a concussion?"

Fina and Haley exchanged a look. Fina grinned, and Haley rolled her eyes.

"Is there a cover on the box?" Fina asked.

"Of course. If there wasn't a cover, he'd just jump right out," he said, in a tone suggesting she was an idiot.

"So you're wondering if he would knock himself unconscious trying to get out?" she clarified.

"Yes." He ate a broccoli floret and gazed at her.

"It depends on how strong the frog is. If he's got strong deltoids and trapezoids like you do"—Fina reached over and squeezed his shoulders— "I don't think he'd have a problem." Chandler giggled. "But if he hasn't been eating his broccoli, then he might bang his soft little head."

"Wow," Haley said, leaning her elbows against the counter. "You're giving this way too much thought."

"It's an interesting question," Fina said. "It deserves a thoughtful answer. What do you think, buddy?" she asked her nephew.

The rest of the meal was a monologue of Chandler's theories and questions, which were as entertaining as they were implausible.

After he finished eating, he resumed his slump on the couch, and Haley cleaned up. As Fina stood to leave, Haley turned off the water and grabbed a paper towel.

"Gammy won't stop talking about the trip," she said, wiping her hands and examining the floor.

"Which trip?" Fina asked.

Haley didn't respond.

"The Miami trip?" Fina asked, eyeing Chandler, who was engrossed in his show.

"Yeah."

"I will put an end to it tonight. I promise."

"Thanks," Haley said.

Fina gave both kids hugs and kisses and let herself out.

Her mom pushed and pushed and pushed, and then she always seemed surprised when Fina pushed back.

This time, Elaine was in for the surprise of her life.

At Nanny's, Fina rummaged around in her closet and pulled out a burner phone. She took it into the living room and pulled up the website for Horizon Mortgage East. Karla Hewett's page listed her e-mail and her cell number. Fina walked over to the window and rested her forehead against the cold pane. She knew that her motives weren't pure, but that didn't negate her actions. Rand deserved everything coming to him, and Karla's kids deserved to be safe. Fina dialed the number.

"Hello."

"Could I please speak with Karla Hewett?" Fina asked.

"This is Karla. How can I help you?"

"Your new boyfriend is a creep, and you should keep him away from your children."

"I'm sorry, who is this?" Karla asked.

"Rand Ludlow is a pedophile, and he likes to hire prostitutes that look like young girls. If you don't believe me, you should ask a woman named Bev Duprey."

"I don't know what you're talking about."

"You can reach Bev at MCI-Framingham," Fina said. "It's a women's prison in Massachusetts. She's an inmate, and I'm sure she'd be happy to enlighten you."

"I don't know who you are, but you don't know what you're talking about. Don't call me again!" Karla said.

"I won't," Fina promised. "You've been warned."

She hung up and went over to the couch. She lay down and pulled Nanny's afghan over her.

It was so draining keeping up with family.

34.

As soon as she woke up, Fina grabbed her phone and called Cristian, but had to settle for leaving a voice mail. She wanted to know if he'd made any progress proving that either Kevin or Vikram was behind the bomb.

The next person she wanted to speak with was Kelly Wegner, but as Fina gathered her belongings, Pamela called.

"I wonder if you could meet me," Pamela said.

"Sure," Fina said, wondering if the moment of truth was approaching.

"How about coffee in the student center?"

"Okay. Give me half an hour."

Pamela was waiting when Fina climbed the broad stairs to the second story of the center. She was seated near a large window in a modern-looking chair covered in striped fabric. There was a coffee cup in her hand.

Fina dragged a chair next to Pamela and sat down.

"What's going on?" Fina asked.

There were dark circles under Pamela's eyes, and her lipstick looked faded.

"I wanted to tell you that I didn't kill Liz Barone."

"I don't think you did," Fina said.

"No?" Pamela asked.

"No. I think you had a motive, but I don't think you acted on it."

Pamela reached forward and placed the coffee cup on a low table in front of them. "So you know."

Fina looked at her. "Why don't you tell me whatever it is that you want to say, Pamela?"

She rotated her watch on her wrist before speaking. "I made a terrible mistake."

"You're going to have to be more specific." Fina adjusted her butt in the chair. Nanny's blue velvet couch may have been ugly, but it was certainly comfortable. "I'm probably the most sympathetic ear you'll have for a while. You can practice on me."

"I don't have a Ph.D. from Stanford. I don't have a Ph.D. at all," she said, the statement coming out in a rush. "I never claimed that I had the degree. Someone else said I did, and then it was too late to correct them."

"When exactly was it too late?" Fina asked. "You've been pretending to have this degree and other related credentials for almost a decade."

"I was at a conference, and the emcee introduced me and said I had a Ph.D. from Stanford," Pamela said, fingering a string of beads around her neck. "I was shocked, but I was so nervous about my presentation that I didn't correct it at the time."

"And afterward?" Fina asked. "Why didn't you correct it that same day? People would have understood that you froze in the moment."

"I forgot about it, and then the next time it came up, too much time had passed. If I set the record straight, it would look like I'd been lying." Pamela dropped her hands to her lap.

"You were lying."

"Not at first," Pamela insisted. "I didn't actively lie at first."

"But I'm assuming some of your advancement can be attributed to your supposed advanced education," Fina said.

"I don't know. I obviously don't need the degree to do my job successfully."

"Maybe," Fina conceded, "but that's hardly the point."

"What are you going to do?" Pamela asked her.

"About this? Nothing. *I'm* not your problem, but I was able to ferret this out pretty easily. If I can do it, others can, too. I'm actually surprised no one has."

"People in academia are very trusting," Pamela said.

Fina watched a few students playing pinball. What did it say about her brothers that their offices resembled a student center?

"Are you telling me this because you secretly hope that I'll spill the beans?" Fina asked. "It would fit the pattern of letting other people decide your fate."

"No," Pamela said testily. "It's nothing that Freudian. I wanted your advice."

"Okay."

"Given your family's history, I thought you might be able to recommend a good PR firm."

"So you're going to go public?" Fina asked.

Pamela sighed. "I'm tired of worrying about being found out. I'm sure once it's public, I'll regret it, but this seems like the lesser of two evils at the moment."

"And then you won't have to worry about someone like Kevin Lafferty holding it over you," Fina commented.

"He told you?"

"No, but I figured that he knew."

"Why?" Pamela asked.

"You were so anxious to tattle on him, and it made sense once I realized you were lying about your degree. He knew, and you were trying to neutralize him."

Pamela's lip curled. "A lot of good that did."

"Oh, I think Kevin is going to get his due," Fina said. "As far as a PR firm is concerned, you should speak with a man named Arthur Drummond. I'll e-mail you his contact info. He's worked with my family and some of our clients."

"I may need some kind of legal representation, too."

"I'm sure Arthur can give you a referral."

There was a loud smacking sound as a student at a nearby pool table racked the balls and broke them with the cue ball.

"Coming clean is the right move," Fina said. "You can craft a statement and make some kind of a deal with the university. And who knows? It might end up being a good time to leave, depending upon how this lawsuit shakes out."

Pamela gazed across the room. "I'll never get another job in academia. No one will hire me."

"Maybe. Maybe not. This is America. Everybody loves a comeback," Fina said, rising to her feet. "I'll send you that e-mail, and if you need help in the meantime, you know how to reach me."

"Thank you, Fina." Pamela dipped her head. "I am ashamed by what I've done."

Fina didn't answer, just walked away.

People often debated the relative morality of lies of commission versus lies of omission; Pamela was a perfect example of the damage wrought by staying silent.

She was embarrassed and ashamed, but there were worse crimes.

Like mayhem and murder.

Kelly and her husband owned a Cape Cod–style house a few streets away from Liz and Jamie's home. Fina parked out front and took note of the family decal on the back of the minivan in the driveway. The house was painted light blue and had a large bay window. Brick steps with a black wrought iron railing led to the door, which was only a few feet from the sidewalk.

Fina rang the bell and peered through the door's glass panel. It was pebbled so you could see movement, but no actual detail. A shadow moved behind it, and Kelly appeared. She didn't look particularly pleased to see Fina when she opened the door.

"Hi," Kelly said.

"I'm sorry to drop by unannounced. I just need a few minutes."

"This isn't a good time. Why don't you call me later and we'll figure something out?"

"Kelly, we need to talk." Fina pulled her shoulders back and looked Kelly in the eye. She wouldn't force herself in, but Fina hoped that her posture communicated the urgency of the matter.

"Okay." Kelly stepped back from the door. "Can you take off your boots? I don't want stuff tracked in."

"Of course." Fina attended to her outerwear, and Kelly moved farther into the room. The front door opened directly onto the staircase and the living room. Kelly sat down on the couch and slipped a stack of papers into a folder, then put the folder into a portable file container.

"You're so organized," Fina commented, joining her on the couch.

Kelly shrugged. "I'm in charge of the spring fair at the kids' school. There's a lot to keep track of."

The room was painted a sandy tone, and there were family photos on the walls and the mantel. A dried-flower arrangement stood on a side table, and a few unburnt logs were assembled in the hearth. The home looked much tidier than Jamie and Liz's, but it was also smaller and darker.

"So what did you need to discuss?" Kelly asked. She pressed her hands between her knees.

Fina got comfortable on the couch. "I'm trying to understand why you're providing Jamie with drugs."

Kelly swallowed and looked away.

"It's just such a bad idea," Fina continued.

"I don't want to talk about this," Kelly said, biting her lower lip.

"I don't blame you, but what you're doing is illegal, not to mention stupid."

"Don't lecture me, Fina." Kelly's tone was more pleading than angry.

"I'm not here to lecture you. I'm here to convince you to stop."

Kelly looked at Fina with tear-filled eyes. "He needs my help."

"Then help him. I've offered to connect him with people, maybe get him into rehab. That's the help he needs."

Kelly smiled bitterly and shook her head. "You sound like Liz."

Fina stared at her. "So Liz knew he was an addict?"

"He's not an addict! Do you know how much pain he's in? How much stress he has?"

"I'm sure that's true, but that doesn't change the fact that he's addicted. You're enabling him, Kelly. You and Gus Sibley."

She started to cry. "He needed help, and Gus and I were willing to provide it, unlike Liz, who was completely unsympathetic."

"She had a lot on her plate, too," Fina noted.

"Don't use the lawsuit as an excuse," Kelly said. "She chose to pursue it."

"Because she was getting worse and was worried about her kids' future," Fina said. "She thought the lawsuit would provide some financial relief."

"And in the meantime, she was racking up lawyers' and doctors' bills, spending money they didn't have. Thirty-seven hundred dollars? You may have that kind of money, but people like us don't."

"She needed to see those lawyers and doctors. Her health—and her family's future—depended on it." Fina held her hands up. "I still don't understand how their financial troubles resulted in you getting drugs for Jamie."

"He needed someone to talk to, and Liz wasn't interested. He needed relief from the pain."

"I'll bet he did."

"It's not like that," Kelly insisted. "The pills were going to be temporary."

"So why are you still doing it?" Fina asked.

"Because Liz died, and things got even worse!"

"And why is he buying pills on the street *and* from Dr. Sibley?"

"Because Gus cut him off for a while," Kelly said, "but I guess he changed his mind."

"Or Jamie threatened to report him if Gus didn't get back in the business," Fina suggested.

Kelly shook her head. "Jamie wouldn't do that."

Fina fought not to roll her eyes. "So Liz is the villain in all this? She doesn't take care of her poor husband at home, so he goes out and finds a woman who will? He's using you, Kelly."

"No, he's not," Kelly said. She crossed her arms tightly. "We have something."

"You're having an affair with a married man and supplying him with drugs. You could lose everything."

"That's not going to happen. We're going to make it work."

"How?" Fina was always amazed that smart women could act so stupid.

"Eventually," Kelly said, wiping her eyes, "we're going to be a family."

"And *then* he's going to stop being a drug addict?"

Kelly sniffled. "You need to leave."

"You realize this gives you a serious motive for murder?" Fina asked.

"Liz was my friend," Kelly said, clenching her hands together.

"Whose husband you were screwing. Some friend." Fina stood and walked back to the front door. She got into her boots and jacket and looked at Kelly, who was wiping more tears from her cheeks. "I'm begging you—at the very least—to stop getting him pills," Fina said. "If your husband or the cops find out, you could be in serious trouble."

Kelly was silent. Fina opened the door and walked back to her car.

There was a heaviness in her chest, for a host of reasons. At the top of the list? Imagining the update she'd have to deliver to Bobbi Barone.

Fina sat in a booth at a diner near police headquarters, waiting for Cristian. She was reluctant to tell him about the little drug trade she'd uncovered, but its existence—and Liz's alleged knowledge of it—cast her death in a new light. If Liz knew that Gus was providing her addicted husband with drugs, she could have turned him in to the cops or the DEA. Kelly seemed to be harboring a fantasy about happily ever after with Jamie, and with his sick, nagging wife out of the way, Jamie's life was less complicated. The whole sorry situation was almost enough to make Fina lose her appetite—almost.

Her phone rang while she studied the menu, and she answered the call from the unidentified number.

"You've been busy," the man on the other end said.

Fina's muscles tensed, and on instinct, she scanned the room.

"Who is this?"

"Come on, Sis, you know who this is."

"What do you want, Rand?" Fina asked.

"You know what I want, but you never seem able to provide it. I want you to butt out of my life."

"And I want you to stay away from Haley and all other little girls," Fina snarled. "You do what I want, and I'll do what you want."

"You don't get to dictate the terms of my life. How dare you interfere with Karla?" Fina could picture him puffing up his chest in outrage.

"I don't know what you mean," she said.

"I know it was you," Rand said. "It's always you."

"This conversation is over," Fina said. "Let's not talk again—ever."

"Oh, but we're going to. In fact, I think it's time for me to visit, don't you? See the family? Catch up?"

Fina balled up her free hand and watched her knuckles whiten. "Don't," she managed to say.

"I'll see you soon."

He ended the call, and Fina placed the phone on the table and rubbed her temples. When she'd hatched her plan to call Karla, she knew there would be fallout, but she'd hadn't spent a lot of time contemplating it. Regardless of the consequences, she had to get her brother away from Karla's kids, but what now? And what about the next girlfriend?

"What's the matter?" Cristian asked, sliding onto the banquette across from her, his face creased in worry.

"It's Rand."

"What now?"

"He's threatening me, saying he's coming to town."

"Why now?" A waitress approached the table, and Cristian waved her off. "Did you do something?"

"Yes, I did something," she snapped. "I stopped him from molesting more little girls."

"Easy, Fina," Cristian said, reaching across the table, taking her hand.

"Fuck. What am I going to do?" She rested her head in her other hand and strained to blink back the tears that were threatening to fall.

"I don't know, but I'll help you figure something out."

"Thanks, Cristian," Fina said, sitting up and pulling her hand back from his.

"So what's the update?" he asked once she'd composed herself.

"First, tell me what's going on with Kevin Lafferty and Vikram Mehra."

"We're waiting on the search warrants, but Kevin's our guy for the bomb."

"Seriously? That douche bag," Fina said, beaming. "Did Zack roll on him?"

"Yeah. Zack got a lawyer who very wisely advised him to make a deal."

"But neither of them built it, right?"

Cristian shook his head. "We're looking for a third guy. I think Kevin hatched and bankrolled the idea, and Zack planted it, but someone else did the actual cooking. We'll find him."

Fina shook her head. "Too bad you can't arrest Vikram for being an ass."

"Actually, your pal Vikram is also in the hot seat."

Fina perked up. "Glad to hear it, but why?"

"When we were at the lab executing a search warrant, one of the other scientists led us around, and he found some things that seemed out of order."

The waitress approached a second time, and Fina ordered a diet soda and a grilled cheese with fries. Cristian opted for black coffee to go.

"What sort of things?" Fina asked.

"Something related to the storage of chemicals. Anyway, this guy called in OSHA, and they're investigating. Looks like Vikram may have been cutting corners."

"I hope he gets radiation poisoning," Fina said.

"Very nice."

"You've met the guy. He's as mean as a snake."

"Okay," Cristian said, pointing at her. "Your turn."

"Okay. Jamie is a drug addict and has been buying pills from Gus Sibley. Kelly Wegner has been the go-between."

Cristian rubbed his chin. "Do you have proof?"

"I have a witness who saw Jamie buy pills in a club, and there are witnesses to Kelly and Gus exchanging something. I've seen the drugs, and Kelly admitted it."

"Did Liz know?" he asked.

"Yes, according to Kelly."

The waitress dropped off the diet soda and coffee. "Things are supposed to be getting clearer, not more complicated," Cristian said.

"Sorry about that," Fina said. "I thought you'd want to know."

"When did you figure this out?" he asked.

"I've been working on it, but I didn't have confirmation until this morning."

"Do you have a theory about how this all fits together? I'm not convinced that Kevin is a murderer in addition to hiring Zack Lawrence."

"I have theories," Fina said, popping open her drink, "but something's off. I can't put my finger on it."

Cristian's phone rang, and he glanced at the screen.

"You need to go?" Fina asked.

"Yeah, but there was something else I wanted to talk to you about."

"Sure."

"The other night . . ."

"Uh-huh." Fina couldn't help but smirk.

"It was great," he said.

"I agree."

"So I was wondering if maybe we should move things in a certain direction," Cristian said.

Fina tilted her head. "What do you mean?"

"Maybe we should actually date," he suggested.

She took a sip of soda. Suspects weren't the only ones who liked to buy time. "But you just ended a relationship because you didn't want to make a commitment."

"To her," Cristian said.

Fina made a silent O with her mouth. She waited for him to say something else.

"I think we could do something different," he added, bringing the to-go cup to his mouth. "I learned a lot in my relationship with Cindy about what I do and don't want."

"So you want to date exclusively?" Fina asked.

"Yeah." He nodded.

"With the idea that it would be serious?"

"Yes."

Fina sighed deeply.

"That's encouraging," Cristian said sourly.

"I don't know what to say. I wasn't expecting this," Fina said. "I like how things are."

"And maybe you'd like them even more this way," he said.

"My head is in so many different places right now, Cristian. I need to think about this."

He nodded, but frowned.

"Well, you didn't actually expect me to agree on the spot, did you?" she asked.

"Think about it," he said, rising from the booth. "Let me know."

"But now you're leaving mad at me," Fina said.

"No, I'm not," he insisted. "I'm leaving frustrated, but I'll get over it." He leaned over and kissed her on the mouth.

Fina watched him walk away.

Why did life have to be so complicated?

Fina showed up at Jamie's office hoping to catch him before he left for the day. She had no doubt that Kelly would have told him about their conversation and that Fina's access to the Barone/Gottlieb household was officially over.

"I don't want to speak with you," Jamie said at the receptionist's desk.

"Fine. Just listen." Fina steered him by the elbow out the glass doors to the elevators. The receptionist gawked at them.

"You need to come clean with Bobbi," Fina said. "No pun intended."

Jamie shook his head. "No, and you can't tell her, either."

"Legally, I'm obligated to tell her. She owns the work product from my investigation, which details your activities." Fina enforced this rule on a case-by-case basis, and chose to invoke it this time. The situation was out of hand, and there were children involved. Not to mention, she didn't work for Jamie; she worked for Bobbi.

"I can't tell her, Fina."

"You have to, or I will."

"Why?" he asked. "Why does she have to know?"

"Because I don't want to be responsible if you wrap your car around a tree with your kids in the backseat. I'm not going to enable your addiction like Kelly does."

He shook his head. "Bobbi won't understand."

The elevator doors opened, depositing a group of young men into the lobby. They exchanged hellos with Jamie before entering the office.

"I think she might understand," Fina said. "I haven't known her long, but Bobbi seems like a fair and decent person. Give her a chance to help you."

"I don't need help."

"Then give her the chance to prove that you do." Fina pushed the down button and faced him. "If you decide you want my help, give me a call."

Jamie hung his head and turned toward the glass office doors. His shoulders sagged. He looked broken, even from behind.

Fina got on the elevator and willed the doors to close quickly.

She could only stomach so much self-destruction.

Fina went to bed early, hoping that sleep might lead to clarity about the case, the Rand situation, and Cristian's revelation. Unfortunately, sleep was elusive; she spent most of the night rolling from side to side, her mind skipping from one quagmire to the next. Fina finally dozed off just after four A.M., only to awaken with a start an hour later.

She sat up in bed, sweat matting her hair to her neck.

She got it now.

It made sense.

But things were definitely going to get worse before they got better.

35.

Fina jumped out of bed and called Cristian. His phone went to voice mail, so she called Pitney instead, who was displeased by the wake-up call. She agreed to meet Fina anyway and promised to get ahold of Cristian.

Fina threw on some clothes and grabbed a Pop-Tart in the kitchen. She ate it in the car on the way, washing it down with water from a nearly empty bottle she found on the car floor. It was still dark, and parts of the road were slick. Fina's car slipped a couple of times, and she backed off the gas. If she got killed on the way, she'd never know if she was right, and she wanted to know.

At the house, Pitney and Cristian climbed out of their unmarked police car and joined her on the front steps.

"This is crazy," Pitney said, "even for you."

"Bear with me," Fina said, ringing the bell. Upstairs, there was a small light on, but otherwise, the house was cloaked in darkness. Fina rang a second time, and just as she felt her desperation growing, the door opened.

A man in his late thirties stood before them, bleary-eyed, in sweats. "You know what time it is?" he asked.

Pitney and Cristian held up their shields.

"We're really sorry to bother you," Cristian said, "but we need to speak with your wife."

"Why?" He rubbed his eyes.

"Is she here?" Pitney asked.

"Yeah, but—" Before he could say more, slippered feet appeared at the top of the stairs. Kelly descended and put her hand on her husband's arm.

"I'll talk to them," Kelly said. "Will you go check on the kids?" She was wearing a pink chenille robe, and her hair was pulled back in a messy knot.

"I don't understand," he said.

"Please, Josh. It's okay," she said, and pushed him gently toward the stairs.

He acquiesced, and Kelly led them into the living room. No one bothered to shed their boots or jackets.

Kelly stared at the floor.

"Okay, Fina. You're up," Pitney said impatiently.

Fina looked at Kelly. "You pushed her. You pushed Liz, and she hit her head. I'm guessing you didn't mean to kill her."

The next moment was laden with anticipation and dread, the four of them holding their breath.

Then Kelly's face crumpled, and a sob escaped her mouth.

"Is that true?" Pitney asked.

Kelly shuffled over to the couch and sat down. She buried her face in her arms and wept. Pitney looked at Fina with a question mark on her face.

"She knew that Liz's latest bill from the lawyer was thirty-seven hundred dollars," Fina said, "but there's no way she could have known that if she weren't in the house that night."

"She told me about it," Kelly cried.

"No, she didn't," Fina said. "Jamie told the cops that they fought about opening the bill that morning, and Liz put it off until later that day. It was on the top of the stack when you stopped by her house. The only other people who saw that were the cops, the EMTs, and anyone who saw the crime scene photos. There's a record of all those people."

Kelly rocked on the couch. "It was just a coincidence that I said that amount. A lucky guess."

"Then why are you so upset, Kelly?" Cristian asked.

She didn't answer.

"It will be better for you if you come clean," Pitney said. "It will help your case if it was an accident."

"Were you fighting about Jamie?" Fina asked.

The three of them were standing over Kelly, asking their questions. Fina considered sitting down, but didn't want to get comfortable.

"I think Liz was angry that you were sleeping with Jamie and enabling his addiction," Fina continued. "Meanwhile, Gus was providing the drugs and withdrawing support from her lawsuit."

Kelly gulped in air. "She was so unforgiving!" she exclaimed.

Pitney snorted. "I wouldn't expect her to be forgiving toward the mistress."

"Liz wasn't doing anything to help him, but she didn't want me helping him, either," Kelly said, brushing her sleeve across her face. "She called me terrible names. I just wanted her to stop."

"Well, you stopped her, all right," Fina said under her breath. "You know the worst part? If you'd called 911, you could have saved her. It didn't have to be a fatal injury."

Kelly's sobbing made Fina cringe—because it was both tragic and selfish.

"Can I go, Lieutenant?" Fina asked.

Pitney nodded. "You may."

Fina squeezed Cristian's arm and left the house, pulling the front door closed behind her. She took a deep breath of cold morning air and returned to her car.

Her work there was done.

Fina slept.

When she opened her eyes, the clock said twelve thirty P.M. She rolled onto her back and looked at the ceiling. Reaching over to the bedside table, Fina grabbed her phone and dialed Bobbi's number.

"I was just talking about you," Bobbi said when she answered.

"Really?"

"Yes. I had a nice chat with your brother Scotty."

"Oh. That's nice. Are you at Ludlow and Associates?" Fina asked.

"Uh-huh. There was a meeting with some potential plaintiffs who might join the suit."

"Great. Are you going to be there for a little while? I need to update you on some things."

"Depends on how long a while is," Bobbi said.

"I can be there in half an hour," Fina said.

"I'll be here."

Fina jumped in the shower, dressed, and was in her car twelve minutes later. She applied some mascara and lip gloss at red lights and arrived at the office right on time.

She found Bobbi in a small meeting room reading some files and sipping a cup of coffee. Fina leaned over and gave her a hug before taking a seat. She reached out and nudged the door closed with her foot.

"How'd the meeting go?" Fina asked.

"It was good." Bobbi's eyes widened. "Definitely an improvement from Thatcher Kinney."

"I would hope so."

"Your dad is getting a bunch of people on board—actually, they're coming out of the woodwork—and he thinks NEU will settle."

"He's a good lawyer," Fina acknowledged. "He fights for his clients."

"How have you been?" Bobbi asked. "You look tired."

"I had an early morning. Speaking of which, have the cops been in touch with you?"

Bobbi shook her head. "No. Why?"

"My early morning started at Kelly Wegner's house." Fina leaned forward, resting her elbows on the table. "Bobbi, she essentially admitted that she fought with Liz and caused her head injury, which in turn caused Liz's death."

She blinked. "What?"

"Kelly killed Liz. I don't think she meant to, but she did."

Bobbi burst into tears. "But why? They were friends."

"Which leads me to my next question," Fina said. "Has Jamie been in touch with you?"

"No. Why?" Bobbi asked, her voice climbing with anxiety.

Fina reached into her bag and pulled out a pack of tissues, which she handed to Bobbi. "I'm sorry to be the one to tell you," Fina said, "but Jamie and Kelly are involved."

"Involved how? An affair?"

Fina nodded. "Not only that, but Jamie has a problem with pills."

Bobbi held up her hand. "Wait, Fina. This is too much."

"I know, but you have a right to know. Do you want some water? Or how about scotch? I can steal some from my father's office."

Bobbi shook her head and blotted her face with a tissue. "Did Liz know all of this?"

"She did. She also knew that Kelly was acting as a go-between for Jamie and Gus Sibley, who was supplying pills."

"Gus Sibley?"

"He first prescribed them when Jamie hurt his knee and then stopped, but their transactions recently started up again."

"Pain pills?" She grimaced.

"Yes. I've spoken to Jamie about rehab or getting some kind of help, but he isn't interested."

"Addicts rarely are," Bobbi said.

"I also told him that he needed to come clean with you about all of this or I would tell you. Obviously, he didn't tell you."

"No, he didn't." Bobbi massaged one of her shoulders with her hand.

"This may seem like a weird suggestion, but I know an amazing massage therapist. The last thing you need is physical pain on top of all of this."

"Is he a miracle worker? That's what I need."

"He kind of is," Fina said. "Tell him that I sent you, and he'll give you a discount." She wrote Milloy's contact information on a piece of paper and tore it off. "You won't regret it."

"Thanks," Bobbi said. "I may need to schedule extra sessions when I get your bill."

"Yeah. I'm not going to send you a bill," Fina said.

Bobbi shook her head. "You've worked hard and did what you said you would. You should be paid."

"Oh, I'm going to be paid, but not by you—by my father."

"But Liz's death wasn't connected to the lawsuit."

"Maybe not directly, but the lawsuit played a role," Fina said. "My dad is going to make plenty of money on the lawsuit. He can eat the cost of the investigation."

Bobbi cried some more. After a few minutes, she seemed to catch her breath. "Thank you, Fina."

"You're welcome. Let's get together soon. We can talk some more about this or something completely different if you like."

Bobbi nodded.

"I told Jamie that I have resources if he decides to get some help," Fina added.

"Okay." She was silent for a moment. "Did Jamie know that Kelly attacked Liz?"

"I don't think so. I haven't asked him, but I don't think that he was holding on to that secret, too. He had enough lies and misery to manage." Fina reached over and squeezed Bobbi's hand. "I can hang out for a little while if you'd like the company."

"Thank you, but no. I'm okay."

They stood and embraced. Fina could feel the wetness from Bobbi's cheek on her own neck.

"I'll talk to you soon," she promised.

Fina left the room and wound through the hallways to her father's office.

"Great. The gang's all here," she said. Carl, Scotty, and Matthew were sitting at the conference table.

"Speak of the devil," said Scotty.

Fina frowned.

"We just heard that you were the target of the car bomb," he said. "I knew it!"

"Woo-hoo! You were right," Fina said, leaning her butt against the credenza. "Who told you?"

"I heard from one of the detectives on the arson bomb squad," Scotty said. "So it was that guy Kevin Lafferty?"

"He didn't attach it to the car, but he was behind it," Fina said.

"Is that the man who was here the other morning?" Carl asked. "The one going berserk?"

"The very one," Fina commented. "He really couldn't stay away from me."

"That was an expensive car, Fina," Carl said, peering at her.

"Cost of doing business, Dad."

"Not my business."

"Are you referring to the business that includes a multimillion-dollar suit against NEU? The case that I brought to the firm?" she asked. "Why don't you just count the car against my finder's fee?"

Carl scowled. "You're not getting a finder's fee."

"Nor am I replacing your SUV," Fina said. "Nor will I be charging Bobbi Barone for the investigation."

"Since when?" Carl asked.

"Since I solved the case. Turn on the TV. I bet they're covering it."

Matthew reached toward Carl's desk and picked up the TV remote. He turned it on and flipped through the channels until he found the local news station. It was the tail end of the weather report, which was calling for snow, snow, and more snow with a little ice thrown in for variety.

The anchor took over from the meteorologist and described an oversized truck wedged under a bridge on Storrow Drive, which was causing a major traffic jam. After a teaser about the Celtics, he announced in solemn tones that a person of interest had been brought in for questioning in the attack on a Hyde Park woman. The story was brief, and Fina filled in the details for Carl and her brothers.

"Well done, Sis," Matthew said.

"You helped," Fina said, punching him playfully on the arm. "You, too, Scotty. I especially appreciate how cool the two of you were under pressure." She grinned.

"The car was on fire," Scotty protested.

"Yeah, I know," Fina said. "I was there, remember? I'm the one who got burned."

"Back to the bill," Carl said. "I thought we agreed that I would foot the bill if her attack had something to do with the lawsuit."

"It does have something to do with the lawsuit," she said, "but I don't want to fight about it right now. Let's just bask in our victory."

"We have too much work to do to bask," Carl said, turning his attention to a file in front of him.

"I'm off, then."

Fina left the office and walked back in the direction of the meeting room where Bobbi had been. The room was empty, so she left the office and headed west on the Mass Pike.

She was in a good mood and wanted to share it.

Frank and Peg weren't home, and neither was Risa, so Fina called Patty. She wasn't home, either, but she suggested Fina wait for her at the house.

Fina stopped and got a frappe on the way. She let herself in and lay down on the couch to watch TV until Patty arrived. She slurped on her drink and channel surfed. Fifteen minutes later, there was a sound in the front hallway.

"Patty!" Fina called out. "I'm in here."

She heard footsteps, and then Elaine appeared in the doorway. She was holding a book of fabric samples in her arms.

"Oh," Fina said. "I thought you were Patty."

"No. I'm not." Elaine dumped the book onto the counter and marched over to the couch. "Turn that off."

"What?" Fina took a long sip through her straw. "I'm watching it."

"Turn it off!" Elaine yelled. Her face was red, and she was shaking.

Fina turned off the TV and sat up. "What is going on?"

"What have you done to your brother?"

"What?"

"Your brother, Josefina!" Elaine hollered. "What have you done?"

Fina stood up and started to brush past her mother. "The right thing. That's what I've done."

Elaine reached out and grabbed Fina's arm, digging her fake nails into her flesh.

"Oww!" Fina yelled. "Let go!"

"No. Not until you explain yourself."

Fina pulled her mother toward her. "Let go or I'll break your wrist."

Elaine released her. "I don't even know who you are. I can't believe I raised a child like this."

"Like this?" Fina shouted. "Like *this*?" She took a step back from Elaine. "You raised a pedophile, that's who you raised! A man who molested his own daughter!"

Her mother sneered. "That's disgusting, Fina!"

"I agree, but it's true. Rand is a pedophile. He should be locked up in jail."

"I don't know what you're talking about," Elaine insisted.

"Of course you don't. Nobody tells you anything, and why would they? You only believe what you want to believe. You live in your own little fantasy land."

"You're lying."

"About your son, the monster? Sorry, it's all true," Fina said.

"Stop it!" Elaine yelled, covering her ears with her hands. "I don't want to hear any more lies!"

"Then stop listening to Rand, Mom. He molested Haley, and he was going to molest Karla's girls, too."

Elaine's face scrunched up. "What did he ever do to you to deserve this treatment?"

"He didn't do anything to me," Fina said. "It's all the other women in his life who've suffered."

"You are a liar. I can't stand the sight of you right now."

Elaine strode out of the room, and the front door slammed. Fina massaged the red marks on her arm and grabbed her things. She couldn't stand to be there one second longer.

Milloy massaged her feet as she lay on the couch. They'd eaten Chinese food and were watching a show about people who lived north of the Arctic Circle. Sure, it was good to know how to hunt your own food and chop your own firewood, but why do it if you didn't have to?

"I think I've started World War Three," Fina said during a commercial.

"You couldn't keep it a secret forever," Milloy said. "The truth would have come out eventually."

"Not like that," she said, rubbing her forehead. "That was not a great move on my part."

"It's unhealthy keeping those kinds of secrets. You'll all be better off now that she knows the truth."

"She's never going to believe it," Fina said bitterly.

He shrugged. "There's nothing you can do about that."

Fina's phone rang. Milloy muted the TV and handed it to her, glancing at the screen. When Fina saw that it was Cristian, she let it go to voice mail.

"You two have a fight?" Milloy asked.

"Hardly."

He looked at her, waiting for her to elaborate.

"He wants to date," Fina said. "Exclusively."

Milloy looked surprised. "What did you say?"

"I didn't say anything. I was too surprised to answer."

"Do you *want* to date him exclusively?"

Fina closed her eyes. "What I want is for you to rub my feet. Can we just do that right now?"

"Of course," Milloy said, and turned the volume back up.

Fina listened as a woman described preparing a scrumptious meal of moose heart and caribou muscle. "These people are crazy," she said, opening her eyes.

"Some people might say the same thing about you," Milloy said, smiling.

Fina nodded and grinned sheepishly. "You're right. Some might."

ACKNOWLEDGMENTS

Although writing is a solitary pursuit, I couldn't do it without the hard work and support of many people.

Thank you to all the readers, booksellers, and librarians who have embraced Fina and the rest of the Ludlows.

Helen Brann, thank you for your unwavering support and advocacy.

Davenie Susi Pereira, Catalina Arboleda, Allison Walker Chader, and Lauri Bortscheller Nakamoto have been amazing readers and cheerleaders throughout this process.

Greg Nakamoto, M.D., and Matthew Bio, Ph.D., let me pick their brains about all things medical and chemical. They provided critical details, and any mistakes are my own. Thanks also to Matina Madrick for coming through in a pinch.

I am so lucky to work with the wonderful teams at Putnam and Penguin Random House. Katie Grinch, Christopher Nelson, Lydia Hirt, Kate Stark, Alexis Welby, Mary Stone, and Meaghan Wagner have been wonderful, and as always, Ivan Held has provided a supportive home for Fina. I pity the writers who don't have Christine Pepe for an editor. She is insightful, always makes Fina better, and always makes me laugh.

Mary Alice Kier and Anna Cottle have worked their butts off to get Fina to Hollywood, and I can't wait to see what's next.

A huge thank-you to my family: Kirsten Thoft, Ted Nadeau, Zoë

Nadeau, Ella Nadeau, Escher Nadeau, Lisa Thoft, Cole Nagel-Thoft, Arden Nagel-Thoft, Erika Thoft-Brown, Chris Thoft-Brown, Owen Thoft-Brown, Sophie Thoft-Brown, Riley Thoft-Brown, and Sharon Padia Stone. Your enthusiasm means the world to me.

My mother, Judith Stone Thoft, and my husband, Doug Berrett, have more than earned this book's dedication. My mom's keen eye and thoughtful feedback are essential to my writing, and everything in life—from book brainstorming to trips to the ER—is more fun with Doug. I couldn't ask for a better partner.